The Voice of S(

Nineteenth-Century Literature

Representative Prose and Verse

Editor: Robert Emmons Rogers

Alpha Editions

This edition published in 2024

ISBN : 9789362991980

Design and Setting By
Alpha Editions
www.alphaedis.com
Email - info@alphaedis.com

As per information held with us this book is in Public Domain.
This book is a reproduction of an important historical work. Alpha Editions uses the best technology to reproduce historical work in the same manner it was first published to preserve its original nature. Any marks or number seen are left intentionally to preserve its true form.

Contents

INTRODUCTION ....- 1 -
MATTHEW ARNOLD ....- 3 -
SIR MICHAEL FOSTER ....- 16 -
THOMAS HENRY HUXLEY ....- 35 -
ON THE PHYSICAL BASIS OF LIFE ....- 46 -
JOHN TYNDALL ....- 62 -
JOHN HENRY, CARDINAL NEWMAN ....- 69 -
ROBERT LOUIS STEVENSON ....- 72 -
JOHN RUSKIN ....- 77 -
MATTHEW ARNOLD ....- 96 -
ARTHUR HUGH CLOUGH ....- 114 -
ALGERNON CHARLES SWINBURNE ....- 116 -
EDWARD FITZGERALD ....- 119 -
ROBERT BROWNING ....- 138 -
ALFRED, LORD TENNYSON ....- 168 -
GEORGE MEREDITH ....- 174 -
WILLIAM E. HENLEY ....- 175 -
THOMAS HARDY ....- 176 -
RALPH WALDO EMERSON ....- 177 -
WALT WHITMAN ....- 212 -

INTRODUCTION

By Henry Greenleaf Pearson

"The Voice of Science in Nineteenth-Century Literature" is a volume of selections put together for use in the third term of a course in English and History offered to the second-year students at the Massachusetts Institute of Technology. The plan of the year's work provides for a study of the record made in English literature by the great movements of thought that distinguished the nineteenth century. First John Stuart Mill's essays on "Liberty" and "Representative Government" furnish an interpretation of the political currents of thought in the first half of the century. Carlyle's "Past and Present," which is read in the second third of the year, is an analysis of economic and social problems in the same period; in the third term the profound effect of science on the thought of the age receives illustration in the writings here brought together.

Broadly stated, the central theme of the book is man's place in the universe, considered in the light of the new knowledge and speculation as to his origin and destiny which the study of science in the nineteenth century has invoked. Some of the selections are more closely related to this theme than are others. Between some of the selections the connection or contrast is obvious ("Rabbi Ben Ezra" and "The Rubaiyat of Omar Khayyam"); in others it is less immediately evident. In some cases the background is the group of ideas roughly classed under the word *evolution*; in others it is some characteristic phase of religious feeling or ethical or theological thought. The contrast in outlook between the American writers, Emerson and Whitman, and their English contemporaries is one of which particularly valuable use may be made. The discovery of these interrelations is what gives zest to the reading for both parties in the classroom; for neither teacher nor students should the work take the form of checking off selections on a minutely correlated syllabus. The course should be pursued on the assumption that the whole is greater than the sum of the parts: the total impression, the height gained at the end, the inspiration of the view there disclosed—these are the goals to be sought for. And the discerning teacher will not be surprised that the pupil presses him so closely up the ascent.

In reading pursued on this plan what should be emphasized on the side of history is not the marshaling of fact, of things done, but the war of thought in one field or another. Without being embroiled in the controversy for this or that belief, the student examines the battleground to learn how the battle was fought. He discovers what befell truths, half-truths, and falsehoods, and under what circumstances of glory or shame. He sees the period with the unity that genius always gives to a subject; at the same time he learns how to make the correction that a piece of contemporary interpretation inevitably requires. On the side of literature, the student's approach is no less special and with its appropriate reward. He sees the man of genius primarily in the setting of his age. The personal adventures and idiosyncracies that often form so large and so unedifying a portion of the treatment afforded in the traditional "historical survey course" here fill a modest space in the background; the attention is concentrated on what this leader did for the men of his own day. These writers lived intensely in the life of their own generation; conscious of a clearer perception of the truth and possessing a voice that men could hear, they sought to lead their companions out of the wilderness. It is the man of genius speaking with authority to those of his own time who is here presented. In such a setting his voice has still its ancient power.

MATTHEW ARNOLD

THE FUNCTION OF CRITICISM[1]

The critical power is of lower rank than the creative. True; but in assenting to this proposition, one or two things are to be kept in mind. It is undeniable that the exercise of a creative power, that a free creative activity, is the true function of man; it is proved to be so by man's finding in it his true happiness. But it is undeniable, also, that men may have the sense of exercising this free creative activity in other ways than in producing great works of literature or art; if it were not so, all but a very few men would be shut out from the true happiness of all men; they may have it in well-doing, they may have it in learning, they may have it even in criticizing. This is one thing to be kept in mind. Another is, that the exercise of the creative power in the production of great works of literature or art, however high this exercise of it may rank, is not, at all epochs, and under all conditions, possible; and that, therefore, labor may be vainly spent in attempting it, and may with more fruit be used in preparing for it, in rendering it possible. This creative power works with elements, with materials; what if it has not those materials, those elements, ready for its use? In that case it must surely wait till they are ready. Now, in literature,—I will limit myself to literature, for it is about literature that the question arises,—the elements with which the creative power works are ideas; the best ideas on every matter which literature touches, current at the time; at any rate, we may lay it down as certain that in modern literature no manifestation of the creative power not working with these can be very important or fruitful. And I say *current* at the time, not merely accessible at the time; for creative literary genius does not principally show itself in discovering new ideas—that is rather the business of the philosopher; the grand work of literary genius is a work of synthesis and exposition, not of analysis and discovery; its gift lies in the faculty of being happily inspired by a certain intellectual and spiritual atmosphere, by a certain order of ideas, when it finds itself in them; of dealing divinely with these ideas, presenting them in the most effective and attractive combinations, making beautiful works with them, in short. But it must have the atmosphere, it must find itself amidst the order of ideas, in order to work freely; and these it is not so easy to command. This is why great creative epochs in literature are so rare; this is why there is so much that is unsatisfactory in the productions of many men of real genius; because, for the creation of a master-work of literature, two powers must concur, the power of the man and the power of the moment, and the man is not enough without the moment; the creative power has, for its happy exercise, appointed elements, and those elements are not in its own control.

Nay, they are more within the control of the critical power. It is the business of the critical power, as I said in the words already quoted, "in all branches of knowledge, theology, philosophy, history, art, science, to see the object as in itself it really is." Thus it tends, at last, to make an intellectual situation of which the creative power can profitably avail itself. It tends to establish an order of ideas, if not absolutely true, yet true by comparison with that which it displaces; to make the best ideas prevail. Presently these new ideas reach society, the touch of truth is the touch of life, and there is a stir and growth everywhere; out of this stir and growth come the creative epochs of literature.

Or, to narrow our range, and quit these considerations of the general march of genius and of society,—considerations which are apt to become too abstract and impalpable,—everyone can see that a poet, for instance, ought to know life and the world before dealing with them in poetry; and life and the world being, in modern times, very complex things, the creation of a modern poet, to be worth much, implies a great critical effort behind it; else it would be a comparatively poor, barren, and short-lived affair. This is why Byron's poetry had so little endurance in it, and Goethe's so much; both had a great productive power, but Goethe's was nourished by a great critical effort providing the true materials for it, and Byron's was not; Goethe knew life and the world, the poet's necessary subjects, much more comprehensively and thoroughly than Byron. He knew a great deal more of them, and he knew them much more as they really are.

It has long seemed to me that the burst of creative activity in our literature, through the first quarter of this century, had about it, in fact, something premature; and that from this cause its productions are doomed, most of them, in spite of the sanguine hopes which accompanied and do still accompany them, to prove hardly more lasting than the productions of far less splendid epochs. And this prematureness comes from its having proceeded without having its proper data, without sufficient materials to work with. In other words, the English poetry of the first quarter of this century, with plenty of energy, plenty of creative force, did not know enough. This makes Byron so empty of matter, Shelley so incoherent, Wordsworth, even, profound as he is, yet so wanting in completeness and variety. Wordsworth cared little for books, and disparaged Goethe. I admire Wordsworth, as he is, so much that I cannot wish him different; and it is vain, no doubt, to imagine such a man different from what he is, to suppose that he could have been different; but surely the one thing wanting to make Wordsworth an even greater poet than he is,—his thought richer, and his influence of wider application,—was that he should have read more books— among them, no doubt, those of that Goethe whom he disparaged without reading him.

But to speak of books and reading may easily lead to a misunderstanding here. It was not really books and reading that lacked to our poetry at this epoch; Shelley had plenty of reading, Coleridge had immense reading. Pindar and Sophocles—as we all say so glibly, and often with so little discernment of the real import of what we are saying—had not many books; Shakespeare was no deep reader. True; but in the Greece of Pindar and Sophocles, in the England of Shakespeare, the poet lived in a current of ideas in the highest degree animating and nourishing to the creative power; society was, in the fullest measure, permeated by fresh thought, intelligent and alive; and this state of things is the true basis for the creative power's exercise; in this it finds its data, its materials, truly ready for its hand; all the books and reading in the world are only valuable as they are helps to this. Even when this does not actually exist, books and reading may enable a man to construct a kind of semblance of it in his own mind, a world of knowledge and intelligence in which he may live and work. This is by no means an equivalent to the artist for the nationally diffused life and thought of the epochs of Sophocles or Shakespeare; but, besides that, it may be a means of preparation for such epochs, it does really constitute, if many share in it, a quickening and sustaining atmosphere of great value. Such an atmosphere the many-sided learning and the long and widely combined critical effort of Germany formed for Goethe, when he lived and worked. There was no national glow of life and thought there, as in the Athens of Pericles or the England of Elizabeth. That was the poet's weakness. But there was a sort of equivalent for it in the complete culture and unfettered thinking of a large body of Germans. That was his strength. In the England of the first quarter of this century there was neither a national glow of life and thought, such as we had in the age of Elizabeth, nor yet a culture and a force of learning and criticism such as were to be found in Germany. Therefore the creative power of poetry wanted, for success in the highest sense, materials and a basis; a thorough interpretation of the world was necessarily denied to it.

At first sight it seems strange that out of the immense stir of the French Revolution and its age should not have come a crop of works of genius equal to that which came out of the stir of the great productive time of Greece, or out of that of the Renaissance, with its powerful episode, the Reformation. But the truth is that the stir of the French Revolution took a character which essentially distinguished it from such movements as these. These were, in the main, disinterestedly intellectual and spiritual movements; movements in which the human spirit looked for its satisfaction in itself and in the increased play of its own activity; the French Revolution took a political, practical character. This Revolution—the object of so much blind love and so much blind hatred—found, indeed, its motive-power in the intelligence of men, and not in their practical sense. This is what distinguishes it from the English Revolution of Charles the First's time; this is what makes it a more spiritual event than our Revolution, an event of much more powerful and world-wide interest, though practically less successful—it appeals to an order of ideas which are universal, certain, permanent. 1789 asked of a thing, Is it rational? 1642 asked of a thing, Is it legal? or, when it went furthest, Is it according to conscience? This is the English fashion, a fashion to be treated, within its own sphere, with the highest respect; for its success, within its own sphere, has been prodigious.

But what is law in one place is not law in another; what is law here to-day is not law even here to-morrow; and as for conscience, what is binding on one man's conscience is not binding on another's; the old woman who threw her stool at the head of the surpliced minister in the Tron Church at Edinburgh obeyed an impulse to which millions of the human race may be permitted to remain strangers. But the prescriptions of reason are absolute, unchanging, of universal validity; *to count by tens is the easiest way of counting*—that is a proposition of which everyone, from here to the Antipodes, feels the force; at least, I should say so if we did not live in a country where it is not impossible that any morning we may find a letter in the "Times" declaring that a decimal coinage is an absurdity. That a whole nation should have been penetrated with an enthusiasm for pure reason, and with an ardent zeal for making its prescriptions triumph, is a very remarkable thing, when we consider how little of mind, or anything so worthy and quickening as mind, comes into the motives which alone, in general, *impel* great masses of men. In spite of the extravagant direction given to this enthusiasm, in spite of the crimes and follies in which it lost itself, the French Revolution derives from the force, truth, and universality of the ideas which it took for its law, and from the passion with which it could inspire a multitude for these ideas, a unique and still living power; it is—it will probably long remain—the greatest, the most animating event in history. And as no sincere passion for the things of the mind, even though it turn out in many respects an unfortunate passion, is ever quite thrown away and quite barren of good, France has reaped from hers one fruit, the natural and legitimate fruit, though not precisely the grand fruit she expected: she is the country in Europe where *the people* is most alive.

But the mania for giving an immediate political and practical application to all these fine ideas of the reason was fatal. Here an Englishman is in his element: on this theme we can all go for hours. And all we are in the habit of saying on it has undoubtedly a great deal of truth. Ideas cannot be too much prized in and for themselves, cannot be too much lived with; but to transport them abruptly into the world of politics and practice, violently to revolutionize this world to their bidding—that is quite another thing. There is the world of ideas and there is the world of practice; the French are often for suppressing the one and the English the other; but neither is to be suppressed. A member of the House of Commons said to me the other day: "That a thing is an anomaly, I consider to be no objection to it whatever." I venture to think he was wrong; that a thing is an anomaly *is* an objection to it, but absolutely and in the sphere of ideas; it is not necessarily, under such and such circumstances, or at such and such a moment, an objection to it in the sphere of politics and practice. Joubert has said beautifully: "C'est la force et le droit qui règlent toutes choses dans le monde; la force en attendant le droit." Force and right are the governors of this world; force till right is ready. *Force till right is ready*; and till right is ready, force, the existing order of things, is justified, is the legitimate ruler. But right is something moral, and implies inward recognition, free assent of the will; we are not ready for right,—*right*, so far as we are concerned, *is not ready*,—until we have attained this sense of seeing it and willing it. The way in which for us it may change and transform force, the existing order of things, and become, in its turn, the legitimate ruler of the world, will depend on the way in which, when our time comes, we see it and will it. Therefore, for other people enamored of their own newly discerned right, to attempt to impose it upon us as ours, and violently to substitute their right for our force, is an act of tyranny, and to be resisted. It sets at nought the second great half of our maxim, *force till right is ready*. This was the grand error of the French Revolution; and its movement of ideas, by quitting the intellectual sphere and rushing furiously into the political sphere, ran, indeed, a prodigious and memorable course, but produced no such intellectual fruit as the movement of ideas of the Renaissance, and created, in opposition to itself, what I may call an *epoch of concentration*.

The great force of that epoch of concentration was England; and the great voice of that epoch of concentration was Burke. It is the fashion to treat Burke's writings on the French Revolution as superannuated and conquered by the event; as the eloquent but unphilosophical tirades of bigotry and prejudice. I will not deny that they are often disfigured by the violence and passion of the moment, and that in some directions Burke's view was bounded, and his observation therefore at fault; but on the whole, and for those who can make the needful corrections, what distinguishes these writings is their profound, permanent, fruitful, philosophical truth; they contain the true philosophy of an epoch of concentration, dissipate the heavy atmosphere which its own nature is apt to engender round it, and make its resistance rational instead of mechanical.

But Burke is so great because, almost alone in England, he brings thought to bear upon politics, he saturates politics with thought; it is his accident that his ideas were at the service of an epoch of concentration, not of an epoch of expansion; it is his characteristic that he so lived by ideas, and had such a source of them welling up within him, that he could float even an epoch of concentration and English Tory politics with them. It does not hurt him that

Dr. Price and the Liberals were displeased with him; it does not hurt him, even, that George the Third and the Tories were enchanted with him. His greatness is that he lived in a world which neither English Liberalism nor English Toryism is apt to enter—the world of ideas, not the world of catchwords and party habits. So far is it from being really true of him that he "to party gave up what was meant for mankind," that at the very end of his fierce struggle with the French Revolution, after all his invectives against its false pretensions, hollowness, and madness, with his sincere conviction of its mischievousness, he can close a memorandum on the best means of combating it,—some of the last pages he ever wrote: the *Thoughts on French Affairs*, in December, 1791,—with these striking words:—

"The evil is stated, in my opinion, as it exists. The remedy must be where power, wisdom, and information, I hope, are more united with good intentions than they can be with me. I have done with this subject, I believe, for ever. It has given me many anxious moments for the last two years. *If a great change is to be made in human affairs, the minds of men will be fitted to it; the general opinions and feelings will draw that way. Every fear, every hope will forward it; and then they who persist in opposing this mighty current in human affairs will appear rather to resist the decrees of Providence itself, than the mere designs of men. They will not be resolute and firm, but perverse and obstinate.*"

That return of Burke upon himself has always seemed to me one of the finest things in English literature, or indeed, in any literature. That is what I call living by ideas: when one side of a question has long had your earnest support, when all your feelings are engaged, when you hear all round you no language but one, when your party talks this language like a steam-engine and can imagine no other—still to be able to think, still to be irresistibly carried, if so it be, by the current of thought to the opposite side of the question, and, like Balaam, to be unable to speak anything *but what the Lord has put in your mouth*. I know nothing more striking, and I must add that I know nothing more un-English.

For the Englishman in general is like my friend the Member of Parliament, and believes, point-blank, that for a thing to be an anomaly is absolutely no objection to it whatever. He is like the Lord Auckland of Burke's day, who, in a memorandum on the French Revolution, talks of "certain miscreants, assuming the name of philosophers, who have presumed themselves capable of establishing a new system of society." The Englishman has been called a political animal, and he values what is political and practical so much that ideas easily become objects of dislike in his eyes, and thinkers "miscreants," because ideas and thinkers have rashly meddled with politics and practice. This would be all very well if the dislike and neglect confined themselves to ideas transported out of their own sphere, and meddling rashly with practice; but they are inevitably extended to ideas as such, and to the whole life of intelligence; practice is everything, a free play of the mind is nothing. The notion of the free play of the mind upon all subjects being a pleasure in itself, being an object of desire, being an essential provider of elements without which a nation's spirit, whatever compensations it may have for them, must, in the long run, die of inanition, hardly enters into an Englishman's thoughts. It is noticeable that the word *curiosity*, which in other languages is used in a good sense, to mean, as a high and fine quality of man's nature, just this disinterested love of a free play of the mind on all subjects, for its own sake— it is noticeable, I say, that this word has in our language no sense of the kind, no sense but a rather bad and disparaging one. But criticism, real criticism, is essentially the exercise of this very quality; it obeys an instinct prompting it to try to know the best that is known and thought in the world, irrespectively of practice, politics, and everything of the kind; and to value knowledge and thought as they approach this best, without the intrusion of any other considerations whatever. This is an instinct for which there is, I think, little original sympathy in the practical English nature, and what there was of it has undergone a long, benumbing period of check and suppression in the epoch of concentration which followed the French Revolution.

But epochs of concentration cannot well endure forever; epochs of expansion, in the due course of things, follow them. Such an epoch of expansion seems to be open here in England. In the first place, all danger of a hostile forcible pressure of foreign ideas upon our practice has long disappeared; like the traveler in the fable, therefore, we begin to wear our cloak a little more loosely. Then, with a long peace, the ideas of Europe steal gradually and amicably in, and mingle, though in infinitesimally small quantities at a time, with our own notions. Then, too, in spite of all that is said about the absorbing and brutalizing influence of our passionate material progress, it seems to me indisputable that this progress is likely, though not certain, to lead in the end to an apparition of intellectual life; and that man, after he has made himself perfectly comfortable and has now to determine what to do with himself next, may begin to remember that he has a mind, and that the mind may be made the source of great pleasure. I grant it is mainly the privilege of faith, at present, to discern this end to our railways, our business, and our fortune-making; but we shall see if, here as elsewhere, faith is not in the end the true prophet. Our ease, our traveling, and our unbounded liberty to hold just as hard and securely as we please to the practice to which our notions have given birth, all tend to beget an inclination to deal a little more freely with these notions themselves, to canvass them a little, to penetrate a little into their real nature. Flutterings of curiosity, in the foreign sense of the word, appear amongst us, and it is in these that criticism must look to find its account. Criticism first; a time of true creative activity, perhaps,—which, as I have said, must inevitably be preceded amongst us by a time of criticism,—hereafter, when criticism has done its work.

It is of the last importance that English criticism should clearly discern what rules for its course, in order to avail itself of the field now opening to it, and to produce fruit for the future, it ought to take. The rules may be given in one word; by being *disinterested*. And how is it to be disinterested? By keeping aloof from practice; by resolutely following the law of its own nature, which is to be a free play of the mind on all subjects which it touches; by steadily refusing to lend itself to any of those ulterior, political, practical considerations about ideas, which plenty of people will be sure to attach to them, which perhaps ought often to be attached to them, which in this country, at any rate, are certain to be attached to them quite sufficiently, but which criticism has really nothing to do with. Its business is, as I have said, simply to know the best that is known and thought in the world, and by in its turn making this known, to create a current of true and fresh ideas. Its business is to do this with inflexible honesty, with due ability; but its business is to do no more, and to leave alone all questions of practical consequences and applications, questions which will never fail to have due prominence given to them. Else criticism, besides being really false to its own nature, merely continues in the old rut which it has hitherto followed in this country, and will certainly miss the chance now given to it. For what is at present the bane of criticism in this country? It is that practical considerations cling to it and stifle it; it subserves interests not its own; our organs of criticism are organs of men and parties having practical ends to serve, and with them those practical ends are the first thing and the play of mind the second; so much play of mind as is compatible with the prosecution of those practical ends is all that is wanted.

It must needs be that men should act in sects and parties, that each of these sects and parties should have its organ, and should make this organ subserve the interests of its action; but it would be well, too, that there should be a criticism, not the minister of these interests, not their enemy, but absolutely and entirely independent of them. No other criticism will ever attain any real authority or make any real way toward its end—the creating a current of true and fresh ideas.

It is because criticism has so little kept in the pure intellectual sphere, has so little detached itself from practice, has been so directly polemical and controversial, that it has so ill accomplished, in England, its best spiritual work; which is to keep man from a self-satisfaction which is retarding and vulgarizing, to lead him toward perfection, by making his mind dwell upon what is excellent in itself, and the absolute beauty and fitness of things. A polemical practical criticism makes men blind even to the ideal imperfection of their practice, makes them willingly assert its ideal perfection, in order the better to secure it against attack; and clearly this is narrowing and baneful for them. If they were reassured on the practical side, speculative considerations of ideal perfection they might be brought to entertain, and their spiritual horizon would thus gradually widen....

It will be said that it is a very subtle and indirect action which I am thus prescribing for criticism, and that, by embracing in this manner the Indian virtue of detachment and abandoning the sphere of practical life, it condemns itself to a slow and obscure work. Slow and obscure it may be, but it is the only proper work of criticism. The mass of mankind will never have any ardent zeal for seeing things as they are; very inadequate ideas will always satisfy them. On these inadequate ideas reposes, and must repose, the general practice of the world. That is as much as saying that whoever sets himself to see things as they are will find himself one of a very small circle; but it is only by this small circle resolutely doing its own work that adequate ideas will ever get current at all. The rush and roar of practical life will always have a dizzying and attracting effect upon the most collected spectator, and tend to draw him into its vortex; most of all will this be the case where that life is so powerful as it is in England. But it is only by remaining collected, and refusing to lend himself to the point of view of the practical man, that the critic can do the practical man any service; and it is only by the greatest sincerity in pursuing his own course, and by at last convincing even the practical man of his sincerity, that he can escape misunderstandings which perpetually threaten him.

For the practical man is not apt for fine distinctions, and yet in these distinctions truth and the highest culture greatly find their account. But it is not easy to lead a practical man—unless you reassure him as to your practical intentions, you have no chance of leading him—to see that a thing which he has always been used to look at from one side only, which he greatly values, and which, looked at from that side, more than deserves, perhaps, all the prizing and admiring which he bestows upon it—that this thing, looked at from another side, may appear much less beneficent and beautiful, and yet retain all its claims to our practical allegiance. Where shall we find language innocent enough, how shall we make the spotless purity of our intentions evident enough, to enable us to say to the political Englishman that the British constitution itself, which, seen from the practical side, looks such a magnificent organ of progress and virtue, seen from the speculative side,—with its compromises, its love of facts, its horror of theory, its studied avoidance of clear thoughts,—that, seen from this side, our august constitution sometimes looks—forgive me, shade of Lord Somers!—a colossal machine for the manufacture of Philistines? How is Cobbett to say this and not be misunderstood, blackened as he is with the smoke of a lifelong conflict in the field of political practice? How is Mr. Carlyle to say it and not be misunderstood, after his furious raid into this field with his

"Latter-day Pamphlets"? How is Mr. Ruskin, after his pugnacious political economy? I say, the critic must keep out of the region of immediate practice in the political, social, humanitarian sphere, if he wants to make a beginning for that more free speculative treatment of things, which may perhaps one day make its benefits felt even in this sphere, but in a natural and thence irresistible manner.

Do what he will, however, the critic will still remain exposed to frequent misunderstandings, and nowhere so much as here in England. For here people are particularly indisposed even to comprehend that, without this free, disinterested treatment of things, truth and the highest culture are out of the question. So immersed are they in practical life, so accustomed to take all their notions from this life and its processes, that they are apt to think that truth and culture themselves can be reached by the processes of this life, and that it is an impertinent singularity to think of reaching them in any other way. "We are all *terræ filii*," cries their eloquent advocate; "all Philistines together. Away with the notion of proceeding by any other way than the way dear to the Philistines; let us have a social movement, let us organize and combine a party to pursue truth and new thought, let us call it *the liberal party*, and let us all stick to each other, and back each other up. Let us have no nonsense about independent criticism, and intellectual delicacy, and the few and the many. Don't let us trouble ourselves about foreign thought; we shall invent the whole thing for ourselves as we go along. If one of us speaks well, applaud him; if one of us speaks ill, applaud him too; we are all in the same movement, we are all liberals, we are all in pursuit of truth." In this way the pursuit of truth becomes really a social, practical, pleasurable affair, almost requiring a chairman, a secretary, and advertisements; with the excitement of a little resistance, an occasional scandal, to give the happy sense of difficulty overcome; but, in general, plenty of bustle and very little thought. To act is so easy, as Goethe says; to think is so hard! It is true that the critic has many temptations to go with the stream, to make one of the party movement, one of these *terræ filii*; it seems ungracious to refuse to be a *terræ filius*, when so many excellent people are; but the critic's duty is to refuse, or, if resistance is vain, at least to cry with Obermann: *Perissons en resistant*.

What then is the duty of criticism here? To take the practical point of view, to applaud the liberal movement and all its works ... for their general utility's sake? By no means; but to be perpetually dissatisfied with these works, while they perpetually fall short of a high and perfect ideal.

In criticism, these are elementary laws; but they never can be popular, and in this country they have been very little followed, and one meets with immense obstacles in following them. That is a reason for asserting them again and again. Criticism must maintain its independence of the practical spirit and its aims. Even with well-meant efforts of the practical spirit, it must express dissatisfaction, if in the sphere of the ideal they seem impoverishing and limiting. It must not hurry on to the goal because of its practical importance. It must be patient, and know how to wait; and flexible, and know how to attach itself to things and how to withdraw from them. It must be apt to study and praise elements that for the fulness of spiritual perfection are wanted, even though they belong to a power that in the practical sphere may be maleficent. It must be apt to discern the spiritual shortcomings or illusions of powers that in the practical sphere may be beneficent. And this without any notion of favoring or injuring, in the practical sphere, one power or the other; without any notion of playing off, in this sphere, one power against the other. When one looks, for instance, at the English Divorce Court,—an institution which perhaps has its practical conveniences, but which in the ideal sphere is so hideous; an institution which neither makes divorce impossible nor makes it decent; which allows a man to get rid of his wife, or a wife of her husband, but makes them drag one another first, for the public edification, through a mire of unutterable infamy,—when one looks at this charming institution, I say, with its crowded trials, its newspaper reports, and its money compensations, this institution in which the gross unregenerate British Philistine has indeed stamped an image of himself, one may be permitted to find the marriage theory of Catholicism refreshing and elevating. Or when Protestantism, in virtue of its supposed rational and intellectual origin, gives the law to criticism too magisterially, criticism may and must remind it that its pretensions, in this respect, are illusive and do it harm; that the Reformation was a moral rather than an intellectual event; that Luther's theory of grace no more exactly reflects the mind of the spirit than Bossuet's philosophy of history reflects it; and that there is no more antecedent probability of the Bishop of Durham's stock of ideas being agreeable to perfect reason than of Pope Pius the Ninth's. But criticism will not on that account forget the achievements of Protestantism in the practical and moral sphere; nor that, even in the intellectual sphere, Protestantism, though in a blind and stumbling manner, carried forward the Renaissance, while Catholicism threw itself violently across its path.

I lately heard a man of thought and energy contrasting the want of ardor and movement which he now found amongst young men in England with what he remembered in his own youth, twenty years ago. "What reformers we were then!" he exclaimed; "what a zeal we had! how we canvassed every institution in Church and State, and were prepared to remodel them all on first principles!" He was inclined to regret, as a spiritual flagging, the lull that he saw. I am disposed rather to regard it as a pause in which the turn to a new mode of spiritual progress is being accomplished. Everything was long seen, by the young and ardent amongst us, in inseparable connection with politics and practical life. We have pretty well exhausted the benefits of seeing things in this connection; we have got all that can be got by so seeing them. Let us try a more disinterested mode of seeing them; let us betake ourselves more to the serener life of the mind and spirit. This life, too, may have its excesses and dangers; but they are not for us at present. Let us think of quietly enlarging our stock of true and fresh ideas, and not, as soon as we get an idea or half an idea, be running out with it into the street, and trying to make it rule there. Our ideas will, in the end, shape the world all the better for maturing a little. Perhaps in fifty years' time it will in the English House of Commons be an objection to an institution that it is an anomaly, and my friend the Member of Parliament will shudder in his grave. But let us in the meanwhile rather endeavor that in twenty years' time it may, in English literature, be an objection to a proposition that it is absurd. That will be a change so vast, that the imagination almost fails to grasp it. *Ab integro sæculorum nascitur ordo.*

If I have insisted so much on the course which criticism must take where politics and religion are concerned, it is because, where these burning matters are in question, it is most likely to go astray. In general, its course is determined for it by the idea which is the law of its being: the idea of a disinterested endeavor to learn and propagate the best that is known and thought in the world, and thus to establish a current of fresh and true ideas. By the very nature of things, as England is not all the world, much of the best that is known and thought in the world cannot be of English growth, must be foreign; by the nature of things, again, it is just this that we are least likely to know, while English thought is streaming in upon us from all sides, and takes excellent care that we shall not be ignorant of its existence; the English critic, therefore, must dwell much on foreign thought, and with particular heed on any part of it which, while significant and fruitful in itself, is for any reason specially likely to escape him. Judging is often spoken of as the critic's one business, and so in some sense it is; but the judgment which almost insensibly forms itself in a fair and clear mind, along with fresh knowledge, is the valuable one; and thus knowledge, and ever fresh knowledge, must be the critic's great concern for himself; and it is by communicating fresh knowledge, and letting his own judgment pass along with it,—but insensibly, and in the second place, not the first, as a sort of companion and clue, not as an abstract lawgiver,—that he will generally do most good to his readers.

Sometimes, no doubt, for the sake of establishing an author's place in literature and his relation to a central standard,—and if this is not done, how are we to get at our *best in the world?*—criticism may have to deal with a subject-matter so familiar that fresh knowledge is out of the question, and then it must be all judgment; an enunciation and detailed application of principles. Here the great safeguard is never to let one's self become abstract, always to retain an intimate and lively consciousness of the truth of what one is saying, and, the moment this fails us, to be sure that something is wrong. Still, under all circumstances, this mere judgment and application of principles is, in itself, not the most satisfactory work to the critic; like mathematics, it is tautological, and cannot well give us, like fresh learning, the sense of creative activity. To have this sense is, as I said at the beginning, the great happiness and the great proof of being alive, and it is not denied to criticism to have it; but then criticism must be sincere, simple, flexible, ardent, ever widening its knowledge. Then it may have, in no contemptible measure, a joyful sense of creative activity; a sense which a man of insight and conscience will prefer to what he might derive from a poor, starved, fragmentary, inadequate creation. And at some epochs no other creation is possible.

Still, in full measure, the sense of creative activity belongs only to genuine creation; in literature we must never forget that. But what true man of letters ever can forget it? It is no such common matter for a gifted nature to come into possession of a current of true and living ideas, and to produce amidst the inspiration of them, that we are likely to underrate it. The epochs of Æschylus and Shakespeare make us feel their preëminence. In an epoch like those is, no doubt, the true life of literature; there is the promised land, toward which criticism can only beckon. That promised land it will not be ours to enter, and we shall die in the wilderness; but to have desired to enter it, to have saluted it from afar, is already, perhaps, the best distinction among contemporaries; it will certainly be the best title to esteem with posterity.

SIR MICHAEL FOSTER

THE GROWTH OF SCIENCE IN THE NINETEENTH CENTURY[2]

The eyes of the young look ever forward; they take little heed of the short though ever-lengthening fragment of life which lies behind them; they are wholly bent on that which is to come. The eyes of the aged turn wistfully again and again to the past; as the old glide down the inevitable slope, their present becomes a living over again the life which has gone before, and the future takes on the shape of a brief lengthening of the past. May I this evening venture to give rein to the impulses of advancing years? May I, at this last meeting of the association in the eighteen hundreds, dare to dwell for a while upon the past, and to call to mind a few of the changes which have taken place in the world since those autumn days in which men were saying to each other that the last of the seventeen hundreds was drawing toward its end?

Dover, in the year of our Lord 1799, was in many ways unlike the Dover of to-day. On moonless nights men groped their way in its narrow streets by the help of swinging lanterns and smoky torches, for no lamps lit the ways. By day the light of the sun struggled into the houses through narrow panes of blurred glass. Though the town then, as now, was one of the chief portals to and from the countries beyond the seas, the means of travel was scanty and dear, available for the most part to the rich alone, and for all beset with discomfort and risk. Slow and uncertain was the carriage of goods, and the news of the world outside came to the town (though it, from its position, learned more than most towns) tardily, fitfully, and often falsely. The people of Dover sat then much in dimness, if not in darkness, and lived in large measure on themselves. They who study the phenomena of living beings tell us that light is the great stimulus of life, and that the fullness of the life of a being or of any of its members may be measured by the variety, the swiftness, and the certainty of the means by which it is in touch with its surroundings. Judged from this standpoint, life at Dover then, as indeed elsewhere, must have fallen far short of the life of to-day.

The same study of living beings, however, teaches us that while from one point of view the environment seems to mould the organism, from another point the organism seems to be master of its environment. Going behind the change of circumstances, we may raise the question, the old question, Was life in its essence worth more then than now? Has there been a real advance?

Let me at once relieve your minds by saying that I propose to leave this question in the main unanswered. It may be, or it may not be, that man's grasp of the beautiful and of the good, if not looser, is not firmer than it was a hundred years ago. It may be, or it may not be, that man is no nearer to absolute truth, to seeing things as they really are, than he was then. I will merely ask you to consider with me for a few minutes how far and in what ways man's laying hold of that aspect of, or part of, truth which we call natural knowledge, or sometimes science, differed in 1799 from what it is to-day, and whether that change must not be accounted a real advance, a real improvement in man.

I do not propose to weary you by what in my hands would be the rash effort of attempting a survey of all the scientific results of the nineteenth century. It will be enough if for a little while I dwell on some few of the salient features distinguishing the way in which we nowadays look upon, and during the coming week shall speak of, the works of nature around us—though those works themselves, save for the slight shifting involved in a secular change, remain exactly the same—from the way in which they were looked upon and might have been spoken of at a gathering of philosophers at Dover in 1799, and I ask your leave to do so.

In the philosophy of the ancients earth, fire, air, and water were called "the elements." It was thought, and rightly thought, that a knowledge of them and of their attributes was a necessary basis of a knowledge of the ways of nature. Translated into modern language, a knowledge of these "elements" of old means a knowledge of the composition of the atmosphere, of water, and of all the other things which we call matter, as well as a knowledge of the general properties of gases, liquids, and solids, and of the nature and effects of combustion. Of all these things our knowledge to-day is large and exact, and, though ever enlarging, in some respects complete. When did that knowledge begin to become exact?

To-day the children in our schools know that the air which wraps round the globe is not a single thing, but is made up of two things, oxygen and nitrogen,[3] mingled together. They know, again, that water is not a single thing, but the product of two things, oxygen and hydrogen, joined together. They know that when the air makes the fire burn and gives the animal life, it is the oxygen in it which does the work. They know that all round them things are undergoing that union with oxygen which we call oxidation, and that oxidation is the ordinary source of heat and light. Let me ask you to picture to yourselves what confusion there would be to-morrow, not only in the discussions at the sectional meetings of our association, but in the world at large, if it should happen that in the coming night some destroying touch should wither up certain tender structures in all our brains and wipe out from our memories all traces of the ideas which cluster in our minds around the verbal tokens, oxygen and oxidation. How could any of us—not the so-called man of science alone, but even the man of business and the man of pleasure—go about his ways lacking those ideas? Yet those ideas were, in 1799, lacking to all but a few.

Although in the third quarter of the seventeenth century the light of truth about oxidation and combustion had flashed out in the writings of John Mayow, it came as a flash only, and died away as soon as it had come. For the rest of that century, and for the greater part of the next, philosophers stumbled about in darkness, misled for most of the time by the phantom conception which they called phlogiston. It was not until the end of the third quarter of the eighteenth century that the new light, which has burned steadily ever since, lit up the minds of the men of science. The light came at nearly the same time from England and from France. Rounding off the sharp corners of controversy, and joining, as we may fitly do to-day, the two countries as twin bearers of a common crown, we may say that we owe the truth to Priestley, to Lavoisier, and to Cavendish. If it was Priestley who was the first to demonstrate the existence of what we now call oxygen, it is to Lavoisier that we owe the true conception of the nature of oxidation and the clear exposition of the full meaning of Priestley's discovery; while the knowledge of the composition of water, the necessity complement of the knowledge of oxygen, came to us through Cavendish and, we may perhaps add, through Watt.

The date of Priestley's discovery of oxygen is 1774; Lavoisier's classic memoir "On the nature of the principle which enters into combination with metals during calcination" appeared in 1775, and Cavendish's paper on the composition of water did not see the light until 1784.

During the last quarter of the eighteenth century this new idea of oxygen and oxidation was struggling into existence. How new was the idea, is illustrated by the fact that Lavoisier himself at first spoke of that which he was afterwards, namely, in 1778, led to call oxygen, the name by which it has since been known, as "the principle which enters into combination." What difficulties its acceptance met with is illustrated by the fact that Priestley himself refused to the end of his life to grasp the true bearings of the discovery which he had made.

In the year 1799 the knowledge of oxygen, of the nature of water and of air, and indeed the true conception of chemical composition and chemical change, was hardly more than beginning to be; and the century had to pass wholly away before the next great chemical idea, which we know by the name of the atomic theory of John Dalton, was made known. We have only to read the scientific literature of the time to recognize that a truth which is now not only woven as a master-thread into all our scientific conceptions, but even enters largely into the everyday talk and thoughts of educated people, was, a hundred years ago, struggling into existence among the philosophers themselves. It was all but absolutely unknown to the large world outside those select few.

If there be one word of science which is writ large on the life of the present time, it is the word "electricity." It is, I take it, writ larger than any other word. The knowledge which it denotes has carried its practical results far and wide into our daily life, while the theoretical conceptions which it signifies pierce deep into the nature of things. We are to-day proud, and justly proud, both of the material triumphs and of the intellectual gains which it has brought us, and we are full of even larger hopes of it in the future.

At what time did this bright child of the nineteenth century have its birth?

He who listened to the small group of philosophers of Dover, who in 1799 might have discoursed of natural knowledge, would perhaps have heard much of electric machines, of electric sparks, of the electric fluid, and even of positive and negative electricity; for frictional electricity had long been known and even carefully studied. Probably one or more of the group, dwelling on the observations which Galvani, an Italian, had made known some twenty years before, developed views on the connection of electricity with the phenomena of living bodies. Possibly one of them was exciting the rest by telling how he had just heard that a professor at Pavia, one Volta, had discovered that electricity could be produced, not only by rubbing together particular bodies, but by the simple contact of two metals, and had thereby explained Galvani's remarkable results. For, indeed, as we shall hear from Professor Fleming, it was in that very year, 1799, that electricity as we now know it took its birth. It was then that Volta brought to light the apparently simple truths out of which so much has sprung. The world, it is true, had to wait for yet some twenty years before both the practical and theoretic worth of Volta's discovery became truly pregnant under the fertilizing influence of another discovery. The loadstone and its magnetic virtues had, like the electrifying power of rubbed amber, long been an old story. But, save for the compass, not much had come from it. And even Volta's discovery might have long remained relatively barren had it been left to itself. When, however, in 1819, Oersted made known his remarkable observations on the relations of electricity to magnetism, he made the contact needed for the flow of a new current of ideas. And it is perhaps not too much to say that those ideas, developing during the years of the rest of the century with an ever-accelerating swiftness, have wholly changed man's material relations to the circumstances of life, and at the same time carried him far in his knowledge of the nature of things.

Of all the various branches of science, none perhaps is to-day, none for these many years past has been, so well known to, even if not understood by, most people as that of geology. Its practical lessons have brought wealth to many;

its fairy tales have brought delight to more; and round it hovers the charm of danger, for the conclusions to which it leads touch on the nature of man's beginning.

In 1799 the science of geology, as we now know it, was struggling into birth. There had been from of old cosmogonies, theories as to how the world had taken shape out of primeval chaos. In that fresh spirit which marked the zealous search after natural knowledge pursued in the middle and latter part of the seventeenth century, the brilliant Stenson, in Italy, and Hooke, in England, had laid hold of some of the problems presented by fossil remains, and Woodward, with others, had labored in the same field. In the eighteenth century, especially in its latter half, men's minds were busy about the physical agencies determining or modifying the features of the earth's crust; water and fire, subsidence from a primeval ocean and transformation by outbursts of the central heat, Neptune and Pluto were being appealed to, by Werner on the one hand and by Demarest on the other, in explanation of the earth's phenomena. The way was being prepared, theories and views were abundant, and many sound observations had been made; and yet the science of geology, properly so called, the exact and proved knowledge of the successive phases of the world's life, may be said to date from the closing years of the eighteenth century.

In 1783 James Hutton put forward in a brief memoir his Theory of the Earth, which, in 1795, two years before his death, he expanded into a book; but his ideas failed to lay hold of men's minds until the century had passed away, when, in 1802, they found an able expositor in John Playfair. The very same year that Hutton published his book, Cuvier came to Paris and almost forthwith began, with Brongniart, his immortal researches into the fossils of Paris and its neighborhood. And four years later, in the year 1799 itself, William Smith's tabular list of strata and fossils saw the light. It is, I believe, not too much to say that out of these, geology, as we now know it, sprang.

It was thus in the closing years of the eighteenth century that was begun the work which the nineteenth century has carried forward to such great results; but at this time only the select few had grasped the truth, and even they only the beginning of it. Outside a narrow circle the thoughts even of the educated about the history of the globe were bounded by the story of the Deluge,— though the story was often told in a strange fashion,—or were guided by fantastic views of the plastic forces of a sportive nature.

In another branch of science, in that which deals with the problems presented by living beings, the thoughts of men in 1799 were also very different from the thoughts of men to-day. It is a very old quest, the quest after the knowledge of the nature of living beings, one of the earliest on which man set out; for it promised to lead him to a knowledge of himself—

a promise which perhaps is still before us, but the fulfillment of which is yet far off. As time has gone on, the pursuit of natural knowledge has seemed to lead man away from himself into the furthermost parts of the universe, and into secret workings of Nature in which he appears to be of little or no account; and his knowledge of the nature of living things, and so of his own nature, has advanced slowly, waiting till the progress of other branches of natural knowledge can bring it aid. Yet in the past hundred years the biologic sciences, as we now call them, have marched rapidly onward.

We may look upon a living body as a machine doing work in accordance with certain laws, and may seek to trace out the working of the inner wheels: how these raise up the lifeless dust into living matter, and let the living matter fall away again into dust, giving out movement and heat. Or we may look upon the individual life as a link in a long chain, joining something which went before to something about to come, a chain whose beginning lies hid in the farthest past, and may seek to know the ties which bind one life to another. As we call up to view the long series of living forms, living now or flitting like shadows on the screen of the past, we may strive to lay hold of the influences which fashion the garment of life. Whether the problems of life are looked upon from the one point of view or the other, we to-day, not biologists only, but all of us, have gained a knowledge hidden even from the philosophers a hundred years ago.

Of the problems presented by the living body viewed as a machine, some may be spoken of as mechanical, others as physical, and yet others as chemical, while some are, apparently at least, none of these. In the seventeenth century William Harvey, laying hold of the central mechanism of the blood stream, opened up a path of inquiry which his own age and the century which followed trod with marked success. The knowledge of the mechanism of the animal and of the plant advanced apace, but the physical and chemical problems had yet to wait. The eighteenth century, it is true, had its physics and its chemistry; but, in relation at least to the problems of the living being, a chemistry which knew not oxygen and a physics which knew not the electricity of chemical action were of little avail. The philosopher of 1799, when he discussed the functions of the animal or of the plant involving chemical changes, was fain, for the most part, as were his predecessors in the century before, to have recourse to such vague terms as "fermentation" and the like; to-day our treatises on physiology are largely made up of precise and exact expositions of the play of physical agencies and chemical bodies in the living organisms. He made use of the words "vital force" or "vital principle," not as an occasional, but as a common, explanation of the phenomena of the living body. During the present century, especially during its latter half, the idea embodied in those words has been driven away from one seat after another; if we use it now when we are dealing with the chemical and physical events of life, we use it with reluctance, as a *deus ex machina* to be appealed to only when everything else has failed.

Some of the problems—and those, perhaps, the chief problems—of the living body have to be solved, neither by physical nor by chemical methods, but by methods of their own. Such are the problems of the nervous system. In respect to these the men of 1799 were on the threshold of a pregnant discovery. During the latter part of this nineteenth century, especially during its last quarter, the analysis of the mysterious processes in the nervous system, and especially in the brain, which issue as feeling, thought, and the power to move, has been pushed forward with a success conspicuous in its practical, and full of promise in its theoretical, gains. That analysis may be briefly described as a following up of threads. We now know that what takes place along a tiny thread which we call a nerve fibre differs from that which takes place along its fellow threads, that differing nervous impulses travel along different nervous fibres, and that nervous and physical events are the outcome of the clashing of nervous impulses as they sweep along the closely woven web of living threads of which the brain is made. We have learned by experiment and by observation that the pattern of the web determines the play of the impulses, and we can already explain many of the obscure problems, not only of nervous disease, but of nervous life, by an analysis which is a tracking out of the devious and linked path of nervous threads. The very beginning of this analysis was unknown in 1799. Men knew that nerves were the agents of feeling and of the movements of muscles; they had learned much about what this part or that part of the brain could do; but they did not know that one nerve fibre differed from another in the very essence of its work. It was just about the end of the eighteenth century, or the beginning of the nineteenth, that an English surgeon began to ponder over a conception which, however, he did not make known until some years later, and which did not gain complete demonstration and full acceptance until still more years had passed away. It was in 1811, in a tiny pamphlet published privately, that Charles Bell put forth his New Idea, that the nervous system is constructed on the principle that "the nerves are not single nerves possessing various powers, but bundles of different nerves, whose filaments are united for the convenience of distribution, but which are distinct in office, as they are in origin, from the brain."

Our present knowledge of the nervous system is to a large extent only an exemplification and expansion of Charles Bell's New Idea, and has its origin in that.

If we pass from the problems of the living organism viewed as a machine to those presented by the varied features of the different creatures who have lived or who still live on the earth, we at once call to mind that the middle years of the nineteenth century mark an epoch in biologic thought such as never came before; for it was then that Charles Darwin gave to the world the "Origin of Species."

That work, however, with all the far-reaching effects which it has had, could have had little or no effect, or, rather, could not have come into existence, had not the earlier half of the century been in travail preparing for its coming. For the germinal idea of Darwin appeals, as to witnesses, to the results of two lines of biologic investigation which were almost unknown to the men of the eighteenth century.

To one of these lines I have already referred. Darwin, as we know, appealed to the geological record; and we also know how that record, imperfect as it was then, and imperfect as it must always remain, has since his time yielded the most striking proofs of at least one part of his general conception. In 1799 there was, as we have seen, no geological record at all.

Of the other line I must say a few words.

To-day the merest beginner in biologic study, or even that exemplar of acquaintance without knowledge, the general reader, is aware that every living being, even man himself, begins its independent existence as a tiny ball, of which we can, even acknowledging to the full the limits of the optical analysis at our command, assert with confidence that in structure, using that word in its ordinary sense, it is in all cases absolutely simple. It is equally well known that the features of form which supply the characters of a grown-up living being, all the many and varied features of even the most complex organism, are reached as the goal of a road, at times a long road, of successive changes; that the life of every being, from the ovum to its full estate, is a series of shifting scenes, which come and go, sometimes changing abruptly, sometimes melting the one into the other, like dissolving views—all so ordained that often the final shape with which the creature seems to begin, or is said to begin, its life in the world is the outcome of many shapes, clothed with which it in turn has lived many lives before its seeming birth.

All, or nearly all, the exact knowledge of the labored way in which each living creature puts on its proper shape and structure is the heritage of the present century. Although the way in which the chick is moulded in the egg was not wholly unknown even to the ancients, and in later years had been told, first in the sixteenth century by Fabricius, then in the seventeenth century, in a more clear and striking manner, by the great Italian naturalist, Malpighi, the teaching thus offered had been neglected or misinterpreted. At the close of the eighteenth century the dominant view was that in the making of a creature out of the egg there was no putting on of wholly new parts, no epigenesis. It was taught that the entire creature lay hidden in the egg, hidden by reason of the very transparency of its substance; lay ready-made, but folded up, as it were; and that the process of development within the egg or within the womb was a mere unfolding, a simple evolution. Nor did men shrink from accepting the logical outcome of such a view—namely, that within the unborn creature itself lay in like manner, hidden and folded up, its offspring also, and within that, again, its offspring in turn, after the fashion of a cluster of ivory balls carved by Chinese hands, one within the other.

This was no fantastic view, put forward by an imaginative dreamer; it was seriously held by sober men, even by men like the illustrious Haller, in spite of their recognizing that, as the chick grew in the egg, some changes of form took place. Though so early as the middle of the eighteenth century Friedrich Casper Wolff, and, later on, others, had strenuously opposed such a view, it held its own, not only to the close of the century, but far on into the next. It was not until a quarter of the nineteenth century had been added to the past that Von Baer made known the results of researches which once and for all swept away the old view. He and others working after him made it clear that each individual puts on its final form and structure, not by an unfolding of preëxisting hidden features, but by the formation of new parts through the continued differentiation of a primitively simple material. It was also made clear that the successive changes which the embryo undergoes in its progress from the ovum to maturity are the expression of morphologic laws; that the progress is one from the general to the special; and that the shifting scenes of embryonic life are hints and tokens of lives lived by ancestors in times long past.

If we wish to measure how far off in biologic thought the end of the eighteenth century stands, not only from the end, but even from the middle of the nineteenth, we may imagine Darwin striving to write the "Origin of Species" in 1799. We may fancy his being told by philosophers how one group of living beings differed from another group because all its members and all their ancestors came into existence at one stroke, when the first-born progenitor of the race, within which all the rest were folded up, stood forth as the result of a creative act. We may fancy him listening to a debate between the philosopher who maintained that all the fossils strewn in the earth were the remains of animals or plants churned up in the turmoil of a violent universal flood, and dropped in their places as the waters went away, and him who argued that such were not really the "spoils of living creatures," but the products of some playful plastic power which, out of the superabundance of its energy, fashioned here and there the lifeless earth into forms which imitated, but only imitated, those of living things. Could he amid such surroundings, by any flight of genius, have beaten his way to the conception for which his name will ever be known?

Here I may well turn away from the past. It is not my purpose, nor, as I have said, am I fitted, nor is this perhaps the place, to tell even in outline the tale of the work of science in the nineteenth century. I am content to have pointed out that the two great sciences of chemistry and geology took their birth, or at least began to stand alone, at the close of the last century, and have grown to be what we know them now within about a hundred years, and that the study of living beings has within the same time been so transformed as to be to-day something wholly different from what it was in 1799. And, indeed, to say more would be to repeat almost the same story about other things. If our present knowledge of electricity is essentially the child of the nineteenth century, so also is our present knowledge of many other branches of physics. And those most ancient forms of exact knowledge, the knowledge of numbers and of the heavens, whose beginning is lost in the remote past, have, with all other kinds of natural knowledge, moved onward during the whole of the hundred years with a speed which is ever increasing. I have said, I trust, enough to justify the statement that in respect to natural knowledge a great gulf lies between 1799 and 1899. That gulf, moreover, is a twofold one: not only has natural knowledge been increased, but men have run to and fro, spreading it as they go. Not only have the few driven far back round the full circle of natural knowledge the dark clouds of the unknown, which wrap us all about, but also the many walk in the zone of light thus increasingly gained. If it be true that the few to-day are, in respect to natural knowledge, far removed from the few of those days, it is also true that nearly all which the few alone knew then, and much which they did not know, has now become the common knowledge of the many.

What, however, I may venture to insist upon here is that the difference in respect to natural knowledge, whatever be the case with other differences between then and now, is undoubtedly a difference which means progress. The span between the science of that time and the science of to-day is beyond all question a great stride onward.

We may say this, but we must say it without boasting. For the very story of the past, which tells of the triumphs of science, bids the man of science put away from him all thoughts of vainglory, and that by many tokens.

Whoever, working at any scientific problem, has occasion to study the inquiries into the same problem by some fellow worker in the years long gone by, comes away from that study humbled by one or other of two different thoughts. On the one hand, he may find, when he has translated the language of the past into the phraseology of to-day, how near was his forerunner of old to the conception which he thought, with pride, was all his own, not only so true but so new. On the other hand, if the ideas of the investigator of old, viewed in the light of modern knowledge, are found to be so wide of the mark as to seem absurd, the smile which begins to play upon the lips of the modern is checked by the thought, Will the ideas which I am now putting forth, and which I think explain so clearly, so fully, the problem in hand, seem to some worker in the far future as wrong and as fantastic as do these of my forerunner to me? In either case his personal pride is checked.

Further, there is written clearly on each page of the history of science, in characters which cannot be overlooked, the lesson that no scientific truth is born anew, coming by itself and of itself. Each new truth is always the offspring of something which has gone before, becoming in turn the parent of something coming after. In this aspect the man of science is unlike, or seems to be unlike, the poet and the artist. The poet is born, not made; he rises up, no man knowing his beginnings; when he goes away, though men after him may sing his songs for centuries, he himself goes away wholly, having taken with him his mantle, for this he can give to none other. The man of science is not thus creative: he is created. His work, however great it be, is not wholly his own: it is in part the outcome of the work of men who have gone before. Again and again a conception which has made a name great has come not so much by the man's own effort as out of the fullness of time. Again and again we may read in the words of some man of old the outlines of an idea which, in later days, has shone forth as a great acknowledged truth. From the mouth of the man of old the idea dropped barren, fruitless; the world was not ready for it, and heeded it not; the concomitant and abutting truths which could give it power to work were wanting. Coming back again in later days, the same idea found the world awaiting it; things were in travail preparing for it, and someone, seizing the right moment to put it forth again, leaped into fame. It is not so much the men of science who make science, as some spirit, which, born of the truths already won, drives the man of science onward and uses him to win new truths in turn.

It is because each man of science is not his own master, but one of many obedient servants of an impulse which was at work long before him, and will work long after him, that in science there is no falling back. In respect to other things there may be times of darkness and times of light; there may be risings, decadences, and revivals. In science there is only progress. The path may not be always a straight line; there may be swerving to this side and to that; ideas may seem to return again and again to the same point of the intellectual compass; but it will always be found that they have reached a higher level—they have moved, not in a circle, but in a spiral. Moreover, science is not fashioned as is a house, by putting brick to brick, that which is once put remaining as it was put, to the end. The growth of science is that of a living being. As in the embryo, phase follows phase, and each member or body puts on in succession different appearances, though all the while the same member, so a scientific conception of one age seems to differ from that of a following age, though it is the same one in the process of being made; and as the dim outlines of the early embryo become, as the being grows more distinct and sharp, like a picture on a screen brought more and more into focus, so the dim gropings and searchings of the men of science of old are by repeated approximations wrought into the clear and exact conclusions of later times.

The story of natural knowledge, of science, in the nineteenth century, as, indeed, in preceding centuries, is, I repeat, a story of continued progress. There is in it not so much as a hint of falling back, not even of standing still. What is gained by scientific inquiry is gained forever; it may be added to, it may seem to be covered up, but it can never be taken away. Confident that the progress will go on, we cannot help peering into the years to come, and straining our eyes to foresee what science will become and what it will do as they roll on. While we do so, the thought must come to us: Will all the increasing knowledge of nature avail only to change the ways of man; will it have no effect on man himself?

The material good which mankind has gained and is gaining through the advance of science is so imposing as to be obvious to everyone, and the praises of this aspect of science are to be found in the mouths of all. Beyond all doubt, science has greatly lessened and has markedly narrowed hardship and suffering; beyond all doubt, science has largely increased and has widely diffused ease and comfort. The appliances of science have, as it were, covered with a soft cushion the rough places of life, and that not for the rich only, but also for the poor. So abundant and so prominent are the material benefits of science, that in the eyes of many these seem to be the only benefits which she brings. She is often spoken of as if she were useful and nothing more; as if her work were only to administer to the material wants of man.

Is this so? We may begin to doubt it when we reflect that the triumphs of science which bring these material advantages are in their very nature intellectual triumphs. The increasing benefits brought by science are the results of man's increasing mastery over nature, and that mastery is increasingly a mastery of mind; it is an increasing power to use the forces of what we call inanimate nature in place of the force of his own or other creatures' bodies; it is an increasing use of mind in place of muscle.

Is it to be thought that that which has brought the mind so greatly into play has had no effect on the mind itself? Is that part of the mind which works out scientific truths a mere slavish machine, producing results it knows not how, having no part in the good which in its workings it brings forth?

What are the qualities, the features, of that scientific mind which has wrought, and is working, such great changes in man's relation to nature? In seeking an answer to this question we have not to inquire into the attributes of genius. Though much of the progress of science seems to take on the form of a series of great steps, each made by some great man, the distinction in science between the great discoverer and the humble worker is one of degree only, not of kind. As I was urging just now, the greatness of many great names in science is often, in large part, the greatness of occasion, not of absolute power. The qualities which guide one man to a small truth silently taking its place among its fellows, as these go to make up progress, are at bottom the same as those by which another man is led to something of which the whole world rings.

The features of the fruitful scientific mind are, in the main, three.

In the first place, above all other things, his nature must be one which vibrates in unison with that of which he is in search; the seeker after truth must himself be truthful, truthful with the truthfulness of nature. For the truthfulness of nature is not wholly the same as that which man sometimes calls truthfulness. It is far more imperious, far more exacting. Man, unscientific man, is often content with the "nearly" and the "almost." Nature never is. It is not her way to call the same two things which differ, though the difference may be measured by less than a thousandth of a milligramme or of a millimetre, or by any other like standard of minuteness. And the man who, carrying the ways of the world into the domain of science, thinks that he may treat nature's differences in any other way than she treats them herself, will find that she resents his conduct; if he, in carelessness or in disdain, overlooks the minute difference which she holds out to him as a signet to guide him in his search, the projecting tip, as it were, of some buried treasure, he is bound to go astray, and the more strenuously he struggles on, the further he will find himself from his true goal.

In the second place, he must be alert of mind. Nature is ever making signs to us; she is ever whispering to us the beginnings of her secrets; the scientific man must be ever on the watch, ready at once to lay hold of nature's hint, however small; to listen to her whisper, however low.

In the third place, scientific inquiry, though it be preeminently an intellectual effort, has need of the moral quality of courage—not so much the courage which helps a man to face a sudden difficulty as the courage of steadfast endurance. Almost every inquiry, certainly every prolonged inquiry, sooner or later goes wrong. The path, at first so straight and clear, grows crooked and gets blocked; the hope and enthusiasm, or even the jaunty ease, with which the inquirer set out, leave him, and he falls into a slough of despond. That is the critical moment calling for courage. Struggling through the slough, he will find on the other side the wicket gate opening up the real path; losing heart, he will turn back and add one more stone to the great cairn of the unaccomplished.

But, I hear someone say, these qualities are not the peculiar attributes of the man of science: they may be recognized as belonging to almost everyone who has commanded or deserved success, whatever may have been his walk of life. That is so. That is exactly what I desire to insist, that the men of science have no peculiar virtues, no special powers. They are ordinary men, their characters are common, even commonplace. Science, as Huxley said, is organized common sense, and men of science are common men drilled in the ways of common sense. For their life has this feature. Though in themselves they are no stronger, no better than other men, they possess a strength which, as I just now urged, is not their own, but is that of the science whose servants they are. Even in his apprenticeship, the scientific inquirer, while learning what has been done before his time, if he learns it aright, so learns it that what is known may serve him, not only as a vantage-ground whence to push off into the unknown, but also as a compass to guide him in his course. And when, fitted for his work, he enters on inquiry itself, what a zealous, anxious guide, what a strict and, because strict, helpful, schoolmistress does Nature make herself to him! Under her care every inquiry, whether it bring the inquirer to a happy issue or seem to end in nought, trains him for the next effort. She so orders her ways that each act of obedience to her makes the next act easier for him; and step by step she leads him on toward that perfect obedience which is complete mastery.

Indeed, when we reflect on the potency of the discipline of scientific inquiry, we cease to wonder at the progress of scientific knowledge. The results actually gained seem to fall so far short of what under such guidance might have been expected to have been gathered in, that we are fain to conclude that science has called to follow her, for the most part, the poor in intellect and the wayward in spirit. Had she called to her service the many acute minds who have wasted their strength struggling in vain to solve hopeless problems, or who have turned their energies to things other than the increase of knowledge; had she called to her service the many just men who have walked straight without the need of a rod to guide them, how much greater than it has been would have been the progress of science, and how many false teachings would the world have been spared! To men of science themselves, when they consider their favored lot, the achievements of the past should serve, not as a boast, but as a reproach.

If there be any truth in what I have been urging, that the pursuit of scientific inquiry is itself a training of special potency, giving strength to the feeble and keeping in the path those who are inclined to stray, it is obvious that the material gains of science, great as they may be, do not make up all the good which science brings, or may bring, to man. We especially, perhaps, in these later days, through the rapid development of the physical sciences, are too apt to dwell on the material gains alone. As a child in its infancy looks upon its mother only as a giver of good things, and does not learn till after days how she was also showing her love by carefully training it in the way it should go, so we, too, have thought too much of the gifts of science, overlooking her power to guide.

Man does not live by bread alone, and science brings him more than bread. It is a great thing to make two blades of grass grow where before one alone grew; but it is no less great a thing to help a man to come to a just conclusion on the questions with which he has to deal. We may claim for science that, while she is doing the one, she may be so used as to do the other also. The dictum just quoted, that science is organized common sense, may be read as meaning that the common problems of life, which common people have to solve, are to be solved by the same methods by which the man of science solves his special problems. It follows that the training which does so much for him may be looked to as promising to do much for them.

Such aid can come from science on two conditions only. In the first place, this her influence must be acknowledged; she must be duly recognized as a teacher no less than as a hewer of wood and a drawer of water. And the pursuit of science must be followed, not by the professional few only, but at least in such measure as will ensure the influence of example by the many. But this latter point I need not urge before this great association, whose chief object during more than half a century has been to bring within the fold of science all who would answer to the call. In the second place, it must be understood that the training to be looked for from science is the outcome, not of the accumulation of scientific knowledge, but of the practice of scientific inquiry. Man may have at his fingers' ends all the accomplished results and all the current opinions of any one or of all the branches of science, and yet remain wholly unscientific in mind; but no one can have carried out even the humblest research without the spirit of science in some measure resting upon him. And that spirit may in part be caught even without entering upon an actual investigation in search of a new truth. The learner may be led to old truths, even the oldest, in more ways than one. He may be brought abruptly to a truth in its finished form, coming straight to it like a thief climbing over the wall; and the hurry and press of modern life tempt many to adopt this quicker way. Or he may be more slowly guided along the path by which the truth was reached by him who first laid hold of it. It is by this latter way of learning the truth, and by this alone, that the learner may hope to catch something at least of the spirit of the scientific inquirer.

This is not the place, nor have I the wish, to plunge into the turmoil of controversy; but if there be any truth in what I have been urging, then they are wrong who think that in the schooling of the young science can be used with profit only to train those for whom science will be the means of earning their bread. It may be that, from the point of view of pedagogic art, the experience of generations has fashioned out of the older studies of literature an instrument of discipline of unusual power, and that the teaching of science is as yet but a rough tool in unpractised hands. That, however, is not an adequate reason why scope should not be given for science to show the value which we claim for it as an intellectual training fitted for all sorts and conditions of men. Nor need the studies of humanity and literature fear her presence in the schools; for if her friends maintain that the teaching is one-sided, and therefore misleading, which deals with the doings of man only, and is silent about the works of nature, in the sight of which he and his doings shrink almost to nothing, she herself would be the first to admit that that teaching is equally wrong which deals only with the works of nature and says nothing about the doings of man, who is, to us at least, nature's centre.

There is yet another general aspect of science on which I would crave leave to say a word. In that broad field of human life which we call politics, in the struggle, not of man with man, but of race with race, science works for good. If we look only on the surface, it may at first sight seem otherwise. In no branch of science has there during these later years been greater activity and more rapid progress than in that which furnishes the means by which man brings death, suffering, and disaster on his fellow men. If the healer can look with pride on the increased power which science has given him to alleviate human suffering and ward off the miseries of disease, the destroyer can look with still greater pride on the power which science has given him to sweep away lives and to work desolation and ruin; while the one has slowly been learning to save units, the other has quickly learned to slay thousands. But, happily, the very greatness of the modern power of destruction is already becoming a bar to its use, and bids fair—may we hope before long—wholly to put an end to it; in the words of Tacitus, though in another sense, the very preparations for war, through the character which science gives them, make for peace.

Moreover, not in one branch of science only, but in all, there is a deep undercurrent of influence sapping the very foundations of all war. As I have already urged, no feature of scientific inquiry is more marked than the dependence of each step forward on other steps which have been made before. The man of science cannot sit by himself in his own cave, weaving out results by his own efforts, unaided by others, heedless of what others have done and are doing. He is but a bit of a great system, a joint in a great machine, and he can only work aright when he is in due touch with his fellow workers. If his labor is to be what it ought to be, and is to have the weight which it ought to have, he must know what is being done, not by himself, but by others, and by others not of his own land and speaking his tongue only, but also of other lands and of other speech. Hence it comes about that to the man of science the barriers of manners and of speech which pen men into nations become more and more unreal and indistinct. He recognizes his fellow worker, wherever he may live, and whatever tongue he may speak, as one who is pushing forward shoulder to shoulder with him toward a common goal, as one whom he is helping and who is helping him. The touch of science makes the whole world kin.

The history of the past gives us many examples of this brotherhood of science. In the revival of learning throughout the sixteenth and seventeenth centuries, and some way on into the eighteenth century, the common use of the Latin tongue made intercourse easy. In some respects, in those earlier days science was more cosmopolitan than it afterwards became. In spite of the difficulties and hardships of travel, the men of science of different lands again and again met each other face to face, heard with their ears, and saw with their eyes, what their brethren had to say or show. The Englishman took the long journey to Italy to study there; the Italian, the Frenchman, and the German wandered from one seat of learning to another; and many a man held a chair in a country not his own. There was help, too, as well as intercourse. The Royal Society of London took upon itself the task of publishing nearly all the works of the great Italian, Malpighi; and the brilliant Lavoisier, two years before his own countrymen in their blind fury slew him, received from the same body the highest token which it could give of its esteem.

In these closing years of the nineteenth century this great need of mutual knowledge and of common action felt by men of science of different lands is being manifested in a special way. Though nowadays what is done anywhere is soon known everywhere, the news of a discovery being often flashed over the globe by telegraph, there is an increasing activity in the direction of organization to promote international meetings and international coöperation. In almost every science, inquirers from many lands now gather together at stated intervals, in international congresses, to discuss matters which they have in common at heart, and go away, each one feeling strengthened by having met his brother. The desire that, in the struggle to lay bare the secrets of nature, the least waste of human energy should be incurred, is leading more and more to the concerted action of nations combining to attack problems the solution of which is difficult and costly. The determination of standards of measurement, magnetic surveys, the solution of great geodetic problems, the mapping of the heavens and of the earth—all these are being carried on by international organizations.

One international scientific effort demands a word of notice. The need which every inquirer in science feels to know, and to know quickly, what his fellow worker, wherever on the globe he may be carrying on his work or making known his results, has done or is doing, led some four years back to a proposal for carrying out by international coöperation a complete current index, issued promptly, of the scientific literature of the world. Though much labor in many lands has been spent upon the undertaking, the project is not yet an accomplished fact. Nor can this, perhaps, be wondered at, when the difficulties of the task are weighed. Difficulties of language, difficulties of driving in one team all the several sciences which, like young horses, wish each to have its head free with leave to go its own way, difficulties mechanical and financial, of press and post, difficulties raised by existing interests—these and yet other difficulties are obstacles not easy to be overcome. The most striking and the most encouraging features of the deliberations which have now been going on for three years have been the repeated expressions, coming not from this or that quarter only, but from almost all quarters, of an earnest desire that the effort should succeed, of a sincere belief in the good of international coöperation, and of a willingness to sink as far as possible individual interests for the sake of the common cause. In the face of such a spirit we may surely hope that the many difficulties will ultimately pass out of sight.

I make no apology for having thus touched on international coöperation. I should have been wanting had I not done so on the memorable occasion of this meeting. A hundred years ago two great nations were grappling with each other in a fierce struggle, which had lasted, with pauses, for many years, and which was to last for many years to come; war was on every lip and in almost every heart. To-day this meeting has, by a common wish, been so arranged that those two nations should, in the persons of their men of science, draw as near together as they can, with nothing but the narrow streak of the Channel between them, in order that they may take counsel together on matters in which they have one interest and a common hope. May we not look upon this brotherly meeting as one of many signs that science, though she works in a silent manner and in ways unseen by many, is steadily making for peace?

Looking back, then, in this last year of the eighteen hundreds, on the century which is drawing to a close, while we may see in the history of scientific inquiry much which, telling the man of science of his shortcomings and his weakness, bids him be humble, we also see much, perhaps more, which gives him hope. Hope is, indeed, one of the watchwords of science. In the latter-day writings of some who know not science much may be read which shows that the writer is losing, or has lost, hope in the future of mankind. There are not a few of these; their repeated utterances make a sign of the times. Seeing in matters lying outside science few marks of progress and many tokens of decline or decay, recognizing in science its material benefits only, such men have thoughts of despair when they look forward to the times to come. But if there be any truth in what I have attempted to urge to-night, if the intellectual, if the moral influences of science are no less marked than her material benefits, if, moreover, that which she has done is but the earnest of that which she shall do, such men may pluck up courage and gather strength by laying hold of her garment.

We men of science at least need not share their views or their fears. Our feet are set, not on the shifting sands of the opinions and the fancies of the day, but on a solid foundation of verified truth, which by the labors of each succeeding age is made broader and more firm. To us the past is a thing to look back upon, not with regret, not as something which has been lost never to be regained, but with content, as something whose influence is with us still, helping us on our further way. With us, indeed, the past points not to itself, but to the future; the golden age is in front of us, not behind us; that which we do know is a lamp whose brightest beams are shed into the unknown before us, showing us how much there is in front, and lighting up the way to reach it. We are confident in the advance because, as each one of us feels that any step forward which he may make is not ordered by himself and is not the result of his own sole efforts in the present, but is, and that in large measure, the outcome of the labors of others in the past, so each one of us has the sure and certain hope that, as the past has helped him, so his efforts, be they great or be they small, will be a help to those to come.

THOMAS HENRY HUXLEY

THREE HYPOTHESES RESPECTING THE HISTORY OF NATURE

So far as I know, there are only three hypotheses which ever have been entertained, or which well can be entertained, respecting the past history of nature. I will, in the first place, state the hypotheses, and then I will consider what evidence bearing upon them is in our possession, and by what light of criticism that evidence is to be interpreted.

Upon the first hypothesis, the assumption is, that phenomena of nature similar to those exhibited by the present world have always existed; in other words, that the universe has existed from all eternity in what may be broadly termed its present condition.

The second hypothesis is, that the present state of things has had only a limited duration, and that, at some period in the past, a condition of the world, essentially similar to that which we now know, came into existence, without any precedent condition from which it could have naturally proceeded. The assumption that successive states of nature have arisen, each without any relation of natural causation to an antecedent state, is a mere modification of this second hypothesis.

The third hypothesis also assumes that the present state of things has had but a limited duration; but it supposes that this state has been evolved by a natural process from an antecedent state, and that from another, and so on; and, on this hypothesis, the attempt to assign any limit to the series of past changes is, usually, given up.

It is so needful to form clear and distinct notions of what is really meant by each of these hypotheses, that I will ask you to imagine what, according to each, would have been visible to a spectator of the events which constitute the history of the earth. On the first hypothesis, however far back in time that spectator might be placed, he would see a world essentially, though perhaps not in all its details, similar to that which now exists. The animals which existed would be the ancestors of those which now live, and similar to them; the plants, in like manner, would be such as we know; and the mountains, plains, and waters would foreshadow the salient features of our present land and water. This view was held more or less distinctly, sometimes combined with the notion of recurrent cycles of change, in ancient times; and its influence has been felt down to the present day.

It is worthy of remark that it is a hypothesis which is not inconsistent with the doctrine of Uniformitarianism, with which geologists are familiar. That doctrine was held by Hutton, and in his earlier days by Lyell. Hutton was struck by the demonstration of astronomers that the perturbations of the planetary bodies, however great they may be, yet sooner or later right themselves; and that the solar system possesses a self-adjusting power by which these aberrations are all brought back to a mean condition. Hutton imagined that the like might be true of terrestrial changes; although no one recognized more clearly than he the fact that the dry land is being constantly washed down by rain and rivers, and deposited in the sea; and that thus, in a longer or shorter time, the inequalities of the earth's surface must be leveled, and its high lands brought down to the ocean. But, taking into account the internal forces of the earth, which, upheaving the sea-bottom, give rise to new land, he thought that these operations of degradation and elevation might compensate each other; and that thus, for any assignable time, the general features of our planet might remain what they are. And inasmuch as, under these circumstances, there need be no limit to the propagation of animals and plants, it is clear that the consistent working-out of the uniformitarian idea might lead to the conception of the eternity of the world. Not that I mean to say that either Hutton or Lyell held this conception—assuredly not; they would have been the first to repudiate it. Nevertheless, the logical development of their arguments tends directly toward this hypothesis.

The second hypothesis supposes that the present order of things, at some no very remote time, had a sudden origin, and that the world, such as it now is, had chaos for its phenomenal antecedent. That is the doctrine which you will find stated most fully and clearly in the immortal poem of John Milton,—the English "Divina Commœdia,"—"Paradise Lost." I believe it is largely to the influence of that remarkable work, combined with the daily teachings to which we have all listened in our childhood, that this hypothesis owes its general wide diffusion as one of the current beliefs of English-speaking people. If you turn to the seventh book of "Paradise Lost," you will find there stated the hypothesis to which I refer, which is briefly this: that this visible universe of ours came into existence at no great distance of time from the present; and that the parts of which it is composed made their appearance, in a certain definite order, in the space of six natural days, in such a manner that, on the first of these days, light appeared; that, on the second, the firmament, or sky, separated the waters above from the waters beneath the firmament; that, on the third day, the waters drew away from the dry land, and upon it a varied vegetable life, similar to that which now exists, made its appearance; that the fourth day was signalized by the apparition of the sun, the stars, the moon, and the planets; that, on the fifth day, aquatic animals originated within the waters; that, on the sixth day, the earth gave rise to our four-footed terrestrial creatures, and to all varieties of terrestrial animals except birds, which had appeared on the preceding day; and, finally, that man appeared upon the earth, and the emergence of the universe from chaos was finished. Milton tells us, without the least ambiguity, what a spectator of these marvelous occurrences would have witnessed. I doubt not that his poem is familiar to all of you, but I should like to recall one passage to your minds, in order that I may be justified in what I have said regarding the perfectly concrete, definite picture of the origin of the animal world which Milton draws. He says:—

The sixth, and of creation last, arose
With evening harps and matin, when God said,
"Let the earth bring forth soul living in her kind,
Cattle and creeping things, and beast of the earth,
Each in their kind!" The earth obeyed, and, straight
Opening her fertile womb, teemed at a birth
Innumerous living creatures, perfect forms,
Limbed and full-grown. Out of the ground uprose,
As from his lair, the wild beast, where he wons
In forest wild, in thicket, brake, or den;
Among the trees in pairs they rose, they walked;
The cattle in the fields and meadows green;
Those rare and solitary; these in flocks
Pasturing at once, and in broad herds upsprung.
The grassy clods now calved; now half appears
The tawny lion, pawing to get free
His hinder parts—then springs, as broke from bonds,
And rampant shakes his brinded mane; the ounce,
The libbard, and the tiger, as the mole
Rising, the crumbled earth above them threw
In hillocks; the swift stag from underground
Bore up his branching head; scarce from his mould
Behemoth, biggest born of earth, upheaved
His vastness; fleeced the flocks and bleating rose
As plants; ambiguous between sea and land,
The river-horse and scaly crocodile.
At once came forth whatever creeps the ground,
Insect or worm.

There is no doubt as to the meaning of this statement, nor as to what a man of Milton's genius expected would have been actually visible to an eye-witness of this mode of origination of living things.

The third hypothesis, or the hypothesis of evolution, supposes that, at any comparatively late period of past time, our imaginary spectator would meet with a state of things very similar to that which now obtains; but that the likeness of the past to the present would gradually become less and less, in proportion to the remoteness of his period of observation from the present day; that the existing distribution of mountains and plains, of rivers and seas, would show itself to be the product of a slow process of natural change operating upon more and more widely different antecedent conditions of the mineral framework of the earth; until, at length, in place of that framework, he would behold only a vast nebulous mass, representing the constituents of the sun and of the planetary bodies. Preceding the forms of life which now exist, our observer would see animals and plants, not identical with them, but like them; increasing their difference with their antiquity and, at the same time, becoming simpler and simpler; until, finally, the world of life would present nothing but that undifferentiated protoplasmic matter which, so far as our present knowledge goes, is the common foundation of all vital activity.

The hypothesis of evolution supposes that, in all this vast progression, there would be no breach of continuity, no point at which we could say, "This is a natural process," and, "This is not a natural process"; but that the whole might be compared to that wonderful process of development which may be seen going on every day under our eyes, in virtue of which there arises, out of the semifluid, comparatively homogeneous substance which we call an egg, the complicated organization of one of the higher animals. That, in a few words, is what is meant by the hypothesis of evolution.

I have already suggested that, in dealing with these three hypotheses, in endeavoring to form a judgment as to which of them is the more worthy of belief, or whether none is worthy of belief,—in which case our condition of mind should be that suspension of judgment which is so difficult to all but trained intellects,—we should be indifferent to all *a priori* considerations. The question is a question of historical fact. The universe has come into existence somehow or other, and the problem is, whether it came into existence in one fashion, or whether it came into existence in another; and, as an essential preliminary to further discussion, permit me to say two or three words as to the nature and the kinds of historical evidence.

The evidence as to the occurrence of any event in past time may be ranged under two heads, which, for convenience' sake, I will speak of as testimonial evidence and as circumstantial evidence. By testimonial evidence I mean human testimony; and by circumstantial evidence I mean evidence which is not human testimony. Let me illustrate by a familiar example what I understand by these two kinds of evidence, and what is to be said respecting their value.

Suppose that a man tells you that he saw a person strike another and kill him: that is testimonial evidence of the fact of murder. But it is possible to have circumstantial evidence of the fact of murder: that is to say, you may find a man dying with a wound upon his head having exactly the form and character of the wound which is made by an axe; and, with due care in taking surrounding circumstances into account, you may conclude with the utmost certainty that the man has been murdered; that his death is the consequence of a blow inflicted by another man with that implement. We are very much in the habit of considering circumstantial evidence as of less value than testimonial evidence; and it may be that, where the circumstances are not perfectly clear and intelligible, it is a dangerous and unsafe kind of evidence; but it must not be forgotten that, in many cases, circumstantial is quite as conclusive as testimonial evidence, and that, not unfrequently, it is a great deal weightier than testimonial evidence. For example, take the case to which I referred just now. The circumstantial evidence may be better and more convincing than the testimonial evidence; for it may be impossible, under the conditions that I have defined, to suppose that the man met his death from any cause but the violent blow of an axe wielded by another man. The circumstantial evidence in favor of a murder having been committed, in that case, is as complete and as convincing as evidence can be. It is evidence which is open to no doubt and to no falsification. But the testimony of a witness is open to multitudinous doubts. He may have been mistaken. He may have been actuated by malice. It has constantly happened that even an accurate man has declared that a thing has happened in this, that, or the other way, when a careful analysis of the circumstantial evidence has shown that it did not happen in that way, but in some other way.

We may now consider the evidence in favor of or against the three hypotheses. Let me first direct your attention to what is to be said about the hypotheses of the eternity of the state of things in which we now live. What will first strike you is, that it is a hypothesis which, whether true or false, is not capable of verification by any evidence. For, in order to obtain either circumstantial or testimonial evidence sufficient to prove the eternity of duration of the present state of nature, you must have an eternity of witnesses or an infinity of circumstances, and neither of these is attainable. It is utterly impossible that such evidence should be carried beyond a certain point of time; and all that could be said, at most, would be, that, so far as the evidence could be traced, there was nothing to contradict the hypothesis. But when you look, not to the testimonial evidence,—which, considering the relative insignificance of the antiquity of human records, might not be good for much in this case,—but to the circumstantial evidence, then you find that this hypothesis is absolutely incompatible with such evidence as we have; which is of so plain and so simple a character that it is impossible in any way to escape from the conclusions which it forces upon us.

You are, doubtless, all aware that the outer substance of the earth, which alone is accessible to direct observation, is not of a homogeneous character, but that it is made up of a number of layers or strata. Each of these groups represents a number of beds of sand, of stone, of clay, of slate, and of various other materials.

On careful examination, it is found that the materials of which each of these layers of more or less hard rock is composed are, for the most part, of the same nature as those which are at present being formed under known conditions on the surface of the earth. For example, the chalk, which constitutes a great part of the Cretaceous formation in some parts of the world, is practically identical in its physical and chemical characters with a substance which is now being formed at the bottom of the Atlantic Ocean, and covers an enormous area; other beds of rock are comparable with the sands which are being formed upon sea-shores, packed together, and so on. Thus, omitting rocks of igneous origin, it is demonstrable that all these beds of stone, of which a total of not less than seventy thousand feet is known, have been formed by natural agencies, either out of the waste and washing of the dry land, or else by the accumulation of the exuviæ of plants and animals. Many of these strata are full of such exuviæ—the so-called "fossils." Remains of thousands of species of animals and plants, as perfectly recognizable as those of existing forms of life which you meet with in museums, or as the shells which you pick up upon the sea-beach, have been imbedded in the ancient sands, or muds, or limestones, just as they are being imbedded now in sandy, or clayey, or calcareous subaqueous deposits. They furnish us with a record, the general nature of which cannot be misinterpreted, of the kinds of things that have lived upon the surface of the earth during the time that is registered by this great thickness of stratified rocks.

But even a superficial study of these fossils shows us that the animals and plants which live at the present time have had only a temporary duration; for the remains of such modern forms of life are met with, for the most part, only in the uppermost, or latest, tertiaries, and their number rapidly diminishes in the lower deposits of that epoch. In the older tertiaries, the places of existing animals and plants are taken by other forms, as numerous and diversified as those which live now in the same localities, but more or less different from them; in the mesozoic rocks, these are replaced by others yet more divergent from modern types; and in the palæozoic formations, the contrast is still more marked. Thus the circumstantial evidence absolutely negatives the conception of the eternity of the present condition of things. We can say with certainty that the present condition of things has existed for a comparatively short period; and that, so far as animal and vegetable nature are concerned, it has been preceded by a different condition. We can pursue this evidence until we reach the lowest of the stratified rocks, in which we lose the indications of life altogether. The hypothesis of the eternity of the present state of nature may, therefore, be put out of court.

We now come to what I will term Milton's hypothesis—the hypothesis that the present condition of things has endured for a comparatively short time; and, at the commencement of that time, came into existence within the course of six days. I doubt not that it may have excited some surprise in your minds that I should have spoken of this as Milton's hypothesis, rather than that I should have chosen the terms which are more customary, such as "the doctrine of creation," or "the Biblical doctrine," or "the doctrine of Moses," all of which denominations, as applied to the hypothesis to which I have just referred, are certainly much more familiar to you than the title of the Miltonic hypothesis. But I have had what I cannot but think are very weighty reasons for taking the course which I have pursued. In the first place, I have discarded the title of the "doctrine of creation," because my present business is not with the question why the objects which constitute nature came into existence, but when they came into existence, and in what order. This is as strictly a historical question as the question when the Angles and the Jutes invaded England, and whether they preceded or followed the Romans. But the question about creation is a philosophical problem, and one which cannot be solved, or even approached, by the historical method. What we want to learn is, whether the facts, so far as they are known, afford evidence that things arose in the way described by Milton, or whether they do not; and, when that question is settled, it will be time enough to inquire into the causes of their origination.

In the second place, I have not spoken of this doctrine as the Biblical doctrine. It is quite true that persons as diverse in their general views as Milton the Protestant and the celebrated Jesuit Father Suarez, each put upon the first chapter of Genesis the interpretation embodied in Milton's poem. It is quite true that this interpretation is that which has been instilled into every one of us in our childhood; but I do not for one moment venture to say that it can properly be called the Biblical doctrine. It is not my business, and does not lie within my competency, to say what the Hebrew text does, and what it does not signify; moreover, were I to affirm that this is the Biblical doctrine, I should be met by the authority of many eminent scholars, to say nothing of men of science, who, at various times, have absolutely denied that any such doctrine is to be found in Genesis. If we are to listen to many expositors of no mean authority, we must believe that what seems so clearly defined in Genesis—as if very great pains had been taken that there should be no possibility of mistake—is not the meaning of the text at all. The account is divided into periods, which we may make just as long or as short as convenience requires. We are also to understand that it is consistent with the original text to believe that the most complex plants and animals may have been evolved by natural processes, lasting for millions of years, out of structureless rudiments. A person who is not a Hebrew scholar can only stand aside and admire the marvelous flexibility of a language which admits of such diverse interpretations. But assuredly, in the face of such contradictions of authority upon matters respecting which he is incompetent to form any judgment, he will abstain, as I do, from giving any opinion.

In the third place, I have carefully abstained from speaking of this as the Mosaic doctrine, because we are now assured upon the authority of the highest critics, and even of dignitaries of the Church, that there is no evidence that Moses wrote the Book of Genesis, or knew anything about it. You will understand that I give no judgment—it would be an impertinence upon my part to volunteer even a suggestion—upon such a subject. But, that being the state of opinion among the scholars and the clergy, it is well for the unlearned in Hebrew lore, and for the laity, to avoid entangling themselves in such a vexed question. Happily, Milton leaves us no excuse for doubting what he means, and I shall therefore be safe in speaking of the opinion in question as the Miltonic hypothesis.

Now we have to test that hypothesis. For my part, I have no prejudice one way or the other. If there is evidence in favor of this view, I am burdened by no theoretical difficulties in the way of accepting it; but there must be evidence. Scientific men get an awkward habit—no, I won't call it that, for it is a valuable habit—of believing nothing unless there is evidence for it; and they have a way of looking upon belief which is not based upon evidence, not only as illogical, but as immoral. We will, if you please, test this view by the circumstantial evidence alone; for, from what I have said, you will understand that I do not propose to discuss the question of what testimonial evidence is to be adduced in favor of it. If those whose business it is to judge are not at one as to the authenticity of the only evidence of that kind which is offered, nor as to the facts to which it bears witness, the discussion of such evidence is superfluous. But I may be permitted to regret this necessity of rejecting the testimonial evidence the less, because the examination of the circumstantial evidence leads to the conclusion, not only that it is incompetent to justify the hypothesis, but that, so far as it goes, it is contrary to the hypothesis.

The considerations upon which I base this conclusion are of the simplest possible character. The Miltonic hypothesis contains assertions of a very definite character relating to the succession of living forms. It is stated that plants, for example, made their appearance upon the third day, and not before. And you will understand that what the poet means by plants are such plants as now live, the ancestors, in the ordinary way of propagation of like by like, of the trees and shrubs which flourish in the present world. It must needs be so: for, if they were different, either the existing plants have been the result of a separate origination since that described by Milton, of which we have no record, or any ground for supposition that such an occurrence has taken place; or else they have arisen by a process of evolution from the original stocks.

In the second place, it is clear that there was no animal life before the fifth day, and that, on the fifth day, aquatic animals and birds appeared. And it is further clear that terrestrial living things, other than birds, made their appearance upon the sixth day, and not before. Hence, it follows that if, in the large mass of circumstantial evidence as to what really has happened in the past history of the globe we find indications of the existence of terrestrial animals, other than birds, at a certain period, it is perfectly certain that all that has taken place since that time must be referred to the sixth day.

In the great Carboniferous formation, whence America derives so vast a proportion of her actual and potential wealth, in the beds of coal which have been formed from the vegetation of that period, we find abundant evidence of the existence of terrestrial animals. They have been described, not only by European but by American naturalists. There are to be found numerous insects allied to our cockroaches. There are to be found spiders and scorpions of large size, the latter so similar to existing scorpions that it requires the practised eye of the naturalist to distinguish them. Inasmuch as these animals can be proved to have been alive in the Carboniferous epoch, it is perfectly clear that, if the Miltonic account is to be accepted, the huge mass of rocks extending from the middle of the Palæozoic formations to the uppermost members of the series must belong to the day which is termed by Milton the sixth.

But, further, it is expressly stated that aquatic animals took their origin upon the fifth day, and not before; hence, all formations in which remains of aquatic animals can be proved to exist, and which therefore testify that such animals lived at the time when these formations were in course of deposition, must have been deposited during or since the period which Milton speaks of as the fifth day. But there is absolutely no fossiliferous formation in which the remains of aquatic animals are absent. The oldest fossils in the Silurian rocks are exuviæ of marine animals; and if the view which is entertained by Principal Dawson and Dr. Carpenter respecting the nature of the Eozoön be well founded, aquatic animals existed at a period as far antecedent to the deposition of the coal as the coal is from us; inasmuch as the Eozoön is met with in those Laurentian strata which lie at the bottom of the series of stratified rocks. Hence it follows, plainly enough, that the whole series of stratified rocks, if they are to be brought into harmony with Milton, must be referred to the fifth and sixth days, and that we cannot hope to find the slightest trace of the products of the earlier days in the geological record. When we consider these simple facts, we see how absolutely futile are the attempts that have been made to draw a parallel between the story told by so much of the crust of the earth as is known to us and the story that Milton tells. The whole series of fossiliferous stratified rocks must be referred to the last two days; and neither the Carboniferous nor any other formation can afford evidence of the work of the third day.

Not only is there this objection to any attempt to establish a harmony between the Miltonic account and the facts recorded in the fossiliferous rocks, but there is a further difficulty. According to the Miltonic account, the order in which animals should have made their appearance in the stratified rocks would be this: fishes, including the great whales, and birds; after them, all varieties of terrestrial animals except birds. Nothing could be further from the facts as we find them; we know of not the slightest evidence of the existence of birds before the Jurassic, or perhaps the Triassic, formation; while terrestrial animals, as we have just seen, occur in the Carboniferous rocks. If there were any harmony between the Miltonic account and the circumstantial evidence, we ought to have abundant evidence of the existence of birds in the Carboniferous, the Devonian, and the Silurian rocks. I need hardly say that this is not the case, and that not a trace of birds makes its appearance until the far later period which I have mentioned.

And again, if it be true that all varieties of fishes and the great whales, and the like, made their appearance on the fifth day, we ought to find the remains of these animals in the older rocks—in those which were deposited before the Carboniferous epoch. Fishes we do find, in considerable number and variety; but the great whales are absent, and the fishes are not such as now live. Not one solitary species of fish now in existence is to be found in the Devonian or Silurian formations. Hence we are introduced afresh to the dilemma which I have already placed before you: either the animals which came into existence on the fifth day were not such as those which are found at present, are not the direct and immediate ancestors of those which now exist,—in which case either fresh creations of which nothing is said, or a process of evolution, must have occurred,—or else the whole story must be given up, as not only devoid of any circumstantial evidence, but as contrary to such evidence as exists.

I placed before you in a few words, some little time ago, a statement of the sum and substance of Milton's hypothesis. Let me now try to state, as briefly, the effect of the circumstantial evidence bearing upon the past history of the earth which is furnished, without the possibility of mistake, with no chance of error as to its chief features, by the stratified rocks. What we find is that the great series of formations represents a period of time of which our human chronologies hardly afford us a unit of measure. I will not pretend to say how we ought to estimate this time, in millions or in billions of years. For my purpose, the determination of its absolute duration is wholly unessential; but unquestionably the time was enormous.

It results from the simplest methods of interpretation, that, leaving out of view certain patches of metamorphosed rocks, and certain volcanic products, all that is now dry land has once been at the bottom of the waters. It is perfectly certain that, at a comparatively recent period of the world's history,—the Cretaceous epoch,—none of the great physical features, which at present mark the surface of the globe, existed. It is certain that the Rocky Mountains were not. It is certain that the Himalaya Mountains were not. It is certain that the Alps and the Pyrenees had no existence. The evidence is of the plainest possible character, and is simply this: we find raised up on the flanks of these mountains, elevated by the forces of upheaval which have given rise to them, masses of Cretaceous rock which formed the bottom of the sea before those mountains existed. It is therefore clear that the elevatory forces which gave rise to the mountains operated subsequently to the Cretaceous epoch; and that the mountains themselves are largely made up of the materials deposited in the sea which once occupied their place. As we go back in time, we meet with constant alternations of sea and land, of estuary and open ocean; and, in correspondence with these alternations, we observe the changes in the fauna and flora to which I have referred.

But the inspection of these changes gives us no right to believe that there has been any discontinuity in natural processes. There is no trace of general cataclysms, of universal deluges, or of sudden destructions of a whole fauna or flora. The appearances which were formerly interpreted in that way have all been shown to be delusive, as our knowledge has increased, and as the blanks which formerly appeared to exist between the different formations have been filled up. That there is no absolute break between formation and formation, that there has been no sudden disappearance of all the forms of life and replacement of them by others, but that changes have gone on slowly and gradually, that one type has died out and another has taken its place, and that thus, by insensible degrees, one fauna has been replaced by another, are conclusions strengthened by constantly increasing evidence. So that within the whole of the immense period indicated by the fossiliferous stratified rocks there is assuredly not the slightest proof of any break in the uniformity of nature's operations, no indication that events have followed other than a clear and orderly sequence.

That, I say, is the natural and obvious teaching of the circumstantial evidence contained in the stratified rocks. I leave you to consider how far, by any ingenuity of interpretation, by any stretching of the meaning of language, it can be brought into harmony with the Miltonic hypothesis.

ON THE PHYSICAL BASIS OF LIFE

In order to make the title of this discourse generally intelligible, I have translated the term "protoplasm," which is the scientific name of the substance of which I am about to speak, by the words "the physical basis of life." I suppose that, to many, the idea that there is such a thing as a physical basis, or matter, of life may be novel, so widely spread is the conception of life as a something which works through matter, but is independent of it; and even those who are aware that matter and life are inseparably connected may not be prepared for the conclusion—plainly suggested by the phrase, "*the* physical basis or matter of life,"—that there is some one kind of matter which is common to all living beings, and that their endless diversities are bound together by a physical, as well as an ideal, unity. In fact, when first apprehended, such a doctrine as this appears almost shocking to common sense.

What, truly, can seem to be more obviously different from one another, in faculty, in form, and in substance, than the various kinds of living beings? What community of faculty can there be between the brightly colored lichen, which so nearly resembles a mere mineral incrustation of the bare rock on which it grows, and the painter, to whom it is instinct with beauty, or the botanist, whom it feeds with knowledge?

Again, think of the microscopic fungus—a mere infinitesimal ovoid particle, which finds space and duration enough to multiply into countless millions in the body of a living fly; and then of the wealth of foliage, the luxuriance of flower and fruit, which lies between this bald sketch of a plant and the giant pine of California, towering to the dimensions of a cathedral spire, or the Indian fig, which covers acres with its profound shadow, and endures while nations and empires come and go around its vast circumference. Or, turning to the other half of the world of life, picture to yourselves the great Finner whale, hugest of beasts that live or have lived, disporting his eighty or ninety feet of bone, muscle, and blubber, with easy roll, among waves in which the stoutest ship that ever left dockyard would founder hopelessly; and contrast him with the invisible animalcules—mere gelatinous specks, multitudes of which could, in fact, dance upon the point of a needle with the same ease as the angels of the Schoolmen could, in imagination. With these images before your minds, you may well ask, what community of form, or structure, is there between the animalcule and the whale, or between the fungus and the fig tree? And, *a fortiori*, between all four?

Finally, if we regard substance, or material composition, what hidden bond can connect the flower that a girl wears in her hair and the blood that courses through her youthful veins; or, what is there in common between the dense and resisting mass of the oak, or the strong fabric of the tortoise, and those broad disks of glassy jelly which may be seen pulsating through the waters of a calm sea, but which drain away to mere films in the hand which raises them out of their element?

Such objections as these must, I think, arise in the mind of everyone who ponders, for the first time, upon the conception of a single physical basis of life underlying all the diversities of vital existence; but I propose to demonstrate to you that, notwithstanding these apparent difficulties, a threefold unity—namely, a unity of power or faculty, a unity of form, and a unity of substantial composition—does pervade the whole living world.

No very abstruse argumentation is needed, in the first place, to prove that the powers, or faculties, of all kinds of living matter, diverse as they may be in degree, are substantially similar in kind.

Goethe has condensed a survey of all the powers of mankind into the well-known epigram:—

Warum treibt sich das Volk so und schreit? Es will sich ernähren,
Kinder zeugen, und die nähren so gut es vermag.
. . . .
Weiter bringt es kein Mensch, stell' er sich wie er auch will.

In physiological language this means that all the multifarious and complicated activities of man are comprehensible under three categories. Either they are immediately directed toward the maintenance and development of the body, or they effect transitory changes in the relative positions of parts of the body, or they tend toward the continuance of the species. Even those manifestations of intellect, of feeling, and of will, which we rightly name the higher faculties, are not excluded from this classification, inasmuch as, to everyone but the subject of them, they are known only as transitory changes in the relative positions of parts of the body. Speech, gesture, and every other form of human action are, in the long run, resolvable into muscular contraction, and muscular contraction is but a transitory change in the relative positions of the parts of a muscle. But the scheme which is large enough to embrace the activities of the highest form of life covers all those of the lower creatures. The lowest plant, or animalcule, feeds, grows, and reproduces its kind. In addition, all animals manifest those transitory changes of form which we class under irritability and contractility; and it is more than probable that, when the vegetable world is thoroughly explored, we shall find all plants in possession of the same powers, at one time or other of their existence.

I am not now alluding to such phenomena, at once rare and conspicuous, as those exhibited by the leaflets of the sensitive plant, or the stamens of the barberry, but to such more widely spread, and, at the same time, more subtle and hidden, manifestations of vegetable contractility. You are doubtless aware that the common nettle owes its stinging property to the innumerable stiff and needle-like, though exquisitely delicate, hairs that cover its surface. Each stinging needle tapers from a broad base to a slender summit, which, though rounded at the end, is of such microscopic fineness that it readily penetrates, and breaks off in, the skin. The whole hair consists of a very delicate outer case of wood, closely applied to the inner surface of which is a layer of semifluid matter, full of innumerable granules of extreme minuteness. This semifluid lining is protoplasm, which thus constitutes a kind of bag, full of a limpid liquid, and roughly corresponding in form with the interior of the hair which it fills. When viewed with a sufficiently high magnifying power, the protoplasmic layer of the nettle hair is seen to be in a condition of unceasing activity. Local contractions of the whole thickness of its substance pass slowly and gradually from point to point, and give rise to the appearance of progressive waves, just as the bending of successive stalks of corn by a breeze produces the apparent billows of a cornfield.

But, in addition to these movements, and independently of them, the granules are driven, in relatively rapid streams, through channels in the protoplasm which seem to have a considerable amount of persistence. Most commonly, the currents in adjacent parts of the protoplasm take similar directions; and, thus, there is a general stream up one side of the hair and down the other. But this does not prevent the existence of partial currents which take different routes; and, sometimes, trains of granules may be seen coursing swiftly in opposite directions, within a twenty-thousandth of an inch of one another; while, occasionally, opposite streams come into direct collision, and, after a longer or shorter struggle, one predominates. The cause of these currents seems to lie in contractions of the protoplasm which bounds the channels in which they flow, but contractions so minute that the best microscopes show only their effects, and not themselves.

The spectacle afforded by the wonderful energies prisoned within the compass of the microscopic hair of a plant, which we commonly regard as a merely passive organism, is not easily forgotten by one who has watched its display, continued hour after hour, without pause or sign of weakening. The possible complexity of many other organic forms, seemingly as simple as the protoplasm of the nettle, dawns upon one; and the comparison of such a protoplasm to a body with an internal circulation, which has been put forward by an eminent physiologist, loses much of its startling character. Currents similar to those of the hairs of the nettle have been observed in a great multitude of very different plants, and weighty authorities have suggested that they probably occur, in more or less perfection, in all young vegetable cells. If such be the case, the wonderful noonday silence of a tropical forest is, after all, due only to the dullness of our hearing; and could our ears catch the murmur of these tiny maelstroms, as they whirl in the innumerable myriads of living cells which constitute each tree, we should be stunned, as with the roar of a great city.

Among the lower plants, it is the rule rather than the exception that contractility should be still more openly manifested at some periods of their existence. The protoplasm of Algæ and Fungi becomes, under many circumstances, partially, or completely, freed from its woody case, and exhibits movements of its whole mass, or is propelled by the contractility of one or more hair-like prolongations of its body, which are called vibratile *cilia*. And, so far as the conditions of the manifestation of the phenomena of contractility have yet been studied, they are the same for the plant as for the animal. Heat and electric shocks influence both, and in the same way, though it may be in different degrees. It is by no means my intention to suggest that there is no difference in faculty between the lowest plant and the highest, or between plants and animals. But the difference between the powers of the lowest plant, or animal, and those of the highest, is one of degree, not of kind, and depends, as Milne-Edwards long ago so well pointed out, upon the extent to which the principle of the division of labor is carried out in the living economy. In the lowest organism all parts are competent to perform all functions, and one and the same portion of protoplasm may successively take on the function of feeding, moving, or reproducing apparatus. In the highest, on the contrary, a great number of parts combine to perform each function, each part doing its allotted share of the work with great accuracy and efficiency, but being useless for any other purpose.

On the other hand, notwithstanding all the fundamental resemblances that exist between the powers of the protoplasm in plants and in animals, they present a striking difference (to which I shall advert more at length presently), in the fact that plants can manufacture fresh protoplasm out of mineral compounds, whereas animals are obliged to procure it ready-made, and hence, in the long run, depend upon plants. Upon what condition this difference in the powers of the two great divisions of the world of life depends, nothing is at present known.

With such qualification as arises out of the last mentioned fact, it may be truly said that the acts of all living things are fundamentally one. Is any such unity predictable of their forms? Let us seek in easily verified facts for a reply to this question. If a drop of blood be drawn by pricking one's finger, and viewed with proper precautions and under a sufficiently high microscopic power, there will be seen, among the innumerable multitude of little circular, discoidal bodies, or corpuscles, which float in it and give it its color, a comparatively small number of colorless corpuscles, of somewhat larger size and very irregular shape. If the drop of blood be kept at the temperature of the body, these colorless corpuscles will be seen to exhibit a marvelous activity, changing their forms with great rapidity, drawing in and thrusting out prolongations of their substance, and creeping about as if they were independent organisms.

The substance which is thus active is a mass of protoplasm, and its activity differs in detail, rather than in principle, from that of the protoplasm of the nettle. Under sundry circumstances the corpuscle dies and becomes distended into a round mass, in the midst of which is seen a smaller spherical body, which existed, but was more or less hidden, in the living corpuscle, and is called its *nucleus*. Corpuscles of essentially similar structure are to be found in the skin, in the lining of the mouth, and scattered through the whole framework of the body. Nay, more: in the earliest condition of the human organism, in that state in which it has but just become distinguishable from the egg in which it arises, it is nothing but an aggregation of such corpuscles, and every organ of the body was, once, no more than such an aggregation.

Thus a nucleated mass of protoplasm turns out to be what may be termed the structural unit of the human body. As a matter of fact, the body, in its earliest state, is a mere multiple of such units; and, in its perfect condition, it is a multiple of such units variously modified.

But does the formula which expresses the essential structural character of the highest animal cover all the rest, as the statement of its powers and faculties covered that of all others? Very nearly. Beast and fowl, reptile and fish, mollusk, worm, and polyp, are all composed of structural units of the same character, namely, masses of protoplasm with a nucleus. There are sundry very low animals, each of which, structurally, is a mere colorless blood-corpuscle, leading an independent life. But, at the very bottom of the animal scale, even this simplicity becomes simplified, and all the phenomena of life are manifested by a particle of protoplasm without a nucleus. Nor are such organisms insignificant by reason of their want of complexity. It is a fair question whether the protoplasm of those simplest forms of life which people an immense extent of the bottom of the sea would not outweigh that of all the higher living beings which inhabit the land put together. And in ancient times, no less than at the present day, such living beings as these have been the greatest of rock-builders.

What has been said of the animal world is no less true of plants. Imbedded in the protoplasm at the broad, or attached, end of the nettle hair, there lies a spheroidal nucleus. Careful examination further proves that the whole substance of the nettle is made up of a repetition of such masses of nucleated protoplasm, each contained in a wooden case, which is modified in form, sometimes into a woody fibre, sometimes into a duct or spiral vessel, sometimes into a pollen grain, or an ovule. Traced back to its earliest state, the nettle arises, as the man does, in a particle of nucleated protoplasm. And in the lowest plants, as in the lowest animals, a single mass of such protoplasm may constitute the whole plant, or the protoplasm may exist without a nucleus.

Under these circumstances it may well be asked, how is one mass of non-nucleated protoplasm to be distinguished from another? Why call one "plant" and the other "animal"?

The only reply is that, so far as form is concerned, plants and animals are not separable, and that, in many cases, it is a mere matter of convention whether we call a given organism an animal or a plant. There is a living body called *Æthalium septicum*, which appears upon decaying vegetable substances, and, in one of its forms, is common upon the surfaces of tan-pits. In this condition it is, to all intents and purposes, a fungus, and formerly was always regarded as such; but the remarkable investigations of De Bary have shown that, in another condition, the *Æthalium* is an actively locomotive creature, and takes in solid matters, upon which, apparently, it feeds, thus exhibiting the most characteristic feature of animality. Is this a plant, or is it an animal? Is it both, or is it neither? Some decide in favor of the last supposition, and establish an intermediate kingdom, a sort of biological "No Man's Land," for all these questionable forms. But, as it is admittedly impossible to draw any distinct boundary line between this no man's land and the vegetable world, on the one hand, and the animal, on the other, it appears to me that this proceeding merely doubles the difficulty which, before, was single.

Protoplasm, simple or nucleated, is the formal basis of all life. It is the clay of the potter, which, bake it and paint it as he will, remains clay, separated by artifice, and not by nature, from the commonest brick or sun-dried clod.

Thus it becomes clear that all living powers are cognate, and that all living forms are fundamentally of one character. The researches of the chemist have revealed a no less striking uniformity of material composition in living matter.

In perfect strictness, it is true that chemical investigation can tell us little or nothing, directly, of the composition of living matter, inasmuch as such matter must needs die in the act of analysis; and upon this very obvious ground, objections, which I confess seem to me to be somewhat frivolous, have been raised to the drawing of any conclusions whatever respecting the composition of actually living matter, from that of the dead matter of life, which alone is accessible to us. But objectors of this class do not seem to reflect that it is also, in strictness, true that we know nothing about the composition of any body whatever, as it is. The statement that a crystal of calc-spar consists of carbonate of lime is quite true, if we only mean that, by appropriate processes, it may be resolved into carbonic acid and quicklime.

If you pass the same carbonic acid over the very quicklime thus obtained, you will obtain carbonate of lime again; but it will not be calc-spar, or anything like it. Can it, therefore, be said that chemical analysis teaches nothing about the chemical composition of calc-spar? Such a statement would be absurd; but it is hardly more so than the talk one occasionally hears about the uselessness of applying the results of chemical analysis to the living bodies that have yielded them.

One fact, at any rate, is out of reach of such refinements, and this is, that all the forms of protoplasm which have yet been examined contain the four elements, carbon, hydrogen, oxygen, and nitrogen, in very complex union, and that they behave similarly toward several reagents. To this complex combination, the nature of which has never been determined with exactness, the name of protein has been applied. And if we use this term with such caution as may properly arise out of our comparative ignorance of the things for which it stands, it may be truly said that all protoplasm is proteinaceous; or, as the white, or albumen, of an egg is one of the commonest examples of a nearly pure protein matter, we may say that all living matter is more or less albuminoid.

Perhaps it would not yet be safe to say that all forms of protoplasm are affected by the direct action of electric shocks; and yet the number of cases in which the contraction of protoplasm is shown to be effected by this agency increases every day.

Nor can it be affirmed with perfect confidence that all forms of protoplasm are liable to undergo that peculiar coagulation at a temperature of from 40 to 50 degrees Centigrade, which has been called "heat-stiffening"; though Kuhne's beautiful researches have proved this occurrence to take place in so many and such diverse living beings, that it is hardly rash to expect that the law holds good for all.

Enough has, perhaps, been said to prove the existence of a general uniformity in the character of the protoplasm, or physical basis of life, in whatever group of living beings it may be studied. But it will be understood that this general uniformity by no means excludes any amount of special modifications of the fundamental substance. The mineral, carbonate of lime, assumes an immense diversity of characters, though no one doubts that, under all these protean changes, it is one and the same thing.

And now, what is the ultimate fate, and what the origin, of the matter of life?

Is it, as some of the older naturalists supposed, diffused throughout the universe in molecules, which are indestructible and unchangeable in themselves, but, in endless transmigration, unite in innumerable permutations, into the diversified forms of life we know? Or, is the matter of life composed of ordinary matter, differing from it only in the manner in which its atoms are aggregated? Is it built up of ordinary matter, and again resolved into ordinary matter when its work is done?

Modern science does not hesitate a moment between these alternatives. Physiology writes over the portals of life:—

Debemur morti nos nostraque,—

with a profounder meaning than the Roman poet attached to that melancholy line. Under whatever disguise it takes refuge, whether fungus or oak, worm or man, the living protoplasm not only ultimately dies and is resolved into its mineral and lifeless constituents, but is always dying, and, strange as the paradox may sound, could not live unless it died.

In the wonderful story of the "Peau de Chagrin," the hero becomes possessed of a magical wild ass's skin, which yields him the means of gratifying all his wishes. But its surface represents the duration of the proprietor's life; and for every satisfied desire the skin shrinks in proportion to the intensity of fruition, until at length life and the last handbreadth of the *peau de chagrin* disappear with the gratification of a last wish.

Balzac's studies had led him over a wide range of thought and speculation, and his shadowing forth of physiological truth in this strange story may have been intentional. At any rate, the matter of life is a veritable *peau de chagrin*, and for every trivial act it is somewhat the smaller. All work implies waste, and the work of life results, directly or indirectly, in the waste of protoplasm.

Every word uttered by a speaker costs him some physical loss; and, in the strictest sense, he burns that others may have light—so much eloquence, so much of his body resolved into carbonic acid, water, and urea. It is clear that this process of expenditure cannot go on forever. But, happily, the protoplasmic *peau de chagrin* differs from Balzac's in its capacity of being repaired, and brought back to its full size, after every exertion.

For example, this present lecture, whatever its intellectual worth to you, has a certain physical value to me, which is conceivably expressible by the number of grains of protoplasm and other bodily substance wasted in maintaining my vital processes during its delivery. My *peau de chagrin* will be distinctly smaller at the end of the discourse than it was at the beginning. By and by, I shall probably have recourse to the substance commonly called mutton, for the purpose of stretching it back to its original size. Now, this mutton was once the living protoplasm, more or less modified, of another animal—a sheep. As I shall eat it, it is the same matter altered, not only by death, but by exposure to sundry artificial operations in the process of cooking.

But these changes, whatever be their extent, have not rendered it incompetent to resume its old functions as matter of life. A singular inward laboratory, which I possess, will dissolve a certain portion of the modified protoplasm; the solution so formed will pass into my veins; and the subtle influences to which it will then be subjected will convert the dead protoplasm into living protoplasm, and transubstantiate sheep into man.

Nor is this all. If digestion were a thing to be trifled with, I might sup on lobster, and the matter of life of the crustacean would undergo the same wonderful metamorphosis into humanity. And were I to return to my own place by sea, and undergo shipwreck, the crustacea might, and probably would, return the compliment, and demonstrate our common nature by turning my protoplasm into living lobster. Or, if nothing better were to be had, I might supply my wants with mere bread, and I should find the protoplasm of the wheat-plant to be convertible into man, with no more trouble than that of the sheep, and with far less, I fancy, than that of the lobster.

Hence it appears to be a matter of no great moment what animal, or what plant, I lay under contribution for protoplasm; and the fact speaks volumes for the general identity of that substance in all living beings. I share this catholicity of assimilation with other animals, all of which, so far as we know, could thrive equally well on the protoplasm of any of their fellows, or of any plant; but here the assimilative powers of the animal world cease. A solution of smelling-salts in water, with an infinitesimal proportion of some other saline matters, contains all the elementary bodies which enter into the composition of protoplasm; but, as I need hardly say, a hogshead of that fluid would not keep a hungry man from starving, nor would it save any animal whatever from a like fate. An animal cannot make protoplasm, but must take it ready-made from some other animal, or some plant—the animal's highest feat of constructive chemistry being to convert dead protoplasm into that living matter of life which is appropriate to itself.

Therefore, in seeking for the origin of protoplasm, we must eventually turn to the vegetable world. The fluid containing carbonic acid, water, and ammonia, which offers such a Barmecide feast to the animal, is a table richly spread to multitudes of plants; and, with a due supply of only such materials, many a plant will not only maintain itself in vigor, but grow and multiply until it has increased a million-fold, or a million-million-fold, the quantity of protoplasm which it originally possessed; in this way building up the matter of life, to an indefinite extent, from the common matter of the universe.

Thus, the animal can only raise the complex substance of dead protoplasm to the higher power, as one may say, of living protoplasm; while the plant can raise the less complex substances—carbonic acid, water, and ammonia—

to the same stage of living protoplasm, if not to the same level. But the plant also has its limitations. Some of the fungi, for example, appear to need higher compounds to start with; and no known plant can live upon the uncompounded elements of protoplasm. A plant supplied with pure carbon, hydrogen, oxygen, and nitrogen, phosphorus, sulphur and the like, would as infallibly die as the animal in his bath of smelling-salts, though it would be surrounded by all the constituents of protoplasm. Nor, indeed, need the process of simplification of vegetable food be carried so far as this, in order to arrive at the limit of the plant's thaumaturgy. Let water, carbonic acid, and all the other needful constituents be supplied with ammonia, and an ordinary plant will still be unable to manufacture protoplasm.

Thus the matter of life, so far as we know it (and we have no right to speculate on any other), breaks up, in consequence of that continual death which is the condition of its manifesting vitality, into carbonic acid, water, and ammonia, which certainly possess no properties but those of ordinary matter. And out of these same forms of ordinary matter, and from none which are simpler, the vegetable world builds up all the protoplasm that keeps the animal world a-going. Plants are the accumulators of the power which animals distribute and disperse.

But it will be observed that the existence of the matter of life depends on the preëxistence of certain compounds; namely, carbonic acid, water, and ammonia. Withdraw any one of these three from the world, and all vital phenomena come to an end. They are related to the protoplasm of the plant, as the protoplasm of the plant is to that of the animal. Carbon, hydrogen, oxygen, and nitrogen are all lifeless bodies. Of these, carbon and oxygen unite in certain proportions, and under certain conditions, to give rise to carbonic acid; hydrogen and oxygen produce water; nitrogen and hydrogen give rise to ammonia. These new compounds, like the elementary bodies of which they are composed, are lifeless. But when they are brought together, under certain conditions, they give rise to the still more complex body, protoplasm, and this protoplasm exhibits the phenomena of life.

I see no break in this series of steps in molecular complication, and I am unable to understand why the language which is applicable to any one term of the series may not be used with any of the others. We think fit to call different kinds of matter carbon, oxygen, hydrogen, and nitrogen, and to speak of the various powers and activities of these substances as the properties of the matter of which they are composed.

When hydrogen and oxygen are mixed in a certain proportion, and an electric spark is passed through them, they disappear, and a quantity of water, equal in weight to the sum of their weights, appears in their place. There is not the slightest parity between the passive and active powers of the water and those of the oxygen and hydrogen which have given rise to it. At 32 degrees Fahrenheit, and far below that temperature, oxygen and hydrogen are elastic gaseous bodies, whose particles tend to rush away from one another with great force. Water, at the same temperature, is a strong though brittle solid, whose particles tend to cohere into definite geometrical shapes, and sometimes build up frosty imitations of the most complex forms of vegetable foliage.

Nevertheless we call these, and many other strange phenomena, the properties of the water, and we do not hesitate to believe that, in some way or another, they result from the properties of the component elements of the water. We do not assume that a something called "aquosity" entered into and took possession of the oxide of hydrogen as soon as it was formed, and then guided the aqueous particles to their places in the facets of the crystal, or among the leaflets of the hoar-frost. On the contrary, we live in the hope and in the faith that, by the advance of molecular physics, we shall by-and-by be able to see our way as clearly from the constituents of water to the properties of water, as we are now able to deduce the operations of a watch from the form of its parts and the manner in which they are put together.

Is the case in any way changed when carbonic acid, water, and ammonia disappear, and in their place, under the influence of preëxisting living protoplasm, an equivalent weight of the matter of life makes its appearance?

It is true that there is no sort of parity between the properties of the components and the properties of the resultant; but neither was there in the case of the water. It is also true that what I have spoken of as the influence of preëxisting living matter is something quite unintelligible; but does anybody quite comprehend the *modus operandi* of an electric spark, which traverses a mixture of oxygen and hydrogen?

What justification is there, then, for the assumption of the existence in the living matter of a something which has no representative, or correlative, in the not-living matter which gave rise to it? What better philosophical status has "vitality" than "aquosity"? And why should "vitality" hope for a better fate than the other "itys" which have disappeared since Martinus Scriblerus accounted for the operation of the meat-jack by its inherent "meat-roasting quality," and scorned the "materialism" of those who explained the turning of the spit by a certain mechanism worked by the draught of the chimney?

If scientific language is to possess a definite and constant signification whenever it is employed, it seems to me that we are logically bound to apply to the protoplasm, or physical basis of life, the same conceptions as those which are held to be legitimate elsewhere. If the phenomena exhibited by water are its properties, so are those presented by protoplasm, living or dead, its properties.

If the properties of water may be properly said to result from the nature and disposition of its component molecules, I can find no intelligible ground for refusing to say that the properties of protoplasm result from the nature and disposition of its molecules.

But I bid you beware lest, in accepting these conclusions, you are placing your feet on the first rung of a ladder which, in most people's estimation, is the reverse of Jacob's, and leads to the antipodes of heaven. It may seem a small thing to admit that the dull, vital actions of a fungus are the properties of its protoplasm, and are the direct results of the nature of the matter of which it is composed. But if, as I have endeavored to prove to you, its protoplasm is essentially identical with, and most readily converted into, that of any animal, I can discover no logical halting-place between the admission that such is the case, and the further concession that all vital action may, with equal propriety, be said to be the result of the molecular forces of the protoplasm which displays it. And if so, it must be true, in the same sense and to the same extent, that the thoughts to which I am now giving utterance, and your thoughts regarding them, are the expression of molecular changes in that matter of life which is the source of our other vital phenomena.

Past experience leads me to be tolerably certain that, when the propositions I have just placed before you are accessible to public comment and criticism, they will be condemned by many zealous persons, and perhaps by some few of the wise and thoughtful. I should not wonder if "gross and brutal materialism" were the mildest phrase applied to them in certain quarters. And, most undoubtedly, the terms of the propositions are distinctly materialistic. Nevertheless two things are certain: the one, that I hold the statements to be substantially true; the other, that I, individually, am no materialist, but, on the contrary, believe materialism to involve grave philosophical error.

This union of materialistic terminology with the repudiation of materialistic philosophy I share with some of the most thoughtful men with whom I am acquainted. And, when I first undertook to deliver the present discourse, it appeared to me to be fitting opportunity to explain how such a union is not only consistent with, but necessitated by, sound logic. I purposed to lead you through the territory of vital phenomena to the materialistic slough in which you find yourselves now plunged, and then to point out to you the sole path by which, in my judgment, extrication is possible.

Let us suppose that knowledge is absolute, and not relative, and, therefore, that our conception of matter represents that which it really is. Let us suppose, further, that we do know more of cause and effect than a certain definite order of succession among facts, and that we have a knowledge of the necessity of that succession,—and hence, of necessary laws,—and I, for my part, do not see what escape there is from utter materialism and necessarianism. For it is obvious that our knowledge of what we call the material world is, to begin with, at least as certain and definite as that of the spiritual world, and that our acquaintance with law is of as old a date as our knowledge of spontaneity. Further, I take it to be demonstrable that it is utterly impossible to prove that anything whatever may not be the effect of a material and necessary cause, and that human logic is equally incompetent to prove that any act is really spontaneous. A really spontaneous act is one which, by the assumption, has no cause; and the attempt to prove such a negative as this is, on the face of the matter, absurd. And while it is thus a philosophical impossibility to demonstrate that any given phenomenon is not the effect of a material cause, anyone who is acquainted with the history of science will admit, that its progress has, in all ages, meant, and now, more than ever, means, the extension of the province of what we call matter and causation, and the concomitant gradual banishment from all regions of human thought of what we call spirit and spontaneity.

I have endeavored, in the first part of this discourse, to give you a conception of the direction in which modern physiology is tending; and I ask you, what is the difference between the conception of life as the product of a certain disposition of material molecules, and the old notion of an Archæus governing and directing blind matter within each living body, except this—that here, as elsewhere, matter and law have devoured spirit and spontaneity? And as surely as every future grows out of past and present, so will the physiology of the future gradually extend the realm of matter and law until it is coextensive with knowledge, with feeling, and with action.

The consciousness of this great truth weighs like a nightmare, I believe, upon many of the best minds of these days. They watch what they conceive to be the progress of materialism, in such fear and powerless anger as a savage feels, when, during an eclipse, the great shadow creeps over the face of the sun. The advancing tide of matter threatens to drown their souls; the tightening grasp of law impedes their freedom; they are alarmed lest man's moral nature be debased by the increase of his wisdom.

If the "New Philosophy" be worthy of the reprobation with which it is visited, I confess their fears seem to me to be well founded. While, on the contrary, could David Hume be consulted, I think he would smile at their perplexities, and chide them for doing even as the heathen, and falling down in terror before the hideous idols their own hands have raised.

For, after all, what do we know of this terrible "matter," except as a name for the unknown and hypothetical cause of states of our own consciousness? And what do we know of that "spirit" over whose threatened extinction by matter a great lamentation is arising, like that which was heard at the death of Pan, except that it is also a name for an unknown and hypothetical cause, or condition, of states of consciousness? In other words, matter and spirit are but names for the imaginary substrata of groups of natural phenomena.

And what are the dire necessity and "iron" law under which men groan? Truly, most gratuitously invented bugbears. I suppose if there be an "iron" law, it is that of gravitation; and if there be a physical necessity, it is that a stone, unsupported, must fall to the ground. But what is all we really know, and can know, about the latter phenomenon? Simply, that, in all human experience, stones have fallen to the ground under these conditions; that we have not the smallest reason for believing that any stone so circumstanced will not fall to the ground; and that we have, on the contrary, every reason to believe that it will so fall. It is very convenient to indicate that all the conditions of belief have been fulfilled in this case, by calling the statement that unsupported stones will fall to the ground "a law of nature." But when, as commonly happens, we change *will* into *must*, we introduce an idea of necessity which most assuredly does not lie in the observed facts, and has no warranty that I can discover elsewhere. For my part, I utterly repudiate and anathematize the intruder. Fact I know, and Law I know, but what is this Necessity, save an empty shadow of my own mind's throwing?

But, if it is certain that we can have no knowledge of the nature of either matter or spirit, and that the notion of necessity is something illegitimately thrust into the perfectly legitimate conception of law, the materialistic position that there is nothing in the world but matter, force, and necessity, is as utterly devoid of justification as the most baseless of theological dogmas. The fundamental doctrines of materialism, like those of spiritualism, and most other "isms," lie outside "the limits of philosophical inquiry"; and David Hume's great service to humanity is his irrefragable demonstration of what these limits are. Hume called himself a skeptic, and therefore others cannot be blamed if they apply the same title to him; but that does not alter the fact that the name, with its existing implications, does him gross injustice.

If a man asks me what the politics of the inhabitants of the moon are, and I reply that I do not know; that neither I, nor anyone else, has any means of knowing; and that, under these circumstances, I decline to trouble myself about the subject at all, I do not think he has any right to call me a skeptic. On the contrary, in replying thus, I conceive that I am simply honest and truthful, and show a proper regard for the economy of time. So Hume's strong and subtle intellect takes up a great many problems about which we are naturally curious, and shows us that they are essentially questions of lunar politics, in their essence incapable of being answered, and therefore not worth the attention of men who have work to do in the world. And he thus ends one of his essays:—

"If we take in hand any volume of Divinity, or school metaphysics, for instance, let us ask, *Does it contain any abstract reasoning concerning quantity or number?* No. *Does it contain any experimental reasoning concerning matter of fact and existence?* No. Commit it then to the flames; for it can contain nothing but sophistry and illusion."

Permit me to enforce this most wise advice. Why trouble ourselves about matters of which, however important they may be, we do know nothing, and can know nothing? We live in a world which is full of misery and ignorance, and the plain duty of each and all of us is to try to make the little corner he can influence somewhat less miserable and somewhat less ignorant than it was before he entered it. To do this effectually, it is necessary to be fully possessed of only two beliefs: the first, that the order of nature is ascertainable by our faculties to an extent which is practically unlimited; the second, that our volition counts for something as a condition of the course of events.

Each of these beliefs can be verified experimentally, as often as we like to try. Each, therefore, stands upon the strongest foundation upon which any belief can rest, and forms one of our highest truths. If we find that the ascertainment of the order of nature is facilitated by using one terminology, or one set of symbols, rather than another, it is our clear duty to use the former; and no harm can accrue, so long as we bear in mind that we are dealing merely with terms and symbols.

In itself it is of little moment whether we express the phenomena of matter in terms of spirit, or the phenomena of spirit in terms of matter: matter may be regarded as a form of thought, thought may be regarded as a property of matter—each statement has a certain relative truth. But with a view to the progress of science, the materialistic terminology is in every way to be preferred. For it connects thought with the other phenomena of the universe, and suggests inquiry into the nature of those physical conditions, or concomitants of thought, which are more or less accessible to us, and a knowledge of which may, in future, help us to exercise the same kind of control over the world of thought that we already possess in respect of the material world; whereas, the alternative, or spiritualistic, terminology is utterly barren, and leads to nothing but obscurity and confusion of ideas.

Thus there can be little doubt that the further science advances, the more extensively and consistently will all the phenomena of nature be represented by materialistic formulæ and symbols.

But the man of science who, forgetting the limits of philosophical inquiry, slides from these formulæ and symbols into what is commonly understood by materialism, seems to me to place himself on a level with the mathematician who should mistake the x's and y's with which he works his problems for real entities—and with this further disadvantage, as compared with the mathematician, that the blunders of the latter are of no practical consequence, while the errors of systematic materialism may paralyze the energies and destroy the beauty of a life.

JOHN TYNDALL

SCOPE AND LIMIT OF SCIENTIFIC MATERIALISM

Partly through mathematical and partly through experimental research, physical science has of late years assumed a momentous position in the world. Both in a material and in an intellectual point of view it has produced, and is designed to produce, immense changes—vast social ameliorations, and vast alterations in the popular conception of the origin, rule, and governance of natural things. By science, in the physical world, miracles are wrought; while philosophy is forsaking its ancient metaphysical channels and pursuing others which have been opened or indicated by scientific research. This must become more and more the case as philosophical writers become more deeply imbued with the methods of science, better acquainted with the facts which scientific men have won and with the great theories which they have elaborated.

If you look at the face of a watch, you see the hour- and minute-hands, and possibly also a second-hand, moving over the graduated dial. Why do these hands move, and why are their relative motions such as they are observed to be? These questions cannot be answered without opening the watch, mastering its various parts, and ascertaining their relationship to each other. When this is done, we find that the observed motion of the hands follows of necessity from the inner mechanism of the watch, when acted upon by the force invested in the spring.

The motion of the hands may be called a phenomenon of art, but the case is similar with the phenomena of nature. These also have their inner mechanism and their store of force to set that mechanism going. The ultimate problem of physical science is to reveal this mechanism, to discern this store, and to show that, from the combined action of both, the phenomena of which they constitute the basis must of necessity flow.

I thought that an attempt to give you even a brief and sketchy illustration of the manner in which scientific thinkers regard this problem would not be uninteresting to you on the present occasion; more especially as it will give me occasion to say a word or two on the tendencies and limits of modern science; to point out the region which men of science claim as their own, and where it is mere waste of time to oppose their advance; and also to define, if possible, the bourne between this and that other region to which the questionings and yearnings of the scientific intellect are directed in vain.

But here your tolerance will be needed. It was the American Emerson, I think, who said that it is hardly possible to state any truth strongly without apparent injustice to some other truth. Truth is often of a dual character, taking the form of a magnet with two poles; and many of the differences which agitate the thinking part of mankind are to be traced to the exclusiveness with which partisan reasoners dwell upon one half of the duality in forgetfulness of the other half. The proper course appears to be to state both halves strongly, and allow each its fair share in the formation of the resultant conviction. But this waiting for the statement of the two sides of the question implies patience. It implies a resolution to suppress indignation if the statement of the one half should clash with our convictions, and to repress equally undue elation if the half-statement should happen to chime in with our views. It implies a determination to wait calmly for the statement of the whole, before we pronounce judgment in the form of either acquiescence or dissent.

This premised and, I trust, accepted, let us enter upon our task. There have been writers who affirmed that the pyramids of Egypt were the productions of nature; and in his early youth Alexander von Humboldt wrote a learned essay with the express object of refuting this notion. We now regard the pyramids as the work of men's hands, aided probably by machinery of which no record remains. We picture to ourselves the swarming workers toiling at these vast erections, lifting the inert stones, and, guided by the volition, the skill, and possibly at times by the whip, of the architect, placing them in their proper positions. The blocks in this case were moved and posited by a power external to themselves, and the final form of the pyramid expresses the thought of its human builder.

Let us pass from this illustration of constructive power to another of a different kind. When a solution of common salt is slowly evaporated, the water which holds the salt in solution disappears, but the salt itself remains behind. At a certain stage of concentration the salt can no longer retain the liquid form: its particles, or molecules, as they are called, begin to deposit themselves as minute solids, so minute, indeed, as to defy all microscopic power. As evaporation continues, solidification goes on, and we finally obtain, through the clustering together of innumerable molecules, a finite crystalline mass of a definite form. What is this form? It sometimes seems a mimicry of the architecture of Egypt. We have little pyramids built by the salt, terrace above terrace from base to apex, forming a series of steps resembling those up which the Egyptian traveler is dragged by his guides. The human is as little disposed to look unquestioning at these pyramidal salt crystals as to look at the pyramids of Egypt without inquiring whence they came. How, then, are those salt pyramids built up?

Guided by analogy, you may, if you like, suppose that, swarming among the constituent molecules of the salt, there is an invisible population, controlled and coerced by some invisible master, and placing the atomic blocks in their positions. This, however, is not the scientific idea, nor do I think your good sense will accept it as a likely one. The scientific idea is that the molecules act upon each other without the intervention of slave labor; that they attract each other and repel each other at certain definite points, or poles, and in certain definite directions; and that the pyramidal form is the result of this play of attraction and repulsion. While, then, the blocks of Egypt were laid down by a power external to themselves, these molecular blocks of salt are self-posited, being fixed in their places by the forces with which they act upon each other.

I take common salt as an illustration because it is so familiar to us all; but any other crystalline substance would answer my purpose equally well. Everywhere, in fact, throughout inorganic nature, we have this formative power, as Fichte would call it—this structural energy ready to come into play and build the ultimate particles of matter into definite shapes. The ice of our winters and of our polar regions is its handiwork, and so equally are the quartz, feldspar, and mica of our rocks. Our chalk-beds are for the most part composed of minute shells, which are almost the product of structural energy; but behind the shell, as a whole, lies a more remote and subtle formative act. These shells are built up of little crystals of calc-spar, and to form these crystals the structural force had to deal with the intangible molecules of carbonate of lime. This tendency on the part of matter to organize itself, to grow into shape, to assume definite forms in obedience to the definite action of force, is, as I have said, all-pervading. It is in the ground on which you tread, in the water you drink, in the air you breathe. Incipient life, as it were, manifests itself throughout the whole of what we call inorganic nature.

The forms of the minerals resulting from this play of polar forces are various, and exhibit different degrees of complexity. Men of science avail themselves of all possible means of exploring their molecular architecture. For this purpose they employ in turn, as agents of exploration, light, heat, magnetism, electricity, and sound. Polarized light is especially useful and powerful here. A beam of such light, when sent in among the molecules of a crystal, is acted on by them, and from this action we infer with more or less of clearness the manner in which the molecules are arranged. That differences, for example, exist between the inner structure of rock salt and crystallized sugar or sugar-candy, is thus strikingly revealed. These differences may be made to display themselves in chromatic phenomena of great splendor, the play of molecular force being so regulated as to remove some of the colored constituents of white light, and to leave others with increased intensity behind.

And now let us pass from what we are accustomed to regard as a dead mineral to a living grain of corn. When *it* is examined by polarized light, chromatic phenomena similar to those noticed in crystals are observed. And why? Because the architecture of the grain resembles the architecture of the crystal. In the grain also the molecules are set in definite positions, and in accordance with their arrangement they act upon the light. But what has built together the molecules of the corn? I have already said regarding crystalline architecture that you may, if you please, consider the atoms and molecules to be placed in position by a power external to themselves. The same hypothesis is open to you now. But if, in the case of crystals, you have rejected this notion of an external architect, I think you are bound to reject it now, and to conclude that the molecules of the corn are self-posited by the forces with which they act upon each other. It would be poor philosophy to invoke an external agent in the one case and reject it in the other.

Instead of cutting our grain of corn into slices and subjecting it to the action of polarized light, let us place it in the earth and subject it to a certain degree of warmth. In other words, let the molecules, both of the corn and of the surrounding earth, be kept in that state of agitation which we call warmth. Under these circumstances, the grain and the substances which surround it interact, and a definite molecular architecture is the result. A bud is formed; this bud reaches the surface, where it is exposed to the sun's rays, which are also to be regarded as a kind of vibratory motion. And as the motion of common heat, with which the grain and the substances surrounding it were first endowed, enabled the grain and these substances to exercise their attractions and repulsions, and thus to coalesce in definite forms, so the specific motion of the sun's rays now enables the green bud to feed upon the carbonic acid and the aqueous vapor of the air. The bud appropriates those constituents of both for which it has an elective attraction, and permits the other constituent to resume its place in the air. Thus the architecture is carried on. Forces are active at the root, forces are active in the blade, the matter of the earth and the matter of the atmosphere are drawn toward both, and the plant augments in size. We have in succession the bud, the stalk, the ear, the full corn in the ear; the cycle of molecular action being completed by the production of grains similar to that with which the process began.

Now there is nothing in this process which necessarily eludes the conceptive or imagining power of the purely human mind. An intellect the same in kind as our own would, if only sufficiently expanded, be able to follow the whole process from beginning to end. It would see every molecule placed in its position by the specific attractions and repulsions exerted between it and other molecules, the whole process and its consummation being an instance of the play of molecular force. Given the grain and its environment, the purely human intellect might, if sufficiently expanded, trace out *a priori* every step of the process of growth, and by the application of purely mechanical principles demonstrate that the cycle must end, as it is seen to end, in the reproduction of forms like that with which it began. A similar necessity rules here to that which rules the planets in their circuits round the sun.

You will notice that I am stating my truth strongly, as at the beginning we agreed it should be stated. But I must go still further, and affirm that in the eye of science *the animal body* is just as much a product of molecular force as the stalk and ear of corn, or as the crystal of salt or sugar. Many of the parts of the body are obviously mechanical. Take the human heart, for example, with its system of valves; or take the exquisite mechanism of the eye or hand. Animal heat, moreover, is the same in kind as the heat of a fire, being produced by the same chemical process. Animal motion, too, is as directly derived from the food of the animal as the motion of Trevethyck's walking engine from the fuel in its furnace. As regards matter, the animal body creates nothing; as regards force, it creates nothing. Which of you by taking thought can add one cubit to his stature? All that has been said, then, regarding the plant may be restated with regard to the animal. Every particle that enters into the composition of a muscle, a nerve, or a bone has been placed in its position by molecular force. And, unless the existence of law in these matters is denied, and the element of caprice introduced, we must conclude that, given the relation of any molecule of the body to its environment, its position in the body might be determined mathematically. Our difficulty is not with the *quality* of the problem, but with its *complexity*; and this difficulty might be met by the simple expansion of the faculties which we now possess. Given this expansion, with the necessary data, and the chick might be deduced as rigorously and as logically from the egg as the existence of Neptune was deduced from the disturbances of Uranus, or as conical refraction was deduced from the undulatory theory of light.

You see, I am not mincing matters, but avowing nakedly what many scientific thinkers more or less distinctively believe. The formation of a crystal, a plant, or an animal is, in their eyes, a purely mechanical problem, which differs from the problems of ordinary mechanics in the smallness of the masses and the complexity of the processes involved. Here you have one half of our dual truth; let us now glance at the other half. Associated with this wonderful mechanism of the animal body, we have phenomena no less certain than those of physics, but between which and the mechanism we discern no necessary connection. A man, for example, can say *I feel, I think, I love*; but how does *consciousness* infuse itself into the problem? The human brain is said to be the organ of thought and feeling; when we are hurt, the brain feels it; when we ponder, it is the brain that thinks; when our passions or affections are excited, it is through the instrumentality of the brain. Let us endeavor to be a little more precise here. I hardly imagine that there exists a profound scientific thinker, who has reflected upon the subject, unwilling to admit the extreme probability of the hypothesis that, for every fact of consciousness, whether in the domain of sense, of thought, or of emotion, a certain definite molecular condition is set up in the brain; who does not hold this relation of physics to consciousness to be invariable, so that, given the state of the brain, the corresponding thought or feeling might be inferred; or, given the thought or feeling, the corresponding state of the brain might be inferred.

But how inferred? It is at bottom not a case of logical inference at all, but of empirical association. You may reply that many of the inferences of science are of this character; the inference, for example, that an electric current of a given direction will deflect a magnetic needle in a definite way; but the cases differ in this, that the passage from the current to the needle, if not demonstrable, is thinkable, and that we entertain no doubt as to the final mechanical solution of the problem. But the passage from the physics of the brain to the corresponding facts of consciousness is unthinkable. Granted that a definite thought and a definite molecular action in the brain occur simultaneously; we do not possess the intellectual organ, nor apparently any rudiment of the organ, which would enable us to pass, by a process of reasoning, from the one to the other. They appear together, but we do not know why. Were our minds and senses so expanded, strengthened, and illuminated as to enable us to see and feel the very molecules of the brain; were we capable of following all their motions, all their groupings, all their electric discharges, if such there be; and were we intimately acquainted with the corresponding states of thought and feeling, we should be as far as ever from the solution of the problem, "How are these physical processes connected with the facts of consciousness?" The chasm between the two classes of phenomena would still remain intellectually impassable. Let the consciousness of *love*, for example, be associated with a right-handed spiral motion of the molecules of the brain, and the consciousness of *hate* with a left-handed spiral motion. We should then know, when we love, that the motion is in one direction, and when we hate, that the motion is in the other; but the *Why?* would remain as unanswerable as before.

In affirming that the growth of the body is mechanical, and that thought, as exercised by us, has its correlative in the physics of the brain, I think the position of the "Materialist" is stated, as far as that position is a tenable one. I think the materialist will be able finally to maintain this position against all attacks; but I do not think, in the present condition of the human mind, that he can pass beyond this position. I do not think he is entitled to say that his molecular groupings and his molecular motions *explain* everything. In reality, they explain nothing. The utmost he can affirm is the association of two classes of phenomena, of whose real bond of union he is in absolute ignorance.

The problem of the connection of body and soul is as insoluble in its modern form as it was in the pre-scientific ages. Phosphorus is known to enter into the composition of the human brain, and a trenchant German writer has exclaimed, "Ohne Phosphor, kein Gedanke."[4] That may or may not be the case; but, even if we knew it to be the case, the knowledge would not lighten our darkness. On both sides of the zone here assigned to the materialist he is equally helpless. If you ask him whence is this "Matter" of which we have been discoursing, who or what divided it into molecules, who or what impressed upon them this necessity of running into organic forms, he has no answer. Science is mute in reply to these questions.

But if the materialist is confounded and science rendered dumb, who else is prepared with a solution? To whom has this arm of the Lord been revealed? Let us lower our heads and acknowledge our ignorance, priest and philosopher, one and all. Perhaps the mystery may resolve itself into knowledge at some future day. The process of things upon this earth has been one of amelioration. It is a long way from the iguanodon and his contemporaries to the President and the Members of the British Association. And whether we regard the improvement from the scientific or from the theological point of view, as the result of progressive development, or as the result of successive exhibitions of creative energy, neither view entitles us to assume that man's present faculties end the series—that the process of amelioration stops at him.

A time may therefore come when this ultra-scientific region by which we are now enfolded may offer itself to terrestrial, if not to human, investigation. Two thirds of the rays emitted by the sun fail to arouse in the eye the sense of vision. The rays exist, but the visual organ requisite for their translation into light does not exist. And so, from this region of darkness and mystery which surrounds us, rays may now be darting which require but the development of the proper intellectual organs to translate them into knowledge as far surpassing ours as ours surpasses that of the wallowing reptiles which once held possession of this planet. Meanwhile the mystery is not without its uses. It certainly may be made a power in the human soul; but it is a power which has feeling, not knowledge, for its base. It may be, and will be, and we hope is, turned to account, both in steadying and strengthening the intellect, and in rescuing man from that littleness to which in the struggle for existence or for precedence in the world he is continually prone.

JOHN HENRY, CARDINAL NEWMAN

CHRISTIANITY AND PHYSICAL SCIENCE[5]

So far, then, as these remarks have gone, Theology and Physics cannot touch each other, have no intercommunion, have no ground of difference or agreement, of jealousy or of sympathy. As well may musical truths be said to interfere with the doctrines of architectural science; as well may there be a collision between the mechanist and the geologist, the engineer and the grammarian; as well might the British Parliament or the French nation be jealous of some possible belligerent power upon the surface of the moon, as Physics pick a quarrel with Theology. And it may be well—before I proceed to fill up in detail this outline, and to explain what has to be explained in this statement—to corroborate it, as it stands, by the remarkable words upon the subject of a writer of the day:[6]—

"We often hear it said," he observes, writing as a Protestant (and here let me assure you, gentlemen, that though his words have a controversial tone with them, I do not quote them in that aspect, or as wishing here to urge anything against Protestants, but merely in pursuance of my own point, that Revelation and Physical Science cannot really come into collision), "we often hear it said that the world is constantly becoming more and more enlightened, and that this enlightenment must be favorable to Protestantism, and unfavorable to Catholicism. We wish that we could think so. But we see great reason to doubt whether this is a well-founded expectation. We see that during the last two hundred and fifty years the human mind has been in the highest degree active; that it has made great advances in every branch of natural philosophy; that it has produced innumerable inventions tending to promote the convenience of life; that medicine, surgery, chemistry, engineering, have been very greatly improved, that government, police, and law have been improved, though not to so great an extent as the physical sciences. Yet we see that, during these two hundred and fifty years, Protestantism has made no conquests worth speaking of. Nay, we believe that, as far as there has been change, that change has, on the whole, been in favor of the Church of Rome. We cannot, therefore, feel confident that the progress of knowledge will necessarily be fatal to a system which has, to say the least, stood its ground in spite of the immense progress made by the human race in knowledge since the days of Queen Elizabeth.

"Indeed, the argument which we are considering seems to us to be founded on an entire mistake. There are branches of knowledge with respect to which the law of the human mind is progress. In mathematics, when once a proposition has been demonstrated, it is never afterwards contested. Every fresh story is as solid a basis for a new superstructure as the original foundation was. Here, therefore, there is a constant addition to the stock of truth. In the inductive sciences, again, the law is progress....

"But with theology the case is very different. As respects natural religion (Revelation being for the present altogether left out of the question), it is not easy to see that a philosopher of the present day is more favorably situated than Thales or Simonides. He has before him just the same evidences of design in the structure of the universe which the early Greeks had.... As to the other great question, what becomes of man after death, we do not see that a highly educated European, left to his unassisted reason, is more likely to be in the right than a Blackfoot Indian. Not a single one of the many sciences, in which we surpass the Blackfoot Indians, throws the smallest light on the state of the soul after the animal life is extinct....

"Natural Theology, then, is not a progressive science. That knowledge of our origin and of our destiny which we derive from Revelation is indeed of very different clearness, and of very different importance. But neither is Revealed Religion of the nature of a progressive science.... In divinity there cannot be a progress analogous to that which is constantly taking place in pharmacy, geology, and navigation. A Christian of the fifth century with a Bible is neither better nor worse situated than a Christian of the nineteenth century with a Bible, candor and natural acuteness being, of course, supposed equal. It matters not at all that the compass, printing, gunpowder, steam, gas, vaccination, and a thousand other discoveries and inventions, which were unknown in the fifth century, are familiar to the nineteenth. None of these discoveries and inventions has the smallest bearing on the question whether man is justified by faith alone, or whether the invocation of saints is an orthodox practice.... We are confident that the world will never go back to the solar system of Ptolemy; nor is our confidence in the least shaken by the circumstance that so great a man as Bacon rejected the theory of Galileo with scorn; for Bacon had not all the means of arriving at a sound conclusion. But when we reflect that Sir Thomas More was ready to die for the doctrine of Transubstantiation, we cannot but feel some doubt whether the doctrine of Transubstantiation may not triumph over all opposition. More was a man of eminent talents. He had all the information on the subject that we have, or *that, while the world lasts, any human being will have.... No progress that science has made, or will make*, can add to what seems to us the overwhelming force of the argument against the Real Presence. We are therefore unable to understand why what Sir Thomas More believed respecting Transubstantiation may not be believed, to the end of time, by men equal in abilities and honesty to Sir Thomas More. But Sir Thomas More is one of the choice specimens of human wisdom and virtue; and the doctrine of Transubstantiation is a kind of proof charge. The faith which stands that test will stand any test....

"The history of Catholicism strikingly illustrates these observations. During the last seven centuries the public mind of Europe has made constant progress in every department of secular knowledge; but in religion we can trace no constant progress.... Four times since the authority of the Church of Rome was established in Western Christendom, has the human intellect risen up against her yoke. Twice that Church remained completely victorious. Twice she came forth from the conflict bearing the marks of cruel wounds, but with the principle of life still strong within her. When we reflect on the tremendous assaults she has survived, we find it difficult to conceive in what way she is to perish."

You see, gentlemen, if you trust the judgment of a sagacious mind, deeply read in history, Catholic Theology has nothing to fear from the progress of Physical Science, even independently of the divinity of its doctrines. It speaks of things supernatural; and these, by the very force of the words, research into nature cannot touch.

ROBERT LOUIS STEVENSON

PULVIS ET UMBRA[7]

We look for some reward of our endeavors, and are disappointed; not success, not happiness, not even peace of conscience, crowns our ineffectual efforts to do well. Our frailties are invincible, our virtues barren; the battle goes sore against us to the going down of the sun. The canting moralist tells us of right and wrong; and we look abroad, even on the face of our small earth, and find them change with every climate, and no country where some action is not honored for a virtue and none where it is not branded for a vice; and we look in our experience, and find no vital congruity in the wisest rules, but at the best a municipal fitness. It is not strange if we are tempted to despair of good. We ask too much. Our religions and moralities have been trimmed to flatter us, till they are all emasculate and sentimentalized, and only please and weaken. Truth is of a rougher strain. In the harsh face of life, faith can read a bracing gospel. The human race is a thing more ancient than the ten commandments; and the bones and revolutions of the Kosmos, in whose joints we are but moss and fungus, more ancient still.

Of the Kosmos in the last resort, science reports many doubtful things, and all of them appalling. There seems no substance to this solid globe on which we stamp: nothing but symbols and ratios. Symbols and ratios carry us and bring us forth and beat us down; gravity, which swings the incommensurable suns and worlds through space, is but a figment varying inversely as the squares of distances; and the suns and worlds themselves, imponderable figures of abstraction, NH_3 and H_2O. Consideration dares not dwell upon this view; that way madness lies; science carries us into zones of speculation, where there is no habitable city for the mind of man.

But take the Kosmos with a grosser faith, as our senses give it us. We behold space sown with rotatory islands, suns and worlds and the shards and wrecks of systems: some, like the sun, still blazing; some rotting, like the earth; others, like the moon, stable in desolation. All of these we take to be made of something we call matter: a thing which no analysis can help us to conceive; to whose incredible properties no familiarity can reconcile our minds. This stuff, when not purified by the lustration of fire, rots uncleanly into something we call life; seized through all its atoms with a pediculous malady; swelling in tumors that become independent, sometimes even (by an abhorrent prodigy) locomotory; one splitting into millions, millions cohering into one, as the malady proceeds through varying stages. This vital putrescence of the dust, used as we are to it, yet strikes us with occasional disgust; and the profusion of worms in a piece of ancient turf, or the air of a marsh darkened with insects, will sometimes check our breathing so that we aspire for cleaner places. But none is clean: the moving sand is infected with lice; the pure spring, where it bursts out of the mountain, is a mere issue of worms; even in the hard rock the crystal is forming.

In two main shapes this eruption covers the countenance of the earth: the animal and the vegetable; one in some degree the inversion of the other; the second rooted to the spot; the first coming detached out of its natal mud, and scurrying abroad with the myriad feet of insects, or towering into the heavens on the wings of birds; a thing so inconceivable that, if it be well considered, the heart stops. To what passes with the anchored vermin, we have little clue; doubtless they have their joys and sorrows, their delights and killing agonies; it appears not how. But of the locomotory, to which we ourselves belong, we can tell more. These share with us a thousand miracles: the miracles of sight, of hearing, of the projection of sound; things that bridge space; the miracles of memory and reason, by which the present is conceived, and, when it is gone, its image kept living in the brains of man and brute; the miracle of reproduction, with its imperious desires and staggering consequences. And to put the last touch upon this mountain mass of the revolting and the inconceivable, all these prey upon each other, lives tearing other lives in pieces, cramming them inside themselves, and by that summary process, growing fat: the vegetarian, the whale, perhaps the tree, not less than the lion of the desert; for the vegetarian is only the eater of the dumb.

Meanwhile our rotatory island, loaded with predatory life, and more drenched with blood, both animal and vegetable, than ever mutinied ship, scuds through space with unimaginable speed, and turns alternate cheeks to the reverberation of a blazing world, ninety million miles away.

What a monstrous spectre is this man, the disease of the agglutinated dust, lifting alternate feet or lying drugged with slumber; killing, feeding, growing, bringing forth small copies of himself; grown upon with hair like grass, fitted with eyes that move and glitter in his face; a thing to set children screaming; and yet, looked at nearlier, known as his fellows know him, how surprising are his attributes! Poor soul, here for so little, cast among so many hardships, filled with desires so incommensurate and so inconsistent, savagely surrounded, savagely descended, irremediably condemned to prey upon his fellow lives: who should have blamed him, had he been of a piece with his destiny, and a being merely barbarous? And we look and behold him instead filled with imperfect virtues: infinitely childish, often admirably valiant, often touchingly kind; sitting down, amidst his momentary life, to debate of right and wrong and the attributes of the deity; rising up to do battle for an egg or die for an idea; singling out his friends and his mate with cordial affection; bringing forth in pain; rearing, with long-suffering solicitude, his young.

To touch the heart of his mystery, we find in him one thought, strange to the point of lunacy: the thought of duty; the thought of something owing to himself, to his neighbor, to his God; an ideal of decency, to which he would rise if it were possible; a limit of shame, below which, if it be possible, he will not stoop. The design in most men is one of conformity; here and there, in picked natures, it transcends itself and soars on the other side, arming martyrs with independence; but in all, in their degrees, it is a bosom thought. Not in man alone, for we trace it in dogs and cats whom we know fairly well; and doubtless some similar point of honor sways the elephant, the oyster, and the louse, of whom we know so little. But in man, at least, it sways with so complete an empire that merely selfish things come second, even with the selfish; that appetites are starved, fears are conquered, pains supported; that almost the dullest shrinks from the reproof of a glance, although it were a child's; and all but the most cowardly stand amid the risks of war; and the more noble, having strongly conceived an act as due to their ideal, affront and embrace death. Strange enough, if, with their singular origin and perverted practice, they think they are to be rewarded in some future life; stranger still, if they are persuaded of the contrary, and think this blow, which they solicit, will strike them senseless for eternity.

I shall be reminded what a tragedy of misconception and misconduct man at large presents: of organized injustice, cowardly violence, and treacherous crime; and of the damning imperfections of the best. They cannot be too darkly drawn. Man is indeed marked for failure in his efforts to do right. But where the best consistently miscarry, how tenfold more remarkable that all should continue to strive; and surely we should find it both touching and inspiring that, in a field from which success is banished, our race should not cease to labor.

If the first view of this creature, stalking in his rotatory isle, be a thing to shake the courage of the stoutest, on this nearer sight he startles us with an admiring wonder. It matters not where we look, under what climate we observe him, in what stage of society, in what depth of ignorance, burthened with what erroneous morality: by camp-fires in Assiniboia, the snow powdering his shoulders, the wind plucking his blanket, as he sits, passing the ceremonial calumet and uttering his grave opinions like a Roman senator: in ships at sea, a man inured to hardship and vile pleasures, his brightest hope a fiddle in a tavern and a bedizened trull who sells herself to rob him, and he, for all that, simple, innocent, cheerful, kindly like a child, constant to toil, brave to drown for others; in the slums of cities, moving among indifferent millions to mechanical employments, without hope of change in the future, with scarce a pleasure in the present, and yet true to his virtues, honest up to his lights, kind to his neighbors, tempted perhaps in vain by the bright gin-palace, perhaps long-suffering with the drunken wife that ruins him; in India (a woman this time) kneeling with broken cries and streaming tears, as she drowns her child in the sacred river; in the brothel, the discard of society, living mainly on strong drink, fed with affronts, a fool, a thief, the comrade of thieves, and even here keeping the point of honor and the touch of pity, often repaying the world's scorn with service, often standing firm upon a scruple, and at a certain cost, rejecting riches—everywhere some virtue cherished or affected, everywhere some decency of thought and carriage, everywhere the ensign of man's ineffectual goodness. Ah! if I could show you this! if I could show you these men and women, all the world over, in every stage of history, under every abuse of error, under every circumstance of failure, without hope, without help, without thanks, still obscurely fighting the lost fight of virtue, still clinging, in the brothel or on the scaffold, to some rag of honor, the poor jewel of their souls! They may seek to escape, and yet they cannot; it is not alone their privilege and glory, but their doom; they are condemned to some nobility; all their lives long, the desire of good is at their heels, the implacable hunter.

Of all earth's meteors, here at least is the most strange and consoling: that this ennobled lemur, this hair-crowned bubble of the dust, this inheritor of a few years and sorrows, should yet deny himself his rare delights, and add to his frequent pains, and live for an ideal, however misconceived. Nor can we stop with man. A new doctrine, received with screams a little while ago by canting moralists, and still not properly worked into the body of our thoughts, lights us a step further into the heart of this rough but noble universe. For nowadays the pride of man denies in vain his kinship with the original dust. He stands no longer like a thing apart. Close at his heels we see the dog, prince of another genus: and in him too we see dumbly testified the same cultus of an unattainable ideal, the same constancy in failure. Does it stop with the dog? We look at our feet, where the ground is blackened with the swarming ant: a creature so small, so far from us in the hierarchy of brutes, that we can scarce trace and scarce comprehend his doings; and here also, in his ordered polities and rigorous justice, we see confessed the law of duty and the fact of individual sin. Does it stop, then, with the ant? Rather, this desire of well-doing and this doom of frailty run through all the grades of life; rather is this earth, from the frosty top of Everest to the next margin of the internal fire, one stage of ineffectual virtues and one temple of pious tears and perseverance.

The whole creation groaneth and travaileth together. It is the common and the god-like law of life. The browsers, the biters, the barkers, the hairy coats of field and forest, the squirrel in the oak, the thousand-footed creeper in the dust, as they share with us the gift of life, share with us the love of an ideal: strive like us,—like us are tempted to grow weary of the struggle,—to do well; like us receive at times unmerited refreshment, visitings of support, returns of courage; and are condemned like us to be crucified between that double law of the members and the will. Are they like us, I wonder, in the timid hope of some reward, some sugar with the drug? Do they, too, stand aghast at unrewarded virtues, at the sufferings of those whom, in our partiality, we take to be just, and the prosperity of such as, in our blindness, we call wicked? It may be; and yet God knows what they should look for. Even while they look, even while they repent, the foot of man treads them by thousands in the dust, the yelping hounds burst upon their trail, the bullet speeds, the knives are heating in the den of the vivisectionist; or the dew falls, and the generation of a day is blotted out. For these are creatures compared with whom our weakness is strength, our ignorance wisdom, our brief span eternity.

And as we dwell, we living things, in our isle of terror and under the imminent hand of death, God forbid it should be man the erected, the reasoner, the wise in his own eyes—God forbid it should be man that wearies in well-doing, that despairs of unrewarded effort, or utters the language of complaint. Let it be enough for faith, that the whole creation groans in mortal frailty, strives with unconquerable constancy—surely not all in vain.

JOHN RUSKIN

THE MYSTERY OF LIFE AND ITS ARTS[8]

When I accepted the privilege of addressing you to-day, I was not aware of a restriction with respect to the topics of discussion which may be brought before this Society[9]—a restriction which, though entirely wise and right under the circumstances contemplated in its introduction, would necessarily have disabled me, thinking as I think, from preparing any lecture for you on the subject of art in a form which might be permanently useful. Pardon me, therefore, in so far as I must transgress such limitation; for indeed my infringement will be of the letter—not of the spirit—of your commands. In whatever I may say touching the religion which has been the foundation of art, or the policy which has contributed to its power, if I offend one, I shall offend all; for I shall take no note of any separations in creeds, or antagonisms in parties: neither do I fear that ultimately I shall offend any, by proving—or at least stating as capable of positive proof—the connection of all that is best in the crafts and arts of man, with the simplicity of his faith, and the sincerity of his patriotism.

But I speak to you under another disadvantage, by which I am checked in frankness of utterance, not here only, but everywhere: namely, that I am never fully aware how far my audiences are disposed to give me credit for real knowledge of my subject, or how far they grant me attention only because I have been sometimes thought an ingenious or pleasant essayist upon it. For I have had what, in many respects, I boldly call the misfortune, to set my words sometimes prettily together; not without a foolish vanity in the poor knack that I had of doing so: until I was heavily punished for this pride, by finding that many people thought of the words only, and cared nothing for their meaning. Happily, therefore, the power of using such pleasant language—if, indeed, it ever were mine—is passing away from me; and whatever I am now able to say at all, I find myself forced to say with great plainness. For my thoughts have changed also, as my words have; and whereas in earlier life, what little influence I obtained was due perhaps chiefly to the enthusiasm with which I was able to dwell on the beauty of the physical clouds, and of their colors in the sky; so all the influence I now desire to retain must be due to the earnestness with which I am endeavoring to trace the form and beauty of another kind of cloud than those: the bright cloud of which it is written, "What is your life? It is even as a vapor that appeareth for a little time, and then vanisheth away."

I suppose few people reach the middle or latter period of their age, without having, at some moment of change or disappointment, felt the truth of those bitter words; and been startled by the fading of the sunshine from the cloud of their life into the sudden agony of the knowledge that the fabric of it was as fragile as a dream, and the endurance of it as transient as the dew. But it is not always that, even at such times of melancholy surprise, we can enter into any true perception that this human life shares in the nature of it, not only the evanescence, but the mystery of the cloud; that its avenues are wreathed in darkness, and its forms and courses no less fantastic, than spectral and obscure; so that not only in the vanity which we cannot grasp, but in the shadow which we cannot pierce, it is true of this cloudy life of ours, that "man walketh in a vain shadow, and disquieteth himself in vain."

And least of all, whatever may have been the eagerness of our passions, or the height of our pride, are we able to understand in its depths the third and most solemn character in which our life is like those clouds of heaven; that to it belongs, not only their transience, not only their mystery, but also their power; that in the cloud of the human soul there is a fire stronger than the lightning, and a grace more precious than the rain; and that, though of the good and evil it shall one day be said alike, that the place that knew them knows them no more, there is an infinite separation between those whose brief presence had there been a blessing, like the mist of Eden that went up from the earth to water the garden, and those whose place knew them only as a drifting and changeful shade, of whom the Heavenly sentence is, that they are "wells without water; clouds that are carried with a tempest, to whom the mist of darkness is reserved forever."

To those among us, however, who have lived long enough to form some just estimate of the rate of the changes which are, hour by hour in accelerating catastrophe, manifesting themselves in the laws, the arts, and the creeds of men, it seems to me that, now at least, if never at any former time, the thoughts of the true nature of our life, and of its powers and responsibilities, should present themselves with absolute sadness and sternness. And although I know that this feeling is much deepened in my own mind by disappointment, which, by chance, has attended the greater number of my cherished purposes, I do not for that reason distrust the feeling itself, though I am on my guard against an exaggerated degree of it; nay, I rather believe that in periods of new effort and violent change, disappointment is a wholesome medicine; and that in the secret of it, as in the twilight so beloved by Titian, we may see the colors of things with deeper truth than in the most dazzling sunshine....

You know, there is a tendency in the minds of many men, when they are heavily disappointed in the main purposes of their life, to feel, and perhaps in warning, perhaps in mockery, to declare, that life itself is a vanity. Because it has disappointed them, they think its nature is of disappointment always, or at best, of pleasure that can be grasped by imagination only; that the cloud of it has no strength nor fire within; but is a painted cloud only, to be delighted in, yet despised. You know how beautifully Pope has expressed this particular phase of thought:—

Meanwhile opinion gilds, with varying rays,
These painted clouds that beautify our days;
Each want of happiness by hope supplied,
And each vacuity of sense, by pride.
Hope builds as fast as Knowledge can destroy;
In Folly's cup, still laughs the bubble joy.
One pleasure past, another still we gain,
And not a vanity is given in vain.

But the effect of failure upon my own mind has been just the reverse of this. The more that my life disappointed me, the more solemn and wonderful it became to me. It seemed, contrarily to Pope's saying, that the vanity of it *was* indeed given in vain; but that there was something behind the veil of it, which was not vanity. It became to me, not a painted cloud, but a terrible and impenetrable one: not a mirage, which vanished as I drew near, but a pillar of darkness, to which I was forbidden to draw near. For I saw that both my own failure, and such success in petty things as in its poor triumph seemed to me worse than failure, came from the want of sufficiently earnest effort to understand the whole law and meaning of existence, and to bring it to noble and due end; as, on the other hand, I saw more and more clearly that all enduring success in the arts, or in any other occupation, had come from the ruling of the lower purposes, not by a conviction of their nothingness, but by a solemn faith in the advancing power of human nature, or in the promise, however dimly apprehended, that the mortal part of it would one day be swallowed up in immortality; and that, indeed, the arts themselves never had reached any vital strength of honor, but in the effort to proclaim this immortality, and in the service either of great and just religion, or of some unselfish patriotism, and law of such national life as must be the foundation of religion.

Nothing that I have ever said is more true or necessary—nothing has been more misunderstood or misapplied—than my strong assertion that the arts can never be right themselves unless their motive is right. It is misunderstood this way: weak painters, who have never learned their business, and cannot lay a true line, continually come to me, crying out, "Look at this picture of mine; it *must* be good, I had such a lovely motive. I have put my whole heart into it, and taken years to think over its treatment." Well, the only answer for these people is,—if one had the cruelty to make it,—"Sir, you cannot think over *any*thing in any number of years,—you haven't the head to do it; and though you had fine motives, strong enough to make you burn yourself in a slow fire, if only first you could paint a picture, you can't paint one, nor half an inch of one; you haven't the hand to do it."

But, far more decisively we have to say to the men who *do* know their business, or may know it if they choose, "Sir, you have this gift, and a mighty one; see that you serve your nation faithfully with it. It is a greater trust than ships and armies: you might cast *them* away, if you were their captain, with less treason to your people than in casting your own glorious power away, and serving the devil with it instead of men. Ships and armies you may replace if they are lost, but a great intellect, once abused, is a curse to the earth forever."

This, then, I meant by saying that the arts must have noble motive. This also I said respecting them, that they never had prospered, nor could prosper, but when they had such true purpose, and were devoted to the proclamation of divine truth or law. And yet I saw also that they had always failed in this proclamation—that poetry, and sculpture, and painting, though great when they strove to teach us something about the gods, never had taught us anything trustworthy about the gods, but had always betrayed their trust in the crisis of it, and, with their powers at the full reach, became ministers to pride and to lust. And I felt also, with increasing amazement, the unconquerable apathy in ourselves the hearers, no less than in these the teachers; and that, while the wisdom and rightness of every act and art of life could only be consistent with a right understanding of the ends of life, we were all plunged as in a languid dream—our hearts fat, and our eyes heavy, and our ears closed, lest the inspiration of hand or voice should reach us—lest we should see with our eyes, and understand with our hearts, and be healed.

This intense apathy in all of us is the first great mystery of life; it stands in the way of every perception, every virtue. There is no making ourselves feel enough astonishment at it. That the occupations or pastimes of life should have no motive, is understandable; but—that life itself should have no motive,—that we neither care to find out what it may lead to, nor to guard against its being forever taken away from us,—here is a mystery indeed. For just suppose I were able to call at this moment to anyone in this audience by name, and to tell him positively that I knew a large estate had been lately left to him on some curious conditions; but that though I knew it was large, I did not know how large, nor even where it was—whether in the East Indies or the West, or in England, or at the Antipodes. I only knew it was a vast estate, and that there was a chance of his losing it altogether if he did not soon find out on what terms it had been left to him. Suppose I were able to say this positively to any single man in this audience, and he knew that I did not speak without warrant, do you think that he would rest content with that vague knowledge, if it were anywise possible to obtain more? Would he not give every energy to find some trace of the facts, and never rest till he had ascertained where this place was, and what it was like? And suppose he were a young man, and all he could discover by his best endeavor was that the estate was never to be his at all, unless he persevered, during certain years of probation, in an orderly and industrious life; but that, according to the rightness of his conduct, the portion of the estate assigned to him would be greater or less, so that it literally depended on his behavior from day to day whether he got ten thousand a year, or thirty thousand a year, or nothing whatever—would you not think it strange if the youth never troubled himself to satisfy the conditions in any way, nor even to know what was required of him, but lived exactly as he chose, and never inquired whether his chances of the estate were increasing or passing away?

Well, you know that this is actually and literally so with the greater number of the educated persons now living in Christian countries. Nearly every man and woman in any company such as this outwardly professes to believe—and a large number unquestionably think they believe—much more than this; not only that a quite unlimited estate is in prospect for them if they please the Holder of it, but that the infinite contrary of such a possession—an estate of perpetual misery—is in store for them if they displease this great Land-Holder, this great Heaven-Holder. And yet there is not one in a thousand of these human souls that cares to think, for ten minutes of the day, where this estate is or how beautiful it is, or what kind of life they are to lead in it, or what kind of life they must lead to obtain it.

You fancy that you care to know this; so little do you care that, probably, at this moment many of you are displeased with me for talking of the matter! You came to hear about the Art of this world, not about the Life of the next, and you are provoked with me for talking of what you can hear any Sunday in church. But do not be afraid. I will tell you something before you go about pictures, and carvings, and pottery, and what else you would like better to hear of than the other world. Nay, perhaps you say, "We want you to talk of pictures and pottery, because we are sure that you know something of them, and you know nothing of the other world." Well—I don't. That is quite true. But the very strangeness and mystery of which I urge you to take notice, is in this—that I do not—nor you either. Can you answer a single bold question unflinchingly about that other world?—Are you sure there is a heaven? Sure there is a hell? Sure that men are dropping before your faces through the pavements of these streets into eternal fire, or sure that they are not? Sure that, at your own death, you are going to be delivered from all sorrow, to be endowed with all virtue, to be gifted with all felicity, and raised into perpetual companionship with a King, compared to whom the kings of the earth are as grasshoppers, and the nations as the dust of his feet? Are you sure of this? or, if not sure, do any of us so much as care to make it sure? and, if not, how can anything that we do be right—how can anything we think be wise? what honor can there be in the arts that amuse us, or what profit in the possessions that please?

Is not this a mystery of life?

But further, you may, perhaps, think it a beneficent ordinance for the generality of men that they do not, with earnestness or anxiety, dwell on such questions of the future, because the business of the day could not be done if this kind of thought were taken by all of us for the morrow. Be it so; but at least we might anticipate that the greatest and wisest of us, who were evidently the appointed teachers of the rest, would set themselves apart to seek out whatever could be surely known of the future destinies of their race; and to teach this in no rhetorical or ambiguous manner, but in the plainest and most severely earnest words.

Now, the highest representatives of men who have thus endeavored, during the Christian era, to search out these deep things, and relate them, are Dante and Milton. There are none who for earnestness of thought, for mastery of word, can be classed with these. I am not at present, mind you, speaking of persons set apart in any priestly or pastoral office, to deliver creeds to us, or doctrines; but of men who try to discover and set forth, as far as by human intellect is possible, the facts of the other world. Divines may perhaps teach us how to arrive there, but only these two poets have in any powerful manner striven to discover, or in any definite words professed to tell, what we shall see and become there; or how those upper and nether worlds are, and have been, inhabited.

And what have they told us? Milton's account of the most important event in his whole system of the universe, the fall of the angels, is evidently unbelievable to himself; and the more so, that it is wholly founded on, and in a great part spoiled and degraded from, Hesiod's account of the decisive war of the younger gods with the Titans. The rest of his poem is a picturesque drama, in which every artifice of invention is visibly and consciously employed; not a single fact being, for an instant, conceived as tenable by any living faith.

Dante's conception is far more intense, and, by himself, for the time, not to be escaped from; it is indeed a vision, but a vision only, and that one of the wildest that ever entranced a soul—a dream in which every grotesque type or fantasy of heathen tradition is renewed, and adorned; and the destinies of the Christian Church, under their most sacred symbols, become literally subordinate to the praise, and are only to be understood by the aid, of one dear Florentine maiden.

I tell you truly that, as I strive more with this strange lethargy and trance in myself, and awake to the meaning and power of life, it seems daily more amazing to me that men such as these should dare to play with the most precious truths (or the most deadly untruths) by which the whole human race listening to them could be informed, or deceived—all the world their audiences forever, with pleased ear, and passionate heart; and yet, to this submissive infinitude of souls, and evermore succeeding and succeeding multitude, hungry for bread of life, they do but play upon sweetly modulated pipes; with pompous nomenclature adorn the councils of hell; touch a troubadour's guitar to the courses of the suns; and fill the openings of eternity, before which prophets have veiled their faces, and which angels desire to look into, with idle puppets of their scholastic imagination, and melancholy lights of frantic faith in their lost mortal love.

Is not this a mystery of life?

But more. We have to remember that these two great teachers were both of them warped in their temper, and thwarted in their search for truth. They were men of intellectual war, unable, through darkness of controversy, or stress of personal grief, to discern where their own ambition modified their utterances of the moral law; or their own agony mingled with their anger at its violation. But greater men than these have been—innocent-hearted—too great for contest. Men, like Homer and Shakespeare, of so unrecognized personality, that it disappears in future ages, and becomes ghostly, like the tradition of a lost heathen god. Men, therefore, to whose unoffended, uncondemning sight, the whole of human nature reveals itself in a pathetic weakness, with which they will not strive; or in mournful and transitory strength, which they dare not praise. And all Pagan and Christian civilization thus becomes subject to them. It does not matter how little, or how much, any of us have read, either of Homer or Shakespeare; everything round us, in substance or in thought, has been moulded by them. All Greek gentlemen were educated under Homer. All Roman gentlemen, by Greek literature. All Italian, and French, and English gentlemen, by Roman literature, and by its principles. Of the scope of Shakespeare, I will say only that the intellectual measure of every man since born, in the domains of creative thought, may be assigned to him according to the degree in which he has been taught by Shakespeare. Well, what do these two men, centres of mortal intelligence, deliver to us of conviction respecting what it most behooves that intelligence to grasp? What is their hope—their crown of rejoicing? what manner of exhortation have they for us, or of rebuke? what lies next their own hearts, and dictates their undying words? Have they any peace to promise to our unrest, any redemption to our misery?

Take Homer first, and think if there is any sadder image of human fate than the great Homeric story. The main features in the character of Achilles are its intense desire of justice and its tenderness of affection. And in that bitter song of the Iliad, this man, though aided continually by the wisest of the gods, and burning with the desire of justice in his heart, becomes yet, through ill-governed passion, the most unjust of men; and, full of the deepest tenderness in his heart, becomes yet, through ill-governed passion, the most cruel of men. Intense alike in love and in friendship, he loses, first his mistress, and then his friend; for the sake of the one, he surrenders to death the armies of his own land; for the sake of the other, he surrenders all. Will a man lay down his life for his friend? Yea, even for his *dead* friend, this Achilles, though goddess-born and goddess-taught, gives up his kingdom, his country, and his life—casts alike the innocent and guilty, with himself, into one gulf of slaughter, and dies at last by the hand of the basest of his adversaries.

Is not this a mystery of life?

But what, then, is the message to us of our own poet, and searcher of hearts, after fifteen hundred years of Christian faith have been numbered over the graves of men? Are his words more cheerful than the Heathen's—is his hope more near—his trust more sure—his reading of fate more happy? Ah, no! He differs from the Heathen poet chiefly in this—that he recognizes, for deliverance, no gods nigh at hand; and that, by petty chance—by momentary folly—by broken message—by fool's tyranny—or traitor's snare, the strongest and most righteous are brought to their ruin, and perish without word of hope. He indeed, as part of his rendering of character, ascribes the power and modesty of habitual devotion to the gentle and the just. The death-bed of Katharine is bright with visions of angels; and the great soldier-king, standing by his few dead, acknowledges the presence of the Hand that can save alike by many or by few. But observe that from those who with deepest spirit meditate, and with deepest passion mourn, there are no such words as these; nor in their hearts are any such consolations. Instead of the perpetual sense of the helpful presence of the Deity, which through all heathen tradition is the source of heroic strength, in battle, in exile, and in the valley of the shadow of death, we find only, in the great Christian poet, the consciousness of a moral law, through which "the gods are just, and of our pleasant vices make instruments to scourge us"; and of the resolved arbitration of the destinies, that conclude into precision of doom what we feebly and blindly began; and force us, when our indiscretion serves us, and our deepest plots do pall, to the confession that "there's a divinity that shapes our ends, rough hew them how we will."

Is not this a mystery of life?

Be it so, then. About this human life that is to be, or that is, the wise religious men tell us nothing that we can trust; and the wise contemplative men, nothing that can give us peace. But there is yet a third class to whom we may turn—the wise practical men. We have sat at the feet of the poets who sang of heaven, and they have told us their dreams. We have listened to the poets who sang of earth, and they have chanted to us dirges and words of despair. But there is one class of men more—men, not capable of vision, nor sensitive to sorrow, but firm of purpose; practised in business; learned in all that can be (by handling) known. Men whose hearts and hopes are wholly in this present world; from whom, therefore, we may surely learn, at least, how, at present, conveniently to live in it. What will *they* say to us, or show us by example? These kings—these councilors—these statesmen and builders of kingdoms—these capitalists and men of business, who weigh the earth, and the dust of it, in a balance. They know the world, surely; and what is the mystery of life to us is none to them. They can surely show us how to live, while we live, and to gather out of the present world what is best.

I think I can best tell you their answer by telling you a dream I had once. For though I am no poet, I have dreams sometimes. I dreamed I was at a child's May-day party, in which every means of entertainment had been provided for them by a wise and kind host. It was in a stately house, with beautiful gardens attached to it; and the children had been set free in the rooms and gardens, with no care whatever but how to pass their afternoon rejoicingly. They did not, indeed, know much about what was to happen next day; and some of them, I thought, were a little frightened, because there was a chance of their being sent to a new school, where there were examinations; but they kept the thoughts of that out of their heads as well as they could, and resolved to enjoy themselves. The house, I said, was in a beautiful garden, and in the garden were all kinds of flowers; sweet, grassy banks for rest; and smooth lawns for play; and pleasant streams and woods; and rocky places for climbing. And the children were happy for a little while; but presently they separated themselves into parties; and then each party declared it would have a piece of the garden for its own, and that none of the others should have anything to do with that piece. Next, they quarrelled violently which pieces they would have; and at last the boys took up the thing, as boys should do, "practically," and fought in the flower-beds till there was hardly a flower left standing; then they trampled down each other's bits of the garden out of spite; and the girls cried till they could cry no more; and so they all lay down at last, breathless, in the ruin, and waited for the time when they were to be taken home in the evening.[10]

Meanwhile, the children in the house had been making themselves happy also in their manner. For them there had been provided every kind of indoor pleasure: there was music for them to dance to; and the library was open, with all manner of amusing books; and there was a museum full of the most curious shells, and animals, and birds; and there was a workshop, with lathes and carpenter's tools, for the ingenious boys; and there were pretty fantastic dresses, for the girls to dress in; and there were microscopes, and kaleidoscopes, and whatever toys a child could fancy; and a table, in the dining-room, loaded with everything nice to eat.

But, in the midst of all this, it struck two or three of the more "practical" children, that they would like some of the brass-headed nails that studded the chairs; and so they set to work to pull them out. Presently, the others, who were reading, or looking at shells, took a fancy to do the like; and, in a little while, all the children, nearly, were spraining their fingers, in pulling out brass-headed nails. With all that they could pull out, they were not satisfied; and then, everybody wanted some of somebody else's. And at last, the really practical and sensible ones declared, that nothing was of any real consequence, that afternoon, except to get plenty of brass-headed nails; and that the books, and the cakes, and the microscopes were of no use at all in themselves, but only, if they could be exchanged for nail-heads. And at last they began to fight for nail-heads, as the others fought for the bits of garden. Only here and there, a despised one shrank away into a corner, and tried to get a little quiet with a book, in the midst of the noise; but all the practical ones thought of nothing else but counting nail-heads all the afternoon, even though they knew they would not be allowed to carry so much as one brass knob away with them. But no—it was, "Who has most nails? I have a hundred, and you have fifty"; or, "I have a thousand, and you have two. I must have as many as you before I leave the house, or I cannot possibly go home in peace." At last, they made so much noise that I awoke, and thought to myself, "What a false dream that is, of *children*!" The child is the father of the man; and wiser. Children never do such foolish things. Only men do.

But there is yet one last class of persons to be interrogated. The wise religious men we have asked in vain; the wise contemplative men, in vain; the wise worldly men, in vain. But there is another group yet. In the midst of this vanity of empty religion, of tragic contemplation, of wrathful and wretched ambition, and dispute for dust, there is yet one great group of persons, by whom all these disputers live—the persons who have determined, or have had it by a beneficent Providence determined for them, that they will do something useful; that whatever may be prepared for them hereafter, or happen to them here, they will, at least, deserve the food that God gives them by winning it honorably: and that, however fallen from the purity, or far from the peace, of Eden, they will carry out the duty of human dominion, though they have lost its felicity; and dress and keep the wilderness, though they no more can dress or keep the garden.

These—hewers of wood and drawers of water; these—bent under burdens, or torn of scourges; these—that dig and weave that plant and build; workers in wood, and in marble, and in iron—by whom all food, clothing, habitation, furniture, and means of delight are produced, for themselves, and for all men beside; men, whose deeds are good, though their words may be few; men, whose lives are serviceable, be they never so short, and worthy of honor, be they never so humble—from these surely, at least, we may receive some clear message of teaching; and pierce, for an instant, into the mystery of life, and of its arts.

Yes; from these, at last, we do receive a lesson. But I grieve to say,—or rather, for that is the deeper truth of the matter, I rejoice to say,—this message of theirs can only be received by joining them, not by thinking about them.

You sent for me to talk to you of art; and I have obeyed you in coming. But the main thing I have to tell you is, that art must not be talked about. The fact that there is talk about it at all, signifies that it is ill done, or cannot be done. No true painter ever speaks, or ever has spoken, much of his art. The greatest speak nothing. Even Reynolds is no exception, for he wrote of all that he could not himself do, and was utterly silent respecting all that he himself did.

The moment a man can really do his work he becomes speechless about it. All words become idle to him—all theories. Does a bird need to theorize about building its nest, or boast of it when built? All good work is essentially done that way—without hesitation, without difficulty, without boasting; and in the doers of the best, there is an inner and involuntary power which approximates literally to the instinct of an animal—nay, I am certain that in the most perfect human artists, reason does *not* supersede instinct, but is added to an instinct as much more divine than that of the lower animals; as the human body is more beautiful than theirs; that a great singer sings not with less instinct than the nightingale, but with more—only more various, applicable, and governable; that a great architect does not build with less instinct than the beaver or the bee, but with more—with an innate cunning of proportion that embraces all beauty, and a divine ingenuity of skill that improvises all construction.

And now, returning to the broader question, what these arts and labors of life have to teach us of its mystery, this is the first of their lessons—that the more beautiful the art, the more it is essentially the work of the people who *feel* themselves wrong, who are striving for the fulfillment of a law, and the grasp of a loveliness, which they have not yet attained, which they feel even further and further from attaining, the more they strive for it. And yet, in still deeper sense, it is the work of people who know also that they are right. The very sense of inevitable error from their purpose marks the perfectness of that purpose, and the continued sense of failure arises from the continued opening of the eyes more clearly to all the sacredest laws of truth.

This is one lesson. The second is a very plain, and greatly precious one: namely—that, whenever the arts and labors of life are fulfilled in this spirit of striving against misrule, and doing whatever we have to do honorably and perfectly, they invariably bring happiness, as much as seems possible to the nature of man. In all other paths by which that happiness is pursued there is disappointment, or destruction: for ambition and for passion there is no rest—no fruition; the fairest pleasures of youth perish in a darkness greater than their past light: and the loftiest and purest love too often does but inflame the cloud of life with endless fire of pain. But, ascending from lowest to highest, through every scale of human industry, that industry, worthily followed, gives peace. Ask the laborer in the field, at the forge, or in the mine; ask the patient, delicate-fingered artisan, or the strong-armed, fiery-hearted worker in bronze, and in marble, and with the colors of light; and none of these, who are true workmen, will ever tell you that they have found the law of heaven an unkind one—that in the sweat of their face they should eat bread, till they return to the ground; nor that they ever found it an unrewarded obedience, if, indeed, it was rendered faithfully to the command, "Whatsoever thy hand findeth to do—do it with thy might."

These are the two great and constant lessons which our laborers teach us of the mystery of life. But there is another, and a sadder one, which they cannot teach us, which we must read on their tombstones.

"Do it with thy might." There have been myriads upon myriads of human creatures who have obeyed this law,—who have put every breath and nerve of their being into its toil,—who have devoted every hour, and exhausted every faculty,—who have bequeathed their unaccomplished thoughts at death,—who, being dead, have yet spoken, by majesty of memory, and strength of example. And, at last, what has all this "Might" of humanity accomplished, in six thousand years of labor and sorrow? What has it *done*? Take the three chief occupations and arts of men, one by one, and count their achievements. Begin with the first,—the lord of them all,—Agriculture. Six thousand years have passed since we were set to till the ground, from which we were taken. How much of it is tilled? How much of that which is, wisely or well? In the very centre and chief garden of Europe,—where the two forms of parent Christianity have had their fortresses,—where the noble Catholics of the Forest Cantons, and the noble Protestants of the Vaudois valleys, have maintained, for dateless ages, their faiths and liberties,—there the unchecked Alpine rivers yet run wild in devastation; and the marshes, which a few hundred men could redeem with a year's labor, still blast their helpless inhabitants into fevered idiotism. That is so, in the centre of Europe! While, on the near coast of Africa, once the Garden of the Hesperides, an Arab woman, but a few sunsets since, ate her child, for famine. And, with all the treasures of the East at our feet, we, in our own dominion, could not find a few grains of rice for a people that asked of us no more; but stood by, and saw five hundred thousand of them perish of hunger.

Then after agriculture, the art of kings, take the next head of human arts—Weaving; the art of queens, honored of all Heathen women, in the person of their virgin goddess—honored of all Hebrew women, by the word of their wisest king—"She layeth her hands to the spindle, and her hands hold the distaff; she stretcheth out her hand to the poor. She is not afraid of the snow for her household, for all her household are clothed with scarlet. She maketh herself covering of tapestry; her clothing is silk and purple. She maketh fine linen, and selleth it, and delivereth girdles to the merchant." What have we done in all these thousands of years with this bright art of Greek maid and Christian matron? Six thousand years of weaving, and have we learned to weave? Might not every naked wall have been purple with tapestry, and every feeble breast fenced with sweet colors from the cold? What have we done? Our fingers are too few, it seems, to twist together some poor covering for our bodies. We set our streams to work for us, and choke the air with fire, to turn our spinning-wheels—and—*are we yet clothed*? Are not the streets of the capitals of Europe foul with sale of cast clouts and rotten rags? Is not the beauty of your sweet children left in wretchedness of disgrace, while, with better honor, nature clothes the brood of the bird in its nest, and the suckling of the wolf in her den? And does not every winter's snow robe what you have not robed, and shroud what you have not shrouded; and every winter's wind bear up to heaven its wasted souls, to witness against you hereafter, by the voice of their Christ,—"I was naked, and ye clothed me not"?

Lastly—take the Art of Building—the strongest—proudest—most orderly—most enduring of the arts of man; that of which the produce is in the surest manner accumulative, and need not perish, or be replaced; but if once well done, will stand more strongly than the unbalanced rocks—more prevalently than the crumbling hills. The art which is associated with all civic pride and sacred principle; with which men record their power—satisfy their enthusiasm—make sure their defence—define and make dear their habitation. And in six thousand years of building, what have we done? Of the greater part of all that skill and strength, *no* vestige is left, but fallen stones, that encumber the fields and impede the streams. But, from this waste of disorder, and of time, and of rage, what *is* left to us? Constructive and progressive creatures that we are, with ruling brains, and forming hands, capable of fellowship, and thirsting for fame, can we not contend, in comfort, with the insects of the forest, or, in achievement, with the worm of the sea? The white surf rages in vain against the ramparts built by poor atoms of scarcely nascent life; but only ridges of formless ruin mark the places where once dwelt our noblest multitudes. The ant and the moth have cells for each of their young, but our little ones lie in festering heaps, in homes that consume them like graves; and night by night, from the corners of our streets, rises up the cry of the homeless: "I was a stranger, and ye took me not in."

Must it be always thus? Is our life forever to be without profit—without possession? Shall the strength of its generations be as barren as death; or cast away their labor, as the wild fig tree casts her untimely figs? Is it all a dream then—the desire of the eyes and the pride of life—or, if it be, might we not live in nobler dream than this? The poets and prophets, the wise men, and the scribes, though they have told us nothing about a life to come, have told us much about the life that is now. They have had—they also—their dreams, and we have laughed at them. They have dreamed of mercy, and of justice; they have dreamed of peace and good-will; they have dreamed of labor undisappointed, and of rest undisturbed; they have dreamed of fulness in harvest, and overflowing in store; they have dreamed of wisdom in council, and of providence in law; of gladness of parents, and strength of children, and glory of gray hairs. And at these visions of theirs we have mocked, and held them for idle and vain, unreal and unaccomplishable. What have we accomplished with our realities? Is this what has come of our worldly wisdom, tried against their folly? this, our mightiest possible, against their impotent ideal? or, have we only wandered among the spectra of a baser felicity, and chased phantoms of the tombs, instead of visions of the Almighty; and walked after the imaginations of our evil hearts, instead of after the counsels of Eternity, until our lives—not in the likeness of the cloud of heaven, but of the smoke of hell—have become "as a vapor, that appeareth for a little time, and then vanisheth away"?

Does it vanish, then? Are you sure of that?—sure that the nothingness of the grave will be a rest from this troubled nothingness; and that the coiling shadow, which disquiets itself in vain, cannot change into the smoke of the torment that ascends forever? Will any answer that they *are* sure of it, and that there is no fear, nor hope, nor desire, nor labor, whither they go? Be it so: will you not, then, make as sure of the Life that now is, as you are of the Death that is to come? Your hearts are wholly in this world—will you not give them to it wisely, as well as perfectly? And see, first of all, that you *have* hearts, and sound hearts, too, to give. Because you have no heaven to look for, is that any reason that you should remain ignorant of this wonderful and infinite earth, which is firmly and instantly given you in possession? Although your days are numbered, and the following darkness sure, is it necessary that you should share the degradation of the brute, because you are condemned to its mortality; or live the life of the moth, and of the worm, because you are to companion them in the dust? Not so; we may have but a few thousands of days to spend, perhaps hundreds only—perhaps tens; nay, the longest of our time and best, looked back on, will be but as a moment, as the twinkling of an eye; still we are men, not insects; we are living spirits, not passing clouds. "He maketh the winds His messengers; the momentary fire, His minister"; and shall we do less than *these*? Let us do the work of men while we bear the form of them; and, as we snatch our narrow portion of time out of Eternity, snatch also our narrow inheritance of passion out of Immortality—even though our lives *be* as a vapor, that appeareth for a little time, and then vanisheth away.

But there are some of you who believe not this—who think this cloud of life has no such close—that it is to float, revealed and illumined, upon the floor of heaven, in the day when He cometh with clouds, and every eye shall see Him. Some day, you believe, within these five, or ten, or twenty years, for every one of us the judgment will be set, and the books opened. If that be true, far more than that must be true. Is there but one day of judgment? Why, for us every day is a day of judgment—every day is a Dies Iræ, and writes its irrevocable verdict in the flame of its west. Think you that judgment waits till the doors of the grave are opened? It waits at the doors of your houses— it waits at the corners of your streets; we are in the midst of judgment—the insects that we crush are our judges—the moments we fret away are our judges—the elements that feed us, judge, as they minister—and the pleasures that deceive us, judge, as they indulge. Let us, for our lives, do the work of Men while we bear the form of them, if indeed those lives are *Not* as a vapor, and do *Not* vanish away.

"The work of men"—and what is that? Well, we may any of us know very quickly, on the condition of being wholly ready to do it. But many of us are for the most part thinking, not of what we are to do, but of what we are to get; and the best of us are sunk into the sin of Ananias, and it is a mortal one—we want to keep back part of the price; and we continually talk of taking up our cross, as if the only harm in a cross was the *weight* of it—as if it was only a thing to be carried, instead of to be—crucified upon. "They that are His have crucified the flesh, with the affections and lusts." Does that mean, think you, that in time of national distress, of religious trial, of crisis for every interest and hope of humanity—none of us will cease jesting, none cease idling, none put themselves to any wholesome work, none take so much as a tag of lace off their footman's coats, to save the world? Or does it rather mean, that they are ready to leave houses, lands, and kindreds—yes, and life, if need be? Life!—some of us are ready enough to throw that away, joyless as we have made it. But "*station* in Life,"—how many of us are ready to quit *that*? Is it not always the great objection, where there is question of finding something useful to do—"We cannot leave our stations in Life"?

Those of us who really cannot—that is to say, who can only maintain themselves by continuing in some business or salaried office, have already something to do; and all that they have to see to is, that they do it honestly and with all their might. But with most people who use that apology, "remaining in the station of life to which Providence has called them" means keeping all the carriages, and all the footmen and large houses they can possibly pay for; and, once for all, I say that if ever Providence *did* put them into stations of that sort,—which is not at all a matter of certainty,—Providence is just now very distinctly calling them out again. Levi's station in life was the receipt of custom; and Peter's, the shore of Galilee; and Paul's, the antechambers of the High Priest—which "station in life" each had to leave, with brief notice.

And whatever our station in life may be, at this crisis, those of us who mean to fulfil our duty ought first, to live on as little as we can; and, secondly, to do all the wholesome work for it we can, and to spend all we can spare in doing all the sure good we can.

And sure good is, first in feeding people, then in dressing people, then in lodging people, and lastly in rightly pleasing people, with arts, or sciences, or any other subject of thought.

I say first in feeding; and, once for all, do not let yourselves be deceived by any of the common talk of "indiscriminate charity." The order to us is not to feed the deserving hungry, nor the industrious hungry, nor the amiable and well-intentioned hungry, but simply to feed the hungry. It is quite true, infallibly true, that if any man will not work, neither should he eat—think of that, and every time you sit down to your dinner, ladies and gentlemen, say solemnly, before you ask a blessing, "How much work have I done to-day for my dinner?" But the proper way to enforce that order on those below you, as well as on yourselves, is not to leave vagabonds and honest people to starve together, but very distinctly to discern and seize your vagabond; and shut your vagabond up out of honest people's way, and very sternly then see that, until he has worked, he does *not* eat. But the first thing is to be sure you have the food to give; and, therefore, to enforce the organization of vast activities in agriculture and in commerce, for the production of the wholesomest food, and proper storing and distribution of it, so that no famine shall any more be possible among civilized beings. There is plenty of work in this business alone, and at once, for any number of people who like to engage in it.

Secondly, dressing people—that is to say, urging everyone within reach of your influence to be always neat and clean, and giving them means of being so. In so far as they absolutely refuse, you must give up the effort with respect to them, only taking care that no children within your sphere of influence shall any more be brought up with such habits; and that every person who is willing to dress with propriety shall have encouragement to do so. And the first absolutely necessary step toward this is the gradual adoption of a consistent dress for different ranks of persons, so that their rank shall be known by their dress; and the restriction of the changes of fashion within certain limits. All which appears for the present quite impossible; but it is only so far even difficult as it is difficult to conquer our vanity, frivolity, and desire to appear what we are not. And it is not, nor ever shall be, creed of mine, that these mean and shallow vices are unconquerable by Christian women.

And then, thirdly, lodging people, which you may think should have been put first, but I put it third, because we must feed and clothe people where we find them, and lodge them afterwards. And providing lodgment for them means a great deal of vigorous legislation, and cutting down of vested interests that stand in the way; and after that, or before that, so far as we can get it, through sanitary and remedial action in the houses that we have; and then the building of more, strongly, beautifully, and in groups of limited extent, kept in proportion to their streams, and walled round, so that there may be no festering and wretched suburb anywhere, but clean and busy streets within, and the open country without, with a belt of beautiful garden and orchard round the walls, so that from any part of the city perfectly fresh air and grass, and sight of far horizon, might be reachable in a few minutes' walk. This the final aim; but in immediate action every minor and possible good to be instantly done, when, and as, we can; roofs mended that have holes in them—fences patched that have gaps in them—walls buttressed that totter—and floors propped that shake; cleanliness and order enforced with our own hands and eyes, till we are breathless, every day. And all the fine arts will healthily follow. I myself have washed a flight of stone stairs all down, with bucket and broom, in a Savoy inn, where they hadn't washed their stairs since they first went up them; and I never made a better sketch than that afternoon.

These, then, are the three first needs of civilized life; and the law for every Christian man and woman is, that they shall be in direct service toward one of these three needs, as far as is consistent with their own special occupation, and if they have no special business, then wholly in one of these services. And out of such exertion in plain duty all other good will come; for in this direct contention with material evil, you will find out the real nature of all evil; you will discern by the various kinds of resistance, what is really the fault and main antagonism to good; also you will find the most unexpected helps and profound lessons given, and truths will come thus down to us which the speculation of all our lives would never have raised us up to. You will find nearly every educational problem solved, as soon as you truly want to do something; everybody will become of use in their own fittest way, and will learn what is best for them to know in that use. Competitive examination will then, and not till then, be wholesome, because it will be daily, and calm, and in practice; and on these familiar arts, and minute, but certain and serviceable knowledges, will be surely edified and sustained the greater arts and splendid theoretical sciences.

But much more than this. On such holy and simple practice will be founded, indeed, at last, an infallible religion. The greatest of all the mysteries of life, and the most terrible, is the corruption of even the sincerest religion, which is not daily founded on rational, effective, humble, and helpful action. Helpful action, observe! for there is just one law, which, obeyed, keeps all religions pure—forgotten, makes them all false. Whenever in any religious faith, dark or bright, we allow our minds to dwell upon the points in which we differ from other people, we are wrong, and in the devil's power. That is the essence of the Pharisee's thanksgiving—"Lord, I thank Thee that I am not as other men are." At every moment of our lives we should be trying to find out, not in what we differ from other people, but in what we agree with them; and the moment we find we can agree as to anything that should be done, kind or good (and who but fools couldn't?) then do it; push at it together: you can't quarrel in a side-by-side push; but the moment that even the best men stop pushing, and begin talking, they mistake their pugnacity for piety, and it's all over. I will not speak of the crimes which in past times have been committed in the name of Christ, nor of the follies which are at this hour held to be consistent with obedience to Him; but I *will* speak of the morbid corruption and waste of vital power in religious sentiment, by which the pure strength of that which should be the guiding soul of every nation, the splendor of its youthful manhood, and spotless light of its maidenhood, is averted or cast away. You may see continually girls who have never been taught to do a single useful thing thoroughly; who cannot sew, who cannot cook, who cannot cast an account, nor prepare a medicine, whose whole life has been passed either in play or in pride; you will find girls like these, when they are earnest-hearted, cast all their innate passion of religious spirit, which was meant by God to support them through the irksomeness of daily toil, into grievous and vain meditation over the meaning of the great Book, of which no syllable was ever yet to be understood but through a deed; all the instinctive wisdom and mercy of their womanhood made vain, and the glory of their pure consciences warped into fruitless agony concerning questions which the laws of common serviceable life would either have solved for them in an instant, or kept out of their way. Give such a girl any true work that will make her active in the dawn, and weary at night, with the consciousness that her fellow creatures have indeed been the better for her day, and the powerless sorrow of her enthusiasm will transform itself into a majesty of radiant and beneficent peace.

So with our youths. We once taught them to make Latin verses, and called them educated; now we teach them to leap and to row, to hit a ball with a bat, and call them educated. Can they plough, can they sow, can they plant at the right time, or build with a steady hand? Is it the effort of their lives to be chaste, knightly, faithful, holy in thought, lovely in word and deed? Indeed it is, with some, nay, with many, and the strength of England is in them, and the hope; but we have to turn their courage from the toil of war to the toil of mercy; and their intellect from dispute of words to discernment of things; and their knighthood from the errantry of adventure to the state and fidelity of a kingly power. And then, indeed, shall abide, for them and for us, an incorruptible felicity, and an infallible religion; shall abide for us Faith, no more to be assailed by temptation, no more to be defended by wrath and by fear;—shall abide with us Hope, no more to be quenched by the years that overwhelm, or made ashamed by the shadows that betray:—shall abide for us, and with us, the greatest of these; the abiding will, the abiding name of our Father. For the greatest of these is Charity.

MATTHEW ARNOLD

MARCUS AURELIUS

Mr. Mill says, in his book on Liberty, that "Christian morality is, in great part, merely a protest against paganism; its ideal is negative rather than positive, passive rather than active." He says, that, in certain most important respects, "it falls far below the best morality of the ancients." The object of systems of morality is to take possession of human life, to save it from being abandoned to passion or allowed to drift at hazard, to give it happiness by establishing it in the practice of virtue; and this object they seek to attain by prescribing to human life fixed principles of action, fixed rules of conduct. In its uninspired as well as in its inspired moments, in its days of languor and gloom as well as in its days of sunshine and energy, human life has thus always a clue to follow, and may always be making way towards its goal. Christian morality has not failed to supply to human life aids of this sort. It has supplied them far more abundantly than many of its critics imagine. The most exquisite document, after those of the New Testament, of all the documents the Christian spirit has ever inspired,—the *Imitation*,—by no means contains the whole of Christian morality; nay, the disparagers of this morality would think themselves sure of triumphing if one agreed to look for it in the *Imitation* only. But even the *Imitation* is full of passages like these: "Vita sine proposito languida et vaga est."—"Omni die renovare debemus propositum nostrum, dicentes: nunc hodie perfecte incipiamus, quia nihil est quod hactenus fecimus."—"Secundum propositum nostrum est cursus profectus nostri."—"Raro etiam unum vitium perfecte vincimus, et ad *quotidianum* profectum non accendimur."—"Semper aliquid certi proponendum est."—"Tibi ipsi violentiam frequenter fac." (*A life without a purpose is a languid, drifting thing.—Every day we ought to renew our purpose, saying to ourselves: This day let us make a sound beginning, for what we have hitherto done is nought.—Our improvement is in proportion to our purpose.—We hardly ever manage to get completely rid even of one fault, and do not set our hearts on* daily *improvement.—Always place a definite purpose before thee.—Get the habit of mastering thine inclination.*) These are moral precepts, and moral precepts of the best kind. As rules to hold possession of our conduct, and to keep us in the right course through outward troubles and inward perplexity, they are equal to the best ever furnished by the great masters of morals—Epictetus and Marcus Aurelius.

But moral rules, apprehended as ideas first, and then rigorously followed as laws, are, and must be, for the sage only. The mass of mankind have neither force of intellect enough to apprehend them clearly as ideas, nor force of character enough to follow them strictly as laws. The mass of mankind can be carried along a course full of hardship for the natural man, can be borne over the thousand impediments of the narrow way, only by the tide of a joyful and bounding emotion. It is impossible to rise from reading Epictetus or Marcus Aurelius without a sense of constraint and melancholy, without feeling that the burden laid upon man is well-nigh greater than he can bear. Honor to the sages who have felt this, and yet have borne it! Yet, even for the sage, this sense of labor and sorrow in his march toward the goal constitutes a relative inferiority; the noblest souls of whatever creed, the pagan Empedocles as well as the Christian Paul, have insisted on the necessity of an inspiration, a living emotion to make moral action perfect; an obscure indication of this necessity is the one drop of truth in the ocean of verbiage with which the controversy on justification by faith has flooded the world. But, for the ordinary man, this sense of labor and sorrow constitutes an absolute disqualification; it paralyzes him; under the weight of it, he cannot make way toward the goal at all. The paramount virtue of religion is, that it has *lighted up* morality; that it has supplied the emotion and inspiration needful for carrying the sage along the narrow way perfectly, for carrying the ordinary man along it at all. Even the religions with most dross in them have had something of this virtue; but the Christian religion manifests it with unexampled splendor. "Lead me, Zeus and Destiny!" says the prayer of Epictetus, "whithersoever I am appointed to go: I will follow without wavering; even though I turn coward and shrink, I shall have to follow all the same." The fortitude of that is for the strong, for the few; even for them the spiritual atmosphere with which it surrounds them is bleak and gray. But, "Let Thy loving spirit lead me forth into the land of righteousness";—"The Lord shall be unto thee an everlasting light, and thy God thy Glory";—"Unto you that fear My Name shall the Sun of Righteousness arise with healing in his wings," says the Old Testament; "born not of blood, nor of the will of the flesh, nor of the will of man, but of God";—"Except a man be born again, he cannot see the kingdom of God";—"Whatsoever is born of God, overcometh the world," says the New. The ray of sunshine is there, the glow of a divine warmth; the austerity of the sage melts away under it, the paralysis of the weak is healed; he who is vivified by it renews his strength; "all things are possible to Him"; "he is a new creature."

Epictetus says: "Every matter has two handles, one of which will bear taking hold of, the other not. If thy brother sin against thee, lay not hold of the matter by this, that he sins against thee; for by this handle the matter will not bear taking hold of. But rather lay hold of it by this, that he is thy brother, thy born mate; and thou wilt take hold of it by what will bear handling." Jesus, being asked whether a man is bound to forgive his brother as often as seven times, answers: "I say not unto thee, until seven times, but until seventy times seven." Epictetus here suggests to the reason grounds for forgiveness of injuries which Jesus does not; but it is vain to say that Epictetus is on that account a better moralist than Jesus, if the warmth, the emotion, of Jesus' answer fires his hearer to the practice of forgiveness of injuries, while the thought in Epictetus's leaves him cold. So with Christian morality in general: its distinction is not that it propounds the maxim, "Thou shalt love God and thy neighbor," with more development, closer reasoning, truer sincerity, than other moral systems; it is that it propounds this maxim with an inspiration which wonderfully catches the hearer and makes him act upon it. It is because Mr. Mill has attained to the perception of truths of this nature, that he is—instead of being, like the school from which he proceeds, doomed to sterility—a writer of distinguished mark and influence, a writer deserving all attention and respect; it is (I must be pardoned for saying) because he is not sufficiently leavened with them, that he falls just short of being a great writer....

The man whose thoughts Mr. Long[11] has thus faithfully reproduced is perhaps the most beautiful figure in history. He is one of those consoling and hope-inspiring marks, which stand forever to remind our weak and easily discouraged race how high human goodness and perseverance have once been carried, and may be carried again. The interest of mankind is peculiarly attracted by examples of signal goodness in high places; for that testimony to the worth of goodness is the most striking which is borne by those to whom all the means of pleasure and self-indulgence lay open, by those who had at their command the kingdoms of the world and the glory of them. Marcus Aurelius was the ruler of the grandest of empires; and he was one of the best of men. Besides him, history presents one or two sovereigns eminent for their goodness, such as Saint Louis or Alfred. But Marcus Aurelius has, for us moderns, this great superiority in interest over Saint Louis or Alfred, that he lived and acted in a state of society modern by its essential characteristics, in an epoch akin to our own, in a brilliant centre of civilization. Trajan talks of "our enlightened age" just as glibly as the "Times" talks of it. Marcus Aurelius thus becomes for us a man like ourselves, a man in all things tempted as we are. Saint Louis inhabits an atmosphere of mediæval Catholicism, which the man of the nineteenth century may admire, indeed, may even passionately wish to inhabit, but which, strive as he will, he cannot really inhabit. Alfred belongs to a state of society (I say it with all deference to the "Saturday Review" critic who keeps such jealous watch over the honor of our Saxon ancestors) half-barbarous. Neither Alfred nor Saint Louis can be morally and intellectually as near to us as Marcus Aurelius.

The record of the outward life of this admirable man has in it little of striking incident. He was born at Rome on the 26th of April, in the year 121 of the Christian era. He was nephew and son-in-law to his predecessor on the throne, Antoninus Pius. When Antoninus died, he was forty years old, but from the time of his earliest manhood he had assisted in administering public affairs. Then, after his uncle's death in 161, for nineteen years he reigned as Emperor. The barbarians were pressing on the Roman frontier, and a great part of Marcus Aurelius's nineteen years of reign was passed in campaigning. His absences from Rome were numerous and long. We hear of him in Asia Minor, Syria, Egypt, Greece; but, above all, in the countries on the Danube, where the war with the barbarians was going on—in Austria, Moravia, Hungary. In these countries much of his "Journal" seems to have been written; parts of it are dated from them; and there, a few weeks before his fifty-ninth birthday, he fell sick and died. The record of him on which his fame chiefly rests is the record of his inward life—his "Journal," or "Commentaries," or "Meditations," or "Thoughts," for by all these names has the work been called. Perhaps the most interesting of the records of his outward life is that which the first book of this work supplies, where he gives an account of his education, recites the names of those to whom he is indebted for it, and enumerates his obligations to each of them. It is a refreshing and consoling picture, a priceless treasure for those, who, sick of the "wild and dreamlike trade of blood and guile," which seems to be nearly the whole that history has to offer to our view, seek eagerly for that substratum of right thinking and well-doing which in all ages must surely have somewhere existed, for without it the continued life of humanity would have been impossible.

"From my mother I learned piety and beneficence, and abstinence not only from evil deeds but even from evil thoughts; and further, simplicity in my way of living, far removed from the habits of the rich." Let us remember that, the next time we are reading the sixth satire of Juvenal. "From my tutor I learned" (hear it, ye tutors of princes!) "endurance of labor, and to want little, and to work with my own hands, and not to meddle with other people's affairs, and not to be ready to listen to slander." The vices and foibles of the Greek sophist or rhetorician—the *Græculus esuriens*—are in everybody's mind; but he who reads Marcus Aurelius's account of his Greek teachers and masters, will understand how it is that, in spite of the vices and foibles of individual *Græculi*, the education of the human race owes to Greece a debt which can never be overrated.

The vague and colorless praise of history leaves on the mind hardly any impression of Antoninus Pius: it is only from the private memoranda of his nephew that we learn what a disciplined, hard-working, gentle, wise, virtuous man he was; a man who, perhaps, interests mankind less than his immortal nephew only because he has left in writing no record of his inner life—*caret quia vate sacro.*

Of the outward life and circumstances of Marcus Aurelius, beyond these notices which he has himself supplied, there are few of much interest and importance. There is the fine anecdote of his speech when he heard of the assassination of the revolted Avidius Cassius, against whom he was marching; *he was sorry,* he said, *to be deprived of the pleasure of pardoning him.* And there are one or two more anecdotes of him which show the same spirit. But the great record for the outward life of a man who has left such a record of his lofty inward aspirations as that which Marcus Aurelius has left, is the clear consenting voice of all his contemporaries,—high and low, friend and enemy, pagan and Christian,—in praise of his sincerity, justice, and goodness. The world's charity does not err on the side of excess, and here was a man occupying the most conspicuous station in the world, and professing the highest possible standard of conduct; yet the world was obliged to declare that he walked worthily of his profession. Long after his death, his bust was to be seen in the houses of private men through the wide Roman Empire. It may be the vulgar part of human nature which busies itself with the semblance and doings of living sovereigns; it is its nobler part which busies itself with those of the dead. These busts of Marcus Aurelius, in the homes of Gaul, Britain, and Italy, bore witness, not to the inmates' frivolous curiosity about princes and palaces, but to their reverential memory of the passage of a great man upon the earth.

Two things, however, before one turns from the outward to the inward life of Marcus Aurelius, force themselves upon one's notice, and demand a word of comment: he persecuted the Christians, and he had for his son the vicious and brutal Commodus. The persecution at Lyons, in which Attalus and Pothinus suffered, the persecution at Smyrna, in which Polycarp suffered, took place in his reign. Of his humanity, of his tolerance, of his horror of cruelty and violence, of his wish to refrain from severe measures against the Christians, of his anxiety to temper the severity of these measures when they appeared to him indispensable, there is no doubt; but, on the one hand, it is certain that the letter, attributed to him, directing that no Christian should be punished for being a Christian, is spurious; it is almost certain that his alleged answer to the authorities of Lyons, in which he directs that Christians persisting in their profession shall be dealt with according to the law, is genuine. Mr. Long seems inclined to try to throw doubt over the persecution at Lyons, by pointing out that the letter of the Lyons Christians relating it alleges it to have been attended by miraculous and incredible incidents. "A man," he says, "can only act consistently by accepting all this letter or rejecting it all, and we cannot blame him for either." But it is contrary to all experience to say that, because a fact is related with incorrect additions, and embellishments, therefore it probably never happened at all; or that it is not, in general, easy for an impartial mind to distinguish between the fact and the embellishments. I cannot doubt that the Lyons persecution took place, and that the punishment of Christians for being Christians was sanctioned by Marcus Aurelius.

But then I must add that nine modern readers out of ten, when they read this, will, I believe, have a perfectly false notion of what the moral action of

Marcus Aurelius, in sanctioning that punishment, really was. They imagine Trajan, or Antoninus Pius, or Marcus Aurelius, fresh from the perusal of the Gospel, fully aware of the spirit and holiness of the Christian saints, ordering their extermination because he loved darkness rather than light. Far from this, the Christianity which these emperors aimed at repressing was, in their conception of it, something philosophically contemptible, politically subversive, and morally abominable. As men, they sincerely regarded it much as well-conditioned people, with us, regard Mormonism; as rulers, they regarded it much as Liberal statesmen, with us, regard the Jesuits. A kind of Mormonism, constituted as a vast secret society, with obscure aims of political and social subversion, was what Antoninus Pius and Marcus Aurelius believed themselves to be repressing when they punished Christians. The early Christian apologists again and again declare to us under what odious imputations the Christians lay, how general was the belief that these imputations were well-grounded, how sincere was the horror which the belief inspired. The multitude, convinced that the Christians were atheists who ate human flesh and thought incest no crime, displayed against them a fury so passionate as to embarrass and alarm their rulers. The severe expressions of Tacitus—"*exitiabilis superstitio*"; "*odio humani generis convicti*"— show how deeply the prejudices of the multitude imbued the educated class also. One asks one's self with astonishment how a doctrine so benign as that of Christ can have incurred misrepresentation so monstrous. The inner and moving cause of the misrepresentation lay, no doubt, in this—that Christianity was a new spirit in the Roman world, destined to act in that world as its dissolvent; and it was inevitable that Christianity in the Roman world, like democracy in the modern world, like every new spirit with a similar mission assigned to it, should at its first appearance occasion an instinctive shrinking and repugnance in the world which it was to dissolve. The outer and palpable causes of the misrepresentation were, for the Roman public at large, the confounding of the Christians with the Jews, that isolated, fierce, and stubborn race, whose stubbornness, fierceness, and isolation, real as they were, the fancy of a civilized Roman yet further exaggerated; the atmosphere of mystery and novelty which surrounded the Christian rites; the very simplicity of Christian theism; for the Roman statesman, the character of secret assemblages which the meetings of the Christian community wore, under a State-system as jealous of unauthorized associations as the Code Napoleon

A Roman of Marcus Aurelius's time and position could not well see the Christians except through the mist of these prejudices. Seen through such a mist, the Christians appeared with a thousand faults not their own; but it has not been sufficiently remarked that faults really their own many of them assuredly appeared with, besides—faults especially likely to strike such an observer as Marcus Aurelius, and to confirm him in the prejudices of his race, station, and rearing. We look back upon Christianity after it has proved what a future it bore within it, and for us the sole representatives of its early struggles are the pure and devoted spirits through whom it proved this; Marcus Aurelius saw it with its future yet unshown, and with the tares among its professed progeny not less conspicuous than the wheat. Who can doubt that, among the professing Christians of the second century, as among the professing Christians of the nineteenth, there was plenty of folly, plenty of rabid nonsense, plenty of gross fanaticism? Who will even venture to affirm that, separated in great measure from the intellect and civilization of the world for one or two centuries, Christianity, wonderful as have been its fruits, had the development perfectly worthy of its inestimable germ? Who will venture to affirm that, by the alliance of Christianity with the virtue and intelligence of men like the Antonines,—of the best product of Greek and Roman civilization, while Greek and Roman civilization had yet life and power,—Christianity and the world, as well as the Antonines themselves, would not have been gainers?

That alliance was not to be. The Antonines lived and died with an utter misconception of Christianity; Christianity grew up in the Catacombs, not on the Palatine. Marcus Aurelius incurs no moral reproach by having authorized the punishment of the Christians; he does not thereby become, in the least, what we mean by a *persecutor*. One may concede that it was impossible for him to see Christianity as it really was, as impossible as for even the moderate and sensible Fleury to see the Antonines as they really were; one may concede that the point of view from which Christianity appeared something anti-civil and anti-social, which the State had the faculty to judge and the duty to suppress, was inevitably his. Still, however, it remains true that this sage, who made perfection his aim and reason his law, did Christianity an immense injustice and rested in an idea of State-attributes which was illusive. And this is, in truth, characteristic of Marcus Aurelius, that he is blameless, yet, in a certain sense, unfortunate; in his character, beautiful as it is, there is something melancholy, circumscribed, and ineffectual.

For of his having such a son as Commodus, too, one must say that he is not to be blamed on that account, but that he is unfortunate. Disposition and temperament are inexplicable things; there are natures on which the best education and example are thrown away; excellent fathers may have, without any fault of theirs, incurably vicious sons. It is to be remembered also, that Commodus was left, at the perilous age of nineteen, master of the whole world; while his father, at that age, was but beginning a twenty years' apprenticeship to wisdom, labor, and self-command, under the sheltering teachership of his uncle Antoninus. Commodus was a prince apt to be led by favorites; and if the story is true which says that he left, all through his reign, the Christians untroubled, and ascribes this lenity to the influence of his mistress Marcia, it shows that he could be led to good as well as to evil; for such a nature to be left at a critical age with absolute power, and wholly without good counsel and direction, was the more fatal. Still one cannot help wishing that the example of Marcus Aurelius could have availed more with his own only son. One cannot but think that with such virtue as his there should go, too, the ardor that removes mountains, and that the ardor that removes mountains might have even won Commodus; the word *ineffectual* again rises to one's mind; Marcus Aurelius saved his own soul by his righteousness, and he could do no more. Happy they who can do this! but still happier, who can do more!

Yet, when one passes from his outward to his inward life, when one turns over the pages of his "Meditations," entries jotted down from day to day, amid the business of the city or the fatigues of the camp, for his own guidance and support; meant for no eye but his own; without the slightest attempt at style, with no care, even, for correct writing; not to be surpassed for naturalness and sincerity—all disposition to carp and cavil dies away, and one is overpowered by the charm of a character of such purity, delicacy, and virtue. He fails neither in small things nor in great; he keeps watch over himself, both that the great springs of action may be right in him, and that the minute details of action may be right also. How admirable in a hard-tasked ruler, and a ruler, too, with a passion for thinking and reading, is such a memorandum as the following:—

"Not frequently nor without necessity to say to anyone, or to write in a letter, that I have no leisure; nor continually to excuse the neglect of duties required by our relation to those with whom we live, by alleging urgent occupation."

And, when that ruler is a Roman emperor, what an "idea" is this to be written down and meditated by him:—

"The idea of a polity in which there is the same law for all, a polity administered with regard to equal rights and equal freedom of speech, and the idea of a kingly government which respects most of all the freedom of the governed."

And, for all men who "drive at practice," what practical rules may not one accumulate out of these "Meditations":—

"The greatest part of what we say or do being unnecessary, if a man takes this away, he will have more leisure and less uneasiness. Accordingly, on every occasion, a man should ask himself, 'Is this one of the unnecessary things?' Now a man should take away not only unnecessary acts, but also unnecessary thoughts, for thus superfluous acts will not follow after."

And again:—

"We ought to check in the series of our thoughts everything that is without a purpose and useless, but most of all the over-curious feeling and the malignant; and a man should use himself to think of those things only about which, if one should suddenly ask, 'What hast thou now in thy thoughts?' with perfect openness thou mightest immediately answer, 'This or That,' so that from thy words it should be plain that everything in thee is simple and benevolent, and such as befits a social animal, and one that cares not for thoughts about sensual enjoyments, or any rivalry or envy and suspicion, or anything else for which thou wouldst blush if thou shouldst say thou hadst it in thy mind."

So, with a stringent practicalness worthy of Franklin, he discourses on his favorite text, "Let nothing be done without a purpose." But it is when he enters the region where Franklin cannot follow him, when he utters his thoughts on the ground-motives of human action, that he is most interesting; that he becomes the unique, the incomparable Marcus Aurelius. Christianity uses language very liable to be misunderstood when it seems to tell men to do good, not, certainly, from the vulgar motives of worldly interest, or vanity, or love of human praise, but "that their Father which seeth in secret may reward them openly." The motives of reward and punishment have come, from the misconception of language of this kind, to be strangely overpressed by many Christian moralists, to the deterioration and disfigurement of Christianity. Marcus Aurelius says, truly and nobly:—

"One man, when he has done a service to another, is ready to set it down to his account as a favor conferred. Another is not ready to do this, but still in his own mind he thinks of the man as his debtor, and he knows what he has done. A third, in a manner, does not even know what he has done, *but he is like a vine which has produced grapes, and seeks for nothing more after it has once produced its proper fruit.* As a horse when he has run, a dog when he has caught the game, a bee when it has made its honey, so a man, when he has done a good act, does not call out for others to come and see, but he goes on to another act, as a vine goes on to produce again the grapes in season. Must a man, then, be one of these, who in a manner acts thus without observing it? Yes."

And again:—

"What more dost thou want when thou hast done a man a service? Art thou not content that thou hast done something conformable to thy nature, and dost thou seek to be paid for it, *just as if the eye demanded a recompense for seeing, or the feet for walking?*"

Christianity, in order to match morality of this strain, has to correct its apparent offers of external reward, and to say: "The kingdom of God is within you."

I have said that it is by its accent of emotion that the morality of Marcus Aurelius acquires a special character, and reminds one of Christian morality. The sentences of Seneca are stimulating to the intellect; the sentences of Epictetus are fortifying to the character; the sentences of Marcus Aurelius find their way to the soul. I have said that religious emotion has the power to *light up* morality: the emotion of Marcus Aurelius does not quite light up his morality, but it suffuses it; it has not power to melt the clouds of effort and austerity quite away, but it shines through them and glorifies them; it is a spirit, not so much of gladness and elation, as of gentleness and sweetness; a delicate and tender sentiment, which is less than joy and more than resignation. He says that in his youth he learned from Maximus, one of his teachers, "cheerfulness in all circumstances as well as in illness; *and a just admixture in the moral character of sweetness and dignity*": and it is this very admixture of sweetness with his dignity which makes him so beautiful a moralist. It enables him to carry, even into his observation of nature, a delicate penetration, a sympathetic tenderness, worthy of Wordsworth; the spirit of such a remark as the following seems to me to have no parallel in the whole range of Greek and Roman literature:—

"Figs, when they are quite ripe, gape open; and in the ripe olives the very circumstance of their being near to rottenness adds a peculiar beauty to the fruit. And the ears of corn bending down, and the lion's eyebrows, and the foam which flows from the mouth of wild boars, and many other things,— though they are far from being beautiful, in a certain sense,—still, because they come in the course of nature, have a beauty in them, and they please the mind; so that, if a man should have a feeling and a deeper insight with respect to the things which are produced in the universe, there is hardly anything which comes in the course of nature which will not seem to him to be in a manner disposed so as to give pleasure."

But it is when his strain passes to directly moral subjects that his delicacy and sweetness lend to it the greatest charm. Let those who can feel the beauty of spiritual refinement read this, the reflection of an emperor who prized mental superiority highly:—

"Thou sayest, 'Men cannot admire the sharpness of thy wits.' Be it so; but there are many other things of which thou canst not say, 'I am not formed for them by nature.' Show those qualities, then, which are altogether in thy power—sincerity, gravity, endurance of labor, aversion to pleasure, contentment with thy portion and with few things, benevolence, frankness, no love of superfluity, freedom from trifling, magnanimity. Dost thou not see how many qualities thou art at once able to exhibit, as to which there is no excuse of natural incapacity and unfitness, and yet thou still remainest voluntarily below the mark? Or art thou compelled, through being defectively furnished by nature, to murmur, and to be mean, and to flatter, and to find fault with thy poor body, and to try to please men, and to make great display, and to be so restless in thy mind? No, indeed; but thou mightest have been delivered from these things long ago. Only, if in truth thou canst be charged with being rather slow and dull of comprehension, thou must exert thyself about this also, not neglecting nor yet taking pleasure in thy dulness."

The same sweetness enables him to fix his mind, when he sees the isolation and moral death caused by sin, not on the cheerless thought of the misery of this condition, but on the inspiring thought that man is blest with the power to escape from it:—

"Suppose that thou hast detached thyself from the natural unity,—for thou wast made by nature a part, but now thou hast cut thyself off,—yet here is this beautiful provision, that it is in thy power again to unite thyself. God has allowed this to no other part—after it has been separated and cut asunder, to come together again. But consider the goodness with which he has privileged man; for he has put it in his power, when he has been separated, to return and to be united and to resume his place."

It enables him to control even the passion for retreat and solitude, so strong in a soul like his, to which the world could offer no abiding city.

"Men seek retreat for themselves, houses in the country, seashores, and mountains; and thou, too, art wont to desire such things very much. But this is altogether a mark of the most common sort of man, for it is in thy power whenever thou shalt choose to retire into thyself. For nowhere either with more quiet or more freedom from trouble does a man retire than into his own soul, particularly when he has within him such thoughts that, by looking into them, he is immediately in perfect tranquillity. Constantly, then, give to thyself this retreat, and renew thyself; and let thy principles be brief and fundamental, which, as soon as thou shalt recur to them, will be sufficient to cleanse the soul completely, and to send thee back free from all discontent with the things to which thou returnest."

Against this feeling of discontent and weariness, so natural to the great for whom there seems nothing left to desire or to strive after, but so enfeebling to them, so deteriorating, Marcus Aurelius never ceased to struggle. With resolute thankfulness he kept in remembrance the blessings of his lot; the true blessings of it, not the false.

"I have to thank Heaven that I was subjected to a ruler and a father [Antoninus Pius] who was able to take away all pride from me, and to bring me to the knowledge that it is possible for a man to live in a palace without either guards, or embroidered dresses, or any show of this kind; but that it is in such a man's power to bring himself very near to the fashion of a private person, without being for this reason either meaner in thought or more remiss in action with respect to the things which must be done for public interest.... I have to be thankful that my children have not been stupid or deformed in body; that I did not make more proficiency in rhetoric, poetry, and the other studies, by which I should perhaps have been completely engrossed, if I had seen that I was making great progress in them;... that I knew Apollonius, Rusticus, Maximus;... that I received clear and frequent impressions about living according to nature, and what kind of a life that is, so that, so far as depended on Heaven and its gifts, help, and inspiration, nothing hindered me from forthwith living according to nature, though I still fall short of it through my own fault, and through not observing the admonitions of Heaven, and, I may almost say, its direct instructions; that my body has held out so long in such a kind of life as mine; that, though it was my mother's lot to die young, she spent the last years of her life with me; that, whenever I wished to help any man in his need, I was never told that I had not the means of doing it; that, when I had an inclination to philosophy, I did not fall into the hands of a sophist."

And, as he dwelt with gratitude on these helps and blessings vouchsafed to him, his mind (so, at least, it seems to me) would sometimes revert with awe to the perils and temptations of the lonely height where he stood, to the lives of Tiberius, Caligula, Nero, Domitian, in their hideous blackness and ruin; and then he wrote down for himself such a warning entry as this, significant and terrible in its abruptness:—

"A black character, a womanish character, a stubborn character, bestial, childish, animal, stupid, counterfeit, scurrilous, fraudulent, tyrannical!"

Or this:—

"About what am I now employing my soul? On every occasion I must ask myself this question, and inquire, What have I now in this part of me which they call the ruling principle, and whose soul have I now—that of a child, or of a young man, or of a weak woman, or of a tyrant, or of one of the lower animals in the service of man, or of a wild beast?"

The character he wished to attain he knew well, and beautifully he has marked it, and marked, too, his sense of shortcoming:—

"When thou hast assumed these names,—good, modest, true, rational, equal minded, magnanimous,—take care that thou dost not change these names; and, if thou shouldst lose them, quickly return to them. If thou maintainest thyself in possession of these names, without desiring that others should call thee by them, thou wilt be another being, and wilt enter on another life. For to continue to be such as thou hast hitherto been, and to be torn in pieces and denied in such a life, is the character of a very stupid man, and one overfond of his life, and like those half-devoured fighters with wild beasts, who though covered with wounds and gore, still entreat to be kept to the following day, though they will be exposed in the same state to the same claws and bites. Therefore fix thyself in the possession of these few names; and if thou art able to abide in them, abide as if thou wast removed to the Happy Islands."

For all his sweetness and serenity, however, man's point of life "between two infinities" (of that expression Marcus Aurelius is the real owner) was to him anything but a Happy Island, and the performances on it he saw through no veils of illusion. Nothing is in general more gloomy and monotonous than declamations on the hollowness and transitoriness of human life and grandeur; but here, too, the great charm of Marcus Aurelius, his emotion, comes in to relieve the monotony and to break through the gloom; and even on this eternally used topic he is imaginative, fresh, and striking:—

"Consider, for example, the times of Vespasian. Thou wilt see all these things, people marrying, bringing up children, sick, dying, warring, feasting, trafficking, cultivating the ground, flattering, obstinately arrogant, suspecting, plotting, wishing for somebody to die, grumbling about the present, loving, heaping up treasure, desiring to be consuls or kings. Well, then that life of these people no longer exists at all. Again, go to the times of Trajan. All is again the same. Their life too is gone. But chiefly thou shouldst think of those whom thou hast thyself known distracting themselves about idle things, neglecting to do what was in accordance with their proper constitution, and to hold firmly to this and to be content with it."

Again:—

"The things which are much valued in life are empty, and rotten, and trifling; and people are like little dogs, biting one another, and little children quarreling, crying, and then straightway laughing. But fidelity, and modesty, and justice and truth are fled

Up to Olympus from the wide-spread earth.

What then is there which still detains thee here?"

And once more:—

"Look down from above on the countless herds of men, and their countless solemnities, and the infinitely varied voyagings in storms and calms, and the differences among those who are born, who live together and die. And consider too the life lived by others in olden time, and the life now lived among barbarous nations, and how many know not even thy name, and how many will soon forget it, and how they who perhaps now are praising thee will very soon blame thee, and that neither a posthumous name is of any value, nor reputation, nor anything else."

He recognized, indeed, that (to use his own words) "the prime principle in man's constitution is the social"; and he labored sincerely to make, not only his acts toward his fellow men, but his thoughts also, suitable to this conviction.

"When thou wishest to delight thyself, think of the virtue of those who live with thee: for instance, the activity of one, and the modesty of another, and the liberality of a third, and some other good quality of a fourth."

Still, it is hard for a pure and thoughtful man to live in a state of rapture at the spectacle afforded to him by his fellow creatures; above all it is hard, when such a man is placed as Marcus Aurelius was placed, and has had the meanness and perversity of his fellow creatures thrust, in no common measure, upon his notice—has had, time after time, to experience how "within ten days thou wilt seem a god to those to whom thou art now a beast and an ape." His true strain of thought as to his relations with his fellow men is rather the following. He has been enumerating the higher consolations which may support a man at the approach of death, and he goes on:—

"But if thou requirest also a vulgar kind of comfort which shall reach thy heart, thou wilt be made best reconciled to death by observing the objects from which thou art going to be removed, and the morals of those with whom thy soul will no longer be mingled. For it is no way right to be offended with men, but it is thy duty to care for them and to bear with them gently; and yet to remember that thy departure will not be from men who have the same principles as thyself. For this is the only thing, if there be any, which could draw us the contrary way and attach us to life—to be permitted to live with those who have the same principles as ourselves. But now thou seest how great is the distress caused by the difference of those who live together, so that thou mayest say: 'Come quick, O death, lest perchance I too should forget myself.'"

O faithless and perverse generation! how long shall I be with you? how long shall I suffer you? Sometimes this strain rises even to passion:—

"Short is the little which remains to thee of life. Live as on a mountain. Let men see, let them know, a real man, who lives as he was meant to live. If they cannot endure him, let them kill him. For that is better than to live as men do."

It is remarkable how little of a merely local and temporary character, how little of those *scoriæ* which a reader has to clear away before he gets to the precious ore, how little that even admits of doubt or question, the morality of Marcus Aurelius exhibits. In general, the action he prescribes is action which every sound nature must recognize as right, and the motives he assigns are motives which every clear reason must recognize as valid. And so he remains the especial friend and comforter of scrupulous and difficult, yet pure-hearted and upward-striving souls, in those ages most especially that walk by sight, not by faith, but yet have no open vision; he cannot give such souls, perhaps, all they yearn for, but he gives them much; and what he gives them, they can receive.

Yet no, it is not for what he thus gives them that such souls love him most! it is rather because of the emotion which gives to his voice so touching an accent, it is because he too yearns as they do for something unattained by him. What an affinity for Christianity had this persecutor of the Christians! The effusion of Christianity, its relieving tears, its happy self-sacrifice, were the very element, one feels, for which his soul longed; they were near him, they brushed him, he touched them, he passed them by. One feels, too, that the Marcus Aurelius one knows must still have remained, even had they presented themselves to him, in a great measure himself; he would have been no Justin. But how would they have affected him? in what measure would it have changed him? Granted that he might have found, like the *Alogi* of modern times, in the most beautiful of the Gospels, the Gospel which has leavened Christendom most powerfully,—the Gospel of St. John,—too much Greek metaphysics, too much *gnosis*; granted that this Gospel might have looked too like what he knew already to be a total surprise to him: what, then, would he have said to the Sermon on the Mount, to the twenty-sixth chapter of St. Matthew? What would have become of his notion of the *exitiabilis superstitio*, of the "obstinacy of the Christians"? Vain question! yet the greatest charm of Marcus Aurelius is that he makes us ask it. We see him wise, just, self-governed, tender, thankful, blameless; yet, with all this, agitated, stretching out his arms for something beyond—*tendentemque manus ripæ ulterioris amore.*

DOVER BEACH

The sea is calm to-night,
The tide is full, the moon lies fair
Upon the straits;—on the French coast the light
Gleams and is gone; the cliffs of England stand,
Glimmering and vast, out in the tranquil bay.
Come to the window, sweet is the night-air!
Only, from the long line of spray
Where the sea meets the moon-blanch'd land,
Listen! you hear the grating roar
Of pebbles which the waves draw back, and fling,

At their return, up the high strand,
Begin, and cease, and then again begin,
With tremulous cadence slow, and bring
The eternal note of sadness in.

Sophocles long ago
Heard it on the Ægæan, and it brought
Into his mind the turbid ebb and flow
Of human misery; we
Find also in the sound a thought,
Hearing it by this distant northern sea.

The Sea of Faith
Was once, too, at the full, and round earth's shore
Lay like the folds of a bright girdle furl'd.
But now I only hear
Its melancholy, long, withdrawing roar,
Retreating, to the breath
Of the night-wind, down the vast edges drear
And naked shingles of the world.
Ah, love, let us be true
To one another! for the world, which seems
To lie before us like a land of dreams,
So various, so beautiful, so new,
Hath really neither joy, nor love, nor light,
Nor certitude, nor peace, nor help for pain;
And we are here as on a darkling plain
Swept with confused alarms of struggle and flight,
Where ignorant armies clash by night.

MORALITY

We cannot kindle when we will
The fire that in the heart resides;
The spirit bloweth and is still,
In mystery our soul abides;
But tasks in hours of insight will'd
Can be through hours of gloom fulfill'd.

With aching hands and bleeding feet
We dig and heap, lay stone on stone;

We bear the burden and the heat
Of the long day, and wish 'twere done.
Not till the hours of light return,
All we have built do we discern.

Then, when the clouds are off the soul,
When thou dost bask in Nature's eye,
Ask, how *she* view'd thy self-control,
Thy struggling task'd morality—
Nature, whose free, light, cheerful air,
Oft made thee, in thy gloom, despair.

And she, whose censure thou dost dread,
Whose eye thou wert afraid to seek,
See, on her face a glow is spread,
A strong emotion on her cheek.
"Ah child," she cries, "that strife divine—
Whence was it, for it is not mine?

"There is no effort on *my* brow—
I do not strive, I do not weep.
I rush with the swift spheres, and glow
In joy, and, when I will, I sleep.
Yet that severe, that earnest air
I saw, I felt it once—but where?

"I knew not yet the gauge of Time,
Nor wore the manacles of Space.
I felt it in some other clime—
I saw it in some other place.
—'Twas when the heavenly house I trod,
And lay upon the breast of God."

SELF-DEPENDENCE

Weary of myself, and sick of asking
What I am, and what I ought to be,
At this vessel's prow I stand, which bears me
Forwards, forwards, o'er the starlit sea.

And a look of passionate desire

O'er the sea and to the stars I send:
"Ye who from my childhood up have calmed me,
Calm me, ah, compose me to the end!

"Ah, once more," I cried, "ye stars, ye waters,
On my heart your mighty charm renew;
Still, still let me, as I gaze upon you,
Feel my soul becoming vast like you!"

From the intense, clear, star-sown vault of heaven,
Over the lit sea's unquiet way,
In the rustling night-air came the answer:
"Wouldst thou *be* as these are? *Live* as they.

"Unaffrighted by the silence round them,
Undistracted by the sights they see,
These demand not that the things without them
Yield them love, amusement, sympathy.

"And with joy the stars perform their shining,
And the sea its long moon-silvered roll;
For self-poised they live, nor pine with noting
All the fever of some differing soul.

"Bounded by themselves, and unregardful
In what state God's other works may be,
In their own tasks all their powers pouring,
These attain the mighty life you see."

O air-born voice! long since, severely clear,
A cry like thine in mine own heart I hear:
"Resolve to be thyself; and know that he,
Who finds himself, loses his misery!"

ARTHUR HUGH CLOUGH

ALL IS WELL

Whate'er you dream, with doubt possessed,
Keep, keep it snug within your breast,
And lay you down and take your rest;
Forget in sleep the doubt and pain,
And when you wake, to work again.
The wind it blows, the vessel goes,
And where and whither, no ones knows.

'Twill all be well: no need of care;
Though how it will, and when, and where,
We cannot see, and can't declare.
In spite of dreams, in spite of thought,
'Tis not in vain, and not for nought,
The wind it blows, the ship it goes,
Though where and whither, no one knows.

TO SPEND UNCOUNTED YEARS OF PAIN

To spend uncounted years of pain,
Again, again, and yet again,
In working out in heart and brain
The problem of our being here;
To gather facts from far and near,
Upon the mind to hold them clear,
And, knowing more may yet appear,
Unto one's latest breath to fear,
The premature result to draw—
Is this the object, end, and law,
And purpose of our being here?

SAY NOT THE STRUGGLE NOUGHT AVAILETH

Say not the struggle nought availeth,
The labor and the wounds are vain,
The enemy faints not, nor faileth,
And as things have been they remain.

If hopes were dupes, fears may be liars;

It may be, in yon smoke concealed,
Your comrades chase e'en now the fliers,
And, but for you, possess the field.

For while the tired waves, vainly breaking,
Seem here no painful inch to gain,
Far back, through creeks and inlets making,
Comes silent, flooding in, the main.

And not by eastern windows only,
When daylight comes, comes in the light;
In front, the sun climbs slow, how slowly;
But westward, look, the land is bright.

ALGERNON CHARLES SWINBURNE

THE GARDEN OF PROSERPINE

Here, where the world is quiet;
Here, where all trouble seems
Dead winds' and spent waves' riot
In doubtful dreams of dreams;
I watch the green field growing
For reaping folk and sowing,
For harvest-time and mowing,
A sleepy world of streams.

I am tired of tears and laughter,
And men that laugh and weep;
Of what may come hereafter
For men that sow to reap:
I am weary of days and hours,
Blown buds of barren flowers,
Desires and dreams and powers
And everything but sleep.

Here life has death for neighbor,
And far from eye or ear
Wan waves and wet winds labor,
Weak ships and spirits steer;
They drive adrift, and whither
They wot not who make thither;
But no such winds blow hither,
And no such things grow here.

No growth of moor or coppice,
No heather-flower or vine,
But bloomless buds of poppies,
Green grapes of Proserpine,
Pale beds of blowing rushes,
Where no leaf blooms or blushes
Save this whereout she crushes
For dead men deadly wine.

Pale, without name or number,
In fruitless fields of corn,
They bow themselves and slumber

All night till light is born;
And like a soul belated,
In hell and heaven unmated,
By cloud and mist abated
Comes out of darkness morn.

Though one were strong as seven,
He too with death shall dwell,
Nor wake with wings in heaven,
Nor weep for pains in hell;
Though one were fair as roses,
His beauty clouds and closes;
And well though love reposes,
In the end it is not well.

Pale, beyond porch and portal,
Crowned with calm leaves, she stands
Who gathers all things mortal
With cold immortal hands;
Her languid lips are sweeter
Than love's who fears to greet her,
To men that mix and meet her
From many times and lands.

She waits for each and other,
She waits for all men born;
Forgets the earth her mother,
The life of fruits and corn;
And spring and seed and swallow
Take wing for her and follow
Where summer song rings hollow
And flowers are put to scorn.

There go the loves that wither,
The old loves with wearier wings,
And all dead years draw thither,
And all disastrous things;
Dead dreams of days forsaken,
Blind buds that snows have shaken,
Wild leaves that winds have taken,
Red strays of ruined springs.

We are not sure of sorrow;

And joy was never sure;
To-day will die to-morrow;
Time stoops to no man's lure;
And love, grown faint and fretful,
With lips but half regretful
Sighs, and with eyes forgetful
Weeps that no loves endure.

From too much love of living,
From hope and fear set free,
We thank with brief thanksgiving
Whatever gods may be
That no life lives for ever;
That dead men rise up never;
That even the weariest river
Winds somewhere safe to sea.

Then star nor sun shall waken,
Nor any change of light:
Nor sound of waters shaken,
Nor any sound or sight:
Nor wintry leaves nor vernal,
Nor days nor things diurnal;
Only the sleep eternal
In an eternal night.

EDWARD FITZGERALD

RUBAIYAT OF OMAR KHAYYAM

I

Wake! For the Sun, who scatter'd into flight
The Stars before him from the Field of Night,
Drives Night along with them from Heav'n, and strikes
The Sultan's Turret with a Shaft of Light.

II

Before the phantom of False morning died,
Methought a Voice within the Tavern cried,
"When all the Temple is prepared within,
Why nods the drowsy Worshipper outside?"

III

And, as the Cock crew, those who stood before
The Tavern shouted—"Open then the Door!
You know how little while we have to stay,
And, once departed, may return no more."

IV

Now the New Year reviving old Desires,
The thoughtful Soul to Solitude retires,
Where the WHITE HAND OF MOSES on the Bough
Puts out, and Jesus from the Ground suspires.

V

Iram indeed is gone with all his Rose,
And Jamshyd's Sev'n-ring'd Cup where no one knows;
But still a Ruby kindles in the Vine,
And many a Garden by the Water blows.

VI

And David's lips are lockt; but in divine
High-piping Pehleví, with "Wine! Wine! Wine!
Red Wine!"—the Nightingale cries to the Rose
That sallow cheek of hers to incarnadine.

VII

Come, fill the Cup, and in the fire of Spring
Your Winter-garment of Repentance fling:
The Bird of Time has but a little way
To flutter—and the Bird is on the Wing.

VIII

Whether at Naishápúr or Babylon,
Whether the Cup with sweet or bitter run,
The Wine of Life keeps oozing drop by drop,
The Leaves of Life keep falling one by one.

IX

Each Morn a thousand Roses brings, you say;
Yes, but where leaves the Rose of Yesterday?
And this first Summer month that brings the Rose
Shall take Jamshyd and Kaikobád away.

X

Well, let it take them! What have we to do
With Kaikobád the Great, or Kaikhosrú?
Let Zál and Rustum bluster as they will,
Or Hátim call to Supper—heed not you.

XI

With me along the strip of Herbage strown
That just divides the desert from the sown,

Where name of Slave and Sultán is forgot—
And Peace to Mahmúd on his golden Throne!

XII

A Book of Verses underneath the Bough,
A Jug of Wine, a Loaf of Bread—and Thou
Beside me singing in the Wilderness—
Oh, Wilderness were Paradise enow!

XIII

Some for the Glories of This World; and some
Sigh for the Prophet's Paradise to come;
Ah, take the Cash, and let the Credit go,
Nor heed the rumble of a distant Drum!

XIV

Look to the blowing Rose about us—"Lo,
Laughing," she says, "into the world I blow,
At once the silken tassel of my Purse
Tear, and its Treasure on the Garden throw."

XV

And those who husbanded the Golden grain,
And those who flung it to the winds like Rain,
Alike to no such aureate Earth are turn'd
As, buried once, Men want dug up again.

XVI

The Worldly Hope men set their Hearts upon
Turns Ashes—or it prospers; and anon,
Like Snow upon the Desert's dusty Face,
Lighting a little hour or two—is gone.

XVII

Think, in this batter'd Caravanserai
Whose Portals are alternate Night and Day,
How Sultan after Sultan with his Pomp
Abode his destined Hour, and went his way.

XVIII

They say the Lion and the Lizard keep
The Courts where Jamshyd gloried and drank deep:
And Bahrám, that great Hunter—the Wild Ass
Stamps o'er his Head, but cannot break his Sleep.

XIX

I sometimes think that never blows so red
The Rose as where some buried Cæsar bled;
That every Hyacinth the Garden wears
Dropt in her Lap from some once lovely Head.

XX

And this reviving Herb whose tender Green
Fledges the River-Lip on which we lean—
Ah, lean upon it lightly! for who knows
From what once lovely Lip it springs unseen!

XXI

Ah, my Belovèd, fill the Cup that clears
TO-DAY of past Regrets and future Fears:
To-morrow!—Why, To-morrow I may be
Myself with Yesterday's Sev'n Thousand Years.

XXII

For some we loved, the loveliest and the best
That from his Vintage rolling Time hath prest,

Have drunk their Cup a Round or two before,
And one by one crept silently to rest.

XXIII

And we, that now make merry in the Room
They left, and Summer dresses in new bloom,
Ourselves must we beneath the Couch of Earth
Descend—ourselves to make a Couch—for whom?

XXIV

Ah, make the most of what we yet may spend,
Before we too into the Dust descend;
Dust into Dust, and under Dust to lie,
Sans Wine, sans Song, sans Singer, and—sans End!

XXV

Alike for those who for TO-DAY prepare,
And those that after some TO-MORROW stare,
A Muezzín from the Tower of Darkness cries,
"Fools! your Reward is neither Here nor There."

XXVI

Why, all the Saints and Sages who discuss'd
Of the Two Worlds so wisely—they are thrust
Like foolish Prophets forth; their Words to Scorn
Are scatter'd, and their Mouths are stopt with Dust.

XXVII

Myself when young did eagerly frequent
Doctor and Saint, and heard great argument
About it and about; but evermore
Came out by the same door where in I went.

XXVIII

With them the seed of Wisdom did I sow,
And with mine own hand wrought to make it grow;
And this was all the Harvest that I reap'd—
"I came like Water, and like Wind I go."

XXIX

Into this Universe, and *Why* not knowing
Nor *Whence*, like Water willy-nilly flowing;
And out of it, as Wind along the Waste,
I know not *Whither*, willy-nilly blowing.

XXX

What, without asking, hither hurried *Whence?*
And, without asking, *Whither* hurried hence!
Oh, many a Cup of this forbidden Wine
Must drown the memory of that insolence!

XXXI

Up from Earth's Centre through the Seventh Gate
I rose, and on the Throne of Saturn sate,
And many a Knot unravel'd by the Road;
But not the Master-knot of Human Fate.

XXXII

There was the Door to which I found no Key;
There was the Veil through which I might not see;
Some little talk awhile of ME and THEE
There was—and then no more of THEE and ME.

XXXIII

Earth could not answer; nor the Seas that mourn
In flowing Purple, of their Lord forlorn;

Nor rolling Heaven, with all his Signs reveal'd
And hidden by the sleeve of Night and Morn.

XXXIV

Then of the THEE IN ME who works behind
The Veil, I lifted up my hands to find
A Lamp amid the Darkness; and I heard,
As from Without—"THE ME WITHIN THEE BLIND!"

XXXV

Then to the Lip of this poor earthen Urn
I lean'd, the Secret of my Life to learn:
And Lip to Lip it murmur'd—"While you live,
Drink!—for, once dead, you never shall return."

XXXVI

I think the Vessel, that with fugitive
Articulation answer'd, once did live,
And drink; and Ah! the passive Lip I kiss'd,
How many Kisses might it take—and give!

XXXVII

For I remember stopping by the way
To watch a Potter thumping his wet Clay;
And with its all-obliterated Tongue
It murmur'd—"Gently, Brother, gently, pray!"

XXXVIII

And has not such a Story from of Old
Down Man's successive generations roll'd
Of such a clod of saturated Earth
Cast by the Maker into Human mould?

XXXIX

And not a drop that from our Cups we throw
For Earth to drink of, but may steal below
To quench the fire of Anguish in some Eye
There hidden—far beneath, and long ago.

XL

As then the Tulip for her morning sup
Of Heav'nly Vintage from the soil looks up,
Do you devoutly do the like, till Heav'n
To Earth invert you—like an empty Cup.

XLI

Perplext no more with Human or Divine,
To-morrow's tangle to the winds resign,
And lose your fingers in the tresses of
The Cypress-slender Minister of Wine.

XLII

And if the Wine you drink, the Lip you press,
End in what All begins and ends in—Yes;
Think then you are TO-DAY what YESTERDAY
You were—TO-MORROW you shall be not less.

XLIII

So when that Angel of the darker Drink
At last shall find you by the river-brink,
And, offering his Cup, invite your Soul
Forth to your Lips to quaff—you shall not shrink.

XLIV

Why, if the Soul can fling the Dust aside,
And naked on the Air of Heaven ride,

Were't not a Shame—were't not a Shame for him
In this clay carcass crippled to abide?

XLV

'Tis but a Tent where takes his one day's rest
A Sultan to the realm of Death addrest;
The Sultan rises, and the dark Ferrásh
Strikes, and prepares it for another Guest.

XLVI

And fear not lest Existence closing your
Account, and mine, should know the like no more;
The Eternal Sákí from that Bowl has pour'd
Millions of Bubbles like us, and will pour.

XLVII

When You and I behind the Veil are past,
Oh, but the long, long while the World shall last,
Which of our Coming and Departure heeds
As the Sea's self should heed a pebble-cast.

XLVIII

A Moment's Halt—a momentary taste
Of BEING from the Well amid the Waste—
And Lo!—the phantom Caravan has reach'd
The NOTHING it set out from—Oh, make haste!

XLIX

Would you that spangle of Existence spend
About THE SECRET—quick about it, Friend!
A Hair perhaps divides the False and True—
And upon what, prithee, may life depend?

L

A Hair perhaps divides the False and True;
Yes; and a single Alif were the clue—
Could you but find it—to the Treasure-house,
And peradventure to THE MASTER too;

LI

Whose secret Presence, though Creation's veins
Running Quicksilver-like, eludes your pains;
Taking all shapes from Máh to Máhi; and
They change and perish all—but He remains;

LII

A moment guess'd—then back behind the Fold
Immerst of Darkness round the Drama roll'd
Which, for the Pastime of Eternity,
He doth Himself contrive, enact, behold.

LIII

But if in vain, down on the stubborn floor
Of Earth, and up to Heav'n's unopening Door,
You gaze TO-DAY, while You are You—how then
TO-MORROW, You when shall be You no more?

LIV

Waste not your Hour, nor in the vain pursuit
Of This and That endeavor and dispute;
Better be jocund with the fruitful Grape
Than sadden after none, or bitter, Fruit.

LV

You know, my Friends, with what a brave Carouse
I made a Second Marriage in my house;

Divorced old barren Reason from my Bed,
And took the Daughter of the Vine to Spouse.

LVI

For "Is" and "Is-not" though with Rule and Line
And "Up-and-down" by Logic I define,
Of all that one should care to fathom, I
Was never deep in anything but—Wine.

LVII

Ah, but my Computations, People say,
Reduced the Year to better reckoning?—Nay,
'Twas only striking from the Calendar
Unborn To-morrow, and dead Yesterday.

LVIII

And lately, by the Tavern Door agape,
Came shining through the Dusk an Angel Shape
Bearing a Vessel on his Shoulder; and
He bid me taste of it; and 'twas—the Grape!

LIX

The Grape that can with Logic absolute
The Two-and-Seventy jarring Sects confute:
The sovereign Alchemist that in a trice
Life's leaden metal into Gold transmute:

LX

The mighty Mahmúd, Allah breathing Lord,
That all the misbelieving and black Horde
Of Fears and Sorrows that infest the Soul
Scatters before him with his whirlwind Sword.

LXI

Why, be this Juice the growth of God, who dare
Blaspheme the twisted tendril as a Snare?
A Blessing, we should use it, should we not?
And if a Curse—why, then, Who set it there?

LXII

I must abjure the Balm of Life, I must,
Scared by some After-reckoning ta'en on trust,
Or lured with Hope of some Diviner Drink,
To fill the Cup—when crumbled into Dust!

LXIII

O threats of Hell and Hopes of Paradise!
One thing at least is certain—*This* Life flies;
One thing is certain and the rest is Lies;
The Flower that once has blown for ever dies.

LXIV

Strange, is it not? that of the myriads who
Before us pass'd the door of Darkness through,
Not one returns to tell us of the Road,
Which to discover we must travel too.

LXV

The Revelations of Devout and Learn'd
Who rose before us, and as Prophets burn'd,
Are all but Stories, which, awoke from Sleep,
They told their comrades, and to Sleep return'd.

LXVI

I sent my Soul through the Invisible,
Some letter of that After-life to spell:

And by and by my Soul return'd to me,
And answer'd, "I myself am Heav'n and Hell":

LXVII

Heav'n but the Vision of fulfill'd Desire,
And Hell the Shadow from a Soul on fire,
Cast on the Darkness into which Ourselves,
So late emerged from, shall so soon expire.

LXVIII

We are no other than a moving row
Of Magic Shadow-shapes that come and go
Round with the Sun-illumined Lantern held
In Midnight by the Master of the Show;

LXIX

But helpless Pieces of the Game He plays
Upon this Chequer-board of Nights and Days;
Hither and thither moves, and checks, and slays,
And one by one back in the Closet lays.

LXX

The Ball no question makes of Ayes and Noes,
But Here or There as strikes the Player goes;
And He that toss'd you down into the Field,
He knows about it all—HE knows—HE knows!

LXXI

The Moving Finger writes; and, having writ,
Moves on: nor all your Piety nor Wit
Shall lure it back to cancel half a Line,
Nor all your Tears wash out a Word of it.

LXXII

And that inverted Bowl they call the Sky,
Whereunder crawling coop'd we live and die,
Lift not your hands to *It* for help—for It
As impotently moves as you or I.

LXXIII

With Earth's first Clay They did the Last Man knead,
And there of the Last Harvest sow'd the Seed:
And the first Morning of Creation wrote
What the Last Dawn of Reckoning shall read.

LXXIV

YESTERDAY *This* Day's Madness did prepare;
TO-MORROW'S Silence, Triumph, or Despair:
Drink! for you know not whence you came, nor why:
Drink! for you know not why you go, nor where.

LXXV

I tell you this—When, started from the Goal,
Over the flaming shoulders of the Foal
Of Heav'n Parwín and Mushtarí they flung,
In my predestined Plot of Dust and Soul

LXXVI

The Vine had struck a fibre: which about
If clings my Being—let the Dervish flout;
Of my Base metal may be filed a Key,
That shall unlock the Door he howls without.

LXXVII

And this I know: whether the one True Light
Kindle to Love, or Wrath—consume me quite,

One Flash of It within the Tavern caught
Better than in the Temple lost outright.

LXXVIII

What! out of senseless Nothing to provoke
A conscious Something to resent the yoke
Of unpermitted Pleasure, under pain
Of Everlasting Penalties, if broke!

LXXIX

What! from his helpless Creature be repaid
Pure Gold for what he lent him dross-allay'd—
Sue for a Debt he never did contract,
And cannot answer—Oh, the sorry trade!

LXXX

O Thou, who didst with pitfall and with gin
Beset the Road I was to wander in,
Thou wilt not with Predestined Evil round
Enmesh, and then impute my Fall to Sin!

LXXXI

O Thou, who Man of baser Earth didst make,
And ev'n with Paradise devise the Snake:
For all the Sin wherewith the Face of Man
Is blacken'd—Man's forgiveness give—and take!

LXXXII

As under cover of departing Day
Slunk hunger-stricken Ramazán away,

Once more within the Potter's house alone
I stood, surrounded by the Shapes of Clay.

LXXXIII

Shapes of all Sorts and Sizes, great and small,
That stood along the floor and by the wall;
And some loquacious Vessels were; and some
Listen'd perhaps, but never talk'd at all.

LXXXIV

Said one among them—"Surely not in vain
My substance of the common Earth was ta'en
And to this Figure moulded, to be broke,
Or trampled back to Shapeless Earth again."

LXXXV

Then said a Second—"Ne'er a peevish Boy
Would break the Bowl from which he drank in joy;
And He that with his hand the Vessel made
Will surely not in after Wrath destroy."

LXXXVI

After a momentary silence spake
Some Vessel of a more ungainly Make;
"They sneer at me for leaning all awry:
What! did the Hand then of the Potter shake?"

LXXXVII

Whereat some one of the loquacious Lot—
I think a Súfi pipkin—waxing hot—
"All this of Pot and Potter—Tell me then,
Who is the Potter, pray, and who the Pot?"

LXXXVIII

"Why," said another, "Some there are who tell
Of one who threatens he will toss to Hell
The luckless Pots he marr'd in making—Pish!
He's a Good Fellow, and 'twill all be well."

LXXXIX

"Well," murmur'd one, "Let whoso make or buy,
My Clay with long Oblivion is gone dry;
But fill me with the old familiar Juice;
Methinks I might recover by and by."

XC

So while the Vessels one by one were speaking,
The little Moon look'd in that all were seeking:
And then they jogg'd each other, "Brother! Brother!
Now for the Porter's shoulder-knot a-creaking!"

. . . .

XCI

Ah, with the Grape my fading Life provide,
And wash the Body whence the Life has died,
And lay me, shrouded in the living Leaf,
By some not unfrequented Garden-side.

XCII

That ev'n my buried Ashes such a snare
Of Vintage shall fling up into the Air
As not a True-believer passing by
But shall be overtaken unaware.

XCIII

Indeed the Idols I have loved so long
Have done my credit in this World much wrong:
Have drown'd my Glory in a shallow Cup,
And sold my Reputation for a Song.

XCIV

Indeed, indeed, Repentance oft before
I swore—but was I sober when I swore?
And then and then came Spring, and Rose-in-hand
My thread-bare Penitence apieces tore.

XCV

And much as Wine has play'd the Infidel,
And robb'd me of my Robe of Honor—Well,
I wonder often what the Vintners buy
One half so precious as the stuff they sell.

XCVI

Yet ah, that Spring should vanish with the Rose!
That Youth's sweet-scented manuscript should close!
The Nightingale that in the branches sang,
Ah, whence, and whither flown again, who knows!

XCVII

Would but the Desert of the Fountain yield
One glimpse—if dimly, yet indeed, reveal'd,
To which the fainting Traveler might spring,
As springs the trampled herbage of the field!

XCVIII

Would but some wingèd Angel ere too late
Arrest the yet unfolded Roll of Fate,

And make the stern Recorder otherwise
Enregister, or quite obliterate!

XCIX

Ah Love! could you and I with Him conspire
To grasp this sorry Scheme of Things entire,
Would not we shatter it to bits—and then
Re-mould it nearer to the Heart's Desire!

. . . .

C

Yon rising Moon that looks for us again—
How oft hereafter will she wax and wane;
How oft hereafter rising look for us
Through this same Garden—and for *one* in vain!

CI

And when like her, oh Sákí, you shall pass
Among the Guests Star-scatter'd on the Grass,
And in your joyous errand reach the spot
Where I made One—turn down an empty Glass!

ROBERT BROWNING

RABBI BEN EZRA

I

Grow old along with me!
The best is yet to be,
The last of life, for which the first was made:
Our times are in His hand
Who saith, "A whole I planned;
Youth shows but half; trust God: see all nor be afraid!"

II

Not that, amassing flowers,
Youth sighed, "Which rose make ours,
Which lily leave and then as best recall?"
Not that, admiring stars,
It yearned, "Nor Jove, nor Mars;
Mine be some figured flame which blends, transcends them all!"

III

Not for such hopes and fears
Annulling youth's brief years,
Do I remonstrate: folly wide the mark!
Rather I prize the doubt
Low kinds exist without,
Finished and finite clods, untroubled by a spark.

IV

Poor vaunt of life indeed,
Were man but formed to feed
On joy, to solely seek and find and feast:
Such feasting ended, then
As sure an end to men;
Irks care the crop-full bird? Frets doubt the maw-crammed beast?

V

Rejoice we are allied
To That which doth provide
And not partake, effect and not receive!
A spark disturbs our clod;
Nearer we hold of God
Who gives, than of His tribes that take, I must believe.

VI

Then, welcome each rebuff
That turns earth's smoothness rough,
Each sting that bids nor sit nor stand but go!
Be our joys three-parts pain!
Strive, and hold cheap the strain;
Learn, nor account the pang; dare, never grudge the throe!

VII

For thence,—a paradox
Which comforts while it mocks,—
Shall life succeed in that it seems to fail:
What I aspired to be,
And was not, comforts me:
A brute I might have been, but would not sink i' the scale.

VIII

What is he but a brute
Whose flesh has soul to suit,
Whose spirit works lest arms and legs want play?
To man, propose this test—
Thy body at its best,
How far can that project thy soul on its lone way?

IX

Yet gifts should prove their use:
I own the Past profuse

Of power each side, perfection every turn:
Eyes, ears took in their dole,
Brain treasured up the whole;
Should not the heart beat once, "How good to live and learn?"

X

Not once beat "Praise be Thine!
I see the whole design,
I, who saw power, see now love perfect too:
Perfect I call Thy plan:
Thanks that I was a man!
Maker, remake, complete,—I trust what Thou shalt do!"

XI

For pleasant is this flesh;
Our soul, in its rose-mesh
Pulled ever to the earth, still yearns for rest;
Would we some prize might hold
To match those manifold
Possessions of the brute,—gain most, as we did best!

XII

Let us not always say,
"Spite of this flesh to-day
I strove, made head, gained ground upon the whole!"
As the bird wings and sings,
Let us cry, "All good things
Are ours, nor soul helps flesh more, now, than flesh helps soul!"

XIII

Therefore I summon age
To grant youth's heritage,
Life's struggle having so far reached its term:
Thence shall I pass, approved

A man, for aye removed
From the developed brute; a god though in the germ.

XIV

And I shall thereupon
Take rest, ere I be gone
Once more on my adventure brave and new:
Fearless and unperplexed,
When I wage battle next,
What weapons to select, what armor to indue.

XV

Youth ended, I shall try
My gain or loss thereby;
Leave the fire ashes, what survives is gold:
And I shall weigh the same,
Give life its praise or blame:
Young, all lay in dispute; I shall know, being old.

XVI

For note, when evening shuts,
A certain moment cuts
The deed off, calls the glory from the gray:
A whisper from the west
Shoots—"Add this to the rest,
Take it and try its worth: here dies another day."

XVII

So, still within this life,
Though lifted o'er its strife,
Let me discern, compare, pronounce at last,
"This rage was right i' the main,
That acquiescence vain:
The Future I may face now I have proved the Past."

XVIII

For more is not reserved
To man, with soul just nerved
To act to-morrow what he learns to-day:
Here, work enough to watch
The Master work, and catch
Hints of the proper craft, tricks of the tool's true play.

XIX

As it was better, youth
Should strive, through acts uncouth,
Toward making, than repose on aught found made:
So, better, age, exempt
From strife, should know, than tempt
Further. Thou waitedest age: wait death nor be afraid!

XX

Enough now, if the Right
And Good and Infinite
Be named here, as thou callest thy hand thine own,
With knowledge absolute,
Subject to no dispute
From fools that crowded youth, nor let thee feel alone.

XXI

Be there, for once and all,
Severed great minds from small,
Announced to each his station in the Past!
Was I, the world arraigned,
Were they, my soul disdained,
Right? Let age speak the truth and give us peace at last!

XXII

Now, who shall arbitrate?
Ten men love what I hate,

Shun what I follow, slight what I receive;
Ten, who in ears and eyes
Match me: we all surmise,
They this thing, and I that: whom shall my soul believe?

XXIII

Not on the vulgar mass
Called "work," must sentence pass,
Things done, that took the eye and had the price;
O'er which, from level stand,
The low world laid its hand,
Found straightway to its mind, could value in a trice:

XXIV

But all, the world's coarse thumb
And finger failed to plumb,
So passed in making up the main account;
All instincts immature,
All purposes unsure,
That weighed not as his work, yet swelled the man's amount:

XXV

Thoughts hardly to be packed
Into a narrow act,
Fancies that broke through language and escaped;
All I could never be,
All, men ignored in me,
This, I was worth to God, whose wheel the pitcher shaped.

XXVI

Ay, note that Potter's wheel,
That metaphor! and feel
Why time spins fast, why passive lies our clay,—
Thou, to whom fools propound,

When the wine makes its round,
"Since life fleets, all is change; the Past gone, seize to-day!"

XXVII

Fool! All that is, at all,
Lasts ever, past recall;
Earth changes, but thy soul and God stand sure:
What entered into thee,
That was, is, and shall be:
Time's wheel runs back or stops: Potter and clay endure.

XXVIII

He fixed thee mid this dance
Of plastic circumstance,
This Present, thou, forsooth, wouldst fain arrest:
Machinery just meant
To give thy soul its bent,
Try thee and turn thee forth, sufficiently impressed.

XXIX

What though the earlier grooves
Which ran the laughing loves
Around thy base, no longer pause and press?
What though, about thy rim,
Skull-things in order grim
Grow out, in graver mood, obey the sterner stress?

XXX

Look not thou down but up!
To uses of a cup,
The festal board, lamp's flash and trumpet's peal,
The new wine's foaming flow,
The Master's lips a-glow!
Thou, heaven's consummate cup, what need'st thou with earth's wheel?

XXXI

But I need, now as then,
Thee, God, who mouldest men;
And since, not even while the whirl was worst,
Did I,—to the wheel of life
With shapes and colors rife,
Bound dizzily,—mistake my end, to slake Thy thirst:

XXXII

So, take and use Thy work:
Amend what flaws may lurk,
What strain o' the stuff, what warpings past the aim!
My times be in Thy hand!
Perfect the cup as planned!
Let age approve of youth, and death complete the same!

AN EPISTLE
CONTAINING THE STRANGE MEDICAL EXPERIENCE OF KARSHISH, THE ARAB PHYSICIAN

Karshish, the picker-up of learning's crumbs,
The not-incurious in God's handiwork
(This man's-flesh He hath admirably made,
Blown like a bubble, kneaded like a paste,
To coop up and keep down on earth a space
That puff of vapor from his mouth, man's soul)
—To Abib, all-sagacious in our art,
Breeder in me of what poor skill I boast,
Like me inquisitive how pricks and cracks
Befall the flesh through too much stress and strain,
Whereby the wily vapor fain would slip
Back and rejoin its source before the term,—
And aptest in contrivance, under God,
To baffle it by deftly stopping such:—
The vagrant Scholar to his Sage at home
Sends greeting (health and knowledge, fame with peace),
Three samples of true snake-stone—rarer still,
One of the other sort, the melon-shaped

(But fitter, pounded fine, for charms than drugs),
And writeth now the twenty-second time.

My journeyings were brought to Jericho;
Thus I resume. Who studious in our art
Shall count a little labor unrepaid?
I have shed sweat enough, left flesh and bone
On many a flinty furlong of this land.
Also the country-side is all on fire
With rumors of a marching hitherward—
Some say Vespasian cometh, some, his son.
A black lynx snarled and pricked a tufted ear;
Lust of my blood inflamed his yellow balls:
I cried and threw my staff and he was gone.
Twice have the robbers stripped and beaten me,
And once a town declared me for a spy;
But at the end, I reach Jerusalem,
Since this poor covert where I pass the night,
This Bethany, lies scarce the distance thence
A man with plague-sores at the third degree
Runs till he drops down dead. Thou laughest here!
'Sooth, it elates me, thus reposed and safe,
To void the stuffing of my travel-scrip
And share with thee whatever Jewry yields.
A viscid choler is observable
In tertians, I was nearly bold to say,
And falling-sickness hath a happier cure
Than our school wots of: there's a spider here
Weaves no web, watches on the ledge of tombs,
Sprinkled with mottles on an ash-gray back;
Take five and drop them ... but who knows his mind,
The Syrian runagate I trust this to?
His service payeth me a sublimate
Blown up his nose to help the ailing eye.
Best wait: I reach Jerusalem at morn
There set in order my experiences,
Gather what most deserves and give thee all—
Or I might add, Judea's gum-tragacanth
Scales off in purer flakes, shines clearer-grained,
Cracks 'twixt the pestle and the porphyry,
In fine exceeds our produce. Scalp disease
Confounds me, crossing so with leprosy—
Thou hadst admired one sort I gained at Zoar—

But zeal outruns discretion. Here I end.

Yet stay: my Syrian blinketh gratefully,
Protesteth his devotion is my price—
Suppose I write what harms not, though he steal?
I half resolve to tell thee, yet I blush,
What set me off a-writing first of all.
An itch I had, a sting to write, a tang!
For, be it this town's barrenness—or else
The Man had something in the look of him—
His case has struck me far more than 'tis worth.
So, pardon if (lest presently I lose
In the great press of novelty at hand
The care and pains this somehow stole from me)
I bid thee take the thing while fresh in mind,
Almost in sight—for, wilt thou have the truth?
The very man is gone from me but now,
Whose ailment is the subject of discourse.
Thus then, and let thy better wit help all.

'Tis but a case of mania—subinduced
By epilepsy, at the turning-point
Of trance prolonged unduly some three days.
When, by the exhibition of some drug
Or spell, exorcisation, stroke of art
Unknown to me and which 'twere well to know,
The evil thing out-breaking all at once
Left the man whole and sound of body indeed,—
But, flinging, so to speak, life's gates too wide,
Making a clear house of it too suddenly,
The first conceit that entered pleased to write
Whatever it was minded on the wall
So plainly at that vantage, as it were
(First come, first served), that nothing subsequent
Attaineth to erase the fancy-scrawls
Which the returned and new-established soul
Hath gotten now so thoroughly by heart
That henceforth she will read or these or none.
And first—the man's own firm conviction rests
That he was dead (in fact they buried him),
That he was dead and then restored to life
By a Nazarene physician of his tribe:
—Sayeth, the same bade, "Rise," and he did rise.

"Such cases are diurnal," thou wilt cry.
Not so this figment!—not, that such a fume,
Instead of giving way to time and health,
Should eat itself into the life of life,
As saffron tingeth flesh, blood, bones and all!
For see, how he takes up the after-life.
The man—it is one Lazarus, a Jew,
Sanguine, proportioned, fifty years of age,
The body's habit wholly laudable,
As much, indeed, beyond the common health
As he were made and put aside to show.
Think, could we penetrate by any drug
And bathe the wearied soul and worried flesh,
And bring it clear and fair, by three days' sleep!
Whence has the man the balm that brightens all?
This grown man eyes the world now like a child.
Some elders of his tribe, I should premise,
Let in their friend, obedient as a sheep,
To bear my inquisition. While they spoke,
Now sharply, now with sorrow,—told the case,—
He listened not except I spoke to him,
But folded his two hands and let them talk,
Watching the flies that buzzed: and yet no fool.
And that's a sample how his years must go.
Look if a beggar, in fixed middle-life,
Should find a treasure, can he use the same
With straightened habits and with tastes starved small,
And take at once to his impoverished brain
The sudden element that changes things,
—That sets the undreamed-of rapture at his hand,
And puts the cheap old joy in the scorned dust?
Is he not such an one as moves to mirth,
Warily parsimonious, when's no need,
Wasteful as drunkenness at undue times?
All prudent counsel, as to what befits
The golden mean, is lost on such an one.
The man's fantastic will is the man's law.
So here—we'll call the treasure knowledge, say—
Increased beyond the fleshy faculty—
Heaven opened to a soul while yet on earth,
Earth forced on a soul's use while seeing Heaven.
The man is witless of the size, the sum,
The value in proportion of all things,

Or whether it be little or be much.
Discourse to him of prodigious armaments
Assembled to besiege his city now,
And of the passing of a mule with gourds—
'Tis one! Then take it on the other side,
Speak of some trifling fact—he will gaze rapt
With stupor at its very littleness—
(Far as I see) as if in that indeed
He caught prodigious import, whole results;
And so will turn to us the bystanders
In ever the same stupor (note this point)
That we too see not with his opened eyes!
Wonder and doubt come wrongly into play,
Preposterously, at cross purposes.
Should his child sicken unto death,—why, look
For scarce abatement of his cheerfulness,
Or pretermission of his daily craft,—
While a word, gesture, glance, from that same child
At play or in the school or laid asleep,
Will start him to an agony of fear,
Exasperation, just as like! demand
The reason why—"'tis but a word," object—
"A gesture"—he regards thee as our lord
Who lived there in the pyramid alone,
Looked at us, dost thou mind, when being young
We both would unadvisedly recite
Some charm's beginning, from that book of his,
Able to bid the sun throb wide and burst
All into stars, as suns grown old are wont.
Thou and the child have each a veil alike
Thrown o'er your heads from under which ye both
Stretch your blind hands and trifle with a match
Over a mine of Greek fire, did ye know!
He holds on firmly to some thread of life—
(It is the life to lead perforcedly)—
Which runs across some vast distracting orb
Of glory on either side that meagre thread,
Which, conscious of, he must not enter yet—
The spiritual life around the earthly life!
The law of that is known to him as this—
His heart and brain move there, his feet stay here.
So is the man perplext with impulses
Sudden to start off crosswise, not straight on,

Proclaiming what is Right and Wrong across
And not along this black thread through the blaze—
"It should be" balked by "here it cannot be."
And oft the man's soul springs into his face
As if he saw again and heard again
His sage that bade him, "Rise," and he did rise.
Something—a word, a tick of the blood within
Admonishes—then back he sinks at once
To ashes, that was very fire before,
In sedulous recurrence to his trade
Whereby he earneth him the daily bread—
And studiously the humbler for that pride,
Professedly the faultier that he knows
God's secret, while he holds the thread of life.
Indeed the especial marking of the man
Is prone submission to the Heavenly will—
Seeing it, what it is, and why it is.
Sayeth, he will wait patient to the last
For that same death which will restore his being
To equilibrium, body loosening soul
Divorced even now by premature full growth:
He will live, nay, it pleaseth him to live
So long as God please, and just how God please.
He even seeketh not to please God more
(Which meaneth, otherwise) than as God please.
Hence I perceive not he affects to preach
The doctrine of his sect whate'er it be—
Make proselytes as madmen thirst to do.
How can he give his neighbor the real ground,
His own conviction? ardent as he is—
Call his great truth a lie, why still the old
"Be it as God please" reassureth him.
I probed the sore as thy disciple should—
"How, beast," said I, "this stolid carelessness
Sufficeth thee, when Rome is on her march
To stamp out like a little spark thy town,
Thy tribe, thy crazy tale and thee at once?"
He merely looked with his large eyes on me.
The man is apathetic, you deduce?
Contrariwise he loves both old and young,
Able and weak—affects the very brutes
And birds—how say I? flowers of the field—
As a wise workman recognizes tools

In a master's workshop, loving what they make.
Thus is the man as harmless as a lamb:
Only impatient, let him do his best,
At ignorance and carelessness and sin—
An indignation which is promptly curbed.
As when in certain travels I have feigned
To be an ignoramus in our art
According to some preconceived design,
And happed to hear the land's practitioners,
Steeped in conceit sublimed by ignorance,
Prattle fantastically on disease,
Its cause and cure—and I must hold my peace!

Thou wilt object—why have I not ere this
Sought out the sage himself, the Nazarene
Who wrought this cure, inquiring at the source,
Conferring with the frankness that befits?
Alas! it grieveth me, the learned leech
Perished in a tumult many years ago,
Accused—our learning's fate—of wizardry.
Rebellion, to the setting up a rule
And creed prodigious as described to me.
His death which happened when the earthquake fell
(Prefiguring, as soon appeared, the loss
To occult learning in our lord the sage
That lived there in the pyramid alone)
Was wrought by the mad people—that's their wont—
On vain recourse, as I conjecture it,
To his tried virtue, for miraculous help—
How could he stop the earthquake? That's their way!
The other imputations must be lies:
But take one—though I loathe to give it thee,
In mere respect to any good man's fame!
(And after all our patient Lazarus
Is stark mad—should we count on what he says?
Perhaps not—though in writing to a leech
'Tis well to keep back nothing of a case.—)
This man so cured regards the curer, then,
As—God forgive me—who but God himself,
Creator and Sustainer of the world,
That came and dwelt in flesh on it awhile!
—Sayeth that such an One was born and lived,
Taught, healed the sick, broke bread at his own house,

Then died, with Lazarus by, for aught I know,
And yet was ... what I said nor choose repeat,
And must have so avouched himself, in fact,
In hearing of this very Lazarus
Who saith—But why all this of what he saith?
Why write of trivial matters, things of price
Calling at every moment for remark?
I noticed on the margin of a pool
Blue-flowering borage, the Aleppo sort,
Aboundeth, very nitrous. It is strange!

Thy pardon for this long and tedious case,
Which, now that I review it, needs must seem
Unduly dwelt on, prolixly set forth.
Nor I myself discern in what is writ
Good cause for the peculiar interest
And awe indeed, this man has touched me with.
Perhaps the journey's end, the weariness
Had wrought upon me first. I met him thus—
I crossed a ridge of short sharp broken hills
Like an old lion's cheek-teeth. Out there came
A moon made like a face, with certain spots
Multiform, manifold, and menacing:
Then a wind rose behind me. So we met
In this old sleepy town at unaware,
The man and I. I send thee what is writ.
Regard it as a chance, a matter risked
To this ambiguous Syrian—he may lose,
Or steal, or give it thee with equal good.
Jerusalem's repose shall make amends
For time this letter wastes, thy time and mine,
Till when, once more thy pardon and farewell!

The very God! think, Abib; dost thou think?
So, the All-Great were the All-Loving too—
So, through the thunder comes a human voice
Saying, "O heart I made, a heart beats here!
Face, my hands fashioned, see it in myself.
Thou hast no power nor may'st conceive of mine,
But love I gave thee, with Myself to love,
And thou must love me who have died for thee!"
The madman saith He said so: it is strange.

CALIBAN UPON SETEBOS
OR, NATURAL THEOLOGY IN THE ISLAND

"Thou thoughtest that I was altogether such a one as thyself."

['Will sprawl, now that the heat of day is best,
Flat on his belly in the pit's much mire,
With elbows wide, fists clenched to prop his chin.
And, while he kicks both feet in the cool slush,
And feels about his spine small eft-things course,
Run in and out each arm, and make him laugh:
And while above his head a pompion-plant,
Coating the cave-top as a brow its eye,
Creeps down to touch and tickle hair and beard,
And now a flower drops with a bee inside,
And now a fruit to snap at, catch and crunch,—
He looks out o'er yon sea which sunbeams cross
And recross till they weave a spider-web
(Meshes of fire, some great fish breaks at times)
And talks to his own self, howe'er he please,
Touching that other, whom his dam called God.
Because to talk about Him vexes—ha,
Could He but know! and time to vex is now,
When talk is safer than in winter-time.
Moreover Prosper and Miranda sleep
In confidence he drudges at their task,
And it is good to cheat the pair, and gibe,
Letting the rank tongue blossom into speech.]

Setebos, Setebos, and Setebos!
'Thinketh, He dwelleth i' the cold o' the moon;
'Thinketh, He made it, with the sun to match,
But not the stars; the stars came otherwise;
Only made clouds, winds, meteors, such as that:
Also this isle, what lives and grows thereon,
And snaky sea which rounds and ends the same.

'Thinketh, it came of being ill at ease:
He hated that He cannot change His cold,
Nor cure its ache. 'Hath spied an icy fish
That longed to 'scape the rock-stream where she lived,
And thaw herself within the lukewarm brine
O' the lazy sea her stream thrusts far amid,
A crystal spike 'twixt two warm walls of wave;

Only, she ever sickened, found repulse
At the other kind of water, not her life
(Green-dense and dim-delicious, bred o' the sun),
Flounced back from bliss she was not born to breathe,
And in her old bounds buried her despair,
Hating and loving warmth alike: so He.

'Thinketh, He made thereat the sun, this isle,
Trees and the fowls here, beast and creeping thing.
Yon otter, sleek-wet, black, lithe as a leech;
Yon auk, one fire-eye in a ball of foam,
That floats and feeds; a certain badger brown
He hath watched hunt with that slant white-wedge eye
By moonlight; and the pie with the long tongue
That pricks deep into oakwarts for a worm,
And says a plain word when she finds her prize,
But will not eat the ants; the ants themselves
That build a wall of seeds and settled stalks
About their hole—He made all these and more,
Made all we see, and us, in spite: how else?
He could not, Himself, make a second self
To be His mate: as well have made Himself:
He would not make what he mislikes or slights,
An eyesore to Him, or not worth His pains:
But did, in envy, listlessness or sport,
Make what Himself would fain, in a manner, be—
Weaker in most points, stronger in a few,
Worthy, and yet mere playthings all the while,
Things He admires and mocks too,—that is it.
Because, so brave, so better though they be,
It nothing skills if He begin to plague.
Look now, I melt a gourd-fruit into mash,
Add honeycomb and pods, I have perceived,
Which bite like finches when they bill and kiss,—
Then, when froth rises bladdery, drink up all,
Quick, quick, till maggots scamper through my brain;
Last, throw me on my back i' the seeded thyme,
And wanton, wishing I were born a bird.
Put case, unable to be what I wish,
I yet could make a live bird out of clay:
Would not I take clay, pinch my Caliban
Able to fly?—for, there, see, he hath wings,
And great comb like the hoopoe's to admire,

And there, a sting to do his foes offence,
There, and I will that he begin to live,
Fly to yon rock-top, nip me off the horns
Of grigs high up that make the merry din,
Saucy through their veined wings, and mind me not.
In which feat, if his leg snapped, brittle clay,
And he lay stupid-like,—why, I should laugh;
And if he, spying me, should fall to weep,
Beseech me to be good, repair his wrong,
Bid his poor leg smart less or grow again,—
Well, as the chance were, this might take or else
Not take my fancy: I might hear his cry,
And give the mankin three sound legs for one,
Or pluck the other off, leave him like an egg,
And lessoned he was mine and merely clay.
Were this no pleasure, lying in the thyme,
Drinking the mash, with brain become alive,
Making and marring clay at will? So He.

'Thinketh, such shows nor right nor wrong in Him,
Nor kind, nor cruel: He is strong and Lord.
'Am strong myself compared to yonder crabs
That march now from the mountain to the sea;
Let twenty pass, and stone the twenty-first,
Loving not, hating not, just choosing so.
'Say, the first straggler that boasts purple spots
Shall join the file, one pincer twisted off;
'Say, this bruised fellow shall receive a worm,
And two worms he whose nippers end in red;
As it likes me each time, I do: so He.

Well then, 'supposeth He is good i' the main,
Placable if His mind and ways were guessed,
But rougher than His handiwork, be sure!
Oh, He hath made things worthier than Himself,
And envieth that, so helped, such things do more
Than He who made them! What consoles but this?
That they, unless through Him, do nought at all,
And must submit: what other use in things?
'Hath cut a pipe of pithless elder joint
That, blown through, gives exact the scream o' the jay
When from her wing you twitch the feathers blue:
Sound this, and little birds that hate the jay

- 155 -

Flock within stone's throw, glad their foe is hurt:
Put case such pipe could prattle and boast forsooth
"I catch the birds, I am the crafty thing,
I make the cry my maker cannot make
With his great round mouth; he must blow through mine!"
Would not I smash it with my foot? So He.

But wherefore rough, why cold and ill at ease?
Aha, that is a question! Ask, for that,
What knows,—the something over Setebos
That made Him, or He, may be, found and fought,
Worsted, drove off and did to nothing, perchance.
There may be something quiet o'er His head,
Out of His reach, that feels nor joy nor grief,
Since both derive from weakness in some way.
I joy because the quails come; would not joy
Could I bring quails here when I have a mind:
This Quiet, all it hath a mind to, doth.
'Esteemeth stars the outposts of its couch,
But never spends much thought nor care that way.
It may look up, work up,—the worse for those
It works on! 'Careth but for Setebos
The many-handed as a cuttle-fish,
Who, making Himself feared through what he does,
Looks up, first, and perceives he cannot soar
To what is quiet and hath happy life;
Next looks down here, and out of very spite
Makes this a bauble-world to ape yon real,
These good things to match those as hips do grapes.
'Tis solace making baubles, ay, and sport.
Himself peeped late, eyed Prosper at his books
Careless and lofty, lord now of the isle:
Vexed, 'stitched a book of broad leaves, arrow-shaped,
Wrote thereon, he knows what, prodigious words;
Has peeled a wand and called it by a name;
Weareth at whiles for an enchanter's robe
The eyed skin of a supple oncelot;
And hath an ounce sleeker than youngling mole,
A four-legged serpent he makes cower and couch,
Now snarl, now hold its breath and mind his eye,
And saith she is Miranda and my wife:
'Keeps for his Ariel a tall pouch-bill crane
He bids go wade for fish and straight disgorge;

Also a sea-beast, lumpish, which he snared,
Blinded the eyes of, and brought somewhat tame,
And split its toe-webs, and now pens the drudge
In a hole o' the rock and calls him Caliban;
A bitter heart that bides its time and bites.
'Plays thus at being Prosper in a way,
Taketh his mirth with make-believes: so He.

His dam held that the Quiet made all things
Which Setebos vexed only: 'holds not so.
Who made them weak, meant weakness He might vex.
Had He meant other, while His hand was in,
Why not make horny eyes no thorn could prick,
Or plate my scalp with bone against the snow,
Or overscale my flesh 'neath joint and joint,
Like an orc's armor? Ay,—so spoil His sport!
He is the One now: only He doth all.

'Saith, He may like, perchance, what profits Him.
Ay, himself loves what does him good; but why?
'Gets good no otherwise. This blinded beast
Loves whoso places flesh-meat on his nose,
But, had he eyes, would want no help, but hate
Or love, just as it liked him: He hath eyes.
Also it pleaseth Setebos to work,
Use all His hands, and exercise much craft,
By no means for the love of what is worked.
'Tasteth, himself, no finer good i' the world
When all goes right, in this safe summer-time,
And he wants little, hungers, aches not much,
Than trying what to do with wit and strength.
'Falls to make something: 'piled yon pile of turfs,
And squared and stuck there squares of soft white chalk,
And, with a fish-tooth, scratched a moon on each,
And set up endwise certain spikes of tree,
And crowned the whole with a sloth's skull a-top,
Found dead i' the woods, too hard for one to kill.
No use at all i' the work, for work's sole sake;
'Shall some day knock it down again; so He.

'Saith He is terrible: watch His feats in proof!
One hurricane will spoil six good months' hope.
He hath a spite against me, that I know,

Just as He favors Prosper, who knows why?
So it is, all the same, as well I find.
'Wove wattles half the winter, fenced them firm
With stone and stake to stop she-tortoises
Crawling to lay their eggs here: well, one wave,
Feeling the foot of Him upon its neck,
Gaped as a snake does, lolled out its large tongue,
And licked the whole labor flat: so much for spite.
'Saw a ball flame down late (yonder it lies)
Where, half an hour before, I slept i' the shade:
Often they scatter sparkles: there is force!
'Dug up a newt He may have envied once
And turned to stone, shut up inside a stone.
Please Him and hinder this?—What Prosper does?
Aha, if He would tell me how! Not He!
There is the sport: discover how or die!
All need not die, for of the things o' the isle
Some flee afar, some dive, some run up trees;
Those at His mercy,—why, they please Him most
When ... when ... well, never try the same way twice!
Repeat what act has pleased, He may grow wroth.
You must not know His ways, and play Him off,
Sure of the issue. 'Doth the like himself:
'Spareth a squirrel that it nothing fears,
But steals the nut from underneath my thumb,
And when I threat, bites stoutly in defense:
'Spareth an urchin that contrariwise,
Curls up into a ball, pretending death
For fright at my approach: the two ways please.
But what would move my choler more than this,
That either creature counted on its life
To-morrow and next day and all days to come,
Saying, forsooth, in the inmost of its heart,
"Because he did so yesterday with me,
And otherwise with such another brute,
So must he do henceforth and always."—Ay?
'Would teach the reasoning couple what "must" means!
'Doth as he likes, or wherefore Lord? So He.

'Conceiveth all things will continue thus,
And we shall have to live in fear of Him
So long as He lives, keeps His strength: no change,
If He have done His best, make no new world

To please Him more, so leave off watching this,—
If He surprise not even the Quiet's self
Some strange day,—or, suppose, grow into it
As grubs grow butterflies: else, here are we,
And there is He, and nowhere help at all.

'Believeth with the life, the pain shall stop.
His dam held different, that after death
He both plagued enemies and feasted friends:
Idly! He doth His worst in this our life,
Giving just respite lest we die through pain,
Saving last pain for worst,—with which, an end.
Meanwhile, the best way to escape His ire
Is, not to seem too happy. 'Sees, himself,
Yonder two flies, with purple films and pink,
Bask on the pompion-bell above; kills both.
'Sees two black painful beetles roll their ball
On head and tail as if to save their lives:
Moves them the stick away they strive to clear.

Even so, 'would have Him misconceive, suppose
This Caliban strives hard and ails no less,
And always, above all else, envies Him;
Wherefore he mainly dances on dark nights,
Moans in the sun, gets under holes to laugh,
And never speaks his mind save housed as now:
Outside, groans, curses. If He caught me here,
O'erheard this speech, and asked "What chucklest at?"
'Would, to appease Him, cut a finger off,
Or of my three kid yearlings burn the best,
Or let the toothsome apples rot on tree,
Or push my tame beast for the orc to taste:
While myself lit a fire, and made a song
And sung it, *"What I hate, be consecrate*
To celebrate Thee and Thy state, no mate
For Thee; what see for envy in poor me?"
Hoping the while, since evils sometimes mend,
Warts rub away and sores are cured with slime,
That some strange day, will either the Quiet catch
And conquer Setebos, or likelier He
Decrepit may doze, doze, as good as die.

[What, what? A curtain o'er the world at once!

Crickets stop hissing; not a bird—or, yes,
There scuds His raven that has told Him all!
It was fool's play, this prattling! Ha! The wind
Shoulders the pillared dust, death's house o' the move
And fast invading fires begin! White blaze—
A tree's head snaps—and there, there, there, there, there,
His thunder follows! Fool to gibe at Him!
Lo! 'Lieth flat and loveth Setebos!
'Maketh his teeth meet through his upper lip,
Will let those quails fly, will not eat this month
One little mess of whelks, so he may 'scape!]

A GRAMMARIAN'S FUNERAL

Let us begin and carry up this corpse,
Singing together.
Leave we the common crofts, the vulgar thorpes,
Each in its tether
Sleeping safe on the bosom of the plain,
Cared-for till cock-crow.
Look out if yonder's not the day again
Rimming the rock-row!
That's the appropriate country—there, man's thought,
Rarer, intenser,
Self-gathered for an outbreak, as it ought,
Chafes in the censer!
Leave we the unlettered plain its herd and crop;
Seek we sepulture
On a tall mountain, citied to the top,
Crowded with culture!
All the peaks soar, but one the rest excels;
Clouds overcome it;
No, yonder sparkle is the citadel's
Circling its summit!
Thither our path lies—wind we up the heights—
Wait ye the warning?
Our low life was the level's and the night's;
He's for the morning!
Step to a tune, square chests, erect the head,
'Ware the beholders!
This is our master, famous, calm, and dead,
Borne on our shoulders.

Sleep, crop and herd! sleep, darkling thorpe and croft,
Safe from the weather!
He, whom we convey to his grave aloft,
Singing together,
He was a man born with thy face and throat,
Lyric Apollo!
Long he lived nameless: how should spring take note
Winter would follow?
Till lo, the little touch, and youth was gone!
Cramped and diminished,
Moaned he, "New measures, other feet anon!
My dance is finished?"
No, that's the world's way! (Keep the mountain-side,
Make for the city.)
He knew the signal, and stepped on with pride
Over men's pity;
Left play for work, and grappled with the world
Bent on escaping:
"What's in the scroll," quoth he, "thou keepest furled?
Show me their shaping,
Theirs, who most studied man, the bard and sage,—
Give!"—So he gowned him,
Straight got by heart that book to its last page:
Learned, we found him!
Yea, but we found him bald too—eyes like lead,
Accents uncertain:
"Time to taste life," another would have said,
"Up with the curtain!"
This man said rather, "Actual life comes next?
Patience a moment!
Grant I have mastered learning's crabbed text,
Still, there's the comment.
Let me know all. Prate not of most or least,
Painful or easy:
Even to the crumbs I'd fain eat up the feast,
Ay, nor feel queasy!"
Oh, such a life as he resolved to live,
When he had learned it,
When he had gathered all books had to give;
Sooner, he spurned it!
Image the whole, then execute the parts—
Fancy the fabric
Quite, ere you build, ere steel strike fire from quartz,

Ere mortar dab brick!

(Here's the town-gate reached: there's the market-place
Gaping before us.)
Yea, this in him was the peculiar grace
(Hearten our chorus),
Still before living he'd learn how to live—
No end to learning.
Earn the means first—God surely will contrive
Use for our earning.
Others mistrust and say, "But time escapes,—
Live now or never!"
He said, "What's Time? leave Now for dogs and apes!
Man has Forever."
Back to his book then: deeper drooped his head;
Calculus racked him:
Leaden before, his eyes grew dross of lead;
Tussis attacked him.
"Now, Master, take a little rest!"—not he!
(Caution redoubled!
Step two abreast, the way winds narrowly.)
Not a whit troubled,
Back to his studies, fresher than at first,
Fierce as a dragon
He (soul-hydroptic with a sacred thirst)
Sucked at the flagon.
Oh, if we draw a circle premature,
Heedless of far gain,
Greedy for quick returns of profit, sure,
Bad is our bargain!
Was it not great? did not he throw on God,
(He loves the burthen—)
God's task to make the heavenly period
Perfect the earthen?
Did not he magnify the mind, shew clear
Just what it all meant?
He would not discount life, as fools do here,
Paid by installment!
He ventured neck or nothing—heaven's success
Found, or earth's failure:
"Wilt thou trust death or not?" he answered "Yes.
Hence with life's pale lure!"
That low man seeks a little thing to do,

Sees it and does it:
This high man, with a great thing to pursue,
Dies ere he knows it.
That low man goes on adding one to one,
His hundred's soon hit:
This high man, aiming at a million,
Misses an unit.
That, has the world here—should he need the next,
Let the world mind him!
This, throws himself on God, and unperplext
Seeking shall find Him.
So, with the throttling hands of Death at strife,
Ground he at grammar;
Still, thro' the rattle, parts of speech were rife.
While he could stammer
He settled *Hoti's* business—let it be!—
Properly based *Oun*—
Gave us the doctrine of the enclitic *De*,
Dead from the waist down.
Well, here's the platform, here's the proper place.
Hail to your purlieus,
All ye highfliers of the feathered race,
Swallows and curlews!
Here's the top-peak! the multitude below
Live, for they can there.
This man decided not to Live but Know—
Bury this man there?
Here—here's his place, where meteors shoot, clouds form,
Lightnings are loosened,
Stars come and go! let joy break with the storm—
Peace let the dew send!
Lofty designs must close in like effects:
Loftily lying,
Leave him—still loftier than the world suspects.
Living and dying.

WHY I AM A LIBERAL

"Why?" Because all I haply can and do,
All that I am now, all I hope to be,—
Whence comes it save from fortune setting free
Body and soul the purpose to pursue,

God traced for both? If fetters, not a few,
Of prejudice, convention, fall from me,
These shall I bid men—each in his degree
Also God-guided—bear, and gayly too?

But little do or can the best of us:
That little is achieved thro' Liberty.
Who then dares hold, emancipated thus,
His fellow shall continue bound? not I,
Who live, love, labor freely, nor discuss
A brother's right to freedom. That is "Why."

FEARS AND SCRUPLES

Here's my case. Of old I used to love him,
This same unseen friend, before I knew:
Dream there was none like him, none above him,—
Wake to hope and trust my dream was true.

Loved I not his letters full of beauty?
Not his actions famous far and wide?
Absent, he would know I vowed him duty,
Present, he would find me at his side.

Pleasant fancy! for I had but letters,
Only knew of actions by hearsay:
He himself was busied with my betters;
What of that? My turn must come some day.

"Some day" proving—no day! Here's the puzzle
Passed and passed my turn is. Why complain?
He's so busied! If I could but muzzle
People's foolish mouths that give me pain!

"Letters?" (hear them!) "You a judge of writing?
Ask the experts!—How they shake the head
O'er these characters, your friend's inditing—
Call them forgery from A to Zed!"

"Actions? Where's your certain proof" (they bother),
"He, of all you find so great and good,
He, he only, claims this, that, the other

Action—claimed by men, a multitude?"

I can simply wish I might refute you,
Wish my friend would,—by a word, a wink,—
Bid me stop that foolish mouth,—you brute, you!
He keeps absent,—why, I cannot think.

Never mind! Tho' foolishness may flout me
One thing's sure enough; 'tis neither frost,
No, nor fire, shall freeze or burn from out me
Thanks for truth—tho' falsehood, gained—tho' lost.

All my days, I'll go the softlier, sadlier,
For that dream's sake! How forget the thrill
Thro' and thro' me as I thought, "The gladlier
Lives my friend because I love him still!"

Ah, but there's a menace some one utters!
"What and if your friend at home play tricks?
Peep at hide-and-seek behind the shutters?
Mean your eyes should pierce thro' solid bricks?

"What and if he, frowning, wake you, dreamy?
Lay on you the blame that bricks—conceal?
Say '*At least I saw who did not see me;
Does see now, and presently shall feel*'?"

"Why, that makes your friend a monster!" say you:
"Had his house no window? At first nod
Would you not have hailed him?" Hush, I pray you!
What if this friend happen to be—God?

EPILOGUE TO "ASOLANDO"

At the midnight in the silence of the sleep-time,
When you set your fancies free,
Will they pass to where—by death, fools think, imprisoned—
Low he lies who once so loved you, whom you loved so,
—Pity me?

Oh, to love so, be so loved, yet so mistaken!

What had I on earth to do
With the slothful, with the mawkish, the unmanly?
Like the aimless, helpless, hopeless, did I drivel
—Being—who?

One who never turned his back but marched breast forward,
Never doubted clouds would break,
Never dreamed, tho' right were worsted, wrong would triumph.
Held we fall to rise, are baffled to fight better,
Sleep to wake.

No, at noonday in the bustle of man's work-time
Greet the unseen with a cheer!
Bid him forward, breast and back as either should be,
"Strive and thrive!" cry, "Speed,—fight on, fare ever
There as here!"

PROSPICE

Fear death?—to feel the fog in my throat,
The mist in my face,
When the snows begin, and the blasts denote
I am nearing the place,
The power of the night, the press of the storm,
The post of the foe;
Where he stands, the Arch Fear in a visible form,
Yet the strong man must go:
For the journey is done and the summit attained,
And the barriers fall,
Though a battle's to fight ere the guerdon be gained,
The reward of it all.
I was ever a fighter, so—one fight more,
The best and the last!
I would hate that death bandaged my eyes, and forbore,
And bade me creep past.
No! let me taste the whole of it, fare like my peers
The heroes of old,
Bear the brunt, in a minute pay glad life's arrears.
Of pain, darkness and cold.
For sudden the worst turns the best to the brave,
The black minute's at end,

And the elements' rage, the fiend-voices that rave,
Shall dwindle, shall blend,
Shall change, shall become first a peace out of pain,
Then a light, then thy breast,
O thou soul of my soul! I shall clasp thee again,
And with God be the rest!

ALFRED, LORD TENNYSON

WAGES

Glory of warrior, glory of orator, glory of song,
Paid with a voice flying by to be lost on an endless sea—
Glory of Virtue, to fight, to struggle, to right the wrong—
Nay, but she aim'd not at glory, no lover of glory she:
Give her the glory of going on, and still to be.

The wages of sin is death: if the wages of Virtue be dust,
Would she have heart to endure for the life of the worm and the fly?
She desires no isles of the blest, no quiet seats of the just,
To rest in a golden grove, or to bask in a summer sky:
Give her the wages of going on, and not to die.

THE HIGHER PANTHEISM

The sun, the moon, the stars, the seas, the hills and the plains—
Are not these, O Soul, the Vision of Him who reigns?

Is not the Vision He? tho' He be not that which He seems?
Dreams are true while they last, and do we not live in dreams?

Earth, these solid stars, this weight of body and limb,
Are they not sign and symbol of thy division from Him?

Dark is the world to thee: thyself art the reason why;
For is He not all but that which has power to feel "I am I"?

Glory about thee, without thee; and thou fulfillest thy doom,
Making Him broken gleams, and a stifled splendor and gloom.

Speak to Him thou, for He hears, and Spirit with Spirit can meet—
Closer is He than breathing, and nearer than hands and feet.

God is law, say the wise; O Soul, and let us rejoice,
For, if He thunder by law, the thunder is yet His voice.

Law is God, say some: no God at all, says the fool;
For all we have power to see is a straight staff bent in a pool;

And the ear of man cannot hear, and the eye of man cannot see;
But if we could see and hear, this Vision—were it not He?

FLOWER IN THE CRANNIED WALL

Flower in the crannied wall,
I pluck you out of the crannies,
I hold you here, root and all, in my hand,
Little flower—but *if* I could understand
What you are, root and all, and all in all,
I should know what God and man is.

IN MEMORIAM

PROEM

Strong Son of God, immortal Love,
Whom we, that have not seen thy face,
By faith, and faith alone, embrace,
Believing where we cannot prove;

Thine are these orbs of light and shade;
Thou madest Life in man and brute;
Thou madest Death; and lo, thy foot
Is on the skull which thou hast made.

Thou wilt not leave us in the dust:
Thou madest man, he knows not why,
He thinks he was not made to die;
And thou hast made him: thou art just.

Thou seemest human and divine,
The highest, holiest manhood, thou:
Our wills are ours, we know not how;
Our wills are ours, to make them thine.

Our little systems have their day;

They have their day and cease to be:
They are but broken lights of thee,
And thou, O Lord, art more than they.

We have but faith: we cannot know;
For knowledge is of things we see;
And yet we trust it comes from thee,
A beam in darkness: let it grow.

Let knowledge grow from more to more,
But more of reverence in us dwell;
That mind and soul, according well,
May make one music as before,

But vaster. We are fools and slight;
We mock thee when we do not fear:
But help thy foolish ones to bear;
Help thy vain worlds to bear thy light.

Forgive what seem'd my sin in me;
What seem'd my worth since I began;
For merit lives from man to man,
And not from man, O Lord, to thee.

Forgive my grief for one removed,
Thy creature, whom I found so fair.
I trust he lives in thee, and there
I find him worthier to be loved.

Forgive these wild and wandering cries,
Confusions of a wasted youth;
Forgive them where they fail in truth,
And in thy wisdom make me wise.

LIV

Oh, yet we trust that somehow good
Will be the final goal of ill,
To pangs of nature, sins of will,
Defects of doubt, and taints of blood;

That nothing walks with aimless feet;

That not one life shall be destroy'd,
Or cast as rubbish to the void,
When God hath made the pile complete;

That not a worm is cloven in vain;
That not a moth with vain desire
Is shrivel'd in a fruitless fire,
Or but subserves another's gain.

Behold, we know not anything;
I can but trust that good shall fall
At last—far off—at last, to all,
And every winter change to spring.

So runs my dream: but what am I?
An infant crying in the night:
An infant crying for the light:
And with no language but a cry.

LV

The wish, that of the living whole
No life may fail beyond the grave,
Derives it not from what we have
The likest God within the soul?

Are God and Nature then at strife,
That Nature lends such evil dreams?
So careful of the type she seems,
So careless of the single life;

That I, considering everywhere
Her secret meaning in her deeds,
And finding that of fifty seeds
She often brings but one to bear,

I falter where I firmly trod,
And falling with my weight of cares
Upon the great world's altar-stairs
That slope thro' darkness up to God,

I stretch lame hands of faith, and grope,

And gather dust and chaff, and call
To what I feel is Lord of all,
And faintly trust the larger hope.

LVI

"So careful of the type?" but no.
From scarped cliff and quarried stone
She cries, "A thousand types are gone:
I care for nothing, all shall go.

"Thou makest thine appeal to me:
I bring to life, I bring to death:
The spirit does but mean the breath:
I know no more." And he, shall he,

Man, her last work, who seem'd so fair,
Such splendid purpose in his eyes,
Who roll'd the psalm to wintry skies,
Who built him fanes of fruitless prayer,

Who trusted God was love indeed
And love Creation's final law—
Tho' Nature, red in tooth and claw
With ravine, shriek'd against his creed—

Who loved, who suffer'd countless ills,
Who battled for the True, the Just,
Be blown about the desert dust,
Or seal'd within the iron hills?

No more? A monster then, a dream,
A discord. Dragons of the prime,
That tare each other in their slime,
Were mellow music match'd with him.

O life as futile, then, as frail!
O for thy voice to soothe and bless!
What hope of answer, or redress?
Behind the veil, behind the veil.

CROSSING THE BAR

Sunset and evening star,
And one clear call for me!
And may there be no moaning of the bar,
When I put out to sea,

But such a tide as moving seems asleep,
Too full for sound and foam,
When that which drew from out the boundless deep
Turns again home.

Twilight and evening bell,
And after that the dark!
And may there be no sadness of farewell,
When I embark;

For tho' from out our bourne of Time and Place
The flood may bear me far,
I hope to see my Pilot face to face
When I have crost the bar.

GEORGE MEREDITH

LUCIFER IN STARLIGHT [12]

On a starred night Prince Lucifer uprose.
Tired of his dark dominion, swung the fiend
Above the rolling ball in cloud part screened,
Where sinners hugged their spectre of repose.
Poor prey to his hot fit of pride were those.
And now upon his western wing he leaned,
And now his huge bulk o'er Afric's sands careened,
And now the black planet shadowed Arctic snows.
Soaring through wider zones that pricked his scars
With memory of the old revolt from Awe,
He reached a middle height, and at the stars,
Which are the brain of heaven, he looked, and sank.
Around the ancient track marched, rank on rank,
The army of unalterable law.

WILLIAM E. HENLEY

INVICTUS

Out of the night that covers me,
Black as a pit from Pole to Pole,
I thank whatever gods may be
For my unconquerable soul.

In the fell clutch of circumstance
I have not winced nor cried aloud;
Under the bludgeonings of chance
My head is bloody but unbowed.

Beyond this place of wrath and tears
Looms but the Horror of the Shade;
And yet the menace of the years
Finds and still finds me unafraid.

It matters not how strait the gate,
How charged with punishments the scroll:
I am the master of my fate;
I am the captain of my soul.

THOMAS HARDY

NEW YEAR'S EVE[13]

"I have finished another year," said God,
"In gray, green, white, and brown;
I have strewn the leaf upon the sod,
Sealed up the worm within the clod,
And let the last sun down."

"And what's the good of it?" I said.
"What reasons made you call
From formless void this earth we tread,
When nine-and-ninety can be read
Why nought should be at all?

"Yea, Sire; why shaped you us, 'who in
This tabernacle groan'?
If ever a joy be found herein,
Such joy no man had wished to win
If he had never known!"

Then he: "My labors—logicless—
You may explain; not I:
Sense-sealed I have wrought, without a guess
That I evolved a Consciousness
To ask for reasons why.

"Strange that ephemeral creatures who
By my own ordering are,
Should see the shortness of my view,
Use ethic tests I never knew,
Or made provision for!"

He sank to raptness as of yore,
And opening New Year's Day
Wove it by rote as theretofore,
And went on working evermore
In his unweeting way.

RALPH WALDO EMERSON

CIVILIZATION[14]

A certain degree of progress from the rudest state in which man is found,—a dweller in caves, or on trees, like an ape,—a cannibal, and eater of pounded snails, worms, and offal,—a certain degree of progress from this extreme, is called Civilization. It is a vague, complex name, of many degrees. Nobody has attempted a definition. M. Guizot, writing a book on the subject, does not. It implies the evolution of a highly-organized man, brought to supreme delicacy of sentiment, as in practical power, religion, liberty, sense of honor, and taste. In the hesitation to define what it is, we usually suggest it by negations. A nation that has no clothing, no iron, no alphabet, no marriage, no arts of peace, no abstract thought, we call barbarous. And after many arts are invented or imported, as among the Turks and Moorish nations, it is often a little complaisant to call them civilized.

Each nation grows after its own genius, and has a civilization of its own. The Chinese and Japanese, though each complete in his way, is different from the man of Madrid or the man of New York. The term imports a mysterious progress. In the brutes is none; and in mankind to-day the savage tribes are gradually extinguished rather than civilized. The Indians of this country have not learned the white man's work; and in Africa, the negro of to-day is the negro of Herodotus. In other races the growth is not arrested; but the like progress that is made by a boy "when he cuts his eye-teeth," as we say,—childish illusions passing daily away, and he seeing things really and comprehensively,—is made by tribes. It is the learning the secret of cumulative power, of advancing on one's self. It implies a facility of association, power to compare, the ceasing from fixed ideas. The Indian is gloomy and distressed when urged to depart from his habits and traditions. He is overpowered by the gaze of the white, and his eye sinks. The occasion of one of these starts of growth is always some novelty that astounds the mind, and provokes it to dare to change. Thus there is a Cadmus, a Pytheas, a Manco Capac at the beginning of each improvement—some superior foreigner importing new and wonderful arts, and teaching them. Of course, he must not know too much, but must have the sympathy, language, and gods of those he would inform. But chiefly the sea-shore had been the point of departure to knowledge, as to commerce. The most advanced nations are always those who navigate the most. The power which the sea requires in a sailor makes a man of him very fast, and the change of shores and population clears his head of much nonsense of his wigwam.

Where shall we begin or end the list of those feats of liberty and wit, each of which feats made an epoch of history? Thus, the effect of a framed or stone house is immense on the tranquillity, power, and refinement of the builder. A man in a cave or in a camp, a nomad, will die with no more estate than the wolf or the horse leaves. But so simple a labor as a house being achieved, his chief enemies are kept at bay. He is safe from the teeth of wild animals, from frost, sunstroke, and weather; and fine faculties begin to yield their fine harvest. Invention and art are born, manners and social beauty and delight. 'Tis wonderful how soon a piano gets into a log-hut on the frontier. You would think they found it under a pine-stump. With it comes a Latin Grammar—and one of those tow-head boys has written a hymn on Sunday. Now let colleges, now let senates, take heed! for here is one who, opening these fine tastes on the basis of the pioneer's iron constitution, will gather all their laurels in his strong hands.

When the Indian trail gets widened, graded, and bridged to a good road, there is a benefactor, there is a missionary, a pacificator, a wealth-bringer, a maker of markets, a vent for industry. Another step in civility is the change from war, hunting, and pasturage to agriculture. Our Scandinavian forefathers have left us a significant legend to convey their sense of the importance of this step. "There was once a giantess who had a daughter, and the child saw a husbandman ploughing in the field. Then she ran and picked him up with her finger and thumb, and put him and his plough and his oxen into her apron, and carried them to her mother, and said, 'Mother, what sort of a beetle is this that I found wriggling in the sand?' But the mother said, 'Put it away, my child; we must begone out of this land, for these people will dwell in it.'" Another success is the post-office, with its educating energy augmented by cheapness and guarded by a certain religious sentiment in mankind; so that the power of a wafer or a drop of wax or gluten to guard a letter, as it flies over sea, over land, and comes to its address as if a battalion of artillery brought it, I look upon as a fine metre of civilization.

The division of labor, the multiplication of the arts of peace, which is nothing but a large allowance to each man to choose his work according to his faculty,—to live by his better hand,—fills the State with useful and happy laborers; and they, creating demand by the very temptation of their productions, are rapidly and surely rewarded by good sale: and what a police and ten commandments their work thus becomes! So true is Dr. Johnson's remark that "men are seldom more innocently employed than when they are making money."

The skillful combinations of civil government, though they usually follow natural leadings, as the lines of race, language, religion, and territory, yet require wisdom and conduct in the rulers, and in their result delight the imagination. "We see insurmountable multitudes obeying, in opposition to their strongest passions, the restraints of a power which they scarcely perceive, and the crimes of a single individual marked and punished at the distance of half the earth."

Right position of woman in the State is another index. Poverty and industry with a healthy mind read very easily the laws of humanity, and love them; place the sexes in right relations of mutual respect, and a severe morality gives that essential charm to woman which educates all that is delicate, poetic, and self-sacrificing, breeds courtesy and learning, conversation and wit, in her rough mate; so that I have thought a sufficient measure of civilization is the influence of good women.

Another measure of culture is the diffusion of knowledge, overrunning all the old barriers of caste, and, by the cheap press, bringing the university to every poor man's door in the newsboy's basket. Scraps of science, of thought, of poetry, are in the coarsest sheet, so that in every house we hesitate to burn a newspaper until we have looked it through.

The ship, in its latest complete equipment, is an abridgment and compend of a nation's arts: the ship steered by compass and chart,—longitude reckoned by lunar observation and by chronometer,—driven by steam; and in wildest sea-mountains, at vast distances from home,—

The pulses of her iron heart
Go beating through the storm.

No use can lessen the wonder of this control, by so weak a creature, of forces so prodigious. I remember I watched, in crossing the sea, the beautiful skill whereby the engine in its constant working was made to produce two hundred gallons of fresh water out of salt water every hour—thereby supplying all the ship's wants.

The skill that pervades complex details; the man that maintains himself; the chimney taught to burn its own smoke; the farm made to produce all that is consumed on it; the very prison compelled to maintain itself and yield a revenue, and, better still, made a reform school, and a manufactory of honest men out of rogues, as the steamer made fresh water out of salt—all these are examples of that tendency to combine antagonisms, and utilize evil, which is the index of high civilization.

Civilization is the result of highly complex organization. In the snake, all the organs are sheathed: no hands, no feet, no fins, no wings. In bird and beast, the organs are released, and begin to play. In man, they are all unbound, and full of joyful action. With this unswaddling he receives the absolute illumination we call Reason, and thereby true liberty.

Climate has much to do with this melioration. The highest civility has never loved the hot zones. Wherever snows falls, there is usually civil freedom.

Where the banana grows, the animal system is indolent and pampered at the cost of higher qualities; the man is sensual and cruel. But this scale is not invariable. High degrees of moral sentiment control the unfavorable influences of climate; and some of our grandest examples of men and of races come from the equatorial regions—as the genius of Egypt, of India, and of Arabia.

These feats are measures or traits of civility; and temperate climate is an important influence, though not quite indispensable; for there have been learning, philosophy, and art in Iceland, and in the tropics. But one condition is essential to the social education of man, namely, morality. There can be no high civility without a deep morality, though it may not always call itself by that name, but sometimes the point of honor, as in the institution of chivalry; or patriotism, as in the Spartan and Roman republics; or the enthusiasm of some religious act which imputes its virtue to its dogma; or the cabalism, or *esprit de corps*, of a masonic or other association of friends.

The evolution of a highly-destined society must be moral; it must run in the grooves of the celestial wheels. It must be catholic in aims. What is *moral?* It is the respecting in action catholic or universal ends. Hear the definition which Kant gives of moral conduct: "Act always so that the immediate motive of thy will may become a universal rule for all intelligent beings."

Civilization depends on morality. Everything good in man leans on what is higher. This rule holds in small as in great. Thus, all our strength and success in the work of our hands depend on our borrowing the aid of the elements. You have seen a carpenter on a ladder with a broad axe chopping upward chips from a beam. How awkward! at what disadvantage he works! But see him on the ground, dressing his timber under him. Now, not his feeble muscles, but the force of gravity brings down the axe; that is to say, the planet itself splits his stick. The farmer had much ill-temper, laziness, and shirking to endure from his hand-sawyers, until one day he bethought him to put his saw-mill on the edge of a waterfall; and the river never tires of turning his wheel: the river is good-natured, and never hints an objection.

We had letters to send: couriers could not go fast enough, nor far enough; broke their wagons, foundered their horses; bad roads in spring, snow-drifts in winter, heats in summer; could not get the horses out of a walk. But we found out that the air and earth were full of electricity, and always going our way—just the way we wanted to send. *Would he take a message?* Just as lief as not; had nothing else to do; would carry it in no time. Only one doubt occurred, one staggering objection—he had no carpetbag, no visible pockets, no hands, not so much as a mouth, to carry a letter. But, after much thought and many experiments, we managed to meet the conditions, and to fold up the letter in such invisible compact form as he could carry in those invisible pockets of his, never wrought by needle and thread—and it went like a charm.

I admire still more than the saw-mill the skill which, on the sea-shore, makes the tides drive the wheels and grind corn, and which thus engages the assistance of the moon, like a hired hand, to grind, and wind, and pump, and saw, and split stone, and roll iron.

Now that is the wisdom of a man, in every instance of his labor, to hitch his wagon to a star, and see his chore done by the gods themselves. That is the way we are strong, by borrowing the might of the elements. The forces of steam, gravity, galvanism, light, magnets, wind, fire, serve us day by day, and cost us nothing.

Our astronomy is full of examples of calling in the aid of these magnificent helpers. Thus, on a planet so small as ours, the want of an adequate base for astronomical measurements is early felt; as, for example, in detecting the parallax of a star. But the astronomer, having by an observation fixed the place of a star, by so simple an expedient as waiting six months, and then repeating his observation, contrived to put the diameter of the earth's orbit, say two hundred millions of miles, between his first observation and his second, and this line afforded him a respectable base for his triangle.

All our arts aim to win this vantage. We cannot bring the heavenly powers to us; but, if we will only choose our jobs in directions in which they travel, they will undertake them with the greatest pleasure. It is a peremptory rule with them, that *they never go out of their road*. We are dapper little busybodies, and run this way and that way superserviceably; but they swerve never from their fore-ordained paths—neither the sun, nor the moon, nor a bubble of air, nor a mote of dust.

And as our handiworks borrow the elements, so all our social and political action leans on principles. To accomplish anything excellent, the will must work for catholic and universal ends. A puny creature, walled in on every side, as Daniel wrote,—

Unless above himself he can
Erect himself, how poor a thing is man!

But when his will leans on a principle, when he is the vehicle of ideas, he borrows their omnipotence. Gibraltar may be strong, but ideas are impregnable, and bestow on the hero their invincibility. "It was a great instruction," said a saint in Cromwell's war, "that the best courages are but beams of the Almighty." Hitch your wagon to a star. Let us not fag in paltry works which serve our pot and bag alone. Let us not lie and steal. No god will help. We shall find all their teams going the other way—Charles's Wain, Great Bear, Orion, Leo, Hercules: every god will leave us. Work rather for those interests which the divinities honor and promote—justice, love, freedom, knowledge, utility.

If we can thus ride in Olympian chariots by putting our works in the path of the celestial circuits, we can harness also evil agents, the powers of darkness, and force them to serve against their will the ends of wisdom and virtue. Thus, a wise government puts fines and penalties on pleasant vices. What a benefit would the American government, not yet relieved of its extreme need, render to itself, and to every city, village, and hamlet in the States, if it would tax whiskey and rum almost to the point of prohibition! Was it Bonaparte who said that he found vices very good patriots? "He got five millions from the love of brandy, and he should be glad to know which of the virtues would pay him as much." Tobacco and opium have broad backs, and will cheerfully carry the load of armies, if you choose to make them pay high for such joy as they give and such harm as they do.

These are traits, and measures, and modes; and the true test of civilization is, not the census, nor the size of cities, nor the crops—no, but the kind of man the country turns out. I see the vast advantages of this country, spanning the breadth of the temperate zone. I see the immense material prosperity—towns on towns, states on states, and wealth piled in the massive architecture of cities; California quartz mountains dumped down in New York to be repiled architecturally along-shore from Canada to Cuba, and thence westward to California again. But it is not New York streets, built by the confluence of workmen and wealth of all nations, though stretching out toward Philadelphia until they touch it, and northward until they touch New Haven, Hartford, Springfield, Worcester, and Boston—not these that make the real estimation. But, when I look over this constellation of cities which animate and illustrate the land, and see how little the government has to do with their daily life, how self-helped and self-directed all families are,—knots of men in purely natural societies,—societies of trade, of kindred blood, of habitual hospitality, house and house, man acting on man by weight of opinion of longer or better-directed industry, the refining influence of women, the invitation which experience and permanent causes open to youth and labor,—when I see how much each virtuous and gifted person, whom all men consider, lives affectionately with scores of excellent people who are not known far from home, and perhaps with great reason reckons these people his superiors in virtue, and in the symmetry and force of their qualities, I see what cubic values America has, and in these a better certificate of civilization than great cities or enormous wealth.

In strictness, the vital refinements are the moral and intellectual steps. The appearance of the Hebrew Moses, of the Indian Buddh,—in Greece, of the Seven Wise Masters, of the acute and upright Socrates, and of the Stoic Zeno,—in Judæa, the advent of Jesus,—and in modern Christendom, of the realists Huss, Savonarola, and Luther,—are casual facts which carry forward races to new convictions, and elevate the rule of life. In the presence of these agencies, it is frivolous to insist on the invention of printing or gunpowder, of steam-power or gas-light, percussion-caps and rubber-shoes, which are toys thrown off from that security, freedom, and exhilaration which a healthy morality creates in society. These arts add a comfort and smoothness to house and street life; but a purer morality, which kindles genius, civilizes civilization, casts backward all that we held sacred into the profane, as the flame of oil throws a shadow when shined upon by the flame of the Bude-light. Not the less the popular measures of progress will ever be the arts and the laws.

But if there be a country which cannot stand any one of these tests—a country where knowledge cannot be diffused without perils of mob-law and statute-law,—where speech is not free,—where the post-office is violated, mailbags opened, and letters tampered with,—where public debts and private debts outside of the State are repudiated,—where liberty is attacked in the primary institution of social life,—where the position of the white woman is injuriously affected by the outlawry of the black woman,—where the arts, such as they have, are all imported, having no indigenous life,—where the laborer is not secured in the earnings of his own hands,—where suffrage is not free or equal,—that country is, in all these respects, not civil, but barbarous; and no advantages of soil, climate, or coast can resist these suicidal mischiefs.

Morality and all the incidents of morality are essential: as, justice to the citizen and personal liberty. Montesquieu says: "Countries are well cultivated, not as they are fertile, but as they are free"; and the remark holds not less, but more true, of the culture of men, than of the tillage of land. And the highest proof of civility is, that the whole public action of the State is directed on securing the greatest good of the greatest number.

ILLUSIONS[15]

Flow, flow the waves hated,
Accursed, adored,
The waves of mutation:
No anchorage is
Sleep is not, death is not;
Who seem to die, live.
House you were born in,
Friends of your spring-time,
Old man and young maid,
Day's toil and its guerdon—
They are all vanishing,

Fleeing to fables,
Cannot be moored.
See the stars through them,
Through treacherous marbles.
Know, the stars yonder,
The stars everlasting
Are fugitive also,
And emulate, vaulted,
The lambent heat-lightning,
And fire-fly's flight.
When thou dost return
On the wave's circulation,
Beholding the shimmer,
The will's dissipation,
And, out of endeavor
To change and to flow,
The gas become solid,
And phantoms and nothings
Return to be things,
And endless imbroglio
Is law and the world,—
Then first shalt thou know,
That in the wild turmoil,
Horsed on the Proteus,
Thou ridest to power,
And to endurance.

Some years ago, in company with an agreeable party, I spent a long summer day in exploring the Mammoth Cave in Kentucky. We traversed, through spacious galleries affording a solid masonry foundation for the town and county overhead, the six or eight black miles from the mouth of the cavern to the innermost recess which tourists visit—a niche or grotto made of one seamless stalactite and called, I believe, Serena's Bower. I lost the light of one day. I saw high domes, and bottomless pits; heard the voice of unseen waterfalls; paddled three quarters of a mile in the deep Echo River, whose waters are peopled with the blind fish; crossed the streams "Lethe" and "Styx"; plied with music and guns the echoes in these alarming galleries; saw every form of stalagmite and stalactite in the sculptured and fretted chambers—icicle, orange-flower, acanthus, grapes, and snowball. We shot Bengal lights into the vaults and groins of the sparry cathedrals, and examined all the masterpieces which the four combined engineers, water, limestone, gravitation, and time, could make in the dark.

The mysteries and scenery of the cave had the same dignity that belongs to all natural objects, and shames the fine things to which we foppishly compare them. I remarked, especially, the mimetic habit, with which Nature, on new instruments, hums her old tunes, making night to mimic day, and chemistry to ape vegetation. But I then took notice, and still chiefly remember, that the best thing which the cave had to offer was an illusion. On arriving at what is called the "Star Chamber," our lamps were taken from us by the guide, and extinguished or put aside, and, on looking upwards, I saw or seemed to see the night heaven thick with stars glimmering more or less brightly over our heads, and even what seemed a comet flaming among them. All the party were touched with astonishment and pleasure. Our musical friends sung with much feeling a pretty song, "The stars are in the quiet sky," etc., and I sat down on the rocky floor to enjoy the serene picture. Some crystal specks in the black ceiling high overhead, reflecting the light of a half-hid lamp, yielded this magnificent effect.

I own, I did not like the cave so well for eking out its sublimities with this theatrical trick. But I have had many experiences like it, before and since; and we must be content to be pleased without too curiously analyzing the occasions. Our conversation with Nature is not just what it seems. The cloud-rack, the sunrise and sunset glories, rainbows, and northern lights, are not quite so spheral as our childhood thought them; and the part our organization plays in them is too large. The senses interfere everywhere, and mix their own structure with all they report of. Once, we fancied the earth a plane, and stationary. In admiring the sunset, we do not yet deduct the rounding, coördinating, pictorial powers of the eye.

The same interference from our organization creates the most of our pleasure and pain. Our first mistake is the belief that the circumstance gives the joy which we give to the circumstance. Life is an ecstasy. Life is sweet as nitrous oxide; and the fisherman dripping all day over a cold pond, the switchman at the railway intersection, the farmer in the field, the negro in the rice-swamp, the fop in the street, the hunter in the woods, the barrister with the jury, the belle at the ball, all ascribe a certain pleasure to their employment, which they themselves give it. Health and appetite impart the sweetness to sugar, bread, and meat. We fancy that our civilization has got on far, but we still come back to our primers.

We live by our imaginations, by our admirations, by our sentiments. The child walks amid heaps of illusions, which he does not like to have disturbed. The boy, how sweet to him is his fancy! how dear the story of barons and battles! What a hero he is, whilst he feeds on his heroes! What a debt is his to imaginative books! He has no better friend or influence than Scott, Shakespeare, Plutarch, and Homer. The man lives to other objects, but who dares affirm that they are more real? Even the prose of the streets is full of refractions. In the life of the dreariest alderman, fancy enters into all details, and colors them with rosy hue. He imitates the air and actions of people whom he admires, and is raised in his own eyes. He pays a debt quicker to a rich man than to a poor man. He wishes the bow and compliment of some leader in the state, or in society; weighs what he says; perhaps he never comes nearer to him for that, but dies at last better contented for this amusement of his eyes and his fancy.

The world rolls, the din of life is never hushed. In London, in Paris, in Boston, in San Francisco, the carnival, the masquerade is at its height. Nobody drops his domino. The unities, the fictions of the piece, it would be an impertinence to break. The chapter of fascinations is very long. Great is paint; nay, God is the painter; and we rightly accuse the critic who destroys too many illusions. Society does not love its unmaskers. It was wittily, if somewhat bitterly, said by D'Alembert, "qu'un état de vapeur était un état très fâcheux, parcequ'il nous faisait voir les choses comme elles sont." I find men victims of illusion in all parts of life. Children, youths, adults, and old men, all are led by one bauble or another. Yoganidra, the goddess of illusion, Proteus, or Momus, or Gylfi's Mocking,—for the Power has many names,— is stronger than the Titans, stronger than Apollo. Few have overheard the gods, or surprised their secret. Life is a succession of lessons which must be lived to be understood. All is riddle, and the key to a riddle is another riddle. There are as many pillows of illusion as flakes in a snowstorm. We wake from one dream into another dream. The toys, to be sure, are various, and are graduated in refinement to the quality of the dupe. The intellectual man requires a fine bait; the sots are easily amused. But everybody is drugged with his own frenzy, and the pageant marches at all hours, with music and banner and badge.

Amid the joyous troop who give in to the charivari, comes now and then a sad-eyed boy, whose eyes lack the requisite refractions to clothe the show in due glory, and who is afflicted with a tendency to trace home the glittering miscellany of fruits and flowers to one root. Science is a search after identity, and the scientific whim is lurking in all corners. At the State Fair, a friend of mine complained that all the varieties of fancy pears in our orchards seem to have been selected by somebody who had a whim for a particular kind of pear, and only cultivated such as had that perfume; they were all alike. And I remember the quarrel of another youth with the confectioners, that, when he racked his wit to choose the best comfits in the shops, in all the endless varieties of sweetmeat he could only find three flavors, or two. What then? Pears and cakes are good for something; and because you, unluckily, have an eye or nose too keen, why need you spoil the comfort which the rest of us find in them?

I knew a humorist who, in a good deal of rattle, had a grain or two of sense. He shocked the company by maintaining that the attributes of God were two—power and risibility; and that it was the duty of every pious man to keep up the comedy. And I have known gentlemen of great stake in the community, but whose sympathies were cold,—presidents of colleges, and governors, and senators,—who held themselves bound to sign every temperance pledge, and act with Bible societies, and missions, and peacemakers, and cry, *Hist-a-boy!* to every good dog. We must not carry comity too far, but we all have kind impulses in this direction. When the boys come into my yard for leave to gather horse-chestnuts, I own I enter into Nature's game, and affect to grant the permission reluctantly, fearing that any moment they will find out the imposture of that showy chaff. But this tenderness is quite unnecessary; the enchantments are laid on very thick. Their young life is thatched with them. Bare and grim to tears is the lot of the children in the hovel I saw yesterday; yet not the less they hung it round with frippery romance, like the children of the happiest fortune, and talked of "the dear cottage where so many joyful hours had flown." Well, this thatching of hovels is the custom of the country. Women, more than all, are the element and kingdom of illusion. Being fascinated, they fascinate. They see through Claude-Lorraines. And how dare anyone, if he could, pluck away the *coulisses*, stage-effects, and ceremonies, by which they live? Too pathetic, too pitiable, is the region of affection, and its atmosphere always liable to *mirage*.

We are not very much to blame for our bad marriages. We live amid hallucinations; and this especial trap is laid to trip up our feet with, and all are tripped up first or last. But the mighty Mother who had been so sly with us, as if she felt that she owed us some indemnity, insinuates into the Pandora-box of marriage some deep and serious benefits, and some great joys. We find a delight in the beauty and happiness of children that makes the heart too big for the body. In the worst-assorted connections there is ever some mixture of true marriage. Teague and his jade get some just relations of mutual respect, kindly observation, and fostering of each other, learn something, and would carry themselves wiselier, if they were now to begin.

'Tis fine for us to point at one or another fine madman, as if there were any exempts. The scholar in his library is none. I, who have all my life heard any number of orations and debates, read poems and miscellaneous books, conversed with many geniuses, am still the victim of any new page; and, if Marmaduke, or Hugh, or Moosehead, or any other, invent a new style or mythology, I fancy that the world will be all brave and right if dressed in these colors, which I had not thought of. Then at once I will daub with this new paint: but it will not stick. 'Tis like the cement which the peddler sells at the door; he makes broken crockery hold with it, but you can never buy of him a bit of the cement which will make it hold when he is gone.

Men who make themselves felt in the world avail themselves of a certain fate in their constitution, which they know how to use. But they never deeply interest us, unless they lift a corner of the curtain, or betray never so slightly their penetration of what is behind it. 'Tis the charm of practical men, that outside of their practicality are a certain poetry and play, as if they led the good horse Power by the bridle, and preferred to walk, though they can ride so fiercely. Bonaparte is intellectual, as well as Cæsar; and the best soldiers, sea-captains, and railway men have a gentleness, when off duty; a good-natured admission that there are illusions, and who shall say that he is not their sport? We stigmatize the cast-iron fellows, who cannot so detach themselves, as "dragon-ridden," "thunder-stricken," and fools of fate, with whatever powers endowed.

Since our tuition is through emblems and indirections, 'tis well to know that there is method in it, a fixed scale, and rank above rank in the phantasms. We begin low with coarse masks, and rise to the most subtle and beautiful. The red men told Columbus, "they had an herb which took away fatigue"; but he found the illusion of "arriving from the east at the Indies" more composing to his lofty spirit than any tobacco. Is not our faith in the impenetrability of matter more sedative than narcotics? You play with jack-straws, balls, bowls, horse and gun, estates and politics; but there are finer games before you. Is not time a pretty toy? Life will show you masks that are worth all your carnivals. Yonder mountain must migrate into your mind. The fine star-dust and nebulous blur in Orion, "the portentous year of Mizar and Alcor," must come down and be dealt with in your household thought. What if you shall come to discern that the play and playground of all this pompous history are radiations from yourself, and that the sun borrows his beams? What terrible questions we are learning to ask! The former men believed in magic, by which temples, cities, and men were swallowed up and all trace of them gone. We are coming on the secret of a magic which sweeps out of men's minds all vestige of theism and beliefs which they and their fathers held and were framed upon.

There are deceptions of the senses, deceptions of the passions, and the structural, beneficent illusions of sentiment and of the intellect. There is the illusion of love, which attributes to the beloved person all which that person shares with his or her family, sex, age, or condition, nay, with the human mind itself. 'Tis these which the lover loves, and Anna Matilda gets the credit of them. As if one shut up always in a tower, with one window, through which the face of heaven and earth could be seen, should fancy that all the marvels he beheld belonged to that window. There is the illusion of time, which is very deep; who has disposed of it? or come to the conviction that what seems the *succession* of thought is only the distribution of wholes into causal series? The intellect sees that every atom carries the whole of Nature; that the mind opens to omnipotence; that, in the endless striving and ascents, the metamorphosis is entire, so that the soul doth not know itself in its own act, when that act is perfected. There is illusion that shall deceive even the elect. There is illusion that shall deceive even the performer of the miracle. Though he make his body, he denies that he makes it. Though the world exist from thought, thought is daunted in presence of the world. One after the other we accept the mental laws, still resisting those which follow, which however must be accepted. But all our concessions only compel us to new profusion. And what avails it that science has come to treat space and time as simply forms of thought, and the material world as hypothetical, and withal our pretension of *property* and even of self-hood are fading with the rest, if, at last, even our thoughts are not finalities; but the incessant flowing and ascension reach these also, and each thought which yesterday was a finality to-day is yielding to a larger generalization?

With such volatile elements to work in, 'tis no wonder if our estimates are loose and floating. We must work and affirm, but we have no guess of the value of what we say or do. The cloud is now as big as your hand, and now it covers a county. That story of Thor, who was set to drain the drinking-horn in Asgard, and to wrestle with the old woman, and to run with the runner Lok, and presently found that he had been drinking up the sea, and wrestling with Time, and racing with Thought, describes us who are contending, amid these seeming trifles, with the supreme energies of Nature. We fancy we have fallen into bad company and squalid condition, low debts, shoe-bills, broken glass to pay for, pots to buy, butcher's meat, sugar, milk, and coal. "Set me some great task, ye gods! and I will show my spirit." "Not so," says the good Heaven; "plod and plough, vamp your old coats and hats, weave a shoestring; great affairs and the best wine by-and-by." Well, 'tis all phantasm; and if we weave a yard of tape in all humility, and as well as we can, long hereafter we shall see it was no cotton tape at all, but some galaxy which we braided, and that the threads were Time and Nature.

We cannot write the order of the variable winds. How can we penetrate the law of our shifting moods and susceptibility? Yet they differ as all and nothing. Instead of the firmament of yesterday, which our eyes require, it is to-day an eggshell which coops us in; we cannot even see what or where our stars of destiny are. From day to day, the capital facts of human life are hidden from our eyes. Suddenly the mist rolls up, and reveals them, and we think how much good time is gone, that might have been saved had any hint of these things been shown. A sudden rise in the road shows us the system of mountains, and all the summits, which have been just as near us all the year, but quite out of mind. But these alternations are not without their order, and we are parties to our various fortune. If life seem a succession of dreams, yet poetic justice is done in dreams also. The visions of good men are good; it is the undisciplined will that is whipped with bad thoughts and bad fortunes. When we break the laws, we lose our hold on the central reality. Like sick men in hospitals, we change only from bed to bed, from one folly to another; and it cannot signify much what becomes of such castaways,— wailing, stupid, comatose creatures,—lifted from bed to bed, from the nothing of life to the nothing of death.

In this kingdom of illusions we grope eagerly for stays and foundations. There is none but a strict and faithful dealing at home, and a severe barring out of all duplicity or illusion there. Whatever games are played with us, we must play no games with ourselves, but deal in our privacy with the last honesty and truth. I look upon the simple and childish virtues of veracity and honesty as the root of all that is sublime in character. Speak as you think, be what you are, pay your debts of all kinds. I prefer to be owned as sound and solvent, and my word as good as my bond, and to be what cannot be skipped, or dissipated, or undermined, to all the *éclat* in the universe. This reality is the foundation of friendship, religion, poetry, and art. At the top or at the bottom of all illusions, I set the cheat which still leads us to work and live for appearances, in spite of our conviction, in all sane hours, that it is what we really are that avails with friends, with strangers, and with fate or fortune.

One would think from the talk of men, that riches and poverty were a great matter; and our civilization mainly respects it. But the Indians say, that they do not think the white man with his brow of care, always toiling, afraid of heat and cold, and keeping within doors, has any advantage of them. The permanent interest of every man is, never to be in a false position, but to have the weight of Nature to back him in all that he does. Riches and poverty are a thick or thin costume; and our life—the life of all of us—identical. For we transcend the circumstance continually, and taste the real quality of existence; as in our employments, which only differ in the manipulations, but express the same laws; or in our thoughts, which wear no silks and taste no ice-creams. We see God face to face every hour, and know the savor of Nature.

The early Greek philosophers Heraclitus and Xenophanes measured their force on this problem of identity. Diogenes of Apollonia said, that unless the atoms were made of one stuff, they could never blend and act with one another. But the Hindoos, in their sacred writings, express the liveliest feeling, both of the essential identity, and of that illusion which they conceive variety to be: "The notions, *I am*, and *This is mine*, which influence mankind, are but delusions of the mother of the world. Dispel, O Lord of all creatures! the conceit of knowledge which proceeds from ignorance." And the beatitude of man they hold to lie in being freed from fascination.

The intellect is stimulated by the statement of truth in a trope, and the will by clothing the laws of life in illusions. But the unities of Truth and of Right are not broken by the disguise. There need never be any confusion in these. In a crowded life of many parts and performers, on a stage of nations, or in the obscurest hamlet in Maine or California, the same elements offer the same choices to each new comer, and, according to his election, he fixes his fortune in absolute nature. It would be hard to put more mental and moral philosophy than the Persians have thrown into a sentence:—

Fooled thou must be, though wisest of the wise:
Then be the fool of virtue, not of vice.

There is no chance, and no anarchy, in the universe. All is system and gradation. Every god is there sitting in his sphere. The young mortal enters the hall of the firmament: there is he alone with them alone, they pouring on him benedictions and gifts, and beckoning him up to their thrones. On the instant, and incessantly, fall snow-storms of illusions. He fancies himself in a vast crowd which sways this way and that, and whose movement and doings he must obey: he fancies himself poor, orphaned, insignificant. The mad crowd drives hither and thither, now furiously commanding this thing to be done, now that. What is he that he should resist their will, and think or act for himself? Every moment, new changes, and new showers of deceptions, to baffle and distract him. And when, by-and-by, for an instant, the air clears, and the cloud lifts a little, there are the gods still sitting around him on their thrones—they alone with him alone.

FATE[16]

Delicate omens traced in air
To the lone bard true witness bare;
Birds with auguries on their wings
Chanted undeceiving things,
Him to beckon, him to warn;
Well might then the poet scorn
To learn of scribe or courier
Hints writ in vaster character;
And on his mind, at dawn of day,
Soft shadows of the evening lay.
For the prevision is allied
Unto the thing so signified;
Or say, the foresight that awaits
Is the same Genius that creates.

It chanced during one winter, a few years ago, that our critics were bent on discussing the theory of the Age. By an odd coincidence, four or five noted men were each reading a discourse to the citizens of Boston or New York, on the Spirit of the Times. It so happened that the subject had the same prominence in some remarkable pamphlets and journals issued in London in the same season. To me, however, the question of the times resolved itself into a practical question of the conduct of life. How shall I live? We are incompetent to solve the times. Our geometry cannot span the huge orbits of the prevailing ideas, behold their return, and reconcile their opposition. We can only obey our own polarity. 'Tis fine for us to speculate and elect our course, if we must accept an irresistible dictation.

In our first steps to gain our wishes, we come upon immovable limitations. We are fired with the hope to reform men. After many experiments, we find that we must begin earlier—at school. But the boys and girls are not docile; we can make nothing of them. We decide that they are not of good stock. We must begin our reform earlier still—at generation: that is to say, there is Fate, or laws of the world.

But, if there be irresistible dictation, this dictation understands itself. If we must accept Fate, we are not less compelled to affirm liberty, the significance of the individual, the grandeur of duty, the power of character. This is true, and that other is true. But our geometry cannot span these extreme points, and reconcile them. What to do? By obeying each thought frankly, by harping, or, if you will, pounding on each string, we learn at last its power. By the same obedience to other thoughts, we learn theirs, and then comes some reasonable hope of harmonizing them. We are sure, that, though we know not how, necessity does comport with liberty, the individual with the world, my polarity with the spirit of the times. The riddle of the age has for each a private solution. If one would study his own time, it must be by this method of taking up in turn each of the leading topics which belong to our scheme of human life, and, by firmly stating all that is agreeable to experience on one, and doing the same justice to the opposing facts in the others, the true limitations will appear. Any excess of emphasis, on one part, would be corrected, and a just balance would be made.

But let us honestly state the facts. Our America has a bad name for superficialness. Great men, great nations, have not been boasters and buffoons, but perceivers of the terror of life, and have manned themselves to face it. The Spartan, embodying his religion in his country, dies before its majesty without a question. The Turk, who believes his doom is written on the iron leaf in the moment when he entered the world, rushes on the enemy's sabre with undivided will. The Turk, the Arab, the Persian, accepts the fore-ordained fate.

On two days, it steads not to run from thy grave,
The appointed, and the unappointed day;
On the first, neither balm nor physician can save,
Nor thee, on the second, the Universe slay.

The Hindoo, under the wheel, is as firm. Our Calvinists, in the last generation, had something of the same dignity. They felt that the weight of the Universe held them down to their place. What could *they* do? Wise men feel that there is something which cannot be talked or voted away—a strap or belt which girds the world.

The Destiny, minister general,
That executeth in the world o'er all,
The purveyance which God hath seen beforne,
So strong it is that tho' the world had sworn
The contrary of a thing by yea or nay,
Yet sometime it shall fallen on a day
That falleth not oft in a thousand year,
For, certainly, our appetites here,
Be it of war, or peace, or hate, or love,
All this is ruled by the sight above.
CHAUCER: *The Knighte's Tale.*

The Greek Tragedy expressed the same sense: "Whatever is fated, that will take place. The great immense mind of Jove is not to be transgressed."

Savages cling to a local god of one tribe or town. The broad ethics of Jesus were quickly narrowed to village theologies, which preach an election or favoritism. And, now and then, an amiable parson, like Jung Stilling, or Robert Huntington, believes in a pistareen-Providence, which, whenever the good man wants a dinner, makes that somebody shall knock at his door, and leave a half-dollar. But Nature is no sentimentalist—does not cosset or pamper us. We must see that the world is rough and surly, and will not mind drowning a man or a woman; but swallows your ship like a grain of dust. The cold, inconsiderate of persons, tingles your blood, benumbs your feet, freezes a man like an apple. The diseases, the elements, fortune, gravity, lightning, respect no persons. The way of Providence is a little rude. The habit of snake and spider, the snap of the tiger and other leapers and bloody jumpers, the crackle of the bones of his prey in the coil of the anaconda— these are in the system, and our habits are like theirs. You have just dined, and, however scrupulously the slaughter-house is concealed in the graceful distance of miles, there is complicity—expensive races—race living at the expense of race. The planet is liable to shocks from comets, perturbations from planets, rendings from earthquake and volcano, alterations of climate, precessions of equinoxes. Rivers dry up by opening of the forest. The sea changes its bed. Towns and counties fall into it. At Lisbon, an earthquake killed men like flies. At Naples, three years ago, ten thousand persons were crushed in a few minutes. The scurvy at sea; the sword of the climate in the west of Africa, at Cayenne, at Panama, at New Orleans, cut off men like a massacre. Our Western prairie shakes with fever and ague. The cholera, the small-pox, have proved as mortal to some tribes, as a frost to the crickets, which, having filled the summer with noise, are silenced by a fall of the temperature of one night. Without uncovering what does not concern us; or counting how many species of parasites hang on a bombyx; or groping after intestinal parasites, or infusory biters, or the obscurities of alternate generation;—the forms of the shark, the *labrus*, the jaw of the sea-wolf paved with crushing teeth, the weapons of the grampus, and other warriors hidden in the sea—are hints of ferocity in the interiors of nature. Let us not deny it up and down. Providence has a wild, rough, incalculable road to its end, and it is of no use to try to whitewash its huge, mixed instrumentalities, or to dress up that terrific benefactor in a clean shirt and white neckcloth of a student in divinity.

Will you say, the disasters which threaten mankind are exceptional, and one need not lay his account for cataclysms every day? Ay, but what happens once, may happen again, and so long as these strokes are not to be parried by us, they must be feared.

But these shocks and ruins are less destructive to us than the stealthy power of other laws which act on us daily. An expense of ends to means is fate—organization tyrannizing over character. The menagerie, or forms and powers of the spine, is a book of fate: the bill of the bird, the skull of the snake, determines tyrannically its limits. So is the scale of races, of temperaments; so is sex; so is climate; so is the reaction of talents imprisoning the vital power in certain directions. Every spirit makes its house; but afterwards the house confines the spirit.

The gross lines are legible to the dull: the cabman is phrenologist so far: he looks in your face to see if his shilling is sure. A dome of brow denotes one thing; a pot-belly another; a squint, a pug-nose, mats of hair, the pigment of the epidermis, betray character. People seem sheathed in their tough organization. Ask Spurzheim, ask the doctors, ask Quetelet, if temperaments decide nothing? or if there be anything they do not decide? Read the description in medical books of the four temperaments, and you will think you are reading your own thoughts which you had not yet told. Find the part which black eyes, and which blue eyes, play severally in the company. How shall a man escape from his ancestors, or draw off from his veins the black drop which he drew from his father's or his mother's life? It often appears in a family, as if all the qualities of the progenitors were potted in several jars—some ruling quality in each son or daughter of the house—and sometimes the unmixed temperament, the rank unmitigated elixir, the family vice, is drawn off in a separate individual, and the others are proportionally relieved. We sometimes see a change of expression in our companion, and say, his father, or his mother, comes to the windows of his eyes, and sometimes a remote relative. In different hours, a man represents each of several of his ancestors, as if there were seven or eight of us rolled up in each man's skin,—seven or eight ancestors at least,—and they constitute the variety of notes for that new piece of music which his life is. At the corner of the street, you read the possibility of each passenger, in the facial angle, in the complexion, in the depth of his eye. His parentage determines it. Men are what their mothers made them. You may as well ask a loom which weaves huckaback, why it does not make cashmere, as expect poetry from this engineer or a chemical discovery from that jobber. Ask the digger in the ditch to explain Newton's laws: the fine organs of his brains have been pinched by overwork and squalid poverty from father to son, for a hundred years. When each comes forth from his mother's womb, the gate of gifts closes behind him. Let him value his hands and feet, he has but one pair. So he has but one future, and that is already predetermined in his lobes, and described in that little fatty face, pig-eye, and squat form. All the privilege and all the legislation of the world cannot meddle or help to make a poet or a prince of him.

Jesus said, "When he looketh on her, he hath committed adultery." But he is an adulterer before he has yet looked on the woman, by the superfluity of animal, and the defect of thought, in his constitution. Who meets him, or who meets her, in the street, sees that they are ripe to be each other's victim.

In certain men, digestion and sex absorb the vital force, and the stronger these are, the individual is so much weaker. The more of these drones perish, the better for the hive. If, later, they give birth to some superior individual, with force enough to add to this animal a new aim, and a complete apparatus to work it out, all the ancestors are gladly forgotten. Most men and most women are merely one couple more. Now and then, one has a new cell or camarilla opened in his brain—an architectural, a musical, or a philological knack, some stray taste or talent for flowers, or chemistry, or pigments, or story-telling, a good hand for drawing, a good foot for dancing, an athletic frame for wide journeying, etc.—which skill nowise alters rank in the scale of nature, but serves to pass the time, the life of sensation going on as before. At last, these hints and tendencies are fixed in one, or in a succession. Each absorbs so much food and force as to become itself a new centre. The new talent draws off so rapidly the vital force, that not enough remains for the animal functions, hardly enough for health; so that, in the second generation, if the like genius appear, the health is visibly deteriorated, and the generative force impaired.

People are born with the moral or with the material bias; uterine brothers with this diverging destination; and I suppose, with high magnifiers, Mr. Frauenhofer or Dr. Carpenter might come to distinguish in the embryo at the fourth day, this is a Whig, and that a Free-soiler.

It was a poetic attempt to lift this mountain of Fate, to reconcile this despotism of race with liberty, which led the Hindoos to say, "Fate is nothing but the deeds committed in a prior state of existence." I find the coincidence of the extremes of eastern and western speculation in the daring statement of Schelling, "There is in every man a certain feeling, that he has been what he is from all eternity, and by no means became such in time." To say it less sublimely—in the history of the individual is always an account of his condition, and he knows himself to be a party to his present estate.

A good deal of our politics is physiological. Now and then, a man of wealth in the heyday of youth adopts the tenet of broadest freedom. In England, there is always some man of wealth and large connection planting himself, during all his years of health, on the side of progress, who, as soon as he begins to die, checks his forward play, calls in his troops, and becomes conservative. All conservatives are such from personal defects. They have been effeminated by position or nature, born halt and blind, through luxury of their parents, and can only, like invalids, act on the defensive. But strong natures, backwoodsmen, New Hampshire giants, Napoleons, Burkes, Broughams, Websters, Kossuths, are inevitable patriots, until their life ebbs, and their defects and gout, palsy and money, warp them.

The strongest idea incarnates itself in majorities and nations, in the healthiest and strongest. Probably, the election goes by avoirdupois weight, and, if you could weigh bodily the tonnage of any hundred of the Whig and the Democratic party in a town, on the Dearborn balance, as they passed the hay scales, you could predict with certainty which party would carry it. On the whole, it would be rather the speediest way of deciding the vote, to put the selectmen or the mayor and aldermen at the hayscales.

In science, we have to consider two things: power and circumstance. All we know of the egg, from each successive discovery, is, *another vesicle*; and if, after five hundred years, you get a better observer, or a better glass, he finds within the last observed another. In vegetable and animal tissue, it is just alike, and all that the primary power or spasm operates, is, still, vesicles, vesicles. Yes— but the tyrannical Circumstance! A vesicle in new circumstances, a vesicle lodged in darkness, Oken thought, became animal; in light, a plant. Lodged in the parent animal, it suffers changes, which end in unsheathing miraculous capability in the unaltered vesicle, and it unlocks itself to fish, bird, or quadruped, head and foot, eye and claw. The Circumstance is Nature. Nature is, what you may do. There is much you may not. We have two things—the circumstance, and the life. Once we thought, positive power was all. Now we learn, that negative power, or circumstance, is half. Nature is the tyrannous circumstance, the thick skull, the sheathed snake, the ponderous, rock-like jaw; necessitated activity; violent direction; the conditions of a tool, like the locomotive, strong enough on its track, but which can do nothing but mischief off it; or skates, which are wings on the ice, but fetters on the ground.

The book of Nature is the book of Fate. She turns the gigantic pages—leaf after leaf—never re-turning one. One leaf she lays down, a floor of granite; then a thousand ages, and a bed of slate; a thousand ages, and a measure of coal; a thousand ages, and a layer of marl and mud; vegetable forms appear; her first misshapen animals, zoöphyte, trilobium, fish, then, saurians—rude forms, in which she has only blocked her future statue, concealing under these unwieldy monsters the fine type of her coming king. The face of the planet cools and dries, the races meliorate, and man is born. But when a race has lived its term, it comes no more again.

The population of the world is a conditional population; not the best, but the best that could live now; and the scale of tribes, and the steadiness with which victory adheres to one tribe, and defeat to another, is as uniform as the superposition of strata. We know in history what weight belongs to race. We see the English, French, and Germans, planting themselves on every shore and market of America and Australia, and monopolizing the commerce of these countries. We like the nervous and victorious habit of our own branch of the family. We follow the step of the Jew, of the Indian, of the Negro. We see how much will has been expended to extinguish the Jew, in vain. Look at the unpalatable conclusions of Knox, in his "Fragment of Races,"—a rash and unsatisfactory writer, but charged with pungent and unforgettable truths. "Nature respects race, and not hybrids." "Every race has its own *habitat.*" "Detach a colony from the race, and it deteriorates to the crab." See the shades of the picture. The German and Irish millions, like the negro, have a great deal of guano in their destiny. They are ferried over the Atlantic, and carted over America, to ditch and to drudge, to make corn cheap, and then to lie down prematurely to make a spot of green grass on the prairie.

One more faggot of these adamantine bandages, is, the new science of Statistics. It is a rule, that the most casual and extraordinary events—if the basis of population is broad enough—become matter of fixed calculation. It would not be safe to say when a captain like Bonaparte, a singer like Jenny Lind, or a navigator like Bowditch, would be born in Boston: but, on a population of twenty or two hundred millions, something like accuracy may be had.[17]

'Tis frivolous to fix pedantically the date of particular inventions. They have all been invented over and over fifty times. Man is the arch machine, of which all these shifts drawn from himself are toy models. He helps himself on each emergency by copying or duplicating his own structure, just so far as the need is. 'Tis hard to find the right Homer, Zoroaster, or Menu; harder still to find the Tubal Cain, or Vulcan, or Cadmus, or Copernicus, or Fust, or Fulton, the indisputable inventor. There are scores and centuries of them. "The air is full of men." This kind of talent so abounds, this constructive tool-making efficiency, as if it adhered to the chemic atoms, as if the air he breathes were made of Vaucansons, Franklins, and Watts.

Doubtless, in every million there will be an astronomer, a mathematician, a comic poet, a mystic. No one can read the history of astronomy, without perceiving that Copernicus, Newton, Laplace, are not new men, or a new kind of men, but that Thales, Anaximenes, Hipparchus, Empedocles, Aristarchus, Pythagoras, Œnopides, had anticipated them; each had the same tense geometrical brain, apt for the same vigorous computation and logic, a mind parallel to the movement of the world. The Roman mile probably rested on a measure of a degree of the meridian. Mahometan and Chinese know what we know of leap-year, of the Gregorian calendar, and of the precession of the equinoxes. As, in every barrel of cowries, brought to New Bedford, there shall be one *orangia*, so there will, in a dozen millions of Malays and Mahometans, be one or two astronomical skulls. In a large city, the most casual things, and things whose beauty lies in their casualty, are produced as punctually and to order as the baker's muffin for breakfast. "Punch" makes exactly one capital joke a week; and the journals contrive to furnish one good piece of news every day.

And not less work the laws of repression, the penalties of violated functions. Famine, typhus, frost, war, suicide, and effete races, must be reckoned calculable parts of the system of the world.

These are pebbles from the mountain, hints of the terms by which our life is walled up, and which show a kind of mechanical exactness, as of a loom or mill, in what we call casual or fortuitous events.

The force with which we resist these torrents of tendency looks so ridiculously inadequate, that it amounts to little more than a criticism or a protest made by a minority of one, under compulsion of millions. I seemed, in the height of a tempest, to see men overboard struggling in the waves, and driven about here and there. They glanced intelligently at each other, but 'twas little they could do for one another; 'twas much if each could keep afloat alone. Well, they had a right to their eye-beams, and all the rest was Fate.

We cannot trifle with this reality, this cropping out in our planted gardens of the core of the world. No picture of life can have any veracity that does not admit the odious facts. A man's power is hooped in by a necessity which, by many experiments, he touches on every side, until he learns its arc.

The element running through entire nature, which we popularly call Fate, is known to us as limitation. Whatever limits us, we call Fate. If we are brute and barbarous, the fate takes a brute and dreadful shape. As we refine, our checks become finer. If we rise to spiritual culture, the antagonism takes a spiritual form. In the Hindoo fables, Vishnu follows Maya through all her ascending changes, from insect and crawfish up to elephant; whatever form she took, he took the male form of that kind, until she became at last woman and goddess, and he a man and a god. The limitations refine as the soul purifies, but the ring of necessity is always perched at the top.

When the gods in the Norse heaven were unable to bind the Fenris Wolf with steel or with weight of mountains,—the one he snapped and the other he spurned with his heel,—they put round his foot a limp band softer than silk or cobweb, and this held him: the more he spurned it, the stiffer it grew. So soft and so staunch is the ring of Fate. Neither brandy, nor nectar, nor sulphuric ether, nor hell-fire, nor ichor, nor poetry, nor genius, can get rid of this limp band. For if we give it the high sense in which the poets use it, even thought itself is not above Fate: that too must act according to eternal laws, and all that is willful and fantastic in it is in opposition to its fundamental essence.

And, last of all, high over thought, in the world of morals, Fate appears as vindicator, leveling the high, lifting the low, requiring justice in man, and always striking soon or late, when justice is not done. What is useful will last; what is hurtful will sink. "The doer must suffer," said the Greeks: "you would soothe a Deity not to be soothed." "God himself cannot procure good for the wicked," said the Welsh triad. "God may consent, but only for a time," said the bard of Spain. The limitation is impassable by any insight of man. In its last and loftiest ascensions, insight itself, and the freedom of the will, is one of its obedient members. But we must not run into generalizations too large, but show the natural bounds or essential distinctions, and seek to do justice to the other elements as well.

Thus we trace Fate, in matter, mind, and morals—in race, in retardations of strata, and in thought and character as well. It is everywhere bound or limitation. But fate has its lord; limitation its limits; is different seen from above and from below; from within and from without. For, though Fate is immense, so is power, which is the other fact in the dual world, immense. If Fate follows and limits power, power attends and antagonizes Fate. We must respect Fate as natural history, but there is more than natural history. For who and what is this criticism that pries into the matter? Man is not order of nature, sack and sack, belly and members, link in a chain, nor any ignominious baggage, but a stupendous antagonism, a dragging together of the poles of the Universe. He betrays his relation to what is below him—thick-skulled, small-brained, fishy, quadrumanous—quadruped ill-disguised, hardly escaped into biped, and has paid for the new powers by loss of some of the old ones. But the lightning which explodes and fashions planets, maker of planets and suns, is in him. On one side, elemental order, sandstone and granite, rock-ledges, peat-bog, forest, sea and shore; and, on the other part, thought, the spirit which composes and decomposes nature—here they are, side by side, god and devil, mind and matter, king and conspirator, belt and spasm, riding peacefully together in the eye and brain of every man.

Nor can he blink the freewill. To hazard the contradiction—freedom is necessary. If you please to plant yourself on the side of Fate, and say, Fate is all; then we say, a part of Fate is the freedom of man. Forever wells up the impulse of choosing and acting in the soul. Intellect annuls Fate. So far as a man thinks, he is free. And though nothing is more disgusting than the crowing about liberty by slaves, as most men are, and the flippant mistaking for freedom of some paper preamble like a "Declaration of Independence," or the statute right to vote, by those who have never dared to think or to act, yet it is wholesome to man to look, not at Fate, but the other way: the practical view is the other. His sound relation to these facts is to use and command, not to cringe to them. "Look not on nature, for her name is fatal," said the oracle. The too much contemplation of these limits induces meanness. They who talk much of destiny, their birth-star, etc., are in a lower dangerous plane, and invite the evils they fear.

I cited the instinctive and heroic races as proud believers in Destiny. They conspire with it; a loving resignation is with the event. But the dogma makes a different impression, when it is held by the weak and lazy. 'Tis weak and vicious people who cast the blame on Fate. The right use of Fate is to bring up our conduct to the loftiness of nature. Rude and invincible except by themselves are the elements. So let man be. Let him empty his breast of his windy conceits, and show his lordship by manners and deeds on the scale of nature. Let him hold his purpose as with the tug of gravitation. No power, no persuasion, no bribe shall make him give up his point. A man ought to compare advantageously with a river, an oak, or a mountain. He shall have not less the flow, the expansion, and the resistance of these.

'Tis the best use of Fate to teach a fatal courage. Go face the fire at sea, or the cholera in your friend's house, or the burglar in your own, or what danger lies in the way of duty, knowing you are guarded by the cherubim of Destiny. If you believe in Fate to your harm, believe it, at least, for your good.

For, if Fate is so prevailing, man also is part of it, and can confront fate with fate. If the Universe have these savage accidents, our atoms are as savage in resistance. We should be crushed by the atmosphere, but for the reaction of the air within the body. A tube made of a film of glass can resist the shock of the ocean, if filled with the same water. If there be omnipotence in the stroke, there is omnipotence of recoil.

But Fate against Fate is only parrying and defense: there are, also, the noble creative forces. The revelation of Thought takes man out of servitude into freedom. We rightly say of ourselves, we were born, and afterward we were born again, and many times. We have successive experiences so important, that the new forgets the old, and hence the mythology of the seven or the nine heavens. The day of days, the great day of the feast of life, is that in which the inward eye opens to the Unity in things, to the omnipresence of law—sees that what is must be, and ought to be, or is the best. This beatitude dips from on high down to us, and we see. It is not in us so much as we are in it. If the air come to our lungs, we breathe and live; if not, we die. If the light come to our eyes, we see; else not. And if truth come to our mind, we suddenly expand to its dimensions, as if we grew to worlds. We are as lawgivers; we speak for Nature; we prophesy and divine.

This insight throws us on the party and interest of the Universe, against all and sundry; against ourselves, as much as others. A man speaking from insight affirms of himself what is true of the mind: seeing its immortality, he says, I am immortal; seeing its invincibility, he says, I am strong. It is not in us, but we are in it. It is of the maker, not of what is made. All things are touched and changed by it. This uses, and is not used. It distances those who share it, from those who share it not. Those who share it not are flocks and herds. It dates from itself; not from former men or better men—gospel, or constitution, or college, or custom. Where it shines, Nature is no longer intrusive, but all things make a musical or pictorial impression. The world of men show like a comedy without laughter:—populations, interests, government, history;—'tis all toy figures in a toy house. It does not overvalue particular truths. We hear eagerly every thought and word quoted from an intellectual man. But, in his presence, our own mind is roused to activity, and we forget very fast what he says, much more interested in the new play of our own thought, than in any thought of his. 'Tis the majesty into which we have suddenly mounted, the impersonality, the scorn of egotisms, the sphere of laws, that engage us. Once we were stepping a little this way, and a little that way; now, we are as men in a balloon, and do not think so much of the point we have left, or the point we would make, as of the liberty and glory of the way.

Just as much intellect as you add, so much organic power. He who sees through the design, presides over it, and must will that which must be. We sit and rule, and, though we sleep, our dream will come to pass. Our thought, though it were only an hour old, affirms an oldest necessity, not to be separated from thought, and not to be separated from will. They must always have coexisted. It apprises us of its sovereignty and godhead, which refuse to be severed from it. It is not mine or thine, but the will of all mind. It is poured into the souls of all men, as the soul itself which constitutes them men. I know not whether there be, as is alleged, in the upper region of our atmosphere, a permanent westerly current, which carries with it all atoms which rise to that height; but I see that, when souls reach a certain clearness of perception, they accept a knowledge and motive above selfishness. A breath of will blows eternally through the universe of souls in the direction of the Right and Necessary. It is the air which all intellects inhale and exhale, and it is the wind which blows the worlds into order and orbit.

Thought dissolves the material universe, by carrying the mind up into a sphere where all is plastic. Of two men, each obeying his own thought, he whose thought is deepest will be the strongest character. Always one man more than another represents the will of Divine Providence to the period.

If thought makes free, so does the moral sentiment. The mixtures of spiritual chemistry refuse to be analyzed. Yet we can see that with the perception of truth is joined the desire that it shall prevail. That affection is essential to will. Moreover, when a strong will appears, it usually results from a certain unity of organization, as if the whole energy of body and mind flowed in one direction. All great force is real and elemental. There is no manufacturing a strong will. There must be a pound to balance a pound. Where power is shown in will, it must rest on the universal force. Alaric and Bonaparte must believe they rest on a truth, or their will can be bought or bent. There is a bribe possible for any finite will. But the pure sympathy with universal ends is an infinite force, and cannot be bribed or bent. Whoever has had experience of the moral sentiment cannot choose but believe in unlimited power. Each pulse from that heart is an oath from the Most High. I know not what the word *sublime* means, if it be not the intimations in this infant of a terrific force. A text of heroism, a name and anecdote of courage, are not arguments, but sallies of freedom. One of these is the verse of the Persian Hafiz, "'Tis written on the gate of Heaven, 'Woe unto him who suffers himself to be betrayed by Fate!'" Does the reading of history make us fatalists? What courage does not the opposite opinion show! A little whim of will to be free gallantly contending against the universe of chemistry.

But insight is not will, nor is affection will. Perception is cold, and goodness dies in wishes; as Voltaire said, 'tis the misfortune of worthy people that they are cowards; "*un des plus grands malheurs des honnêtes gens c'est qu'ils sont des lâches.*" There must be a fusion of these two to generate the energy of will. There can be no driving force, except through the conversion of the man into his will, making him the will, and the will him. And one may say boldly, that no man has a right perception of any truth, who has not been reacted on by it, so as to be ready to be its martyr.

The one serious and formidable thing in nature is a will. Society is servile from want of will, and therefore the world wants saviours and religions. One way is right to go: the hero sees it, and moves on that aim, and has the world under him for root and support. He is to others as the world. His approbation is honor; his dissent, infamy. The glance of his eye has the force of sunbeams. A personal influence towers up in memory only worthy, and we gladly forget numbers, money, climate, gravitation, and the rest of Fate.

We can afford to allow the limitation, if we know it is the meter of the growing man. We can stand against Fate, as children stand up against the wall in their father's house, and notch their height from year to year. But when the boy grows to man, and is master of the house, he pulls down that wall, and builds a new and bigger. 'Tis only a question of time. Every brave youth is in training to ride, and rule this dragon. His science is to make weapons and wings of these passions and retarding forces. Now whether, seeing these two things, fate and power, we are permitted to believe in unity? The bulk of mankind believe in two gods. They are under one dominion here in the house, as friend and parent, in social circles, in letters, in art, in love, in religion: but in mechanics, in dealing with steam and climate, in trade, in politics, they think they come under another; and that it would be a practical blunder to transfer the method and way of working of one sphere into the other. What good, honest, generous men at home, will be wolves and foxes on change! What pious men in the parlor will vote for what reprobates at the polls! To a certain point, they believe themselves the care of a Providence. But in a steamboat, in an epidemic, in war, they believe a malignant energy rules.

But relation and connection are not somewhere and sometimes, but everywhere and always. The divine order does not stop where their sight stops. The friendly power works on the same rules, in the next farm and the next planet. But where they have not experience, they run against it, and hurt themselves. Fate, then, is a name for facts not yet passed under the fire of thought—for causes which are unpenetrated.

But every jet of chaos which threatens to exterminate us is convertible by intellect into wholesome force. Fate is unpenetrated causes. The water drowns ship and sailor, like a grain of dust. But learn to swim, trim your bark, and the wave which drowned it will be cloven by it, and carry it, like its own foam, a plume and a power. The cold is inconsiderate of persons, tingles your blood, freezes a man like a dew-drop. But learn to skate, and the ice will give you a graceful, sweet, and poetic motion. The cold will brace your limbs and brain to genius, and make you foremost men of time. Cold and sea will train an imperial Saxon race, which nature cannot bear to lose, and, after cooping it up for a thousand years in yonder England, gives a hundred Englands, a hundred Mexicos. All the bloods it shall absorb and domineer: and more than Mexicos—the secrets of water and steam, the spasms of electricity, the ductility of metals, the chariot of the air, the ruddered balloon, are awaiting you.

The annual slaughter from typhus far exceeds that of war; but right drainage destroys typhus. The plague in the sea-service from scurvy is healed by lemon juice and other diets portable or procurable; the depopulation by cholera and small-pox is ended by drainage and vaccination; and every other pest is not less in the chain of cause and effect, and may be fought off. And, whilst art draws out the venom, it commonly extorts some benefits from the vanquished enemy. The mischievous torrent is taught to drudge for man; the wild beasts he makes useful for food, or dress, or labor; the chemic explosions are controlled like his watch. These are now the steeds on which he rides. Man moves in all modes, by legs of horses, by wings of wind, by steam, by gas of balloon, by electricity, and stands on tiptoe threatening to hunt the eagle in his own element. There is nothing he will not make his carrier.

Steam was, till the other day, the devil which we dreaded. Every pot made by any human potter or brazier had a hole in its cover, to let off the enemy, lest he should lift pot and roof, and carry the house away. But the Marquis of Worcester, Watt, and Fulton bethought themselves that where was power was not devil, but was God; that it must be availed of, and not by any means let off and wasted. Could he lift pots and roofs and houses so handily? he was the workman they were in search of. He could be used to lift away, chain, and compel other devils, far more reluctant and dangerous, namely, cubic miles of earth, mountains, weight or resistance of water, machinery, and the labors of all men in the world; and time he shall lengthen, and shorten space.

It has not fared much otherwise with higher kinds of steam. The opinion of the million was the terror of the world, and it was attempted, either to dissipate it, by amusing nations, or to pile it over with strata of society—a layer of soldiers; over that, a layer of lords; and a king on the top; with clamps and hoops of castles, garrisons, and police. But, sometimes, the religious principle would get in, and burst the hoops, and rive every mountain laid on top of it. The Fultons and Watts of politics, believing in unity, saw that it was a power, and, by satisfying it (as justice satisfies everybody), through a different disposition of society,—grouping it on a level, instead of piling it into a mountain,—they have contrived to make of this terror the most harmless and energetic form of a State.

Very odious, I confess, are the lessons of Fate. Who likes to have a dapper phrenologist pronouncing on his fortunes? Who likes to believe that he has hidden in his skull, spine, and pelvis, all the vices of a Saxon or Celtic race, which will be sure to pull him down—with what grandeur of hope and resolve he is fired—into a selfish, huckstering, servile, dodging animal? A learned physician tells us, the fact is invariable with the Neapolitan that, when mature, he assumes the forms of the unmistakable scoundrel. That is a little overstated—but may pass.

But these are magazines and arsenals. A man must thank his defects, and stand in some terror of his talents. A transcendent talent draws so largely on his forces, as to lame him; a defect pays him revenues on the other side. The sufferance, which is the badge of the Jew, has made him, in these days, the ruler of the rulers of the earth. If Fate is ore and quarry, if evil is good in the making, if limitation is power that shall be, if calamities, oppositions, and weights are wings and means—we are reconciled.

Fate involves the melioration. No statement of the universe can have any soundness, which does not admit its ascending effort. The direction of the whole, and of the parts, is toward benefit, and in proportion to the health. Behind every individual closes organization: before him opens liberty—the better, the best. The first and worst races are dead. The second and imperfect races are dying out, or remain for the maturing of higher. In the latest race, in man, every generosity, every new perception, the love and praise he extorts from his fellows, are certificates of advance out of fate into freedom. Liberation of the will from the sheaths and clogs of organization which he has outgrown, is the end and aim of this world. Every calamity is a spur and valuable hint; and where his endeavors do not yet fully avail, they tell as tendency. The whole circle of animal life,—tooth against tooth,—devouring war, war for food, a yelp of pain and a grunt of triumph, until, at last, the whole menagerie, the whole chemical mass, is mellowed and refined for higher use—pleases at a sufficient perspective.

But to see how fate slides into freedom, and freedom into fate, observe how far the roots of every creature run, or find, if you can, a point where there is no thread of connection. Our life is consentaneous and far-related. This knot of nature is so well tied, that nobody was ever cunning enough to find the two ends. Nature is intricate, overlapped, inter-weaved, and endless. Christopher Wren said of the beautiful King's College chapel, "that, if anybody would tell him where to lay the first stone, he would build such another." But where shall we find the first atom in this house of man, which is all consent, inosculation, and balance of parts?

The web of relation is shown in *habitat*, shown in hibernation. When hibernation was observed, it was found, that, whilst some animals become torpid in winter, others were torpid in summer: hibernation then was a false name. The *long sleep* is not an effect of cold, but is regulated by the supply of food proper to the animal. It becomes torpid when the fruit or prey it lives on is not in season, and regains its activity when its food is ready.

Eyes are found in light; ears in auricular air; feet on land; fins in water; wings in air; and each creature where it was meant to be, with a mutual fitness. Every zone has its own *Fauna*. There is adjustment between the animal and its food, its parasite, its enemy. Balances are kept. It is not allowed to diminish in numbers, nor to exceed. The like adjustments exist for man. His food is cooked when he arrives; his coal in the pit; the house ventilated; the mud of the deluge dried; his companions arrived at the same hour, and awaiting him with love, concert, laughter, and tears. These are coarse adjustments, but the invisible are not less. There are more belongings to every creature than his air and his food. His instincts must be met, and he has predisposing power that bends and fits what is near him to his use. He is not possible until the invisible things are right for him, as well as the visible. Of what changes, then, in sky and earth, and in finer skies and earths, does the appearance of some Dante or Columbus apprise us!

How is this effected? Nature is no spendthrift, but takes the shortest way to her ends. As the general says to his soldiers, "If you want a fort, build a fort," so nature makes every creature do its own work and get its living—is it planet, animal, or tree. The planet makes itself. The animal cell makes itself; then, what it wants. Every creature—wren or dragon—shall make its own lair. As soon as there is life, there is self-direction, and absorbing and using of material. Life is freedom—life in the direct ratio of its amount. You may be sure, the new-born man is not inert. Life works both voluntarily and supernaturally in its neighborhood. Do you suppose he can be estimated by his weight in pounds, or that he is contained in his skin—this reaching, radiating, jaculating fellow? The smallest candle fills a mile with its rays, and the papillæ of a man run out to every star.

When there is something to be done, the world knows how to get it done. The vegetable eye makes leaf, pericarp, root, bark, or thorn, as the need is; the first cell converts itself into stomach, mouth, nose, or nail, according to the want; the world throws its life into a hero or a shepherd, and puts him where he is wanted. Dante and Columbus were Italians in their time: they would be Russians or Americans to-day. Things ripen, new men come. The adaptation is not capricious. The ulterior aim, the purpose beyond itself, the correlation by which planets subside and crystallize, then animate beasts and men, will not stop, but will work into finer particulars, and from finer to finest.

The secret of the world is, the tie between person and event. Person makes event and event person. The "times," "the age," what is that, but a few profound persons and a few active persons who epitomize the times?— Goethe, Hegel, Metternich, Adams, Calhoun, Guizot, Peel, Cobden, Kossuth, Rothschild, Astor, Brunel, and the rest. The same fitness must be presumed between a man and the time and event, as between the sexes, or between a race of animals and the food it eats, or the inferior races it uses. He thinks his fate alien, because the copula is hidden. But the soul contains the event that shall befall it, for the event is only the actualization of its thoughts; and what we pray to ourselves for is always granted. The event is the print of your form. It fits you like your skin. What each does is proper to him. Events are the children of his body and mind. We learn that the soul of Fate is the soul of us, as Hafiz sings—

Alas! till now I had not known,
My guide and fortune's guide are one.

All the toys that infatuate men, and which they play for,—houses, land, money, luxury, power, fame,—are the self-same thing, with a new gauze or two of illusion overlaid. And of all the drums and rattles by which men are made willing to have their heads broke, and are led out solemnly every morning to parade, the most admirable is this by which we are brought to believe that events are arbitrary, and independent of actions. At the conjurer's we detect the hair by which he moves his puppet, but we have not eyes sharp enough to descry the thread that ties cause and effect.

Nature magically suits the man to his fortunes, by making these the fruit of his character. Ducks take to the water, eagles to the sky, waders to the sea margin, hunters to the forest, clerks to counting-rooms, soldiers to the frontier. Thus events grow on the same stem with persons; are sub-persons. The pleasure of life is according to the man that lives it, and not according to the work or the place. Life is an ecstasy. We know what madness belongs to love—what power to paint a vile object in hues of heaven. As insane persons are indifferent to their dress, diet, and other accommodations, and, as we do in dreams, with equanimity, the most absurd acts, so, a drop more of wine in our cup of life will reconcile us to strange company and work. Each creature puts forth from itself its own condition and sphere, as the slug sweats out its slimy house on the pear-leaf, and the woolly aphides on the apple perspire their own bed, and the fish its shell. In youth, we clothe ourselves with rainbows, and go as brave as the zodiac. In age, we put out another sort of perspiration—gout, fever, rheumatism, caprice, doubt, fretting, and avarice.

A man's fortunes are the fruit of his character. A man's friends are his magnetisms. We go to Herodotus and Plutarch for examples of Fate; but we are examples. *"Quisque suos patimur manes."* The tendency of every man to enact all that is in his constitution is expressed in the old belief, that the efforts which we make to escape from our destiny only serve to lead us into it; and I have noticed, a man likes better to be complimented on his position, as the proof of the last or total excellence, than on his merits.

A man will see his character emitted in the events that seem to meet, but which exude from and accompany him. Events expand with the character. As once he found himself among toys, so now he plays a part in colossal systems, and his growth is declared in his ambition, his companions, and his performance. He looks like a piece of luck, but is a piece of causation—the mosaic, angulated and ground to fit into the gap he fills. Hence in each town there is some man who is, in his brain and performance, an explanation of the tillage, production, factories, banks, churches, ways of living, and society, of that town. If you do not chance to meet him, all that you see will leave you a little puzzled: if you see him, it will become plain. We know in Massachusetts who built New Bedford, who built Lynn, Lowell, Lawrence, Clinton, Fitchburg, Holyoke, Portland, and many another noisy mart. Each of these men, if they were transparent, would seem to you not so much men, as walking cities, and, wherever you put them, they would build one.

History is the action and reaction of these two,—Nature and Thought,—two boys pushing each other on the curbstone of the pavement. Everything is pusher or pushed: and matter and mind are in perpetual tilt and balance so. Whilst the man is weak, the earth takes him up. He plants his brain and affections. By-and-by he will take up the earth, and have his gardens and vineyards in the beautiful order and productiveness of his thought. Every solid in the universe is ready to become fluid on the approach of the mind, and the power to flux it is the measure of the mind. If the wall remain adamant, it accuses the want of thought. To a subtler force, it will stream into new forms, expressive of the character of the mind.

What is the city in which we sit here, but an aggregate of incongruous materials, which have obeyed the will of some man? The granite was reluctant, but his hands were stronger, and it came. Iron was deep in the ground, and well combined with stone, but could not hide from his fires. Wood, lime, stuffs, fruits, gums, were dispersed over the earth and sea, in vain. Here they are, within the reach of every man's day-labor—what he wants of them.

The whole world is the flux of matter over the wires of thought to the poles or points where it would build. The races of men rise out of the ground preoccupied with a thought which rules them, and divided into parties ready armed and angry to fight for this metaphysical abstraction. The quality of the thought differences the Egyptian and the Roman, the Austrian and the

American. The men who come on the stage at one period are all found to be related to each other. Certain ideas are in the air. We are all impressionable, for we are made of them; all impressionable, but some more than others, and these first express them. This explains the curious contemporaneousness of inventions and discoveries. The truth is in the air, and the most impressionable brain will announce it first, but all will announce it a few minutes later. So women, as most susceptible, are the best index of the coming hour. So the great man, that is, the man most imbued with the spirit of the time, is the impressionable man—of a fibre irritable and delicate, like iodine to light. He feels the infinitesimal attractions. His mind is righter than others, because he yields to a current so feeble as can be felt only by a needle delicately poised.

The correlation is shown in defects. Möller, in his "Essay on Architecture," taught that the building which was fitted accurately to answer its end would turn out to be beautiful, though beauty had not been intended. I find the like unity in human structures rather virulent and pervasive: that a crudity in the blood will appear in the argument; a hump in the shoulder will appear in the speech and handiwork. If his mind could be seen, the hump would be seen. If a man has a seesaw in his voice, it will run into his sentences, into his poem, into the structure of his fable, into his speculation, into his charity. And, as every man is hunted by his own dæmon, vexed by his own disease, this checks all his activity.

So each man, like each plant, has his parasites. A strong, astringent, bilious nature, has more truculent enemies than the slugs and moths that fret my leaves. Such an one has curculios, borers, knife-worms: a swindler ate him first, then a client, then a quack, then a smooth, plausible gentleman, bitter and selfish as Moloch.

This correlation really existing can be divined. If the threads are there, thought can follow and show them. Especially when a soul is quick and docile; as Chaucer sings,—

Or if the soul of proper kind
Be so perfect as men find,
That it wot what is to come,
And that he warneth all and some,
Of every of their aventures,
By previsions or figures;
But that our flesh hath not might
It to understand aright,
For it is warned too darkly.

Some people are made up of rhyme, coincidence, omen, periodicity, and presage: they meet the person they seek: what their companion prepares to say to them, they first say to him; and a hundred signs apprise them of what is about to befall.

Wonderful intricacy in the web, wonderful constancy in the design, this vagabond life admits. We wonder how the fly finds its mate, and yet year after year we find two men, two women, without legal or carnal tie, spend a great part of their best time within a few feet of each other. And the moral is, that what we seek we shall find; what we flee from flees from us; as Goethe said, "what we wish for in youth, comes in heaps on us in old age," too often cursed with the granting of our prayer; and hence the high caution, that, since we are sure of having what we wish, we beware to ask only for high things.

One key, one solution to the mysteries of human condition, one solution to the old knots of fate, freedom, and foreknowledge, exists, the propounding, namely, of the double consciousness. A man must ride alternately on the horses of his private and his public nature, as the equestrians in the circus throw themselves nimbly from horse to horse, or plant one foot on the back of one, and the other foot on the back of the other. So when a man is the victim of his fate, has sciatica in his loins, and cramp in his mind; a club-foot and a club in his wit; a sour face, and a selfish temper; a strut in his gait, and a conceit in his affection; or is ground to powder by the vice of his race; he is to rally on his relation to the universe which his ruin benefits. Leaving the dæmon who suffers, he is to take sides with the Deity who secures universal benefit by his pain.

To offset the drag of temperament and race, which pulls down, learn this lesson—namely, that by the cunning co-presence of two elements, which is throughout nature, whatever lames or paralyzes you draws in with it the divinity, in some form, to repay. A good intention clothes itself with sudden power. When a god wishes to ride, any chip or pebble will bud and shoot out winged feet, and serve him for a horse.

Let us build altars to the Blessed Unity which holds nature and souls in perfect solution, and compels every atom to serve an universal end. I do not wonder at a snow-flake, a shell, a summer landscape, or the glory of the stars; but at the necessity of beauty under which the universe lies; that all is and must be pictorial; that the rainbow, and the curve of the horizon, and the arch of the blue vault, are only results from the organism of the eye. There is no need for foolish amateurs to fetch me to admire a garden of flowers, or a sun-gilt cloud, or a waterfall, when I cannot look without seeing splendor and grace. How idle to choose a random sparkle here or there, when the indwelling necessity plants the rose of beauty on the brow of chaos, and discloses the central intention of nature to be harmony and joy.

Let us build altars to the Beautiful Necessity. If we thought men were free in the sense that in a single exception one fantastical will could prevail over the law of things, it were all one as if a child's hand could pull down the sun. If, in the least particular, one could derange the order of nature—who would accept the gift of life?

Let us build altars to the Beautiful Necessity, which secures that all is made of one piece; that plaintiff and defendant, friend and enemy, animal and planet, food and eater, are of one kind. In astronomy is vast space, but no foreign system; in geology, vast time, but the same laws as to-day. Why should we be afraid of nature, which is no other than "philosophy and theology embodied"? Why should we fear to be crushed by savage elements, we who are made up of the same elements? Let us build to the Beautiful Necessity, which makes man brave in believing that he cannot shun a danger that is appointed, nor incur one that is not; to the Necessity which rudely or softly educates him to the perception that there are no contingencies; that Law rules throughout existence, a Law which is not intelligent but intelligence,—not personal nor impersonal,—it disdains words and passes understanding; it dissolves persons; it vivifies nature, yet solicits the pure in heart to draw on all its omnipotence.

WALT WHITMAN

SONG OF THE OPEN ROAD

I

Afoot and light-hearted I take to the open road,
Healthy, free, the world before me,
The long brown path before me leading wherever I choose.

Henceforth I ask not good-fortune, I myself am good fortune,
Henceforth I whimper no more, postpone no more, need nothing,
Done with indoor complaints, libraries, querulous criticisms,
Strong and content I travel the open road.

The earth, that is sufficient,
I do not want the constellations any nearer,
I know they are very well where they are,
I know they suffice for those who belong to them.

(Still here I carry my old delicious burdens,
I carry them, men and women, I carry them with me wherever I go,
I swear it is impossible for me to get rid of them,
I am fill'd with them, and I will fill them in return.)

II

You road I enter upon and look around, I believe you are not all that is here,
I believe that much unseen is also here.
Here the profound lesson of reception, nor preference nor denial,
The black with his woolly head, the felon, the diseas'd, the illiterate person, are not denied;
The birth, the hasting after the physician, the beggar's tramp, the drunkard's
stagger, the laughing party of mechanics,
The escap'd youth, the rich person's carriage, the fop, the eloping couple.
The early market-man, the hearse, the moving of furniture into the town, the return back from the town,
They pass, I also pass, anything passes, none can be interdicted,
None but are accepted, none but shall be dear to me.

III

You air that serves me with breath to speak!
You objects that call from diffusion my meanings and give them shape!
You light that wraps me and all things in delicate equable showers!
You paths worn in the irregular hollows by the roadsides!
I believe you are latent with unseen existences, you are so dear to me.

You flagg'd walks of the cities! you strong curbs at the edges!
You ferries! you planks and posts of wharves! you timber-lin'd sides! you distant ships!
You rows of houses! you window-pierc'd façades! you roofs!
You porches and entrances! you copings and iron guards!
You windows whose transparent shells might expose so much!
You doors and ascending steps! you arches!
You gray stones of interminable pavements! you trodden crossings!
From all that has touch'd you I believe you have imparted to yourselves, and
now would impart the same secretly to me,
From the living and the dead you have peopled your impassive surfaces, and
the spirits thereof would be evident and amicable with me.

IV

The earth expanding right hand and left hand,
The picture alive, every part in its best light,
The music falling in where it is wanted, and stopping where it is not wanted,
The cheerful voice of the public road, the gay fresh sentiment of the road.

O highway I travel, do you say to me, *Do not leave me?*
Do you say, *Venture not—if you leave me you are lost?*
Do you say, *I am already prepared, I am well-beaten and undenied, adhere to me?*

O public road, I say back I am not afraid to leave you, yet I love you,
You express me better than I can express myself,
You shall be more to me than my poem.

I think heroic deeds were all conceiv'd in the open air, and all free poems also,
I think I could stop here myself and do miracles,

I think whatever I shall meet on the road I shall like, and whoever beholds me
shall like me.
I think whoever I see must be happy.

V

From this hour I ordain myself loos'd of limits and imaginary lines,
Going where I list, my own master total and absolute,
Listening to others, considering well what they say,
Pausing, searching, receiving, contemplating,
Gently, but with undeniable will, divesting myself of the holds that would hold me.

I inhale great draughts of space,
The east and the west are mine, and the north and the south are mine.

I am larger, better than I thought,
I did not know I held so much goodness.

All seems beautiful to me,
I can repeat over to men and women, You have done such good to me I would do the same to you,
I will recruit for myself and you as I go,
I will scatter myself among men and women as I go,
I will toss a new gladness and roughness among them,
Whoever denies me it shall not trouble me,
Whoever accepts me he or she shall be blessed and shall bless me.

VI

Now if a thousand perfect men were to appear it would not amaze me,
Now if a thousand beautiful forms of women appear'd it would not astonish me.

Now I see the secret of the making of the best persons,
It is to grow in the open air and to eat and sleep with the earth.

Here a great personal deed has room
(Such a deed seizes upon the hearts of the whole race of men,
Its effusion of strength and will overwhelms law and mocks all authority

and
all argument against it).

Here is the test of wisdom,
Wisdom is not finally tested in schools,
Wisdom cannot be pass'd from one having it to another not having it,
Wisdom is of the soul, is not susceptible of proof, is its own proof,
Applies to all stages and objects and qualities and is content,
Is the certainty of the reality and immortality of things, and the excellence of
things;
Something there is in the float of the sight of things that provokes it out of the soul.

Now I reëxamine philosophies and religions,
They may prove well in lecture-rooms, yet not prove at all under the spacious
clouds and along the landscape and flowing currents.
Here is realization,
Here is a man tallied—he realizes here what he has in him,
The past, the future, majesty, love—if they are vacant of you, you are vacant
of them.

Only the kernel of every object nourishes;
Where is he who tears off the husks for you and me?
Where is he that undoes stratagems and envelopes for you and me?

Here is adhesiveness, it is not previously fashion'd, it is apropos;
Do you know what it is as you pass to be loved by strangers?
Do you know the talk of those turning eye-balls?

VII

Here is the efflux of the soul,
The efflux of the soul comes from within through embower'd gates, ever provoking questions,
These yearnings why are they? these thoughts in the darkness why are they?
Why are there men and women that while they are nigh me the sunlight expands
my blood?

Why when they leave me do my pennants of joy sink flat and lank?
Why are there trees I never walk under but large and melodious thoughts
descend upon me?
(I think they hang there winter and summer on those trees and always drop
fruit
as I pass.)
What is it I interchange so suddenly with strangers?
What with some driver as I ride on the seat by his side?
What with some fisherman drawing his seine by the shore as I walk by and
pause?
What gives me to be free to a woman's and man's good-will? what gives
them
to be free to mine?

VIII

The efflux of the soul is happiness, here is happiness,
I think it pervades the open air, waiting at all times,
Now it flows unto us, we are rightly charged.

Here rises the fluid and attaching character,
The fluid and attaching character is the freshness and sweetness of man
and
woman
(The herbs of the morning sprout no fresher and sweeter every day out of
the
roots of themselves, than it sprouts fresh and sweet continually out of
itself).
Toward the fluid and attaching character exudes the sweat of the love of
young
and old,
From it falls distill'd the charm that mocks beauty and attainments,
Toward it heaves the shuddering, longing ache of contact.

IX

Allons! whoever you are, come travel with me!
Traveling with me you find what never tires.

The earth never tires,
The earth is rude, silent, incomprehensible at first, Nature is rude and

incomprehensible at first.
Be not discouraged, keep on, there are divine things well envelop'd,
I swear to you there are divine things more beautiful than words can tell.

Allons! we must not stop here,
However sweet these laid-up stores, however convenient this dwelling, we cannot remain here,
However shelter'd this port and however calm these waters we must not anchor
here,
However welcome the hospitality that surrounds us we are permitted to receive it
but a little while.

X

Allons! the inducements shall be greater,
We will sail pathless and wild seas,
We will go where winds blow, waves dash, and the Yankee clipper speeds by
under full sail.

Allons! with power, liberty, the earth, the elements,
Health, defiance, gayety, self-esteem, curiosity;
Allons! from all formules!
From your formules, O bat-eyed and materialistic priests.

The stale cadaver blocks up the passage—the burial waits no longer.

Allons! yet take warning!
He traveling with me needs the best blood, thews, endurance,
None may come to the trial till he or she bring courage and health,
Come not here if you have already spent the best of yourself,
Only those may come who come in sweet and determin'd bodies,
No diseas'd person, no rum-drinker or venereal taint is permitted here.
(I and mine do not convince by arguments, similes, rhymes,
We convince by our presence.)

XI

Listen! I will be honest with you,
I do not offer the old smooth prizes, but offer rough new prizes,
These are the days that must happen to you:

You shall not heap up what is call'd riches,
You shall scatter with lavish hand all that you earn or achieve,
You but arrive at the city to which you were destin'd, you hardly settle yourself
to satisfaction before you are call'd by an irresistible call to depart,
You shall be treated to the ironical smiles and mockings of those who remain
behind you,
What beckonings of love you receive you shall only answer with passionate kisses of parting,
You shall not allow the hold of those who spread their reach'd hands toward you.

XII

Allons! after the great Companions, and to belong to them!
They too are on the road—they are the swift and majestic men—they are the
greatest women,
Enjoyers of calms of seas and storms of seas,
Sailors of many a ship, walkers of many a mile of land,
Habitués of many distant countries, habitués of far-distant dwellings,
Trusters of men and women, observers of cities, solitary toilers,
Pausers and contemplators of tufts, blossoms, shells of the shore,
Dancers at wedding-dances, kissers of brides, tender helpers of children, bearers of children,
Soldiers of revolts, standers by gaping graves, lowerers-down of coffins,
Journeyers over consecutive seasons, over the years, the curious years each emerging from that which preceded it,
Journeyers as with companions, namely their own diverse phases,
Forth-steppers from the latent unrealized baby-days,
Journeyers gayly with their own youth, journeyers with their bearded and well-grain'd manhood,
Journeyers with their womanhood, ample, unsurpass'd, content,
Journeyers with their own sublime old age of manhood or womanhood,
Old age, calm, expanded, broad with the haughty breadth of the universe,
Old age, flowing free with the delicious near-by freedom of death.

XIII

Allons! to that which is endless as it was beginningless,
To undergo much, tramps of days, rests of nights,
To merge all in the travel they tend to, and the days and nights they tend to,
Again to merge them in the start of superior journeys,
To see nothing anywhere but what you may reach it and pass it,
To conceive no time, however distant, but what you may reach it and pass it,
To look up or down no road but it stretches and waits for you, however long but
it stretches and waits for you,
To see no being, not God's or any, but you also go thither,
To see no possession but you may possess it, enjoying all without labor or purchase, abstracting the feast yet not abstracting one particle of it,
To take the best of the farmer's farm and the rich man's elegant villa, and the
chaste blessings of the well-married couple, and the fruits of orchards and flowers of gardens,
To take to your use out of the compact cities as you pass through,
To carry buildings and streets with you afterward where-ever you go,
To gather the minds of men out of their brains as you encounter them, to gather
the love out of their hearts,
To take your lovers on the road with you, for all that you leave them behind you,
To know the universe itself as a road, as many roads, as roads for traveling souls.

All parts away for the progress of souls,
All religion, all solid things, arts, governments—all that was or is apparent upon
this globe or any globe, falls into niches and corners before the procession of souls along the grand roads of the universe.

Of the progress of the souls of men and women along the grand roads of the
universe, all other progress is the needed emblem and sustenance.

Forever alive, forever forward,
Stately, solemn, sad, withdrawn, baffled, mad, turbulent, feeble, dissatisfied,

Desperate, proud, fond, sick, accepted by men, rejected by men,
They go! they go! I know that they go, but I know not where they go,
But I know that they go toward the best—toward something great.

Whoever you are, come forth! or man or woman come forth!
You must not stay sleeping and dallying there in the house, though you built it,
or though it has been built for you.
Out of the dark confinement! out from behind the screen!
It is useless to protest, I know all and expose it.

Behold through you as bad as the rest,
Through the laughter, dancing, dining, supping of people,
Inside of dresses and ornaments, inside of those wash'd and trimm'd faces,
Behold a secret silent loathing and despair.

No husband, no wife, no friend, trusted to hear the confession,
Another self, a duplicate of every one, skulking and hiding it goes,
Formless and wordless through the streets of the cities, polite and bland in the
parlors,
In the cars of railroads, in steamboats, in the public assembly,
Home to the houses of men and women, at the table, in the bedroom, everywhere,
Smartly attired, countenance smiling, form upright, death under the breast-bones,
hell under the skull-bones,
Under the broadcloth and gloves, under the ribbons and artificial flowers,
Keeping fair with the customs, speaking not a syllable of itself,
Speaking of anything else but never of itself.

XIV

Allons! through struggles and wars!
The goal that was named cannot be countermanded.

Have the past struggles succeeded?
What has succeeded? yourself? your nation? Nature?
Now understand me well—it is provided in the essence of things that from any
fruition of success, no matter what, shall come forth something to make a greater struggle necessary.

My call is the call of battle, I nourish active rebellion,
He going with me must go well arm'd,
He going with me goes often with spare diet, poverty, angry enemies, desertions.

XV

Allons! the road is before us!
It is safe—I have tried it—my own feet have tried it well—be not detain'd!
Let the paper remain on the desk unwritten, and the book on the shelf unopen'd!
Let the tools remain in the workshop! let the money remain unearn'd!
Let the school stand! mind not the cry of the teacher!
Let the preacher preach in his pulpit! let the lawyer plead in the court, and the
judge expound the law.

Camerado, I give you my hand!
I give you my love more precious than money,
I give you myself before preaching or law;
Will you give me yourself? will you come travel with me?
Shall we stick by each other as long as we live?

CROSSING BROOKLYN FERRY

I

Flood-tide below me! I see you face to face!
Clouds of the west—sun there half an hour high—I see you also face to face.

Crowds of men and women attired in the usual costumes, how curious you are
to me!
On the ferry-boats the hundreds and hundreds that cross, returning home, are
more curious to me than you suppose,
And you that shall cross from shore to shore years hence are more to me,

and
more in my meditations, than you might suppose.

II

The impalpable sustenance of me from all things at all hours of the day,
The simple, compact, well-join'd scheme, myself disintegrated, everyone disintegrated yet part of the scheme,
The similitudes of the past and those of the future,
The glories strung like beads on my smallest sights and hearings, on the walk in
the street and the passage over the river,
The current rushing so swiftly and swimming with me far away,
The others that are to follow me, the ties between me and them,
The certainty of others, the life, love, sight, hearing of others.
Others will enter the gates of the ferry and cross from shore to shore,
Others will watch the run of the flood-tide,
Others will see the shipping of Manhattan north and west, and the heights of
Brooklyn to the south and east,
Others will see the islands large and small;
Fifty years hence, others will see them as they cross, the sun half an hour high,
A hundred years hence, or ever so many hundred years hence, others will see
them,
Will enjoy the sunset, the pouring-in of the flood-tide, the falling-back to the sea
of the ebb-tide.

III

It avails not, time nor place—distance avails not,
I am with you, you men and women of a generation, or ever so many generations
hence,
Just as you feel when you look on the river and sky, so I felt,
Just as any of you is one of a living crowd, I was one of a crowd,
Just as you are refresh'd by the gladness of the river and the bright flow, I was
refresh'd,

Just as you stand and lean on the rail, yet hurry with the swift current, I stood yet
was hurried,
Just as you look on the numberless masts of ships and the thick-stemm'd pipes
of steamboats, I look'd.

I too many and many a time cross'd the river of old,
Watched the Twelfth-month sea-gulls, saw them high in the air floating with
motionless wings, oscillating their bodies,
Saw how the glistening yellow lit up parts of their bodies and left the rest in strong
shadow,
Saw the slow-wheeling circles and the gradual edging toward the south,
Saw the reflection of the summer sky in the water,
Had my eyes dazzled by the shimmering track of beams,
Look'd at the fine centrifugal spokes of light round the shape of my head in the
sunlit water,
Look'd on the haze on the hills southward and south-westward,
Look'd on the vapor as it flew in fleeces tinged with violet,
Look'd toward the lower bay to notice the vessels arriving,
Saw their approach, saw aboard those that were near me,
Saw the white sails of schooners and sloops, saw the ships at anchor,
The sailors at work in the rigging or out astride the spars,
The round masts, the swinging motion of the hulls, the slender serpentine
pennants,
The large and small steamers in motion, the pilots in their pilot-houses,
The white wake left by the passage, the quick tremulous whirl of the wheels,
The flags of all nations, the falling of them at sunset,
The scallop-edged waves in the twilight, the ladled cups, the frolicsome crests
and glistening,
The stretch afar growing dimmer and dimmer, the gray walls of the granite
storehouses by the docks,
On the river the shadowy group, the big steam-tug closely flank'd on each side
by the barges, the hay-boat, the belated lighter,
On the neighboring shore the fires from the foundry chimneys burning high and
glaringly into the night,

Casting their flicker of black contrasted with wild red and yellow light over the
tops of houses, and down into the clefts of streets.

IV

These and all else were to me the same as they are to you,
I loved well those cities, loved well the stately and rapid river,
The men and women I saw were all near to me,
Others the same—others who look back on me because I look'd forward to them
(The time will come, though I stop here to-day and to-night).

V

What is it then between us?
What is the count of the scores or hundreds of years between us?

Whatever it is, it avails not—distance avails not, and place avails not,
I too lived, Brooklyn of ample hills was mine,
I too walk'd the streets of Manhattan Island, and bathed in the waters around it,
I too felt the curious abrupt questionings stir within me,
In the day among crowds of people sometimes they came upon me,
In my walks home late at night or as I lay in my bed they came upon me,
I too had been struck from the float forever held in solution,
I too had receiv'd identity by my body,
That I was I knew was of my body, and what I should be
I knew I should be of my body.

VI

It is not upon you alone the dark patches fall,
The dark threw its patches down upon me also,
The best I had done seem'd to me blank and suspicious,
My great thoughts as I supposed them, were they not in reality meagre?
Nor is it you alone who know what it is to be evil,
I am he who knew what it was to be evil,
I too knitted the old knot of contrariety,
Blabb'd, blush'd, resented, lied, stole, grudg'd,
Had guile, anger, lust, hot wishes I dared not speak,

Was wayward, vain, greedy, shallow, sly, cowardly, malignant,
The wolf, the snake, the hog, not wanting in me,
The cheating look, the frivolous word, the adulterous wish, not wanting,
Refusals, hates, postponements, meanness, laziness, none of these wanting,
Was one with the rest, the days and haps of the rest,
Was call'd by my nighest name by clear loud voices of young men as they saw
me approaching or passing,
Felt their arms on my neck as I stood, or the negligent leaning of their flesh against
me as I sat,
Saw many I lov'd in the street or ferry-boat or public assembly, yet never told
them a word,
Liv'd the same life with the rest, the same old laughing, gnawing, sleeping,
Play'd the part that still looks back on the actor or actress,
The same old rôle, the rôle that is what we make it, as great as we like,
Or as small as we like, or both great and small.

VII

Closer yet I approach you,
What thought you have of me now, I had as much of you—I laid in my stores in
advance,
I consider'd long and seriously of you before you were born.

Who was to know what should come home to me?
Who knows but I am enjoying this?
Who knows, for all the distance, but I am as good as looking at you now, for all
you cannot see me?

VIII

Ah, what can ever be more stately and admirable to me than mast-hemm'd Manhattan?
River and sunset and scallop-edg'd waves of flood-tide?
The sea-gulls oscillating their bodies, the hay-boat in the twilight, and the belated
lighter?

What gods can exceed these that clasp me by the hand, and with voices I love
call me promptly and loudly by my nighest name as I approach?
What is more subtle than this which ties me to the woman or man that looks in
my face?
Which fuses me into you now, and pours my meaning into you?

We understand then, do we not?
What I promis'd without mentioning it, have you not accepted?
What the study could not teach—what the preaching could not accomplish is
accomplish'd, is it not?

IX

Flow on, river! flow with the flood-tide, and ebb with the ebb-tide!
Frolic on, crested and scallop-edg'd waves!
Gorgeous clouds of the sunset! drench with your splendor me, or the men and
women generations after me!
Cross from shore to shore, countless crowds of passengers!
Stand up, tall masts of Mannahatta! stand up, beautiful hills of Brooklyn!
Throb, baffled and curious brain! throw out questions and answers!
Suspend here and everywhere, eternal float of solution!
Gaze, loving and thirsting eyes, in the house or street or public assembly!
Sound out, voices of young men! loudly and musically call me by my nighest
name!
Live, old life! play the part that looks back on the actor or actress!
Play the old rôle, the rôle that is great or small according as one makes it!
Consider, you who peruse me, whether I may not in unknown ways be looking
upon you;
Be firm, rail over the river, to support those who lean idly, yet haste with the
hasting current;
Fly on, sea-birds! fly sideways, or wheel in large circles high in the air;
Receive the summer sky, you water, and faithfully hold it till all downcast eyes
have time to take it from you!

Diverge, fine spokes of light, from the shape of my head, or anyone's head, in the
sunlit water!
Come on, ships from the lower bay! pass up or down, white-sail'd schooners,
sloops, lighters!
Flaunt away, flags of all nations! be duly lower'd at sunset!
Burn high your fires, foundry chimneys! cast black shadows at nightfall! cast red
and yellow light over the tops of the houses!
Appearances, now or henceforth, indicate what you are,
You necessary film, continue to envelop the soul,
About my body for me, and your body for you, be hung our divinest aromas,
Thrive, cities—bring your freight, bring your shows, ample and sufficient rivers,
Expand, being than which none else is perhaps more spiritual,
Keep your places, objects than which none else is more lasting.

You have waited, you always wait, you dumb, beautiful ministers,
We receive you with free sense at last, and are insatiate henceforward,
Not you any more shall be able to foil us, or withhold yourselves from us,
We use you, and do not cast you aside—we plant you permanently within us,
We fathom you not—we love you—there is perfection in you also,
You furnish your parts toward eternity,
Great or small, you furnish your parts toward the soul.

A SONG OF JOYS

O to make the most jubilant song!
Full of music— full of manhood, womanhood, infancy!
Full of common employments—full of grain and trees.

O for the voices of animals—O for the swiftness and balance of fishes!
O for the dropping of raindrops in a song!
O for the sunshine and motion of waves in a song!

O for the joy of my spirit—it is uncaged—it darts like lightning!
It is not enough to have this globe or a certain time,
I will have thousands of globes and all time.

O the engineer's joys! to go with a locomotive!
To hear the hiss of steam, the merry shriek, the steam-whistle, the laughing
locomotive!
To push with resistless way and speed off in the distance.

O the gleesome saunter over fields and hillsides!
The leaves and flowers of the commonest weeds, the moist fresh stillness
of the
woods,
The exquisite smell of the earth at daybreak, and all through the forenoon.

O the horseman's and horsewoman's joys!
The saddle, the gallop, the pressure upon the seat, the cool gurgling by the
ears
and hair.

O the fireman's joys!
I hear the alarm at dead of night,
I hear bells, shouts! I pass the crowd, I run!
The sight of the flames maddens me with pleasure.

O the joy of the strong-brawn'd fighter, towering in the arena in perfect
condition,
conscious of power, thirsting to meet his opponent.
O the joy of that vast elemental sympathy which only the human soul is
capable of
generating and emitting in steady and limitless floods.

O the mother's joys!
The watching, the endurance, the precious love, the anguish, the patiently
yielded
life.

O the joy of increase, growth, recuperation,
The joy of soothing and pacifying, the joy of concord and harmony.

O to go back to the place where I was born,
To hear the birds sing once more,
To ramble about the house and barn and over the fields once more,
And through the orchard and along the old lanes once more.

O to have been brought up on bays, lagoons, creeks, or along the coast,

To continue and be employ'd there all my life,
The briny and damp smell, the shore, the salt weeds exposed at low water,
The work of fishermen, the work of the eel-fisher and clam-fisher;
I come with my clam-rake and spade, I come with my eel-spear.
Is the tide out? I join the group of clam-diggers on the flats,
I laugh and work with them, I joke at my work like a mettlesome young man;
In winter I take my eel-basket and eel-spear and travel out on foot on the ice—I
have a small axe to cut holes in the ice,
Behold me well-clothed going gayly or returning in the afternoon, my brood of
tough boys accompanying me,
My brood of grown and part-grown boys, who love to be with no one else so
well as they love to be with me.

Another time in warm weather out in a boat, to lift the lobster-pots where they
are sunk with heavy stones (I know the buoys),
O the sweetness of the Fifth-month morning upon the water as I row just before
sunrise toward the buoys,
I pull the wicker pots up slantingly, the dark green lobsters are desperate with
their claws as I take them out, I insert wooden pegs in the joints of their pincers,
I go to all the places one after another, and then row back to the shore,
There in a huge kettle of boiling water the lobsters shall be boil'd till their color
becomes scarlet.

Another time mackerel-taking,
Voracious, mad for the hook, near the surface, they seem to fill the water for
miles;
Another time fishing for rock-fish in Chesapeake bay, I one of the brown-faced
crew;
Another time trailing for blue-fish off Paumanok, I stand with braced body,
My left foot is on the gunwale, my right arm throws far out the coils of slender

rope,
In sight around me the quick veering and darting of fifty skiffs, my companions.

O boat on the rivers,
The voyage down the St. Lawrence, the superb scenery, the steamers,
The ships sailing, the Thousand Islands, the occasional timber-raft and the raftsmen with long-reaching sweep-oars,
The little huts on the rafts, and the stream of smoke when they cook supper at
evening.

(O something pernicious and dread!
Something far away from a puny and pious life!
Something unproved! something in a trance!
Something escaped from the anchorage and driving free.)

O to work in mines, or forging iron,
Foundry casting, the foundry itself, the rude high roof, the ample and shadow'd
space,
The furnace, the hot liquid pour'd out and running.

O to resume the joys of the soldier!
To feel the presence of a brave commanding officer—to feel his sympathy!
To behold his calmness—to be warm'd in the rays of his smile!
To go to battle—to hear the bugles play and the drums beat!
To hear the crash of artillery—to see the glittering of the bayonets and musket-barrels in the sun!
To see men fall and die and not complain!
To taste the savage taste of blood—to be so devilish!
To gloat so over the wounds and deaths of the enemy.

O the whaleman's joys! O I cruise my old cruise again!
I feel the ship's motion under me, I feel the Atlantic breezes fanning me,
I hear the cry again sent down from the mast-head, *There—she blows!*
Again I spring up the rigging to look with the rest—we descend, wild with excitement,
I leap in the lower'd boat, we row toward our prey where he lies,
We approach stealthy and silent, I see the mountainous mass, lethargic, basking,
I see the harpooneer standing up, I see the weapon dart from his vigorous arm;

O swift again far out in the ocean the wounded whale, settling, running to windward, tows me,
Again I see him rise to breathe, we now close again,
I see a lance driven through his side, press'd deep, turn'd in the wound,
Again we back off, I see him settle again, the life is leaving him fast,
As he rises he spouts blood, I see him swim in circles narrower and narrower,
swiftly cutting the water—I see him die,
He gives one convulsive leap in the centre of the circle, and then falls flat and still
in the bloody foam.

O the old manhood of me, my noblest joy of all!
My children and grand-children, my white hair and beard,
My largeness, calmness, majesty, out of the long stretch of my life.

O ripen'd joy of womanhood! O happiness at last!
I am more than eighty years of age, I am the most venerable mother,
How clear is my mind—how all people draw nigh to me!
What attractions are these beyond any before? what bloom more than the bloom
of youth?
What beauty is this that descends upon me and rises out of me?

O the orator's joys!
To inflate the chest, to roll the thunder of the voice out from the ribs and throat,
To make the people rage, weep, hate, desire, with yourself,
To lead America—to quell America with a great tongue.

O the joy of my soul leaning pois'd on itself, receiving identity through materials
and loving them, observing characters and absorbing them,
My soul vibrated back to me from them, from sight, hearing, touch, reason,
articulation, comparison, memory, and the like,
The real life of my senses and flesh transcending my senses and flesh,
My body done with materials, my sight done with my material eyes,
Proved to me this day beyond cavil that it is not my material eyes which finally
see,
Nor my material body which finally loves, walks, laughs, shouts, embraces, procreates.

O the farmer's joys!
Ohioan's, Illinoisian's, Wisconsinese', Kanadian's, Iowan's, Kansian's, Missourian's, Oregonese' joys!
To rise at peep of day and pass forth nimbly to work,
To plough land in the fall for winter-sown crops,
To plough land in the spring for maize,
To train orchards, to graft the trees, to gather apples in the fall.

O to bathe in the swimming-bath, or in a good place along shore,
To splash the water! to walk ankle-deep, or race naked along the shore.

O to realize space!
The plenteousness of all, that there are no bounds,
To emerge and be of the sky, of the sun and moon and flying clouds, as one with
them.

O the joy of a manly self-hood!
To be servile to none, to defer to none, not to any tyrant known or unknown,
To walk with erect carriage, a step springy and elastic,
To look with calm gaze or with a flashing eye,
To speak with a full and sonorous voice out of a broad chest,
To confront with your personality all the other personalities of the earth.

Know'st thou the excellent joys of youth?
Joys of the dear companions and of the merry word and laughing face?
Joy of the glad light-beaming day, joy of the wide-breath'd games?
Joy of sweet music, joy of the lighted ball-room and the dancers?
Joy of the plenteous dinner, strong carouse, and drinking?

Yet O my soul supreme!
Know'st thou the joys of pensive thought?
Joys of the free and lonesome heart, the tender, gloomy heart?
Joys of the solitary walk, the spirit bow'd yet proud, the suffering and the struggle?
The agonistic throes, the ecstasies, joys of the solemn musings day or night?
Joys of the thought of Death, the great spheres, Time and Space?
Prophetic joys of better, loftier love's ideals, the divine wife, the sweet, eternal,
perfect comrade?

Joys all thine own, undying one, joys worthy thee, O soul?

O while I live to be the ruler of life, not a slave,
To meet life as a powerful conqueror,
No fumes, no ennui, no more complaints or scornful criticisms,
To these proud laws of the air, the water and the ground, proving my interior soul
impregnable,
And nothing exterior shall ever take command of me.

For not life's joys alone I sing, repeating—the joy of death!
The beautiful touch of Death, soothing and benumbing a few moments, for
reasons,
Myself discharging my excrementitious body to be burn'd, or render'd to powder, or buried,
My real body doubtless left to me for other spheres,
My voided body nothing more to me, returning to the purifications, further offices,
eternal uses of the earth.

O to attract by more than attraction!
How it is I know not—yet behold! the something which obeys none of the rest,
It is offensive, never defensive—yet how magnetic it draws.

O to struggle against great odds, to meet enemies undaunted!
To be entirely alone with them, to find how much one can stand!
To look strife, torture, prison, popular odium, face to face!
To mount the scaffold, to advance to the muzzles of guns with perfect nonchalance!
To be indeed a God!

O to sail to sea in a ship!
To leave this steady unendurable land,
To leave the tiresome sameness of the streets, the sidewalks and the houses,
To leave you, O you solid motionless land, and entering a ship,
To sail and sail and sail!

O to have life henceforth a poem of new joys!
To dance, clap hands, exult, shout, skip, leap, roll on, float on!
To be a sailor of the world bound for all ports,

A ship itself (see indeed these sails I spread to the sun and air),
A swift and swelling ship full of rich words, full of joys.